No Suspicious Circumstances

THE MULGRAY TWINS

Allison & Busby Limited
13 Charlotte Mews
London W1T 4EJ
www.allisonandbusby.com

Hardcover published in Great Britain in 2007.
This paperback edition published in 2008.

Extract on page 138 from 'Edinburgh' by Alfred Noyes,
used by kind permission of the Society of Authors,
Literary Representative of the Estate of Alfred Noyes.

A CIP catalogue record for this book is available from
the British Library.

10 9 8 7 6 5 4 3 2 1

ISBN 978-0-7490-8059-4

Typeset in Sabon by
Terry Shannon

Printed and bound in the UK by
CPI Bookmarque, Croydon, CR0 4TD

From the moment that, as premature twins, they were placed end to end beside a radiator in an Edinburgh nursing home, HELEN AND MORNA MULGRAY have lived together. The identical twins have also pursued an identical career path, and after retiring from teaching, they now live and write together. They also love to travel when they are not plotting and writing DJ Smith mysteries at home in Edinburgh.

Acknowledgements

Our grateful thanks to our friend Irene Fekete who started us on the road to publication, and our agent Frances Hanna of Acacia House Publishing, Brantford, Ontario, who over the years never lost faith in DJ Smith and Gorgonzola.

To Edith and Harry for being themselves.

In research matters we are indebted to the following:
Cherry and Ray Legg for matters nautical, in particular the properties of inflatable boats and drowned bodies.

Linda of Headstart hairdressing salon, Joppa, Edinburgh, for her invaluable advice on the awful pitfalls of amateur hair dyeing – and disaster recovery.

Elizabeth Scott who kept us right on matters feline.

For those readers interested in the phenomenon of cats that paint (or find the idea totally incredible), we refer you to the amazing works of art in *Why Cats Paint – a theory of feline aesthetics* by Burton Silver and Heather Busch. Published by Seven Dials, Orion Publishing Group, London. Pocket edition published by Ten Speed Press, California and Toronto.

For Alanna
in thanks and friendship

CHAPTER ONE

My closest friends know me as DJ Smith, investigator for Her Majesty's Revenue and Customs (Drugs Division). My enemies, I hope, don't know me at all. In my line of work I try to keep the lowest of profiles. Cloaked in secrecy. Under wraps. Undercover. That's me. For the kind of enemies I make would be glad to see me dead. It's always at the back of my mind.

That was why I should have paid more attention to the bell-boy with a couple of suitcases on his trolley. I'd summoned the lift to take me down from one of the penthouse suites. A sudden violent blow on the back slammed me against the stainless-steel shaft doors. They shouldn't have opened. But someone had made sure they did. I pitched forward and down...

Whoever made the attempt on my life hadn't taken into account the position of the lift, which was at the floor below. So my fall was not the intended twelve storeys, but a mere six feet; my injuries were a few cuts, bruises and more than a little shock to the system. I survived, but I can't say the same for my undercover career as leisure hostess cum personal shopper.

* * *

The Department were quite good about the fact that I'd screwed up that carefully set up operation. My next assignment was, thankfully, not to Siberia but to Scotland.

'Just a routine nose around, Deborah. Treat it as a holiday for you and the cat. It'll be a rest for you after that last little bit of bother.' Jim Orr, my Head of Section, selected a slim file from the neat stack on his desk.

A bit of bother! I'd almost been *killed*. But a six-foot fall instead of twelve storeys – if you look at it that way, I suppose you *could* call it 'a bit of bother'...

He held the file out to me. 'We've had a tip-off about a country house hotel not far from Edinburgh. It's all in there, such as it is. The East of Scotland Drug Squad have been reporting a big increase in heroin traffic over the past year. They suspect the stuff's coming in somewhere along the coastline between Edinburgh and the English border.'

I opened the file. The first plastic pocket held a photograph of a big grey-stone house in the Scottish Baronial style of architecture.

'The White Heather Hotel, your base while you're up there.' He hummed a snatch of 'The Bonnie Banks of Loch Lomond'. 'Proprietors Murdo and Morag Mackenzie. They've no previous convictions.'

I studied the mug shot. A harmless-looking couple, but that didn't mean a thing. Murdo Mackenzie's heavy features frowned back at me. That deep line between the eyes showed him to be one of life's worriers. One of those anxieties seemed to involve premature hair loss as he'd combed dark strands of hair across his scalp in a vain attempt to disguise a receding hairline. Morag was four years older. Her black hair was flecked with iron grey, and tied back in the severe hairstyle of an old-fashioned bun at the nape of the neck. Her hard face and thin lips gave the impression that she was the more dominant of the two.

Jim flicked a hand at a fly about to make a six-point landing on a stack of files on his desk. 'The woman's in the clear, but her husband's distinctly shady. The local police have been interested in him for the last couple of years. Nothing ever proved, though.' He gazed pensively at the fly, undeterred and now nosing through a pile of confidential papers. 'Our source reckons there's a *possibility* that Mackenzie might be involved in the distribution of the heroin. It shouldn't take you long to check the place out. The Operation code name is Scotch Mist.' He whipped a canister of fly-spray from a drawer. *Pssssssh*. The fly flopped on its back, one leg waving a final farewell, lips sealed forever. 'But I don't think this will come to anything.' I was treated to another snatch of 'The Bonnie Banks of Loch Lomond'. 'Yes, just treat it as a holiday for yourself and the cat.'

It was the middle of June, but all the way from the border with England that notorious Scottish east coast mist made driving difficult. Cold and dismal, it hung low over the fields and hills, bleaching out the summer colours of the countryside and reducing the famed beauty of the landscape to grey, indistinct shapes that loomed, then vanished quickly behind. I peered through the windscreen. If I'd taken the main dual carriageway instead of the scenic route, I'd have checked into the White Heather Hotel an hour ago. I'd now be putting my feet up and having a coffee, or sampling one of Scotland's pure malts. I rolled the names over my tongue. Glenmorangie, Laphroaig, Cragganmore, Dalwhinnie, Macallan, Royal Lochnagar, Tallisker...

That mist was thicker than ever. The insides of the car windows were steaming up too. I grabbed for the cloth lying on the back seat. In the driving mirror my eyes met Customs Officer Gorgonzola's copper ones. She gave me her Cheshire Cat grin, designed to show off each sharp tooth to perfect advantage.

In case you're wondering, Customs Officer Gorgonzola, extraordinarily gifted sniffer-out of drugs, is a cat, a large Red Persian of tatty and disreputable appearance. She has the typical sweet nature of the breed, the copper eyes, but not the long luxuriant coat. Some Don Juan of an alley cat must have seduced her mother, hence the moth-eaten appearance. At times, for no apparent reason, her eyes narrow into slits, she sheathes and unsheathes her claws and hisses quietly to herself, perhaps dwelling upon the harrowing circumstance of her near-drowning at birth.

The White Heather Hotel couldn't be far away now, but visibility was very poor, only a couple of hundred yards or so. I lowered the window and stuck out my head. A low dry-stone wall loomed to the right, and beyond it I could hear the faint crash of waves on the shore. A little way ahead, insubstantial in the mist, a huge monkey-puzzle tree spread a dark tangle of arms. As I crept level, a puff of wind swirled and eddied the mist to reveal a white signboard suspended from a branch overhanging the road. On it in fancy lettering:

WHITE HEATHER COUNTRY HOUSE HOTEL.

I'd reached my goal. I brought the car to an abrupt halt, depositing Gorgonzola in an astonished heap on the floor.

'It's your own fault,' I growled unsympathetically. 'You should have let me clip you into your harness instead of poncing about on the back seat.'

Ignoring such coarseness, she leapt back onto the seat and curled up. One open eye watched me sulkily as I stepped out of the car.

WHITE HEATHER COUNTRY HOUSE HOTEL
SELF-CATERING COTTAGES
JACUZZI, SOLARIUM, SAUNA
NO PETS.
Proprietors Mr & Mrs M Mackenzie

Beneath hung a smaller notice: *Vacancies*.

The *No Pets* edict was not a problem. I'd often faced this sort of tricky situation. 'Nothing that our well-rehearsed routine can't cope with, eh, G?'

Never one to hold a grudge for long, she stepped daintily out of the car and wound herself round my legs in affectionate agreement.

The hotel was miles from anywhere – a breakdown would provide an excellent excuse for not having booked ahead. I turned off the ignition, propped up the bonnet, and sawed vigorously at the drive belt with the scissors kept in my bag for 'emergencies'. A minute or two of effort, and I surveyed the ragged cut with satisfaction. I pulled the severed belt off its pulley and threw it into the nearest clump of bushes.

Now for the luggage. I leant into the boot and whipped out a large blue holdall inscribed *MINE*, and an equally large red one, surprisingly heavy for its size, inscribed *YOURS*, containing a fluffy towel, a soft sheepskin rug (G's bed, she liked her comforts), and fifteen large cans of an obscure but expensive brand of cat food, her favourite. I locked the car, gathered up the two holdalls, and set off. Gorgonzola, moth-eaten tail held high, stalked ahead.

Despite the hampering mist I could see that the grounds of the hotel were extensive and well-kept – lawns of billiard table smoothness, silvery with moisture, lapped two huge beds of heather (white, of course). Half a dozen cars were parked on the gravelled forecourt from which wide stone steps led up to the front door of the house, its rather grim grey stone softened by the finely sculptured leaves of a rampant Virginia creeper. Of Gorgonzola, there was no sign. She always knew when to make herself scarce.

I scrunched over the wet gravel and up the steps. An elegant potted plant in a classy white jardinière graced the large vestibule. Beside it on a small spindly legged walnut table reposed a tastefully designed card bearing in copperplate script a glowing description of the hotel. A well-polished brass plaque introduced a somewhat curter note.

THE MANAGEMENT REGRETS NO PETS CAN BE ENTERTAINED.

Entertained? An audience of cats and dogs in the drawing room solemnly listening to a string quartet? Mustn't laugh, I could be on CCTV.

Through the glass door, I could see carpeted stairs and, standing guard at their foot, an imposing grandfather clock with yellowed dial. I pulled open the door, and deposited the holdalls in front of the polished reception desk. Spread open before me lay an open ledger and, beside it, a porcelain hand bell with the notice *Please ring for attention*. I rang as requested. No response. I seized the opportunity and swivelled the ledger to scan the entries.

'Can I be of assistance…madam?' The cold, steely voice paused perceptibly before the *madam*. The speaker had noted my action and did not approve.

I spun round guiltily, as if I'd sneaked a quick glance at a doctor's notes and been caught in the act. Confronting me was a tall angular woman, her black hair flecked with iron grey. Mrs Morag Mackenzie.

'You have a vacancy?' I asked.

She inclined her head in aristocratic assent. 'Hotel, or self-catering cottage?'

'Oh, hotel!' I said. 'I do like my little luxuries!'

Her gaze rested on the two holdalls. 'A single or a double room, madam?'

'A double,' I replied blandly. 'Though I'm by myself, I prefer the extra space.'

Her eyes scrutinised me for a long moment, as if to x-ray my morals. 'Sign here, please.' She pushed the register towards me and selected a key from the board behind her.

I signed my name with a flourish. My real name, that is. Using an alias, I've found, only leads to unnecessary complications.

'Ms Deborah Smith. Smith…' She pursed her thin lips,

savouring the word as if it was something rather nasty she had found in the salad. Again her eyes homed in on the *YOURS* holdall like an Exocet missile on its way to its target.

'Yes, it's plain Smith, not spelt with y or e, I'm afraid, Mrs...er...' I smiled disarmingly.

'Mackenzie.' There was no reciprocating smile from the Gorgon. 'I'll show you to your room. It's number 4 on the first floor.'

I picked up the holdalls. Now to dispel any lurking suspicion that my arrival was anything other than chance. 'Is there a phone in the room? I'm afraid my car's broken down just outside your driveway, and I'll have to contact a garage.'

'Room telephone, madam? *Of course*. This way.' She stalked ahead of me up the ornately balustraded staircase.

The weather should be a safe enough topic. 'Do you often get mist as thick as this?'

'Haar,' replied Mrs Mackenzie, 'haar.'

West Country accent, Devon or Cornwall. Orr's briefing on the hotel and its owners had not included any such connections. Perhaps this was going to be a lead worth following up.

'Haar?' I echoed encouragingly, hoping she would reveal more.

She paused beside a magnificent Victorian stained-glass window on the half-landing. Her thin lips compressed into what might have been a condescending smile. 'Haar,' she spoke slowly and clearly as if explaining to a person of limited understanding, 'is the local word for the sea mist that tends to linger for several days after a spell of hot weather.'

'How interesting,' I said truthfully.

Room 4 faced to the rear, just above a small tree whose branches overhung the sloping roof of a conservatory running the length of the building. I wouldn't have to smuggle Gorgonzola in under my jacket as I sometimes had to do if access proved beyond her mountaineering skills.

When I was alone, I threw up the lower half of the sash window with as much noise as I could decently make. In anyone's books, this dreadful weather counted as winter. I was confident I wouldn't have to wait long.

G couldn't bear being wet or cold – not surprising in view of her near-death experience as a kitten. After a misalliance, pedigree breeders can be unforgiving. I'd found her late one autumn afternoon, a wet and shivering ball clinging desperately to an old log jammed against the river bank. Beside her floated the drowned bodies of her brothers and sisters. I'd scooped her up and taken her home wrapped in my woolly hat. No alternative, was there? I couldn't leave her there to die.

I dried her, made up an intensive care unit from a hot water bottle and an old jersey, and started a regime of two-hourly feeds from a pipette. There wasn't much sign of life. She was so weak that I had to put the tip in her mouth and stroke her throat so that she would swallow the slow trickle of warm liquid. Then it was retire to bed, set the alarm, stagger up, eyes glued with sleep. Each time, to my surprise, the little ball of ginger fur was still alive.

The next morning a pink tongue licked my finger. 'Welcome to the world, Kitten,' I'd said. 'You can stay here till I find you a good home.'

I didn't give her a name, just called her Kitten. Keeping a cat was really out of the question for me, so it was better not to become too attached to this tiny creature. At the time I trained dogs for HM Revenue and Customs, taking three or four home and testing them by hiding an object in the house. That way I found out which of them had potential as a Sniffer.

I kept her out of the way of the dogs at first, but she soon showed she could take care of herself. Any dog that overstepped the mark received a sharp reminder to behave. Puppies came and went. Kitten stayed. She played with the dogs, ate with the dogs, slept with the dogs. I suppose she grew up thinking she *was* a dog. I shortened her name to Kit and didn't try too hard to find her that good home.

Training sessions may look like games, but they're a serious business. The dogs mustn't be distracted, so I shut Kit in her basket, when I could catch her, but more often than not the process became a game of hide and seek. She hid. I'd seek. Sometimes I shut her out in the garden, and then she would peer in at us, gingery face pressed disconsolately against the glass.

Kit's career with Revenue and Customs began the day I chose a ripe cheese as my test for the dogs. To make it a tough one, I liberally squirted a can of lavender-scented polish on every wooden surface in the lounge, paying particular attention to the bookcase. In the six-inch gap between carpet and base I laid my pongy morsel of cheese, pushing it as far back as I could. Only a dog with the very best 'nose' would pass a grade A test like this.

Before going to fetch the dogs, I went in search of Kit. She was lying on my bed curled up, face buried in tail in her *Do Not Disturb* posture. I gave her a quick stroke and left her to it. No need to put her in her basket today. I let the puppies, Jenny and Roger, out of their kennels, attached a leash to each collar and led them into the house.

I tied Jenny securely to the stair rail and knelt down beside Roger. In my hand I held another piece of the smelly cheese.

When he'd had a good sniff, I slipped the leash, and pointed at the open lounge door. 'Search!'

The puppy bounded forward, barking with excitement, tail wagging, while I stood in the doorway, stopwatch and notebook in hand. Chair, settee, cupboard, chair again, pawing and sniffing. Bookcase. A cursory sniff underneath, then back to the settee again and another scamper round the various pieces of furniture. He trotted back past the bookcase again, but showed no interest in it. In the end I had to write, *Roger – Fail.*

Then it was Jenny's turn for the cheese test. I slipped the leash. 'Search!'

Tail wagging, she made straight for the bookcase. Nose down, rear in air, snuffle, sniff, frantic wagging. I had my pencil poised to rate Jenny as a pass, when she lost interest in the bookcase. Off she rushed to investigate the easy chair by the fire, then a cushion on the settee. She completed a second tour round the room, but made no return to the bookcase. Regretfully, I wrote, *Jenny – Fail.*

'Just goes to show,' I thought. 'You never can tell.' I'd been pretty sure that Jenny would find the cheese. It was really disappointing. I'd give them both a second chance tomorrow.

I took the dogs to their kennels, and went back to the lounge to retrieve the cheese. To save too much scrabbling and peering, I'd placed it directly in line with the *Complete Guide to Dog Care*, but when I reached in, my fingers touched only carpet. I made a sweeping motion to right and left. Nothing. I stretched out full length and squinted into the gap. Two eyes peered back. Two copper eyes and a self-satisfied ginger smile. Hanging from a whisker were two crumbs, all that was left of the cheese.

It didn't take me long to figure out the chain of events. Kit had known it was training time and had wanted a part of the action, so while I was away collecting the dogs, she'd sneaked into the lounge. Beneath the strong scent of lavender polish was the cheesy smell that had been on my hand when I'd stroked her. She'd recognised it – and tracked it down. The dogs hadn't failed their test. There had been no cheese left to detect.

Intrigued by her exploit, I reran the cheese test. Only this time there were three participants. Roger failed, Jenny locked on in 60 seconds, Kit in 30. After that, I allowed her to join the dogs in their sniffing games. Time after time, she proved that her sense of smell and intelligence were outstanding. What else could I do but recommend her for training?

On the day she passed her final test, I decided that her new role deserved a new name and called her after the cheese that had triggered her change of status.

'Welcome to HM Customs, Gorgonzola,' I said, and gave her a hug. The unwanted ugly duckling, left to drown, had matured into a swan. We'd been a team ever since.

I didn't have to wait long at the open window of the White Heather Hotel. Two minutes later, there was a scrabbling in the tree over the conservatory and Gorgonzola, looking rather like a bedraggled dish mop, stepped daintily over the sill, leaving a trail of wet paw prints across Mrs Mackenzie's pristine carpet. 'Haar,' she spat petulantly.

I was impressed. She had already set herself to learn the local lingo. Slamming the window shut, I delved in the red *YOURS* holdall and pulled out her fluffy towel – like all prima donnas, she expected to be cosseted.

I enveloped her in the towel and rubbed gently. 'There, that's better, isn't it?' I crooned.

Tap tap on the bedroom door. I hadn't locked it. To have done so would have aroused suspicion, and I had to assume the Mackenzies were guilty till I found otherwise.

The handle turned at the same moment as Mrs Mackenzie's sharp, 'Can I trouble you a minute, Miss Smith?'

With one swift movement, I rolled up G in the towel and hurled the swaddled bundle under the bed. She gave a surprised squeak, then silence. She'd recognised an emergency. And that's what there'd be if Mrs Mackenzie threw me out of the hotel for entertaining an expressly forbidden pet. A quick glance at the open holdall reassured me that she'd see nothing more incriminating than the sheepskin rug.

Mrs M's angular body appeared in the open doorway. 'I just came up to ask if everything was all right.' Her eyes swivelled round the room, raking it for evidence of anything untoward.

'Everything's fine, thank you, Mrs Mackenzie.'

Her glance flicked to the open holdall, but she seemed satisfied. She gave the room a final once-over, and turned to go. 'Guests are expected to keep reasonable hours. The hotel is locked at midnight.' With a curt nod she went out. The door clicked shut behind her.

So…she'd checked up on me. Interesting. I stepped softly to the door and stood there with my ear pressed to the panelling. Three seconds, four, five… Then I heard her moving away and the *creak creak* as she descended the stairs. Quietly, I turned the key in the lock.

I stooped to look under the bed, 'OK, you can—'

I heard the *crunch* of tyres on gravel and crossed to the window just in time to see a van disappearing into the depths of the enormous double garage set back at a little distance from the rear of the house. The door swung down silently behind the van. Concealed by the curtain, I waited. Murdo Mackenzie, co-owner of the White Heather Hotel, emerged from a small access port carrying a plastic-wrapped package. Was it my imagination, or was there something shifty about the way he was glancing around? He moved towards the house and I lost sight of him.

From the holdall I drew out a rather old-fashioned mobile phone, in reality a state-of-the-art encrypted camera-phone. Holding it close to my mouth, I began my report.

'June 19th, 20.00 hours. Operation Scotch Mist. In position at target. Double garage at rear looks interesting. Blue transit van just arrived. Driver M, in possession of plastic-covered package.'

I switched off and moved back to the window. The mist seemed to be thinning a little, for I could now see, on the far side of the damp lawn, a large pond and the outline of two small buildings that might be the self-catering cottages. I opened the window and listened. Silence, except for muffled dripping from the saturated tree that had served as G's entrance route.

She was still under the bed. I lifted the valance sheet and peered beneath. A pair of furious copper eyes glared back at me. It took much wheedling and coaxing, and a dish piled high with her favourite salmon flakes, before, mollified, she condescended to emerge.

I waited till her tongue had rasped up the last morsel. Then, 'Sorry, G, it's time for work. You're on duty.' I reached into the holdall for the broad black collar she wore when on drug-detecting duty. Incorporated in it was a miniaturised transmitter.

The awful realisation struck that she was about to be sent out into the damp grey world. One moment she was grooming her coat, the next she'd flopped into a relaxed heap, eyes closed, heavy breathing, denoting a deep and exhausted slumber that not even the most cold-hearted taskmaster would dream of interrupting.

'Nice try, Gorgonzola.' Unfeelingly, I snapped the collar round her neck. 'Remind me to nominate you for an Oscar, Actress of the Year award.'

Training won. With only a token protest, she allowed herself to be bundled up in my arms and carried to the window. I pointed at the garage. 'Search!'

Moth-eaten tail twitching to indicate deep and continuing displeasure, she leapt lightly into the branches of that conveniently placed tree. Rustling leaves and the patter of displaced mist droplets marked her progress to the ground. With a final expressive twitch of her tail, she disappeared round the side of the garage.

I turned from the window and tuned an innocent-looking iPod to receiving frequency, then lay back on my bed, hands behind my head, waiting. Five minutes…ten minutes… The collar-transmitter was sound-activated, so there would be nothing from the receiver unless her search was successful.

My eyelids grew heavy... It had been a long drive from London and that mist had made the stretch from the Scottish border particularly tiring. My thoughts began to drift...

Rrrrrr rrrrrrr. The low crooning call from the 'iPod' brought me fully awake. It looked as if the Mackenzie establishment would indeed merit further investigation.

CHAPTER TWO

Bright sunlight filtering into the room woke me at 6.30 a.m., half an hour before the time set on my alarm. I yawned and threw back the duvet. There was no sign of Gorgonzola, who had already left on her early morning stroll. Cool air billowed out the thin curtains as I padded to the window.

The mist had cleared. For the first time I could see the full extent of the grounds behind the house. A broad green lawn stretched past the garage with its interesting contents to where, in the middle distance, a large irregularly shaped pond glinted in the pale sunlight. On the far side were two chalet-style buildings, the shapes I'd glimpsed from my window last night. A dense shrubbery of rhododendron and laurel screened them from the drive.

Sun at last. I whistled cheerfully as I made leisurely preparations to go down to breakfast. I locked the *MINE* holdall against prying eyes. I left unsecured the *YOURS* holdall with its large stock of assorted cat food and pile of sales leaflets and order forms designed to mislead anyone of an inquisitive disposition – and Mrs Mackenzie certainly fell into that category. When I was ready, I closed the window, a sign to Gorgonzola that she was expected to stay outside.

It was 7.15. That gave me almost an hour to reconnoitre

the grounds under the guise of a pre-breakfast stroll. I made my way downstairs. The early morning sunshine slanting through the Victorian stained-glass window carpeted the parquet flooring of the hall in patches of red and blue. As I had hoped, there was nobody about, though the distant clatter of dishes showed the kitchen staff was already busy.

Time to do a little snooping. A few steps and I was behind the reception desk scanning the most recent entries in the ledger, still in position. *Miss F Lannelle* from London. Two Americans, *Hiram J Spinks* from San Francisco, and *Waldo M Hinburger Jnr* from New York. A *Signora Gina Lombardini* from Milan, Italy. An English couple, *Mr and Mrs John Smythe* from Liverpool. Had Mrs Mackenzie treated Smythe with a y, pronounced, of course, Sm-eye-th, with the same scepticism she'd accorded to a plain common Smith? That's the trouble with my surname. It sometimes arouses more attention and comment than a much more exotic name like...like Lombardini or Hinburger...or...

Distracted by these thoughts, I failed to hear the soft scrape of a footfall behind me. A shadow fell across the open page.

An American voice drawled, 'I wouldn't like to be in your shoes, ma'am, if the old battleaxe, Mackenzie, catches you eyeballing that book of hers.'

A strangely clad figure was regarding me with a wide and friendly grin. A yellow and black tartan cap sat at a jaunty angle on his crew-cut head, a green T-shirt printed with a map pinpointing the major golf courses in Scotland was tucked into a pair of tweedy plus-fours. Yellow socks colour coordinated with the tartan cap.

I returned the grin. 'I can see you take the ancient art of golf seriously.' I indicated the putter he was carrying. 'Out for some early morning practice, Mr er...'

'Hiram J Spinks from San Francisco, US of A. Gotta get forty putts in before breakfast.' With a cheery wave he made for the front door, slipped the latch, and went out.

I gazed thoughtfully after the cheerful Spinks and changed my mind about that pre-breakfast stroll. If one guest was engaging in early morning golfing activity, another guest could jog without comment. A jogger blends innocently into the background. The Mackenzies had something to hide. I might arouse attention by wandering through the grounds, but jogging...

It took only a few minutes for me to return to my room and emerge clad in a rather scruffy black tracksuit reserved for the occasions when I desire to blend in with the landscape. I passed once more through the hall, but paused with my hand on the latch of the front door. My eye had been caught by a dainty ceramic hand pointing along a carpeted corridor. Underneath were the words, *This way to the Jacuzzi, Sauna, Solarium*. Curious to see the kind of facility offered by Mrs Mackenzie's northern establishment, I put on hold the early morning pleasure of investigative jogging and followed the pointing finger.

Two other plaques, equally tasteful, adorned the door at the far end of the passage. The first cooed, *We hope you enjoy our Jacuzzi – Sauna – Solarium. Guests may partake of these facilities between the hours of 7 a.m. and 9.30 p.m.* The second admonished in stern Scottish Presbyterian vein, ever mindful of human frailty, *GUESTS ARE REQUESTED TO DRESS IN A SEEMLY MANNER AT ALL TIMES.*

I pushed open the door and was enveloped in warm, humid air, heavy with the fragrance of pine. I had envisaged a plain, white-tiled room, vaguely Victorian, the tub a modernised version of a hip-bath. Instead, I made the pleasant discovery of fashionably classical tiles on walls and floor, and a Jacuzzi of the latest design.

In a proprietorial gesture, the sole occupant of the tub had flung a soft white towelling bathrobe carelessly over both of the stylish white loungers. He glared at me, patently resentful of the intrusion. I didn't fancy sharing the tub with that thickset heavy-jowled Grouch, and abandoned the temptation to have a relaxing soak in the warm bubbling waters.

'Back in a minute,' I lied, giving him a warm smile. That should keep him on edge and spoil his enjoyment. I closed the door and beat a leisurely retreat.

Outside in the open air I took a deep invigorating breath, and for the benefit of eyes that might be watching from one of the windows, did a few warm-up exercises before commencing a circuit of the grounds. My main aim was a closer examination of the garage, but before that a carefully casual jog round the front lawn would allay any suspicion. I set off, steering well clear of the intensely concentrating figure of Hiram J Spinks, head down over his putter, oblivious of anything except the white ball in front of him and the small flag he had planted a few yards away.

After two token circuits I veered round the side of the house, making towards the back lawn and my target, the garage. I was in luck. Its main door was fully raised, allowing me to see that the walls were lined with large cardboard boxes stacked from floor to ceiling. I slowed to a halt and commenced some running on the spot, followed by energetic arm and leg exercises designed to let me see as much as possible of the interior. Slow motion t'ai chi would have been less exhausting, but to have pranced up to the open door, arm fully extended like some figure from an ancient Egyptian wall painting, would certainly have been a lot more obtrusive. The blue van I'd seen last night was still there, its rear doors open. Loading – or unloading?

From inside the garage came whistles and grunts of effort and the sound of heavy boxes being dragged across the floor. My exercises halted in mid-swing. Stepping boldly to the open door, I stuck my head round the jamb. Stretching right to the back of the garage were more large cardboard boxes, stamped *MACKENZIE'S TASTE OF SCOTLAND*. I squinted through the gloom and could just make out Murdo Mackenzie hauling a heavy packing case across the floor. Swearing and cursing, he braced himself, knees bent, to heave the box into the back of the van.

'Hello there, Jimmy! No haar the day, then,' I called cheerfully. Two expressions in the Scots lingo – and before breakfast. I was proud of myself.

'What the f—' he swung round. The weight he was carrying caught him off balance and the box crashed to the floor spilling its contents in all directions. A large tartan tin rolled to my feet. His face contorted and flushed a rather alarming shade of purple. Even his scalp, visible through the combed and plastered hair, turned an interesting colour.

'My fault!' I cried. 'Do let me help you pick them up.'

Without giving him the chance to refuse, I pounced on the nearest tins and returned them to the box. They bore the same slogan as on the cardboard packing cases.

'Oh, there's another over there,' I squeaked.

I rushed to the front of the van, knelt, and picked up two cans. When I turned to face him I was holding up only one. The other was wedged somewhat uncomfortably under the waistband of my tracksuit.

'Terribly sorry if I startled you, Jimmy, but I see that van's a Ford. I was wondering if you would happen to have a spare drive belt?'

That vertical frown line between his eyes deepened, lengthened. Incomprehensible guttural sounds issued from his lips. I waited politely until he stopped to draw breath.

'Sorry. Didn't quite catch that. I have a little difficulty making out the Scottish accent,' I soothed.

The purple flush of his face darkened to aubergine. The guttural sounds increased in ferocity. Time to leave.

'But I see I've caught you at a somewhat inconvenient time, er… Jimmy,' I added hastily. 'If you find a spare drive belt, just give me a shout. Room 4. The name's Smith, without a y or an e.'

I ducked back through the doorway and jogged away in the direction of the distant clump of rhododendron bushes, elbow pressed to side to keep my prize secured. In a couple of minutes I was passing the two wooden chalets beside the pond. One, all its curtains closed, looked unoccupied, the other's window and door were open. At this early hour, somebody else was up and about.

I stopped as if to admire the view, but in fact to hitch up the tin that was threatening to escape from its precarious position and slide down my leg. I kept the pond to my left and jogged on till I reached the shrubbery to the right of the cottages.

An ornate metal signpost offered a choice of route along grassy paths. *Cottages, Walled Garden, Dovecote, Hermit's Grotto*. I took none of them, but threaded my way through to the middle of the dense clump of rhododendrons and laurels to examine my trophy. It was a tin of haggis... Had Mackenzie flown off the handle because half a kilo of haggis had landed on his toe? Or was he overreacting because I'd interrupted something shady? It could be worth sending a sample of the contents to forensic. I sniggered. At being asked to test a haggis, the boys at the lab would be sniggering too. If the results were negative, I'd never live it down. Haggis Smith, and all that...

I heard a faint rustle from the bushes behind me. I changed the snigger into a throat-clearing cough and swung round in time to see the lower branches of a rhododendron spring back into position as if released by an unseen hand. The unmistakable feeling of being watched sent a prickle down my spine. I never ignore this sixth sense. It has saved my life more than once. There I was, the stolen tin of haggis in my hand. Was the unseen watcher Mackenzie planning an ambush to retrieve his stolen property? A jumble of excuses spilt into my mind. *Just fell over it. Doing some weightlifting exercises. I'm a haggis freak on a secret binge*. All equally far-fetched.

Another rustle, this time from the clump of rhododendrons to my right. Another branch trembled and swayed. It was not likely to be Mackenzie. From what I had seen of him in action, he wouldn't be creeping about on hands and knees patiently waiting his chance. He'd be homing in on his tin of haggis with all the subtlety of an iron filing clamping itself to a magnet. Whoever it was, I had better get rid of the evidence. With a quick flick of the wrist, I lobbed that incriminating tin into the shrubbery.

Two things happened. From the bushes in front of me skirled a high-pitched shriek followed by a stream of unladylike remarks. At precisely the same moment, Gorgonzola stepped daintily out of the undergrowth, tail held high. She crouched, looked up at me with narrowed eyes and growled the growl of a half-starved cat whose breakfast is long overdue. The bushes surged, billowed, parted as a plump lady of majestic proportions, wild-eyed, indignant, erupted through the greenery brandishing the tin of haggis.

'That could have *killed* me. I could have been brained by that missile. I *demand an explanation* of this hooligan conduct! And don't insult my intelligence by telling me that you were teaching that cat to fetch.' The Plump One paused, her ample bosom heaving in agitation.

G twitched the tip of her tail, dangerously offended at being downgraded to the level of a puppy under training. Searching was a skill, a professional challenge. In no way could it be compared to a *dog* bounding after a stick.

I took a deep breath. 'I...er, *have* no explanation. At least,' I gushed, 'none that *excuses* hitting you with a projectile.'

The formidable lady seemed on the point of launching a nasty assault on my person.

I improvised hastily. 'You will have heard, however, of the Scottish Highland Games?'

An impatient nod.

'And of the sport of tossing the caber?'

Another impatient nod.

'Well, instead of tossing that great heavy lump of wood,' I continued smoothly, 'ladies can compete in tossing something much lighter, a half kilo tin of haggis. I was just indulging in a little practice. I had no idea, of course, that there was anyone nearby. I'm most *awfully* sorry. I hope the tin didn't strike too painfully?' I pinned on a worried frown.

Yikes, the virago still seemed firmly intent on GBH.

I tried a distracting gambit. 'Of course, though I've...er...thrown a haggis, I've never actually eaten the stuff. I believe it's an acquired taste.'

I seemed to have found the magic formula. The angry features softened.

'I can assure you that the haggis – at least as served here – is ab-saw-loot-ly delicious. I'll let you into a secret.' Her eyes raked the shrubbery for potential eavesdroppers. 'I'm writing an article about the culinary pleasures of this establishment. In my report I intend to award it a five-fork rating. This delicacy is served the local way with *tatties* and *neeps*—' seeing my look of mystification, she added, 'potatoes and turnips. Or alone with a glass of whisky. Quite the gastronome's delight. The vegetables are all grown, organically of course, in the Kitchen Garden over there.'

'Could I be speaking to...?' I allowed a note of awe to creep into my voice.

'Yes, Felicity Lannelle, the food writer of *Gastronome Monthly*. When I was almost *brained* by your tin, I was researching the Scottish truffle, normally thought of as a French delicacy. But would you believe it, a *prize-winning* one was found hereabouts last year!'

'No!' I exclaimed genuinely unimpressed. 'Well, I'll

certainly take the opportunity to try the haggis while I'm here, coming as it does with the highest recommendation.'

The deep resonant echoes of a gong drifted across lawn and pond.

'Ah, breakfast.' She handed me the tin. 'I recommend the porridge. Taken with sugar and cream, though, of course, true *aficionados* take it without sugar and standing up.'

Felicity Lannelle, truffle researcher, headed purposefully for the hotel intent on savouring another gastronomic delight. At which point, Gorgonzola forcibly reminded me of *her* presence by treading heavily on my foot. I stuffed the tin back into my tracksuit. One female placated, time now to placate a second.

It was 8.30 a.m. and breakfast was well underway. The airy conservatory, all white paint and cream muslin curtains, held a dozen circular tables set for two or four. Elegant little vases of summer flowers stood on crisp white cloths. I stood in the doorway trying to spot an empty seat. There was one beside Ms Lannelle in the corner, but she had spread the whole surface of the table with a variety of dishes and a large notebook. Research was obviously in progress. Another presence would certainly be unwelcome. Better not to incur her wrath again so soon.

Above the low hum of breakfast conversation, the nasal drawl of Hiram J Spinks held forth. The words 'putter', 'iron', 'bunker', drifted my way. The recipient of his discourse was an olive-skinned young woman, dark-haired, sophisticated. Could she be the Italian, Gina Lombardini? She was looking slightly bored in a polite kind of way.

The only other vacant place was beside a large potted palm. At a table for two, the Grouch of the Jacuzzi, now clad in an expensive lightweight suit of American cut, was tucking into a plate of bacon and eggs while reading a copy of the *New York Times* propped up against the coffee pot. The Waldo M Hinburger on the hotel register?

'Fine morning,' I remarked pulling back the chair and sitting down opposite. 'You don't mind if I join you?'

I hoped he was in a better mood now. He wasn't. I was rewarded with an uncommunicative grunt. I spotted the corner of the menu, just visible under the folds of the newspaper.

'Excuse me,' I reached across and tweaked it out.

The only response was the irritated rustle of newsprint from the other side of the table.

In keeping with the country house ambiance of the hotel, the choice for breakfast commenced with fruit juices, continued through cereals and Swiss muesli, porridge and cream, and Loch Fyne kippers, and culminated in the authentically Victorian dish of bacon, eggs, and devilled kidneys.

My usual breakfast is orange juice, toast and coffee but that little jog round the grounds had built up quite an appetite. I addressed the *New York Times*. 'Anything you can recommend? Did you try the porridge?'

The American waxed eloquent. 'Nope.' He turned to another page.

So, I would have to order without the benefit of his advice, but if the porridge was good enough for the gastronome, it was good enough for me. I ordered porridge and cream.

While I waited, I gave the nearest guests the once over. At the next table was a family with two well-behaved children. Mrs Mackenzie, of course, would not tolerate any rowdy behaviour. They seemed to be in deep discussion of holiday plans. Beyond them sat a newly married couple with eyes only for each other. At regular intervals they blew little kisses and fed each other morsels of toast.

'Your porridge and cream, madam.' The waitress set down a bowl and a jug. 'Some of our guests like to take it with a sprinkling of sugar. I'll bring the coffee and croissants later.'

I poured the cream and looked for the sugar. There it was. Just out of reach beside Old Grouch's coffee cup.

I leant forward. 'Please—'

The newspaper twitched violently, the coffee pot rocked, brown spots spattered over Mrs Mackenzie's pure white tablecloth.

'Cops give me a pain in the ass. What rap are ya trying to pin on me?' The American's eyes bored into mine, pupils large and black like the twin barrels of a sawn-off shotgun.

Shit. How had he blown my cover? Operation Scotch Mist seemed over before it had even begun.

'Er, what—'

'Y' said y' were a cop, didn't yuh?'

'Cop? Don't know what you mean.' Well, it was worth a try.

'Police,' he snapped impatiently.

'No, no, I was just about to say *please* pass the sugar.' I gave a nervous giggle.

A grunt, 'If y' ain't the cops, who are ya?' Suspicion still glinted in the black eyes.

When faced with a question like that, my usual fall-back is to reply that I am in the insurance business, an effective turn-off for most people. But this time, perhaps not wise. Being in the insurance business to a gangster means only one thing – the protection racket. So I said smoothly, 'DJ Smith, Cat Food Wholesale Supplies.' I fished in my pocket, and with a flourish produced a business card illustrated with a smiling cat, napkin round neck, knife and fork poised.

It had the desired effect. He visibly relaxed, his lip curling in instant contempt. DJ Smith dismissed as a patsy, no threat, no danger.

'Guess it takes all sorts,' he grunted. He folded his newspaper. 'Have to call New York. Got unfinished business with some guys.'

I looked at my watch, feigning bewilderment. 'But it'll be after midnight there.'

'Yup'. The twin-bore barrels swivelled towards me, daring me to ask more.

I busied myself dabbing cravenly at the damp spots of coffee on the tablecloth.

The waitress bustled up. 'Did you enjoy your breakfast, Mr Hinburger?'

This was met with another ambivalent grunt. He squared his broad shoulders under the expensive suit and headed purposefully out of the breakfast room.

I stared thoughtfully after him. Waldo M Hinburger's affairs would undoubtedly bear investigation. This afternoon I'd send his name and description to London with the rest of my report.

CHAPTER THREE

Hot afternoon sun blazed from a blue sky. No trace today of that awful mist. Tourists thronged the pavements of Edinburgh's Royal Mile. Boutiques, craft galleries, restaurants, and cafés all jostled for position on the narrow street. Hung around with camera and laden with guidebooks, I strolled up towards the castle, shopping for a store of experiences to swap with the other guests in the lounge after dinner.

Kit Yourself out in a Kilt. There's one for you!!! I paused at one of the many tartan shops, its window awash with every conceivable tartan garment to clothe man, woman, and child from head to foot as a member of the Clan Macdonald, Stewart, Buchanan or Campbell. Not for me. I'd leave that sort of thing to Hiram J Spinks. As I turned away, my eye caught a quirky notice on a basket by the door. *Accessorise your Pet. Match your Tartan. Coats, Hats, Bootees, Collars and Leads – His, Hers, and Its.* Gorgonzola and I like teasing each other. This would be just the thing to send her up the wall. I rummaged till I found the very thing – a pet's coat of a particularly virulent violet, red, and yellow, designed to fit a small dog – or a very large cat. I smirked. This would be something to get out on the occasions when she was being deliberately perverse. I went in and bought it.

Opposite the shop was an interesting house with its upper floors jutting precariously over the street. I crossed the road to read the plaque at the door.

> *Gladstone's Land. National Trust for Scotland.*
> 17th *century tenement home of a prosperous Edinburgh Merchant.*

Half an hour of wandering round the panelled rooms with their ornately painted ceilings would give me plenty of ammunition for after-dinner conversation in the lounge. I added it to my 'shopping basket'.

When I came out, it was nearly 3.30 p.m. I'd just have time to collect one more 'piece of shopping'. Should I voyage through Scotland's turbulent past in the Scottish Whisky Heritage Centre's barrels? Or eyeball the Scottish crown jewels and Coronation Stone of Destiny in the castle? What about visiting the 140-year-old Camera Obscura to marvel at the views in the revolving rooftop mirror? Yes, I'd do that. It wouldn't take more than quarter of an hour. Then I'd catch a bus back to the hotel. By then, the local garage should have turned up to repair the damage I'd inflicted on my car, and I'd be in good time for dinner and a chat about my 'shopping'.

One of a small group, I climbed the steps in the Camera Obscura tower to a small room at the top where lenses reflected the outside scene onto the concave surface of a circular table. Spread before me was the Royal Mile and the Tartan Shop in which I'd purchased G's coat. We all oohed and aahed as the white surface pulsed and glowed with lifelike colour in the darkened room. The faces of the passengers on an open-topped bus at the traffic lights stood out as sharp and clear as if we were standing on the pavement. I didn't like the thought that unseen eyes had watched *me* on my way up the Royal Mile.

The camera panned to the upper part of the High Street to focus on tourists consulting maps and reading the sign outside the entrance to the Whisky Heritage Centre. One of them looked up, and the shotgun eyes of Waldo M Hinburger bored coldly into mine. For one heart-stopping moment I thought he could see *me*. Beside him in a distinctive bright red jacket was the dark-haired, sophisticated young woman I had seen at breakfast, the bored recipient of Hiram J Spinks's golfing experiences. Hinburger turned towards her, the heavy jowls moving in earnest conversation.

'That's all, ladies and gentlemen.' The camera operator pulled a lever. Hinburger's image faded. 'Hope you enjoyed the show.'

By the time I'd hurried down the stairs two at a time to emerge blinking into bright sunlight, Hinburger and the woman had disappeared. Perhaps they'd gone into the Whisky Heritage Centre? Cautiously, I pushed open the door. Inside, a small queue waited to buy tickets. There was no trace of Hinburger and his companion.

I looked up and down the High Street. The throng on the pavement thinned momentarily and I caught a flash of red disappearing down a narrow alleyway. By the time I'd pushed through the hampering crowds, the passageway stretched emptily ahead. The gold lettering on the wall announced that this was *Lady Stair's Close*. Pretending to consult a guidebook, I slowed my pace to a stroll.

A few yards down the Close, the rough walls opened out into a spacious split-level courtyard. It was deserted. I hesitated, looking round as if to get my bearings. To my right, a Y-shaped stone staircase gave access to four doors, all firmly shut. Directly opposite me, below the inscription *Feare the Lord and depart from evil*, was an open door. I read the sign on the wall, *Lady Stair's House is a museum open to the public*. I looked inside, but saw no red-coated figure.

Stymied. I looked about me uncertainly, but the small-paned windows gazed blindly back, and the studded wooden doors kept their secrets. If I lurked here in the courtyard, and she had gone down those steep steps at the other end, she'd be walking away from me with every second that passed. On the other hand, she might be behind one of these firmly closed doors. Should I linger on the chance she might emerge, or should I hurry on? I tossed a mental coin and plunged on.

Abruptly the Close ended, and I found myself halfway up the hill that leads from Princes Street to the castle. *Eureka*. There Gina was, walking briskly down the hill towards Princes Street. Alone. I followed at a discreet distance, the crowded pavements providing good cover, though she didn't once look back.

She made a beeline for the Tourist Information Centre near the railway station and the Balmoral Hotel. The Centre's big room was crowded with people, so I did not feel the same need for caution now. What could be more natural than two tourists meeting in such a place? Nevertheless, I thought it better not to advertise my presence. I picked up a holiday newspaper and hid behind it, watching her as she waited in a long queue at a counter with the sign *Excursions*. At last, it was her turn. As she stepped forward, I moved closer, taking up position behind a conveniently placed leaflet rack.

'The Inchcolm Island boat trip?' the assistant's voice carried clearly. 'Yes, it runs every afternoon, but it would be advisable to book in advance. It's very popular, you know... Shall I reserve you a place?'

An inaudible mutter from my quarry.

'Your name and the hotel where you're staying?'

Another inaudible mutter.

The assistant thumbed through a book of tickets. 'Right then, Ms Lombardini, there are a few places left for Thursday and Friday. Which would you prefer?'

Speak up, I wanted to shout. I leant forward... The carrier bag containing Gorgonzola's new coat nudged against a stand of precariously stacked leaflets. As they began a silent slither to the floor, I made an ineffectual grab at them. The trickle became a rush, then a cascade. I peered apprehensively at the counter. Gina was turning round.

'*Mon Dieu! Quelle catastrophe!*' I cried, turning my head away and scrabbling for the leaflets.

A young assistant was bearing down on me. '*N'importe, madame. Puis-je vous aider?*' she asked helpfully.

By the time we'd tidied up the leaflets and restored them to their proper position and I could look around once more, Gina Lombardini had gone.

Why was she going to the island of Inchcolm? Because I'd seen her speaking with Hinburger, I was definitely interested in finding out.

The young assistant was still hovering helpfully. '*Madame? Vous voulez prendre un billet d'excursion?*'

Merde, I'd have to keep up this pretence of being French. '*Oui*.'

She directed me to stand in the queue and was still within earshot when it was my turn to be served, so I summoned up my best French-accented English for the red-head behind the counter. 'I like to go on boat journey to ze island Eenshcoom. Ven eez ze first joorney possible?'

'Thursday – there – are – still – tickets.' She spoke the words slowly and carefully.

Had Gina decided on Thursday, or Friday? I played safe, 'You have anozzer time thees week?'

She consulted her computer. 'There – are – also – tickets – for – Friday.'

'*Bon*. I zall book for zee two days.' I announced firmly.

Her voice rose in astonishment. 'You wish to book for Thursday *and* Friday?'

'*Mais oui*. In ze case that ze sea is...' I hesitated as if searching for the right word. I made up and down motions with the hands and clutched my stomach, more polite than making throwing-up noises. 'I have ze *mal de mer*, ze sickness of the sea, you understand?'

She nodded with a twitch of a smile.

'So,' I continued, 'I go ze day ze sea is not...' I waved my hands up and down once again.

That should ensure I was on the same boat as Gina Lombardini. But then I had an awful thought. I might have to make the trip on both days, if she didn't turn up on the Thursday. On possibly choppy seas. My *mal de mer* was not wholly fictional. *Merde*.

* * *

The bus deposited me a few yards from the driveway of the White Heather Hotel. There was no sign of my car by the side of the road where I'd abandoned it the night before. I hoped that meant that the mechanic had left it in the hotel car park as instructed.

I heard the click of putter against ball as I reached the bend in the drive. I rounded the curve to see Hiram J Spinks engaged in another bout of golfing practice. Here was an opportunity to size up one of the residents. Stepping over the *Keep off the Putting Green* notice, I strolled across the grass towards him. He gave me only the briefest of glances before taking up a huddled semi-stooped position, knees firmly together. A frown of concentration creased his forehead.

'Hi ma'am! Just observe this putt.'

I watched politely. *Thwack*. The ball sped across the grass, hit a tussock, bounced over the hole, rolled several yards down the slope of the lawn, and ended up in the heather bed.

Straightening up, Spinks turned towards me. 'Made a real goof there—' Suddenly, he threw down his putter and strode off towards the hotel without a backward glance.

The embarrassment of a missed putt couldn't matter *that* much, could it? Strange. I turned to make my way back to legitimate territory before Mrs Mackenzie spotted me treading on the hallowed turf of the putting green.

Gorgonzola, a moth-eaten furry mound, was stretching and yawning in the middle of the drive. Did Spinks have cat phobia? Could that be the explanation for his abrupt departure? Well, I felt much the same way about spiders. Bathed in a glow of sympathetic fellow feeling, I retrieved the ball from amongst the heather and laid it and the hastily discarded putter neatly beside the hole. No doubt he'd come back and collect them later when he'd recovered.

G rubbed against my legs, then sat down and looked up at me with an ostentatious licking of her lips, reminding me that I had been a little remiss.

'Past your teatime, G? OK, it's coming.'

I spotted my car parked close to the edge of one of the heather beds. Too close. The rear wheels were crushing the life out of a clump of Mrs Mackenzie's cherished white heathers. I'd better remedy *that* before she added the damage to my bill. I fished in my pocket for the car keys, and came up with a few coins and a used bus ticket. I must have left the spare set in my room.

I directed G to the back of the hotel. 'Tradesman's Entrance for you.'

She walked haughtily off, twitching her tail to show offence had been taken. I gently swung the carrier bag containing her tartan coat, and smiled meanly.

Spinks had left the front door ajar. The lobby was deserted, the tick of the grandfather clock loud in the silence. I eyed my room key lying beside an envelope in the pigeon-hole. If I went behind the desk to retrieve it, Mrs Mackenzie would be sure to materialise like a genie from a bottle. I behaved myself and summoned her with the porcelain hand bell.

Her bony face split into a joyless smile of greeting. 'The mechanic has left his bill with your keys.' She reached into the pigeon-hole. 'I trust you had a pleasant day, Miss Smith?' She lingered thoughtfully on 'Smith'.

I enthused as expected, omitting any reference to the Royal Mile and the Tourist Information Centre, building up my cover by adding, 'Of course, it wasn't all holiday. I was also taking the opportunity to find trade outlets. You know, cat owners can be fanatical about their pets' diet. The trouble is, I've got to carry samples that will...'

I went on to expatiate at some length on the trials of a travelling sales rep's life. Mrs Mackenzie's sour features stiffened into boredom.

Back in my room, I came to some decisions. Tomorrow, I'd open that tin of haggis and send a sample to forensic. Gorgonzola could have the rest. It would be her introduction to Scottish food. After all, when abroad one should sample the native cuisine. Tonight, there was just time before dinner to feed her, and transmit my report to London via the encrypted mobile link.

I opened the window. No sign of Gorgonzola yet, as making me wait was her way of asserting her independence. I had finished my report and was logging off, when I heard a faint scrabbling, and she slithered in over the windowsill. Ignoring me, she padded straight to the YOURS holdall and sat pointedly washing her paws.

'OK, G, let's see what's on the menu tonight.' I reached into the YOURS holdall and stopped with my hand on the tin. It didn't appear to have been searched, but eyes *had* been prying. The cat food retail lists were now in a different order.

I had purposely left the YOURS unzipped for prying eyes to view. I had positioned the MINE holdall so that the letter M matched up with a long scratch on the edge of the luggage rack. It was still perfectly aligned. My ruse had worked. Whoever had wanted to find out about me seemed to have been satisfied by all that innocent-looking cat info.

With a sharp nudge Gorgonzola pressed hard against me, the moth-eaten tail dusting my nostrils, semaphoring 'tired of waiting'. When she acts uppity I like to show her who's boss. I unwrapped the hideous tartan coat and held it up. 'Look what I've bought for you, G. This will keep you warm and dry in that horr-rr-id Scottish haar.'

Her eyes grew large as she took in the vile red, violet, and yellow monstrosity.

'Would you like to dress for dinner?' I advanced upon her, coat held out invitingly.

Her back arched and with a derisory *Haar* she shot under the bed. Satisfied that I'd established who was boss, I opened a tin of Scottish salmon from the *YOURS* holdall.

I hoped my own dinner would prove equally appetising. I arrived at the dining room just after the gong, only to find that the other guests had already seated themselves for dinner in anticipation of Mrs Mackenzie's culinary talent. As I hesitated in the doorway, Felicity Lannelle looked up and, to my surprise, made an unmistakable gesture for me to join her.

My bottom was still hovering above the chair when she leant forward across the table. 'Do introduce yourself, Ms... I've quite forgiven you for that fright you gave me this morning, or at least I will,' she lowered her voice confidentially, 'when you tell me where you acquired that tin of haggis.'

'Er...' I rotated my wineglass in uneasy circles over the tablecloth.

She placed a hand over mine, as soft and pudgy as rising dough. 'It's ab-saw-loot-ly essential for my research that I compare the tinned variety with the delicious haggis we are served at dinner. Very often the canning process affects the flavour – makes it, well, you know,' she sought for the right word, failed, and settled on 'tinny'.

She paused discreetly while the waitress came to take my order. When the girl had gone, she glanced round and lowered her voice further so I had to strain to hear. 'I asked if I could have a tin. Would you believe it? Mrs Mackenzie refused *me*, Felicity Lannelle, gastronome *extraordinaire*, and laughed in the most horribly condescending way.' Miss Lannelle's plump cheeks glowed pink at the recollected humiliation. '"My dear," she said to me, "our haggis is a culinary triumph that can be experienced only in our dining room, or abroad in high class specialist outlets. Tins simply *cannot* be obtained here. They are for export only."

'"Well," I said to her, "in that case why does one of the *other* guests have a tin?" The dragon favoured me with a stony stare and snapped, "I refuse to believe that!"'

Shit, shit, shit. I managed to school my expression to one of polite interest.

Felicity Lannelle glanced round the room to reassure herself that no one was listening. 'Of course, she asked me to identify that guest. Unfortunately, I didn't know your name...' she paused, eyebrows raised in interrogation.

'Deborah Smith,' I mumbled. Thank God she *hadn't* known who I was.

'But I described you. Early thirties, short brown hair, healing cuts on hands – have you been in an accident recently, dear?' Without waiting for a reply, she steam-rollered on. 'I assured her that you *definitely* had a tin.'

Scuppered. There were only a couple of other guests in my

age group, and neither of them had cuts on their hands.

'When did this conversation take place?' Though my pulse was racing, I kept my voice casual.

'Just a few minutes ago, before dinner.' The gastronome gave a fruity chuckle. 'By her reaction, one would have thought you had stolen the crown jewels.'

I could visualise the scene all too well.

'Perhaps,' I said slowly, desperately searching for something to say, 'the recipe *is* a family heirloom, a sort of industrial secret.'

This was something Felicity Lannelle could understand, her eyes gleamed. 'You simply *must* tell me where you got that tin.' She shot me a calculating look. 'You could, of course, sell it to me.' She opened her handbag and rummaged. 'How much do you want for it?'

I thought quickly. 'No, no… It's not a matter of money. I would gladly give you the tin for your research, Miss Lannelle…'

'Ms,' she corrected automatically.

'Ms Lannelle,' I continued, thankful for the few seconds extra thinking time. 'But the fact is, when I was coming down to dinner just now, Mrs Mackenzie caught me on the stairs and demanded it back. That's why I was a little late.'

She closed her handbag with a disappointed snap. 'You see, I've taken a self-catering apartment here *precisely* so that I can make my tests, on site as it were. There's so much more freedom with self-catering. Of course, I have my little travelling stove for places that don't have cooking facilities.' She fell silent, toying with the half-eaten roll on her plate. 'Mrs Mackenzie's repossessed the tin, you say?'

I nodded.

'What a pity! Such a golden opportunity to find out if this establishment has managed to retain the flavour of their gourmet food *after* the canning process.'

I relaxed. That plausible lie of mine had worked.

All of a sudden Ms Lannelle brightened. 'You can still tell me *where* you got the tin.' She played her ace. 'I gather Mrs Mackenzie didn't give you it in the first place, so just how *did* you acquire it?'

My turn to fall silent. I couldn't tell her the literal truth, 'fallen off the back of a lorry' – or in this case a van. There'd be no harm, I suppose, in telling her that I had got the tin from the garage. If she tried to filch one, her amateurish attempt would perhaps help to divert suspicion from DJ Smith...

That seemed to satisfy her, but I finished the meal without much recollection of what I had eaten.

As soon as I decently could, I excused myself and hurried up to my room. I'd hidden the tin of haggis in the *YOURS* holdall underneath the other tins of cat food. It had still been there on my return from Edinburgh. I seized the holdall and without ceremony upended it on the bed. Out rolled tins of turkey, salmon, pâté de foie gras, caviar, and cream dessert.

But of the tin of *Mackenzie's Taste of Scotland* there was no sign, no sign at all.

CHAPTER FOUR

Pensively, I made my way downstairs. Was my cover blown? The haggis tin had been in the same holdall as the cat food so, with a bit of luck, the Mackenzies might think that I had taken it to add to my samples. That would be the line I would take if they brought up the matter.

In Mackenzie avoidance mode, I paused at the final turn of the stairs and scanned the hall below. The reception desk was unmanned, though the door behind it stood ajar. From behind the closed door of the lounge filtered the muffled sounds of television, male voices, and a high-pitched female laugh. I'd head for the lounge and seek safety in numbers.

I was tiptoeing past the reception desk when I heard Mackenzie voices raised in bitter argument, 'Bloody woman...tin...'

I crept round the desk to the door behind and eased it further open to reveal a narrow corridor, dark uncarpeted stairs, and at the bottom a shaft of light streaming out of an open doorway.

I heard Murdo whine defensively above the faint clash of dishes. 'But, Morag, how was I...?'

'Mackenzie, a bairn of ten wouldn't be as gormless as you...' The steely voice sliced off his words with the efficiency of an unsheathed skean-dhu.

A tongue-lashing followed. I was quite enjoying Mrs M's inventiveness, but I knew I mustn't risk being caught eavesdropping.

I was just easing the door shut again, about to tiptoe away, when I heard her snap, 'Perhaps no harm has been done, but when you go off to the meeting tomorrow afternoon, you'd better keep quiet about that tin of haggis, or it won't just be me you've got to deal with.'

Mackenzie said something indecipherable in reply. The shaft of light from the open door widened. Time to leave. A couple of strides took me across to the lounge door. I could hear the scrape of footsteps ascending the stairs from the kitchen.

Sudden tell-tale sound burst from the lounge as I opened the door, a dead giveaway to the Mackenzie on the stairs who'd hear it and realise that whoever was in the hall might very well have overheard the argument in the kitchen.

I slipped into the room, swiftly closing the door behind me, and subsided onto the sofa beside Felicity Lannelle. A breathless, 'Sorry, had to rush away from the table. Phone call to make. Can't wait to hear your verdict on the meal.'

'Oh! You did give me a bit of a turn there,' she clutched hand to heart dramatically. 'It does upset the digestion so. You see, stress can cause acid production in the stomach and...'

Over her shoulder, I was aware of the angular Mrs Mackenzie framed in the doorway. She glanced round speculatively. After an interminably prolonged inspection, she announced, 'Hot drinks and biscuits will be available, here in the lounge, between 9 p.m. and 10 p.m.' She withdrew with a last suspicious look round the room.

'...you will, won't you?' Felicity was looking at me expectantly, obviously waiting for a reply.

I had been listening with only half an ear. 'Er, well...yes, of course,' I hazarded.

She gave a delighted cry. 'I knew you'd help when I explained how *important* it was to get hold of some haggis.' She leant forward confidentially. 'Now, I've been thinking. We won't have to break into the garage to get a tin—'

'Break into the garage? *We?*' *My* acid levels took a hike. 'We won't?'

'No.' She folded her arms and sat back triumphantly. 'Because they prepare it in the *kitchen*. I've smelt it. Such a heavenly aroma!' Her eyes rolled ecstatically.

Oh God, I seemed to have committed myself to assisting Felicity in a raid. Too late, I tried to extricate myself.

'But I don't think I could... No,' I said firmly, 'I certainly couldn't.' I cast round for a convincing excuse.

Ms Lannelle's soft brown eyes narrowed and grew hard as olive stones.

'Oh, but you *must*,' she urged softly. Leaning forward, she patted my arm. 'If you don't, I'll have to tell Mrs Mackenzie your little secret.'

How could she know anything about Operation Scotch Mist? I stared at her with wide-open insincere eyes. 'But I haven't *got* a secret.'

She put a plump finger to her lips, then reached for the television remote control and twitched up the volume a couple of notches. 'Fib!' she cried playfully. 'I saw you letting that scruffy stray cat into your room. But don't you worry. I'm a cat lover myself.' She looked pointedly at the scratches on my hands. 'Take my advice, dear, stick to pedigree cats. They're less likely to turn on you. Help me with my little problem, and the whole affair will be just our little secret.' She closed an eye in an exaggerated conspiratorial wink. Considerations of ethics patently played no part in a gastronome's scheme of things.

Hell hath no fury like a Foodie scorned. I felt a grudging admiration for Ms Lannelle's tactics. But Operation Scotch Mist would be seriously jeopardised if I were thrown out of the hotel and could no longer keep the Mackenzies under close observation. Though I knew I was beaten, I made one last attempt to wriggle out of her cunning trap.

'But, Ms Lannelle,' I said with not-altogether feigned astonishment, 'I don't see why you need my help. I'm quite sure that you could manage perfectly well on your own. All you'll have to do is sneak across from your cottage in the middle of the night and help yourself to a sample of haggis from the kitchen. I'll give you my key to the front door.'

She sighed. 'Well now, I have my own little confession to make.' A rush of words, 'I have this silly fear of the dark, have to keep a night light on in my room. If there's a power cut at night,' her massive frame shuddered, 'I just go to pieces!' She gave an embarrassed giggle.

At 2.05 a.m. a triangle of light, too bright for a night bulb, escaped from between the curtains of Felicity Lannelle's self-catering cottage, evidence that she was awake, eagerly awaiting my arrival with the coveted haggis.

I turned away from the window and crossed to the bedroom door. Gorgonzola lazily opened one eye, curiosity wrestling with comfort. Comfort won. She decided my activities had nothing to do with her, and went back to sleep.

A black shape amid the shadows of the upper landing, I stood at the top of the stairs, letting my eyes adjust to the dim glow of the emergency lights. The rays of a full moon stained the stair carpet with the patterns of the Victorian window, its bright colours of daytime now washed out and anaemic. I listened to the sounds of the sleeping house, vague creaks and rustlings, the measured tick...tock...from the old grandfather clock down in the hall. Satisfied there was nobody else about, I carefully made my way downstairs.

The lock on the door behind the reception desk was no match for the gadget I took from my pocket. One twist and the levers clicked back. I flicked on a pencil torch, picked my way down the steps to the basement kitchen, and played its narrow ray on the door at the foot of the stairs. No antiquated Victorian lock, this, or even a modern five-levered mortise, but a device that might be a match for even my sophisticated equipment. Overdoing the security for the kitchen of a country house hotel, weren't they? Evidence of something to hide?

It took a full ten minutes before the lock yielded to my pick-lock gadget and the door swung open. The moon was shining through the large window, the brightness of its rays intensified by the white and stainless steel surfaces of an ultra-modern kitchen.

Nothing out of the ordinary here, except for two huge stainless-steel vats that stood against the back wall beside a large white cabinet. A quick inspection brought disappointment. Empty.

I turned my attention to the white cabinet. A faint hum suggested it was some kind of refrigerator. I pulled open the door.

Inside were stacked several large containers of Felicity Lannelle's precious haggis and a plastic canister full of a thick dark brown liquid labelled *Gravy for Haggis*. 'Eureka!' I breathed. I took a spoon from a drawer and filled Felicity's bowl with haggis. As an afterthought, I poured on a generous quantity of the gravy. I'd better give her the whole cordon bleu offering, or I'd find myself making a return visit to the kitchen to fetch that missing ingredient. More in hope than expectation, I spooned a sample of the haggis into an empty film canister to send to London.

It was frustrating that a thorough search had revealed nothing suspicious. But that security lock was too expensive for so ordinary a kitchen. Perhaps there was an entirely innocent explanation, such as an attempt to protect a traditional family recipe? No. Gut feeling told me that the Mackenzies were guarding a more sinister secret. When Murdo went to that meeting in a few hours, I would follow him to find out.

I looked round once more. Satisfied that I had left no trace of my presence, I made my way back upstairs to the lobby. By now the coloured pattern from the window had moved from stairs to wall. Controlling my breathing, listening to the loud ticking of the grandfather clock, I stood in the shadows behind the reception desk. I counted slowly to a hundred before I crossed to the glass inner door and slid back the Yale latch. The heavy key in the outer wooden door turned smoothly. No high security locks here.

A huge moon floodlit the lawn and glittered on the surface of the pond, laying a silvery path across the dark water to the lighted window of the self-catering cottage and an eager Felicity Lannelle. I glanced back at the house. No lights, but eyes *could* be watching, so it took me fifteen minutes to take a circuitous route to the shrubbery, but once under its cover, it was easy to move swiftly to the rear of her cottage.

A faint glow filtered through tartan curtains. At my discreet tap the light dimmed.

A shadowy figure inched the window open a crack, and hissed, 'Is that you, dear? Have you got it?'

'Yes to both,' I muttered, resisting the temptation of, 'It's Mrs Mackenzie come to see what's cooking!'

Felicity was wearing a vibrant orange caftan protected by a large white apron. Behind her, I glimpsed a pot standing on the cooker, and on the worktop a notepad and pen laid out ready for use.

'Oh, thank you so much, dear.' She seized the bowl of haggis. 'I just can't *wait* to test it. In fact, I'm *not* waiting. I'm going to try out a little recipe of my own right now!'

A plump hand waved in dismissive farewell. Ms Lannelle was already lost in her own foodie world.

Gorgonzola did not take kindly to being disturbed twice by my coming and going, or to be exact, going and coming, in the middle of the night. She took her revenge by making numerous perambulations of her own. I drifted in and out of a troubled sleep, punctuated by a half-remembered dream...

...a Felicity cum Gorgonzola figure, clad in a tartan caftan, sat at a white-clothed table, napkin knotted round neck, knife and fork poised. Gorgonzola with Felicity's body, or Felicity with G's face? I was still trying to figure it out when Mrs Mackenzie, smiling proudly, marched up holding a tray piled high with bowls of steaming haggis. With a flourish, she placed bowl after bowl on the table until Gorgonzola Lannelle disappeared behind a haggis rampart.

'I want some too,' I cried. With my right foot zipped into the *MINE* holdall, and my left in the *YOURS*, I shuffled across the dining room waving a large wooden spoon. Mrs Mackenzie held up her tray, now engraved with the message, *The management regrets no Smiths can be entertained*. Her thin lips moved, but all that emerged was the high-pitched purring croon that Gorgonzola had been trained to utter when she detected illicit drugs...

The bleep of my alarm woke me. Prising open one heavy eyelid, I tried to focus on the dial. 7.30 a.m. Sleepily, I turned over, then with a supreme effort of will flung back the duvet. Curled up on the end of the bed, Gorgonzola didn't even stir.

'A night on the tiles at our age catches up with us, doesn't it, G?' I murmured as I headed for the shower. I mustn't be late for breakfast. That would draw unwelcome attention to myself. Keep a low profile. Give Mrs Mackenzie no cause to notice me.

There was no sign of Felicity Lannelle at breakfast. Hardly surprising, considering the time she must have spent tasting and making detailed notes. She probably wouldn't have been able to face breakfast anyway, after consuming that bowl of haggis – unless, as with wine-sampling, it was a case of taste and spit.

Also missing from his usual position beside the potted plant was godfather figure, Waldo M Hinburger. I checked out the other tables. Not there either. Perhaps he had spent most of the night contacting his associates in the States. I'd arrange for a tap to be put on the phone line, but that would necessitate a warrant, a lot of supporting evidence, and, therefore, time. At least he wouldn't get between me and my breakfast today.

I sat in my car, gloomily contemplating the boring hours I might have to spend waiting for Mackenzie's blue van to set off to that meeting, and for the umpteenth time looked at the dashboard clock. 12.15. My position in the lay-by, three hundred yards or so from the White Heather Hotel, should give me a clear view of the van. I stretched a cramped leg and yawned. The car interior was stiflingly hot even with the windows down. It was becoming a real effort to stay awake...

The nose of the blue van edged out from the driveway. A clash of gears, a spurt of gravel, and the van set off in the direction of the capital. I allowed a couple of cars to pass me, then slipped in behind and followed at a discreet distance. This could be the breakthrough we'd been waiting for.

CHAPTER FIVE

I stood under a casuarina tree wearing wrap-around sunglasses and a silk headscarf, a thin disguise but it would have to do. The glasshouses of Edinburgh Botanic Gardens seemed an odd place to hold a meeting, but Mackenzie had made straight there, looking neither to right nor left. And he had not come to talk to the plants, I was sure of that.

I peered through the cascading blue-green waterfall of branches. The Temperate House with its variety of greens – pale, dark, olive, bottle, and grey – could equally well have been called the Temperate Jungle. Shrubs grew head-high, trees tapped at the glass roof sixty feet above – mimosa, magnolia, banksia, bottlebrush, some kind of oak, everything so luxuriant that I couldn't see the small group of tourists making their way along another path, only track their progress by their chatter.

'Just look at those purple berries...'

'Not purple. I'd say they were cobalt blue...'

'Never seen a fuchsia with flowers like that...'

'A *tomato* tree, well I never...'

Which of the paths through the thick foliage had Mackenzie taken? The nearest wound under a high-level concrete walkway thickly covered in climbing plants that held its upper railing in a stranglehold and trailed predatory tendrils down towards the path below. No trace of him down here. He must have gone to the higher level. Leaving the cover of the casuarina tree, I hurried towards the flight of steps.

From above my head came Mackenzie's unmistakable whine, 'I don't see why we have to change the drop site. It's perfectly safe. The new place will be a lot more difficult to—'

'*We'll* decide that,' a gravelly American voice cut him short. 'Your job is to do what you're told, fella.' The tone was menacing, the voice familiar. Waldo M Hinburger.

I heard the squeak of a door opening, and the words were abruptly cut off as it closed. I raced up the steps. By the time I got there, the walkway was deserted, but the South American House was only a few yards to the left. Through the glass I could see a hump-backed bridge over a pool surrounded by giant bromeliads. On guard near the door was the sort of plant I visualised Hinburger cultivating in his yard, a murderous-looking agave, the tips of its ferocious leaves looking as if they'd been dipped in blood.

Nobody was on the bridge, nobody on the path round the pool. With no need for caution, I ran across the bridge to glance in the adjoining Arid House. Spiky cacti, green against the dusty red, buff, and grey of low stone outcrops, stared aggressively back. A few people were wandering round, but Mackenzie and Hinburger weren't among them.

I'd turned left at the top of the stairs, so Mackenzie and his companion must have gone right. I rushed back the way I'd come, slowing to a more decorous pace when I joined other visitors on the walkway. More hurry, less speed. A meandering family group, infant in pushchair, grandad with stick, blocked my path. I stepped to the left, grandad shuffled left. I stepped right, the old man stopped dead. His stick swung out at an angle, threatening to entangle itself with my legs, collision avoided by a hair's breadth.

'Excuse me... So sorry...' Mumbling suitable apologies, I dodged past and hurried on. A magnificent red passion flower scrambling over the railings stretched out tendrils to clutch at my neck and pluck at my clothes. No time to read its label, no time to admire that purple flower with its velvety leaves, sniff at the fluffy yellow balls of the mimosa, or view close-up the frozen blue-green cascades of the casuarina tree.

Which way now? To the right, the corridor led to the orchids and cycads. Ahead loomed the steamed up doors of the Tropical Aquatic House. Through the misted glass, hazy and indistinct like a Monet painting, I could make out a pool carpeted with giant water lilies, and, moving away, a blurred burly figure.

Warm, humid air gusted into my face as I opened the door and slipped in. The hiss of humidifiers and the steady drip of moisture from trees massed between glass and water sounded unnaturally loud. The pool took up most of the area. Huge water lilies, fragile green pads turned up at the rim like enormous spiky flan dishes, spread across the surface of the dark water.

At the far end of the glasshouse, the door was slowly closing on its weight. Assuming Mackenzie and Hinburger had gone into the next house, there was no cover on the wide path if they took it into their heads to return. On the other hand, they'd probably not notice a woman in headscarf and sunglasses taking an intense interest in those croton leaves streaked Jackson Pollock-style, red, yellow, green and orange.

With my hand on the Fern House door I had second thoughts. It might be better to retreat now, while the going was good. After all, I had made *some* progress – I'd established that there was definitely a link between Mackenzie and an American gangster, and I'd overheard a reference to 'drop sites'. Better a small success than a fatal setback for Scotch Mist if they were put on their guard. On the other hand, what I had learnt so far wasn't enough to act on. I took a calculated risk and pushed open the door.

The drop in temperature was marked as the cold mistiness of the Fern House enveloped me, the damp air heavy with the smell of mouldering vegetation. I stopped just inside the doorway, concentrating on the sounds around me – a hiss of mist nozzles, the pit-pat of moisture dripping from the fronds of tree ferns, their intricately incised leaves gracefully arching high overhead, the noisy burbling of a small stream. And off to the right, the faint murmur of voices.

There was not enough cover along a central path, but another to the left twisted through crowding trunks and giant ferns. I crept along it. The voices were louder now, an American twang, a woman's derisive laugh, but the words were muffled by the gurgling of the stream and the thick vegetation. Frustrated, I hesitated in mid-creep. Just tourists. I'd foolishly jumped to conclusions when I'd glimpsed that blurred figure through the glass. Disconsolately, I rubbed a finger along a tree fern's woolly cinnamon stem. They'd be well away by—

'No, I tell you!' Hinburger's raised voice made me jump.

Then, a woman's voice, indistinct.

A murmur from Hinburger.

Silence.

I inched closer, straining to hear.

Mackenzie whined petulantly, 'There's nothing wrong with the castle. It's the best place.'

Hinburger, Mackenzie – and perhaps Gina Lombardini? I raised a hand to ease apart the fronds, when, loud and clear from Hinburger, 'Yeah, but...'

Loud and clear. That meant they were... I turned and ran back the way I had come. The noisy stream that I had cursed for blocking out their conversation now concealed the scrape of my feet on the wet stone. If they caught even a glimpse of me... There's nothing more suspicion-rousing than a running figure. Too late I realised I should have relied on the camouflage of the commonplace, whipped out my notebook and crouched down amongst the ferns in artist's drawing mode.

The door of the Fern House swung closed behind me.

Long before I could make my escape from the Tropical House, they would come through that same door. Crisis. There was no one else here to engage in conversation, no group to mingle with. I looked round for a hiding place. The mass of foliage – tropical shrubs, banana plant, coffee bush, colourful croton – was closely packed, but I'd leave a trail of damage that the three of them couldn't fail to notice. I might as well put up a sign announcing, *Somebody hiding here!*

There was no other cover, none at all. Only that thick clump of sugar cane growing in the brown waters of the pool...

I stuffed my headscarf and glasses into my pocket, thankful that there was no one to create a fuss as I slid into the pool. I lay stretched out, submerged in the dark water, the back of my head towards the Fern House door. My ears would tell me what was happening. I waited, body shielded by the giant spiky pad of a water lily, head hidden by the thick stems of sugar cane.

I heard the door opening and footsteps passing by, very close. The woman was saying, 'We decide this after I been there, yes?' Foreign accent.

Hinburger growled a reply.

Something nibbled at my hand. I had a vision of a darting mass of piranha, my arm terminating in white skeletal fingers. I was being a silly fool. They wouldn't allow dangerous fish in a pool accessible to children's hands. I gritted my teeth and flicked my fingers as vigorously as I dared. Little mouths snacked on my other hand. Something large brushed against my leg.

Ignoring for a moment the fishy diners feasting on my hands, I squinted past the long aspidistra-like leaves of a beautifully patterned plant. I'd been right, the woman was indeed Gina Lombardini.

She was striding ahead of the others, calling impatiently over her shoulder, 'Come, come! Let us get out of here quickly. You know I not like being shut up in these so-closed places!'

With a soft thud the door closed behind them. I mulled over what she had said. *We decide this after I been there*. Where? Was that her reason for going on that excursion to Inchcolm? And were they arguing about where to bring ashore their drug consignments? Could this be a link between Mackenzie,

Hinburger *and* Lombardini? Progress at last.

A sharp nip from a would-be piranha brought me back to my present predicament. I sat up. I heard a clatter of little footsteps behind me and a childish voice piping, 'Mummy, why is that lady having a bath?' A curly haired child in pink dungarees and floppy sun hat was staring round-eyed at me. 'Mummy, can I have a bath too?'

I gazed back gravely. 'It's really rather nasty in here. Those little red fish eat you.'

She sucked a finger while she considered the matter. Then the little face crumpled. With a loud wail she turned to look for her mother.

I heaved myself onto dry land, and with as much dignity as possible marched, dripping muddy water, past her open-mouthed parent. I had almost reached the door, when it was flung open by a burly member of the Botanic Garden's police force.

'So you're not drowned, lassie?' He sounded relieved. 'Someone down below in the underwater viewing area was looking through the observation glass at the fish, and saw the outline of a body floating up here in the big pool. Gave her quite a fright,' he added reprovingly.

I flashed him my most winning smile and my ID card, fortunately laminated and waterproof.

'Revenue and Customs investigations,' I hissed enigmatically. *'Top Secret.'* I left him gazing after me.

I dripped my way back along the walkway and down the stairs. Heads turned, but no one said anything, foreigners mystified, British too polite, I suppose.

Outside, there was no sign of Hinburger and his

companions. The sun blazed down from the bluest of skies and only the faintest of breezes stirred the yellow daisies in the herbaceous border beside the glasshouses, but in my sopping clothes I was chilled. Better try to dry out first. I didn't fancy a horribly uncomfortable drive back to the hotel. I'd follow the example of the citizens of Edinburgh who were stretched out on the grassy lawns, arms neatly folded over bodies, legs decorously crossed at the ankle, as if pole-axed by the unaccustomed heat and laid out ready for burial by some zealous undertaker. I found a sunny spot sheltered from the wind and laid myself out, arranging my limbs in what seemed to be the approved position. As a faint grey ectoplasm of steam rose slowly from my wet clothes, I closed my eyes and let the warmth of the sun seep into me. My thoughts drifted...

An American voice interrupted the half-doze, 'Waal, hi there, ma'am!' Looming above me was Hiram J Spinks's hideous yellow and black tartan cap in Macleod tartan, or perhaps more accurately, MacLoud. He was staring at my steaming clothes with undisguised curiosity.

'Fell in the pond,' I said quickly, before he could ask. 'I overbalanced while trying to feed the ducks. Don't ask me more. I'm too embarrassed. And it would be simply *awful* if anybody at the hotel heard about it.'

He clucked sympathetically, 'You can sure rely on me, ma'am.' He put a finger to his lips.

I hoped I could. It wouldn't do at all if Hinburger, Mackenzie and the Signora heard that I had visited the Botanics at precisely the same time as themselves. As the yellow and black cap vanished behind a giant clump of pampas grass, I raised my face to the sun again, vaguely wondering why, on such a perfect day, Hiram J Spinks had preferred to come here rather than tramp round one of his beloved golf courses.

Much later, water-stained and crumpled, but nearly dry, I drove back. An ambulance shot out of the hotel drive just as I was about to turn in, forcing me to brake sharply. In the mirror I watched the receding blue light. Had there been an accident in the kitchen? Had a guest suffered a heart attack? I drove slowly up the drive.

A knot of people stood in an animated huddle in front of the house. I parked the car and, conscious of my bedraggled appearance, made for the door, hoping they would be too engrossed to notice me.

As I sidled past, I caught snatches of conversation.

'...perfectly OK last night.'

'...found in her room.'

'...unconscious and white as a corpse. She was breathing in a very funny way. Botulism, I shouldn't wonder...'

'My God! What was she eating last night?' A tubby little man stared wildly round. His eyes lit up as they fell on me sneaking past. 'I say, weren't you sitting at her table last night? Did she eat—' his voice quavered, '—the mussels?'

Five pairs of eyes skewered me.

'I'm sorry,' I stammered. 'I don't know what...who...?' I tailed off.

'Miss Lannelle. We're talking about Miss Lannelle. Haven't you heard?'

'What's happened?' I hoped I sounded only mildly

interested. 'She seemed to be in good health last night in the lounge.'

'Well, she would, wouldn't she? It can take several hours for food poisoning to strike.' The tubby man clutched desperately at my arm. 'Well, *did* she eat the mussels?'

I looked him straight in the eye.

'Why, yes,' I said untruthfully, calculating correctly that the resulting consternation would enable me to slip quietly away.

As I made my way through the hall, through the open door of the dining room conservatory I caught a glimpse of an uncharacteristically flustered and agitated Mrs Mackenzie supervising the setting of tables for the evening meal.

Once in my room, I went over to the window to let in Gorgonzola. On the far side of the pond, I could see that the door of Felicity's cottage was open. *Was* she suffering from food poisoning? Her build, lifestyle and occupation made her a prime candidate for a coronary. *Could* she have had a heart attack? As I watched, Mackenzie came out and pulled the door shut. He seemed to be having some difficulty with the lock because he was holding something in his left hand. *Shit*, I'd left my binoculars in the car. I narrowed my eyes in an effort to focus better. Yes, there was definitely something in his hand, something white, but his body was screening it from view as he walked briskly along the path that led through the shrubbery back to the hotel. Concealed behind the filmy curtain, I waited for him to reappear.

When he did, his hands were empty. Whatever he'd been carrying, he didn't have it now.

CHAPTER SIX

Dinner that night was a sombre and silent affair. Eyes suspiciously scrutinised Mrs Mackenzie's best culinary efforts, making a careful forensic examination of each plate of food. By nine o'clock the dining room was empty, the lounge deserted. Those who had not already checked out had retreated behind the closed doors of their rooms to await in fearful anticipation the first symptoms of the dreaded botulism. I, too, had sought the privacy of my room, but for a very different reason – to await the reply to my urgent email request for priority analysis of the haggis sample and a medical report on Ms Lannelle's collapse.

Sample – Negative. I pursed my lips in disappointment. Perhaps the medical report would be more illuminating. I stared at the screen...*a massive heroin overdose.* I switched off the 'iPod' and mulled over the information. Felicity Lannelle, a heroin addict? No way! That overdose *must* somehow be linked to her midnight feast. But the haggis she'd eaten came from the *same* container as the sample that had tested negative... I couldn't figure it out.

G tapped softly on my foot, ready for *her* dinner. In view of the current seafood scare in the Mackenzie establishment, it would be insensitive to choose anything even slightly fishy. I busied myself spooning out succulent chunks of *Dawn-shot Highland Grouse* while I pondered the riddle of Felicity's overdose. There must be an answer. I watched idly while Gorgonzola rapidly demolished her heaped plate. A final rasping at the empty plate with her tongue, then she looked up, eyes wide and appealing, all part of her well-tried can-I-have-some-more Oliver Twist routine. Pretending I hadn't noticed, I moved over to the window and looked over to the self-catering cottage. The answer might lie there.

'You're going to have company on your midnight stroll tonight, G,' I said.

The hotel was a black shape against the faintly luminous night sky. A dull light glowed from behind the tightly drawn curtains of one window of the hotel. The full moon had not yet risen to silver lawn and pond, and my dark jeans and jacket merged with the night. I was still edgy, but once Felicity's cottage shielded me from the hotel, I relaxed a little. I'd sent Gorgonzola out wearing her working collar. Now I summoned her with the cat whistle, and, while I waited, inserted my pick-lock in the chalet door.

Click. I pushed open the back door into the kitchen and played the narrow beam of my pencil torch over an overturned chair. On the table stood a bottle of wine and a half-full glass, Felicity's pen and open notepad beside them.

A tail curling round my legs announced Gorgonzola's arrival.

'This could be *Flannan Isle* or the *Marie Celeste,* eh, G?'

I pulled the door shut behind us. Though the curtains were drawn over the windows, I couldn't risk putting on the light.

In the bedroom my torch picked out Felicity's voluminous nightdress, neatly folded, lying on a chair. The bed had not been slept in.

'She must have been taken ill pretty soon after eating the haggis. What do you think, G?'

Gorgonzola ventured no opinion, merely scratched her ear and yawned.

I moved back to the kitchen. Mackenzie had definitely taken *something* from the chalet. And disposed of it. A tablecloth was on the table, but no dishes or cutlery. I pulled open cupboards till I found the one where the pots were stored. A rack held two pots and a frying pan. There was one empty space. A cooking pot was missing – and the bowl I had used to carry the haggis from the kitchen. A room maid might have washed up, but she wouldn't have removed pot and bowl. And surely she'd have picked up the overturned chair. I checked the other cupboards in case she'd stacked the bowl with the other crockery. No bowl.

It seemed pretty clear that Mrs Mackenzie's hen-pecked spouse had removed the tell-tale evidence of Felicity's midnight feast. He'd carried it away in a kitchen bin liner from the spares under the sink. And disposed of it in the shrubbery. That's what I'd seen from my window. Perhaps he'd been afraid that Public Health Inspectors would come to investigate a case of food poisoning.

'Well, G,' I scooped her up, opened the door and deposited her outside on the step. 'It's up to you to find out if it's still there.'

I was halfway along the path back to the hotel when I heard her crooning call. Only a few minutes of searching the shrubbery and she'd sniffed out the bin liner bag. Behind me and off to the left. I started to feel my way through the shrubbery. A faint glimmer in the sky from the rising moon silhouetted the tops of the bushes, but under foot it was pitch black. The torch remained in my pocket, unused. Every window at the rear of the hotel was a potential eye to observe its beam or the reflection of its light on leaves and ground.

'It's all right for you, G,' I muttered as I stumbled over roots and low branches. 'You can see in the dark. And you're—'

I could just make out a denser rounded patch of black ahead, a low mound topped by a smaller ball, like a giant's woollen hat with a bobble. A crooning bobble.

'That didn't take you long, clever cat. That deserves a little reward when we get back. How do you fancy a bit of roast duck?'

The croon changed to a deep reverberating purr. The bobble heaved, grew four legs and a bushy tail, and detached itself from the mound. I edged forward, one step…two… My foot caught on something sharp and metallic, and I pitched forward, landing heavily on the soft earth. As I lay there winded, disorientated by the sudden shock of the fall, I was treated to a mouse-eye view of Gorgonzola's concerned face. She reached out an enquiring paw and gently patted my nose.

I got shakily to my feet and risked playing the beam over the ground. Sunk into the grass was an ornate metal sign bearing the words *Hermit's Grotto*. Set into the mound was a low doorway, and inside, tucked behind a clump of ferns, a plastic bag containing the cooking pot, spoon and bowl.

As the contents were pretty much dried and crusted, it was easy to collect a scraping of each into my sample containers. I stored each carefully labelled canister in an inner pocket. By confirming the presence of heroin in Felicity's haggis meal, G had given me the hard evidence I'd needed of a *connection* between the Mackenzies and the drug.

Gorgonzola was waiting for me when I got back to Room 4, sitting beside the *YOURS* holdall, metaphorical knife and fork in paw, napkin under chin.

'I wasn't forgetting, G.' I picked out a tin of roast duck in gravy and ladled out the promised reward.

She crouched there daintily eating, muted *slurps* punctuated now and then by rumbling *purrs* of satisfaction. Her tail twitched gently from side to side, a swingometer of enjoyment.

'All that eating's putting on the fat, Gorgonzola. Shall I cut out tomorrow's breakfast?' This said with kindly concern, one female to another.

She stopped in mid-chew and looked up, a glistening drop of gravy clinging to one whisker.

Gravy. I made the connection. Last night I had taken the haggis sample. And then I had added *gravy* to Felicity's bowl. That innocent-looking sauce in the Mackenzie's fridge was nothing other than heroin in liquid form. Concentrated, deadly. Otherwise known as 'Polish Soup'.

I scooped up an astonished cat and planted a triumphant kiss on her nose.

The soft buzz of the alarm woke me at seven a.m. Tentatively, I opened one eye. No bright sunlight this morning. What I could see of the sky through a gap in the curtains was grey and stormy. Was that the sound of rain pattering against the window? Last night's intention to rise early for another investigative jog no longer seemed such a good idea. I pulled the duvet over my head. What a day! I snuggled down and decisively closed the opened eye. No need, really, to get up for another half hour…

Gorgonzola had other ideas. The bed shuddered and creaked as a heavy weight landed on my legs. An impatient paw pushed aside the duvet and an indignant furry face peered in accusingly at me. *She* was ready for her early morning jog. I groaned and gave in.

After I'd shut the window behind her, I reluctantly made up my mind to face getting dressed. My eye fell on the soft white bathrobe hanging behind the door. A soak in a warm tub would be just the thing on such a morning. Keeping my fingers crossed that the disgruntled Grouch would not already have taken up residence, I slipped the robe over my swimsuit and made my way down to the Jacuzzi.

As I turned the corner of the stairs, I heard the *click* of the front door quietly closing. Through the door's patterned glass, I glimpsed a tall shadowy figure and the unmistakable yellow and black of Hiram J Spinks's golfing cap. I had to hand it to someone who could face that awful weather just to knock a little ball about. There was no one else around at that early hour, and it looked as if I would have the Jacuzzi all to myself.

I poked my head round the door. If the bad-tempered American was there, I might reconsider. The room was satisfyingly empty, though someone had left a bathrobe in a crumpled heap on the tiled floor. Probably that slob, the Grouch, hadn't bothered to take it back to his room. I virtuously made a point of hanging up mine on one of the hooks.

The green waters boiled and frothed invitingly. I dipped a

foot in, feeling for the step invisible under the turbulence. I found it and stood there for a moment in the welcoming warmth. Lowering myself in, I lay along the seat allowing the jets to pummel my legs. The bubbles foamed against my shoulders. I closed my eyes. Utter relaxation. I must make a point of doing this more often. No wonder people went in for Jacuzzis in a big way, even installing them in their gardens.

A droplet splashed in my eye. I sat up, swinging my legs down off the seat. My foot touched something soft. I explored further with my toes. They touched fabric. *And what felt horribly like skin.*

I jerked my legs away, jumped to my feet – and stood on what was definitely a *face. Arrrgh,* I leapt out of the Jacuzzi, and leant against the tiled wall, trembling, eyes closed.

Beside me, the tub bubbled and seethed. Unexceptional, familiar, its grim secret hidden. With shaking hand, I leant over and pressed the stop button. Slowly the effervescence subsided. The seething surface stilled. Through the clear green waters, the shotgun eyes of Waldo M Hinburger delivered a final heart-stopping blast. His mouth gaped wide, as if in surprise and outrage that Death had served a subpoena from which there was no escape.

In a career as investigator for the Drugs Division of Her Majesty's Revenue and Customs, dead bodies are an occupational hazard I usually can handle, but to share a Jacuzzi with *a corpse*... A wave of nausea swept over me, my knees buckled, and I collapsed onto a lounger.

I had seen no obvious signs of violence, but I couldn't rule out foul play. The local police would investigate that. Meanwhile, what was the best thing to do? My first instinct was to creep away and leave the discovery of the body to someone else. Cowardly – and impracticable. On my way here I'd seen the golfer Spinks, though he had not seen me. So there was a strong possibility that I too might be spotted as, clad in the tell-tale bathrobe, I made my way back to my room.

After a moment, I took a deep breath and steeled myself for another look into the Jacuzzi. Mistake. One more blast from those shotgun eyes and I fled the scene. I pulled my robe from the peg, wrapped it round me, flung open the door, and heedless of the damp trail on the carpet, ran along the corridor towards Reception.

At this early hour the hall was still deserted. The greyness of the sky and the sombre ticking of the grandfather clock made the place unusually gloomy. From below stairs, massed voices droned a mournful Scottish psalm, some early morning radio programme the Mackenzies had tuned into – quite well-timed as a funeral service for Waldo M Hinburger, and definitely all the mourning he would get.

It didn't take any acting ability to bang the bell hysterically and gasp out my story to a frowning Mrs Mackenzie.

'I think poor Mr Hinburger must have had a heart attack,' I finished.

Her frown deepened. Her lips compressed into a thin hard line. 'The Management takes no responsibility for misuse of the Jacuzzi. There is a notice to that effect.' Her hand hovered over the phone. 'There's no chance that you could be...mistaken?' Her tone indicated that I might be indulging in some tasteless English practical joke.

I shook my head, as if not trusting myself to speak. She gave a long-suffering sigh and vanished downstairs to reappear a moment later with her grumbling husband in tow. He hurried sullenly off in the direction of the Jacuzzi.

The proprietress of the White Heather Hotel stood grim and silent. One hand tapped out an impatient tattoo, the other pinned the telephone receiver down onto its rest as if to prevent the transmission of Bad Publicity. Her narrowed eyes homed in on the damp trail on the carpet.

It was a shaken Mackenzie who reappeared a few moments later. In answer to her unspoken question, he nodded his head. 'I've locked the door, Morag,' he grunted.

Without another word, he disappeared downstairs. The mournful Scottish psalm was turned up to full volume.

Mrs M released her imprisoning grip on the receiver to point with a reproving finger at my wet handprints marring the polished surface of the counter. With the soft sleeve of my bathrobe, I scrubbed apologetically at the wet patches while she set about the distasteful task of reporting to the police the sudden early morning checkout of guest Waldo M Hinburger.

'...Yes, discovered by another of the guests, a Ms Smith... Yes, he's definitely dead... And none of your sirens and blue lights,' she snapped. 'Come in by the rear entrance. I don't want my guests disturbed.'

Guiltily aware of the pool that was forming beneath my feet, I beat a hasty retreat, while she was still occupied. I had time to dress and send a report before I was called for questioning. The police were very solicitous about my shocking experience. I didn't feel the need to reveal my official status, and the interview didn't take long.

Later, from behind the curtains of my room, I admired the discreet way the whole business was handled as Hinburger's bulky white-sheeted form was whisked into the ambulance waiting at the rear beside the garage. Mrs Mackenzie was right, of course, to insist on secrecy. Only yesterday, guests had watched the prostrate form of another guest being carried away. Seeing an obvious corpse carted off today would have emptied the hotel quicker than the time it took to say Waldo M Hinburger. And that would have left me dangerously exposed to the suspicions of Gina Lombardini and the Mackenzies.

By now the other guests would be at breakfast, looking round with nervous curiosity to see who had survived the night. Well, Waldo had, and yet he hadn't survived till breakfast. If anyone noted his absence, Mrs Mackenzie would stonewall, and the only person interested enough to pursue the matter of his non-appearance would be Gina. Most guests would merely assume that he had checked out. I thought about breakfast. If I went down, it would be hard to explain later why I hadn't said anything to the assembled guests. My non-appearance, on the other hand, would be understandable in view of the shock of finding the body. And I *did* feel a little queasy after that foot-to-face meeting with a corpse.

Gina. She was now the only link with the Mackenzies. That snatch of conversation I'd overheard at the Botanics, *I tell you there's nothing wrong with the castle. It's the best place...* She knew what Mackenzie was referring to. And I might find the answer in her room. This was an ideal opportunity to search it while she was at breakfast. If I could find out which castle was involved and discover the lines of supply...

Had she already gone down to breakfast? And if so, how long before she returned? A few quiet steps took me along to her room. I pressed my ear to the wooden door. No sound from within. If this had been a flimsy modern door, I could have been sure that the room was empty, but the thick wood deadened everything. I straightened and rapped sharply on the panelling. If she answered, I would say that there had been an accident and Mrs Mackenzie wanted everyone down to breakfast as soon as possible. From within, no movement or shouted question. I tried again. Still no response. Slowly, I turned the handle. As expected, it was locked.

I'd inserted the pick in the lock, when I heard a creak of the stair and the soft brush of shoes on carpet. Time to retreat. Gina's room would have to wait.

CHAPTER SEVEN

At a quarter to two, I was standing on the quayside at South Queensferry looking up at the spider's web tracery of the Forth Railway Bridge. The honey-coloured stone columns supporting the rust-red ironwork dwarfed the little yachts bobbing uneasily in the swell. Wispy clouds had thickened, and under a faded blue sky the colour of washed-out jeans, the pale grey sea was heaving itself up into peaks and mountains.

There was no sign of Gina Lombardini. I joined the dozen or so people queuing to present their tickets for boarding. It would be better to be on board before she arrived, though almost impossible to avoid coming face to face with her on such a small vessel.

I found myself a position in the saloon from where I would have a good view of the jetty. *The Maid of the Forth* filled up rapidly. Few chose the exposed upper deck, most, like myself, preferring the comfort and shelter of the cabin. A noisy couple with a young child discussed at loud length where to sit, then spread their belongings on the bench behind me. So much for a peaceful cruise on the river. I felt a thump, then another, as the back of my seat shuddered under the playful onslaught of the child's foot. I pressed my lips firmly together and gazed out through one of the large observation windows. No sign yet of the Italian. Overhead, seagulls performed a noisy aerial ballet. A bank of clouds drifted slowly over the sun, turning the sea into a gunmetal sheet shot with silver highlights.

At precisely two o'clock the ship's engines rumbled into life and the crew began to pull in the gangway. It looked as if this was going to be a wasted journey, she was not going to turn up. And then I saw her, a figure in an ankle-length black coat hurrying along beside the sea wall. I found I'd been unconsciously holding my breath, and released it in a long sigh. Just as the last rope was being untied and the boat was preparing to pull away from the quayside, she scrambled aboard. The tactics of a professional, making sure anyone following would be given the slip.

Bypassing the saloon, she made immediately for the top deck. If I managed to keep a low profile, the results could be promising. I unfolded the tourist map I had purchased from the ship's bar and settled down to behave like a genuine tourist.

With much threshing of engines we reversed, swinging upstream towards the soaring span of the Road Bridge before turning to begin the four mile journey down the River Forth to the island of Inchcolm. Once clear of the shelter of the shore, the ship began to pitch and roll as its bow ploughed into the white-crested waves.

'I'm going to be sick, Mummy!' the child behind me announced tremulously. 'Now!'

Just what I needed when my own stomach was beginning to churn ominously. I tried to close my ears to the ensuing gurgles and studied the map of the island. I'd no idea where

Gina was likely to go. I ran my finger along the route from the landing stage to the ruined abbey, a good place for a rendezvous with all those visitors wandering round.

To the left of the landing stage, on the eastern tip of the island, were wartime gun emplacements and an ammunition tunnel... Promising, but too public a place for a drugs drop, and the fortifications were located on top of cliffs, with only one access, and that was direct from the landing stage. Tourists are inquisitive creatures. They'd be sure to stumble upon any hidden cache sooner or later. And with the custodian's cottage close by, nocturnal activity would run an extremely high risk of discovery. I crossed the gun emplacement off my list of possibilities.

I scanned the map again. Could Gina's rendezvous be at East Jetty on the far south-west tip of the island? In the short time available for a visit, few tourists would make their way there. I pursed my lips and gazed thoughtfully into space.

The childish treble screeched a few inches from my ear. 'I'm feeling better, Mummy! Look, look!'

While my attention had been on the map, a long low green island had appeared over the bow. Inchcolm. Quarter of an hour later, the ship nosed its way into a sheltered little harbour guarded by cliffs of brown volcanic rock, and the square tower of the 12th century abbey came into view.

Gina Lombardini had taken up position at the gangway ready for a quick getaway. The problem would be how to follow her without being detected. As if sensing that she was being watched, her head began to turn in my direction. I restrained an impulse to duck. A sudden movement like that would be sure to draw her attention.

I was saved by a click, a cough, from the ship's public address system. Heads jerked up to listen. 'Ladies and gentlemen, this is an important announcement.' The tinny voice paused, using silence to corral attention. 'If weather conditions should deteriorate further this afternoon, you will be recalled earlier than stated on the itinerary. If you hear three blasts on the klaxon, I must ask you to return immediately. The ship will leave ten minutes after the signal.'

The child delivered a farewell salvo of kicks to the back of my seat, but I sat still. Ignoring the hectic rush to disembark, I took care to be one of the last to get off. Gina had set off briskly, not in the direction of the East Jetty but towards the ruins of the abbey. As the majority of the visitors were also heading that way, I found it easy to mingle with them. I hoped that she hadn't spotted me, but there was nothing I could do about it if she had.

Her black-clad figure disappeared through the entrance arch of the abbey, and, by the time I reached the same spot, was nowhere to be seen. I gazed around. The plan on the wall showed that I was standing at one corner of a four-sided cloister, not the airy open-sided cloister familiar in English abbeys, but solid walls pierced at infrequent intervals by small arched windows. I could see along two sides, but the passage enclosed by the other two sides was hidden from view. It was impossible to know if anyone was standing there.

Somebody passed one of the arched windows – Gina, or just another tourist? It was the perfect place to shake off any pursuit – or to observe without being seen. Were eyes watching *me* at this very moment? The back of my neck prickled. Hurriedly, I moved out of line with the window.

The old walls seemed to swallow up any sound from the outside world. It was eerily silent. Even my footsteps were muffled as I walked quickly along the east side of the cloister. At the end of the passage a low doorway led into the church. A couple of people were peering at the explanatory notices. They moved off, leaving me alone. Though I had no obvious reason for the feeling, again I had the sensation that someone was watching me.

There was still no sign of Gina. From one corner of the church, worn stone steps led steeply up to a dark doorway. I paused on the topmost step to listen. Was that a faint murmur of voices? Perhaps they were only tourists, but my pulse quickened as I stepped through the doorway, very conscious that I would be momentarily outlined against the lighter gloom of the church. When my eyes adjusted to the semi-darkness, I could just make out two figures studying a piece of paper at the far end of the long shadowy room. One wore an ankle-length coat. Gina.

I took a careful step back. My foot scuffed on one of the uneven flagstones, the sound magnified in the stillness. The murmur of voices stopped abruptly. I let the map slip from my fingers and flutter to the floor. I made a show of scrabbling for it, and when I looked up, they had gone.

Oooong Oooong Oooong. Three strident blasts blared from the direction of the landing stage. As the echoes of the ship's klaxon died away, I could hear footsteps clattering downwards. Passengers rushing back to the jetty? Or Gina and her co-conspirator making their escape? Abandoning caution, I ran across the room to the narrow spiral staircase, ducked through the low arch, and hurried as fast as I dared down the twisting precipitous stairway.

At a dark opening in the stair wall I hesitated. The footsteps continued steadily downwards. I risked taking steps two at a time, my harsh breathing noisy in my ears.

I failed to register the faint whisper of sound behind me till it was too late. The violent push was sudden and effective. As I pitched forward, I desperately flung up an arm to protect my head. For a split second I was aware of the worn steps hurtling up to meet me.

Then nothing.

CHAPTER EIGHT

'Yes, there are vacancies.' An elongated Mrs Mackenzie towered over me. 'Double beds for Smythes, single beds for Smyths, rooms without bed for Smiths. And, of course, twin beds for twins and cat beds for cats.'

The floor was very hard. I banged the bell at reception. Mrs Mackenzie's head floated up from under the desk.

'I want to change my name to Smythe,' I whined.

'Once a Smith, always a Smythe,' her head said before floating away.

My whole body ached, and when I moved my head, excruciating pain shot through it and brought on a wave of nausea. I squeezed my eyes shut and lay motionless in the hope that it would pass. Nausea... My mind woozily tried to pinpoint the cause. Hadn't there been a scare in the hotel about food poisoning... Botulism, that was it. Somebody had been struck down, a shrouded form carried off on a stretcher. I had the feeling that it was important to remember who, but it was all too much effort...

Consciousness ebbed and flowed. A soft *tap tap tap*. The sound of approaching footsteps. I must escape...*must*... Again, I felt those hands on my back sending me hurtling headlong down the steep stone stairs. *Panic*.

The footsteps were much closer now, the unknown assailant coming to finish the job. Perhaps if I lay without moving... Now I could sense the presence of someone standing over me. My heart hammered against my ribs. I heard a sharp intake of breath and a man's voice booming and echoing unintelligibly. A hand touched my shoulder. As I tried to twist away, an amazing fireworks display erupted in my head, to be almost instantly extinguished by darkness once more as I slid into unconsciousness.

My eyelids painfully flickered open. My head ached dreadfully, my eyes refused to focus. I felt as if I had been squashed through the rollers of a giant mangle. Every movement hurt. Mrs Mackenzie's beds were very hard. Someone ought to complain...

The click of a door opening jerked me into wakefulness. In hotels, I make it a habit to lock my bedroom door. Again, I felt that rush of terror. As I struggled to raise my head, there was a movement beside me, and I found myself looking up into an unfamiliar bearded face.

'It's a braw, bricht, moonlicht nicht the nicht, lassie,' said the face cheerfully in a broad Scots accent.

As I stared in astonishment, the hairy features subtly transformed themselves into Gorgonzola's best Cheshire Cat grin, all teeth. Comforted by her presence, I drifted off into an uneasy sleep.

Next time I awoke, I still hurt all over. A trial movement of my head brought not much more than a moment's dizziness. I eased myself up on the pillows and gazed round the room, puzzled by its unfamiliarity. Where was I? Blue and green checked curtains fluttered at the open window, revealing a sky of palest eggshell blue. The furniture was a light pine, the wallpaper cheerful and sunny. This was certainly not the impersonal, deliberately old-fashioned style favoured by Mrs Mackenzie at the White Heather Hotel. What was I doing here? I propped myself up against the pillows and tried to work out an answer, but my mind seemed wrapped in cotton wool.

A light tap at the door was followed by a bearded face, vaguely familiar. The face, surmounted by a mop of unruly ginger hair, peered in at me.

'Glad to see you're awake at last,' the man advanced into the room with a beaming smile. 'I was really worried about you, lassie. Real wabbit, you were. That was a right tumble you took. We wanted the doctor to take a look at you, but the storm was too bad for him to come across.'

'Storm? Tumble...? Doctor...?'

'Och, I'm forgetting you'll maybe not remember much about it, seeing it's likely you'll be having concussion. I'm Iain Fraser. My wife and I are the curators here on Inchcolm. When *The Maid* had to leave in a hurry yesterday because of the storm, they reported that they were one passenger missing, so I had a wee look around the Abbey and found you at the foot of the dormitory stairs.' He paused. 'You're looking a lot better today.'

I gazed at him in astonishment. 'The last thing I remember,' I said slowly, 'is getting on the boat at the Forth Bridge.'

He patted my hand comfortingly, 'I wouldn't worry about it, lassie. That's quite common after concussion. The doctor from Aberdour will be here soon. He'll tell you the same. Just you have a wee rest till he comes.'

With an encouraging smile, he went out, closing the door quietly behind him. I let my body relax against the soft pillows, but my mind refused to settle. Elusive images flitted tantalisingly on the verge of recall... My eyelids drooped and I fell into a fitful doze...

'Another day in bed, and you'll be fit to travel,' the doctor assured me when he came. 'But by bus, not car, Ms Smith.'

So, the next day I sat in the bus on my way back to the White Heather Hotel, staring out of the window and striving desperately to remember *anything* that had happened after I had boarded *The Maid of the Forth*. Try as I might, those vital hours remained infuriatingly and disturbingly blank.

After the bus deposited me at the gates, I walked slowly up the drive. I stumbled a little as I mounted the entrance steps. That short walk had been a lot more exhausting than I'd bargained for. I pushed open the door, and saw with relief that, as usual, the hall was deserted and there was no one behind the imposing reception desk. I didn't feel I could cope with the formidable Mrs Mackenzie. In fact, I didn't want to meet anybody. Until I could recall what had happened during those missing hours on Inchcolm, I felt instinctively that it was important to be on my guard.

As I leant over the desk and stretched out my hand for the key with its heavy brass tag, a muffled cough from my left startled me. Mr Mackenzie's straggle of dark hair, then that fissure of a frown line, slowly appeared above the polished expanse of the desktop. His eyes widened in astonishment when he saw me, his mouth opening and closing like a newly caught fish landed on the river bank. He recovered, opened the door to the basement and yelled, 'Morag, she's back!'

Mrs Mackenzie popped up from the lower regions, her expression sour. I couldn't blame them for jumping to the conclusion that I had left without paying my bill. I got in first, to forestall an angry outburst.

'I'm terribly sorry, Mrs Mackenzie, but I had rather a bad accident on Friday. I realise, of course, that the two nights I have been away will be charged at normal rates.'

Her expression uncurdled infinitesimally, but she slapped my key down sharply, showing no sign whatsoever of enquiring solicitously after my health.

It was perhaps unwise to antagonise her, but, put it down to my concussed state, I couldn't resist the temptation. 'And how is Miss Lannelle?' I asked sweetly.

Her expression recurdled.

I delivered a second thrust. Feigning a look of concern, I added, 'I hope not too many other guests have been taken ill?'

That implied aspersion cast on the White Heather cuisine elicited a squeak of indignation from Murdo and a sharp intake of outraged breath from Morag. I turned and limped my way upstairs as quickly as my shaky state allowed.

As soon as I had locked the door of my room behind me, I went straight to the window. Though, in a crisis, Gorgonzola was perfectly capable of looking after herself by catching wildlife – mice, rather than the feathered kind, I hoped – I was always a little anxious when I had to leave her for a long period of time. Once I'd opened the window, I flung myself on the bed. It didn't matter how long I had to wait. I'd just rest till Gorgonzola came...

…Whiskers tickled my face, followed by a tap on my cheek, gentle, then harder. Gorgonzola was peering down at me crossly. When she saw she had gained my attention, she leapt lightly off the bed and sat beside the holdall of tins, running her tongue meaningfully over her lips.

I was in the midst of spooning out a generous helping of duck onto her plate, when the faint boom of the dinner gong rippled up the stairs. I didn't feel very much like eating, but I'd better put in an appearance or Mrs Mackenzie might take it as another deliberate insult, might even ask me to leave. And that wouldn't do at all. I was more convinced than ever that the key to Operation Scotch Mist lay in the Mackenzie kitchen…

Purrrr…purrrr…purr purr. Grrrrrrrr… Tantalised beyond endurance by the raised spoon, Gorgonzola lost patience. She twined herself tightly round my legs in an anaconda embrace more akin to a rugby tackle than an affectionate reminder.

'OK, OK, sorry, sorry, sorry.' Penitently, I added a generous amount of gravy to the plate and placed it in front of her.

Chomp. Slurp. Chomp. I closed the door behind me.

I was halfway down the stairs when the soft black curtain that had been drawn across my mind suddenly lifted, and a fleeting memory from those missing hours returned… Gina and a shadowy figure whispering in the gloom…

I realised I might come face to face with her in the dining room. And perhaps, with her shadowy accomplice too. Suddenly, I remembered the hand thudding into my back, saw the dormitory steps rushing up to meet me.

'Pull yourself together,' I scolded, mouth dry, resentful of my own weakness. 'It's an ideal opportunity to see her reaction when you walk in.' I might even get a lead on the identity of that shadowy figure.

I took a deep breath and made my way into the dining room. Keyed up as I was, a glance round the room brought disappointment. No sign of Gina. Casually, I made my way towards an empty table with a good view of the door. As soon as she entered, we'd see each other.

On my way past Hiram J Spinks's table, I brushed against the heavily starched folds of the tablecloth, knocking a spoon to the floor. He looked up, and the leaflet he had been studying fluttered from his grasp.

'Excuse me,' I bent down to retrieve the fallen items.

His hand closed over the leaflet an instant before mine. When I straightened up, a wave of dizziness caused Spinks and the room to sway alarmingly. I clutched at the tablecloth to steady myself, and with a loud clatter the rest of his cutlery followed his spoon onto the highly polished floor. Mrs Mackenzie's reproving figure materialised in the doorway like a malevolent genie.

'Oh, I'm so sorry, Mr Spinks,' I stammered. 'Still a bit wobbly after Friday's accident, I'm afraid.'

Mrs M began fussing over Spinks and resetting the table, casting pained glances in my direction.

His eyes examined me closely. 'Accident?' he drawled. 'You sure look as if you've been in the rough, ma'am, if you'll excuse a golfing expression. I hope you weren't hospitalised?'

'No, but—'

He sprang to his feet and pulled out a chair for me. 'Why don't you sit down here, ma'am, and tell me all the details from A to Zee.'

Though I hadn't intended to speak to anyone, I sank onto the chair with some relief, my mind still geared to watching for Gina.

I might as well try out my story. 'I can't remember anything at all about the accident,' I said slowly. 'I'd gone on a boat trip to Inchcolm and I was found at the foot of some stairs in the church there – they call it the abbey, I think.'

Mrs Mackenzie placed our soup on the table.

'And you can't remember a thing about it?' His eyes studied me over his soup-spoon.

I shook my head. 'Must have tripped on the steps, I suppose.'

'Now hold it right there.' He took a last mouthful of soup and leant forward eagerly. 'Folks don't just trip for no reason. Maybe the lighting was bad, or a step needed fixing?' His eyebrows were thin twin interrogation marks. 'I can put you in touch with a swell personal injury lawyer, if it comes to a matter of litigation.'

'I'm afraid it must have been my own fault, Mr Spinks.' My smile was rueful. 'I'm a bit disaster prone. Falling into the pond at the Botanics – and now this!'

He stared at me. 'You really can't remember a thing?'

There was something in his voice that troubled me, but the need for an immediate reply was postponed by the arrival of Mrs Mackenzie with our second course. While she removed our soup plates and proudly laid her culinary masterpieces before us, I tried to analyse the underlying tone in his last question. I finally identified it. Relief, definitely *relief*. I felt the knotting of muscles in the pit of my stomach. *Could* Gina's accomplice be Hiram J Spinks? *Spinks*, the idea seemed preposterous. And yet...he *had* been at the Botanics the day I had followed Mackenzie there. And there was that early morning glimpse of his distinctive yellow golfing cap *just before* my discovery of Hinburger's body in the Jacuzzi. The hairs on the nape of my neck bristled.

'You really can't remember a thing?' he repeated.

I'd see how he reacted when... Furrowing my brow as if trying hard to recall what had happened, I said slowly, 'I have just remembered something.'

His elbow jerked convulsively and his cutlery made a second descent to the floor. Mrs Mackenzie, her looks thunderous, rematerialised to restore order, giving me a precious moment to think of my next move. I hadn't been too clever. My hole-in-one looked like turning out to be an own goal, if I didn't convince him pretty quickly that what I remembered wasn't at all significant.

I leant forward. 'Yes, I remember the blinding pain as my head hit the stone floor. But,' I rattled on, giving my best rendition of a wry smile, 'the doctor said that I'm suffering from post-traumatic amnesia, so it's very unlikely that I'll *ever* remember the accident itself. In fact, I can't remember *anything* after getting on the boat at the Forth Bridge.'

His eyes stared into mine for what seemed a lifetime. Then he picked up his fork and turned his attention to the herring fried in oatmeal, one of Mrs Mackenzie's specialities.

Had I convinced him? My life might well depend on it. The vision of Waldo's dead face floated in front of me, a bit like Banquo's ghost at the Macbeth dinner table. For the rest of the meal I did my best to chatter brightly about trivial touristy matters, anything that would convince him that I really did not remember events before the accident, and so harboured no suspicions at all.

At last Spinks pushed back his chair. 'Gotta leave you now, ma'am.' He gave a swing of an imaginary club. 'Must get in some practice while the light's still good.' The stringy figure made its way to the door.

I sagged back in my chair. That had been a close call. I could only hope that I had talked my way out of immediate danger, but one thing's for sure – I'd certainly not be taking another Jacuzzi in the White Heather Hotel.

A brightly coloured Tourist Board guide to East Lothian was wedged under Spinks's plate. I reached over and drew it towards me. I skimmed quickly through it. Nothing for Operation Scotch Mist there. Just places of interest and recreation, with the golf courses circled in heavy black marker.

I was folding the leaflet ready to slip it back under his plate, when I noticed the faint pencil marks. Two places on the coast had been lightly underlined. I held the shiny paper up to the light. He might come back and catch me reading the leaflet…but it was worth the risk.

Jackpot. The underlined place names were *castles*, Tantallon and Fast Castle. In those snatches of conversation I'd overheard at the Botanics, hadn't Mackenzie insisted that 'the castle' was the best place for – something?

Hands moist with nerves and excitement, I stuffed the leaflet back under the plate and made a strategic withdrawal from the dining room. Not a moment too soon. My foot was on the bottom step of the stairs when Spinks, putter in hand, hurried by to retrieve his map.

By the time I reached my room, reaction had set in. My head was pounding and my limbs felt weighted with lead as the after-effects of concussion took their toll. I looked longingly at the bed. How wonderful to be able to lie back against its soft pillows and fall blissfully asleep, like Gorgonzola, who was comfortably curled up in the centre of the bed digesting her belated dinner.

Instead, I retrieved the mobile from the holdall and sent a coded progress report on Operation Scotch Mist. *Hiram J Spinks prime suspect in Hinburger death. Request no action meantime. Tantallon and Fast Castle, East Lothian, possible drop sites. Investigation proceeding.*

I closed down. If Spinks was busy putting, and Gina was out and about somewhere, there wouldn't be a better opportunity to search her room. G was now lying on her back enjoying the softness of the bed, feet relaxed and purring contentedly. I tapped her briskly on the shoulder. The purring stopped, she stiffened and lay as one dead.

'Time for duty,' I said heartlessly, slipping on her working collar.

One resentful eye opened, she yawned, stretched, and deliberately took her time to get into gear. I waited patiently for her to finish her little demonstration of independence. When she had jumped lightly to the floor, I quietly pulled open the door of my room and slipped out into the corridor.

There was no interruption this time as I wielded the electronic pick-lock. Two seconds was all it took, and Gorgonzola and I were inside with the door locked behind us. Though there was probably little chance of Gina returning unexpectedly, I took the precaution of leaving the pick in the lock to prevent a key being inserted from the outside.

It's more difficult to search a meticulously tidy room and leave no traces, but Gina Lombardini was one of those untidy people who leave their belongings scattered around in chaotic disarray. Someone like that wouldn't notice the difference if a whirlwind hit the room and swirled everything around.

'Search, G.'

She padded across the floor, tail erect, the tip twitching as if it too was sniffing out forbidden substances. I commenced my own methodical search of the room, working clockwise. After ten fruitless minutes, my headache was worse than ever. Gorgonzola, too, had given up, and was now sitting on one of Gina Lombardini's expensive dresses watching a large bluebottle buzzing angrily against the window.

I felt as frustrated as the bluebottle. She *must* have noted something down somewhere, yet I hadn't found it. Disorganised people have scatty, disorganised minds. They have to write important things down or they would never remember them.

I stared irritably at the buzzing bluebottle. Gorgonzola stared at it. Suddenly, she pounced. Insolently, the bluebottle circled her head. A retaliatory swipe of her paw missed its target completely and knocked to the floor Mrs Mackenzie's stand-in for the Gideon Bible, a novel by Sir Walter Scott, placed in each room for the edification of guests. The bluebottle did a victory roll. Pretending that was what she had intended in the first place, Gorgonzola converted the follow-through of the swipe to a rub of her ear.

I bent down to pick up the book, *The Bride of Lammermuir*. In it, acting as a makeshift bookmark, was a piece of paper roughly torn from an Italian magazine. Was it likely that someone who was not a fluent English speaker would choose to read so difficult a book? Hoping against hope, I opened it at the marker. Halfway down the page, the words *Wolf's Crag* were heavily underlined in red ink, and scrawled untidily in the margin opposite was the word *Tantallon*. I almost missed the smaller piece of paper nestling behind the bookmark. In the same flamboyant handwriting was written *Lunedi 23 14.30* and underneath, *Mercoledi 25 19.00*.

I'd found what I was looking for.

I felt like hugging Gorgonzola – and Gina too if she had been here, though neither lady would have appreciated it.

At that moment of euphoria, the door handle rattled. Someone tried to fit a key in the lock. More rattlings. I tiptoed to the door and put my ear to the panel. Muttered imprecations in Italian were followed by the *clack* of retreating footsteps. I reckoned I had barely two minutes to make my escape before she returned with one of the Mackenzies.

It took less than half that time to replace the book on the windowsill, scoop up Gorgonzola, and slip quietly back to my room.

CHAPTER NINE

It was one p.m., a full hour and a half earlier than necessary, when, car mobile once again, I drove past the lane leading to Tantallon Castle, and parked as inconspicuously as possible beside some cottages. Since I was engaged in surveillance, it would be too conspicuous to use the official car park, as there'd be few other cars on such a foul day as this. With yet another dense Scottish haar blanking out all but my immediate surroundings, it felt like winter rather than the height of summer. Definitely more like November than June.

I hunched deeper into my jacket as I made my way on foot up the castle drive. The approaching car, engine note muffled by the fog, was almost upon me before I heard it. A hundred yards ahead, the dipped yellow beams of headlights attempted to stab their way through the thick misty blanket. I pressed myself hard against the dripping foliage of one of the large bushes lining the road. The dark shape of a small car crawled by. As far as I could tell, there seemed to be only one occupant. The mist swirled and eddied in the vehicle's wake before closing in again as impenetrably as before. I disentangled myself from the bushes, uncomfortably aware of moisture soaking coldly through the shoulders of my jacket from a shower of drips. I was here in the course of duty and I felt a twinge of sympathy for those tourists inexorably programmed for sightseeing, sun, rain – or Scottish haar.

It was now five past one. Gina's scribbled note in Mrs Mackenzie's book had set the rendezvous for half past two. There'd be time to look round the castle and find a suitable position from which to monitor her movements, but tracking her would be difficult in this mist.

The official car park, as I'd thought, was almost empty, occupied only by a Vauxhall, a Renault, a battered blue Ford and a tour bus, bodywork dulled, windows opaque with a thin film of mist. Good thinking to have left my car beside the cottages. Gina would have been sure to spot it.

Behind the wooden hut that served as a ticket office, the ground rose in a series of green humps and mounds, and beyond, through the billowing haar, loomed the dark rectangular bulk of the castle. On the side of the hut was a board with a list of admission charges and opening times. When I tapped on the steamed-up window, it slid smartly open.

The grey-haired custodian tore a ticket from a machine. 'Good morning, with this weather I didn't expect any more visitors.' He handed me my change. 'You're only the fourth we've had today, apart from the scheduled bus party.'

'It must be a pretty boring job on a day like this.' I picked up a leaflet and flicked through it. *Tantallon Castle, built in 1350...besieged by Cromwell...visited by Queen Victoria...* There on the back page was what I was looking for – a plan of the castle.

'You'll find that leaflet quite interesting.' He settled his arms more comfortably on the window ledge.

My heart sank. He was obviously getting ready for a lengthy chat. I paid for the leaflet and began to edge away.

He leant forward confidingly. 'I'm afraid Scots don't know much about their own castles. I have to say that English visitors like yourself seem to be more knowledgeable.'

I nodded and inched away a little more.

He warmed to what was obviously a well-loved theme. 'I don't know what they teach them in schools nowadays. School kids seem to know nothing at all about Scottish history. All they seem to have heard about is Robert the Bruce and his encounter with the spider. And all they know about William Wallace is what they've seen in that film *Braveheart*. It's a disgrace that foreigners know more about Scottish history than the Scots. Now...'

I smiled politely and shifted from one foot to another, hoping that my impatience did not show.

'...only half an hour ago a foreign lady, Italian I think she was, actually wanted to know if there was any danger from *wolves* here. I thought at first she was getting mixed up with the Wolf of Badenoch's castle near Newtonmore – but it turned out that she had actually read Walter Scott's novel, *The Bride of Lammermuir*, and wanted to see its castle, Wolf's Crag. Well, I had to tell her she'd made a mistake with the castle. Wolf's Crag is not Tantallon, but Fast Castle further down the coast. You won't find many Scots nowadays who've read that book, or *any* of his novels, let alone know that he was writing about Fast Castle...' he trailed off, a faraway look in his eye.

So Gina was already here. By not being in position early enough, I'd committed one of the most elementary mistakes in surveillance.

I tried to sound casual. 'What a coincidence! An Italian lady staying at my hotel told me about Sir Walter Scott, Tantallon, and *The Bride of Lammermuir*. I expect she was interested because of its connection with the opera. It *must* be her. Perhaps I can catch her up. Or has she left yet?'

'The coach party's still here, and the chap from France.' He rubbed his hand over his chin. 'I think the American's gone. Been several times, he has. He didn't stay long this time, though. I suppose the weather must have put him off. I'm surprised he bothered to come at all today. Paid his money and away again in twenty minutes. Well, that's Americans for you! Money doesn't mean the same to them, does it? But I think the Italian lady's still here. It's gratifying when people take a proper interest.'

That reference to an American jolted me like a hammer blow. Could that American be Hiram J Spinks?

'Thank you. I'll just see if I can find her.' With a smile I turned away and walked over the wet grass towards the outer walls of the castle. I quickened my step. It looked like I'd missed the rendezvous, but I might still learn something if I could find Gina.

I passed through the remains of the outer gate. The ruined bulk of the inner castle reared ahead of me, blurred, dark, vaguely menacing. The faint swish of the sea on my right swelled to a hollow boom as I made my way over a stretch of closely cropped grass towards a fence. Far below, through the swirling mist, I could just make out the moving surface of the sea and the tips of jagged rocks. I shivered and turned away.

The haar eddied, then lightened. Like a fade-up on a film screen, the castle materialised on the edge of the cliff. Ruined red sandstone, lichened curtain-walls topped by a high tower, reared upward for forty to fifty feet. I crossed another drawbridge to a low arched doorway below an eroded coat of arms.

There was no sign of Gina in the inner courtyard of the castle. The only vantage point was the crumbling wall of the mid-tower. The ancient stones, wet and dripping from the haar, soared floorless till roofed four storeys above by a grey-white blankness of sky. The only sounds were the whisper of my shoes on the smooth flagstones and the flutter of pigeons disturbed from their nesting places in the old fireplaces. I moved on.

I might be able to spot Gina from the top of that covered staircase leading to the battlements. I started up the hollowed foot-worn steps, the only light-source artificial sconces and narrow slit windows through which the haar insinuated ghostly grey fingers. A huge spider's web, insubstantial and dusty, hung from the roof like some ancient moth-eaten battle standard. Had I been a bona fide holidaymaker, I would have enjoyed the Gothic atmosphere.

As it was, when I finally emerged onto the battlements, all I felt was frustration. Grey mist blocked all vision to right and left. Enclosed in a narrow grey-walled corridor, I strained my ears for any sign of human presence – a voice, a footstep – but the only sound was the mournful, muffled surge of the sea. There seemed no point in climbing higher. With such poor visibility I wouldn't be able to see anything useful.

A breath of wind momentarily tugged aside the grey blanket to reveal another narrow staircase, this time leading steeply downward. I took it and found myself in the central courtyard of the castle. At this level, the mist had retreated, an invader repulsed by the old red walls. Over to my left, Japanese tourists, heads covered by plastic rain hoods, were studying with serious expressions the remains of an old tower. They'd make excellent cover. I made my way over to join them.

'These stairs...' The Scottish guide was pointing to weathered steps hugging the walls and spiralling ever upwards to a small patch of grey sky. 'Just think how many feet have climbed them.' He looked expectantly at his flock. The Japanese gazed back with inscrutable politeness and varying degrees of comprehension.

He'd got *me* thinking. I studied the worn treads. What fears and hopes...?

Out of the corner of my eye, I caught a glimpse of red as a figure disappeared into a doorway on the opposite side of the courtyard. Gina Lombardini wore a red coat.

I walked quickly across the courtyard, running the last few yards, and peered in the doorway through which the figure had vanished. *Pit Prison*. A small notice pointed down through a series of arches. The dank smell of damp earth, mould and stagnant air drifted up unpleasantly from below, the smell of despair and death. Poor wretches had been thrown down there, never to emerge. From such a place there was only one entrance – and no exit. All I would have to do was conceal myself behind a convenient pillar and wait.

After several minutes, I heard the soft scuffle of footsteps ascending the narrow stairs. A dark head appeared, then red shoulders. One of the Japanese tourists. There was nothing particularly memorable about the woman's features, but her hairstyle was quite distinctive, a broad gold streak dyed into her coal-black hair. Was this woman Gina's contact? An Asian connection would give a whole new dimension to Operation Scotch Mist. I watched her make her way across the courtyard and join the rest of the group. If possible, I'd catch up with her later and take her photograph.

I withdrew behind the pillar and waited. Gina could still be down there. She wouldn't leave the Pit Prison until a decent interval had elapsed.

Ten minutes later, with no sign of Gina, I knew I'd wasted my time. There was no one down there. *Shit*. It had been a mistake to assume that someone wearing a red coat might be Gina. After all, she hadn't been wearing red on those visits to Inchcolm and the Botanics...

With the clarity of a video replay, I saw myself lying submerged in the warm waters of the Tropical House... Gina striding ahead of Hinburger and Mackenzie, and calling impatiently over her shoulder in her heavily accented English, 'Come, come! Let us get out of here quickly. You know *I no like being shut up in these so closed places*!' Gina was claustrophobic and wouldn't have tolerated even one minute in the dark foul atmosphere of the Pit Prison. *Shit, Shit, Shit*.

There was no point in wasting energy in self-recrimination. The haar was staging another counter-attack, closing in. The Japanese tourists were barely visible.

One minute, they were earnestly following their guide towards the edge of the cliff top, the next, the men were pointing and gesticulating, the women were standing with their hands to their mouths, their eyes frightened and staring. I ran across the grass and peered over the rain-hatted heads.

And found Gina Lombardini.

A buttressed tower loomed through the mist, its red sandstone walls an extension of the cliff face. From a tall narrow window protruded the head and shoulders of Gina, panic-stricken, her mouth a round O of terror. She seemed to be trying to lever herself out of the narrow opening. Both arms were flailing in a frenzy that battered her hands mercilessly against the rough walls. Her body shuddered and convulsed. From her lips came a peculiar mewing sound. Sixty feet below, as the sea surged and fell back, sharp rocks bared their teeth in anticipation.

I pushed my way to the front of the group. 'Gina! *Gina*! Go back.'

I waved and shouted, but the wide staring eyes were incapable of seeing. She was obviously beyond rational thought. I elbowed my way through the silent, staring Japanese and ran.

It took only a few seconds to reach the wide entrance at the base of the tower. Inside, to the left, was a small studded door. Frantically, I lifted the iron latch, pulled and tugged at the massive door. The door didn't budge. Could it be locked? But there was no key in the huge keyhole.

'Gina! *Gina*!' Heedless of bruised knuckles, I hammered on the thick wooden panels. There was no response.

I peered through the keyhole into a tiny enclosed space that would be terrifying to the claustrophobic Gina. There was only one small window and Gina's body was blocking out most of the light. It took a few seconds for my eye to become accustomed to the darkness. Then I could just make out the stones of the wall and, occasionally, a wildly waving foot.

Behind me I heard a jangle of keys. I turned to find the custodian, his chest heaving with the effort of running, and at his shoulder the guide, red-faced and agitated.

The custodian gazed at the empty keyhole, his brow furrowed. 'That lock was so rusted up the key wouldn't turn. Can't understand it, Dave. The key was there this morning when I opened up and made my rounds. It must have been taken by one of those souvenir hunters, they're always making off with bits of the castle. Don't know how the buggers did it, though.' He searched the ground with his eyes, as if willing the key to materialise. 'Don't think there's much chance of getting that door open.' He pushed back his cap and scratched his head. 'We'll have to break it down.'

That would need the fire brigade and a battering ram. I knew we didn't have time.

'Perhaps if you rattle one of those other keys around a bit, she'll realise that help is coming,' I suggested.

'Good idea.' Muttering to himself, he selected the largest from his bunch of keys and moved it vigorously from side to side in the lock.

A thin film of sweat beaded my forehead. How long before she lost all reason and threw herself out of the window...?

I pressed my ear to the door. Feet scrabbled on sandstone... Abruptly the sound stopped.

Filled with foreboding, I applied my eye to the keyhole. The tiny room was no longer dark. The obstruction in the window had gone. I could see only a segment of the room, and it was empty.

'I think she's *jumped*,' I burst out, my voice shaking.

We ran back to the fence on the cliff top, stumbling in our

haste over the uneven ground. The Japanese tourists stood in a huddled, silent group, staring across at the window. Heart thumping, I followed their gaze.

Gina had not jumped. In her frenzy to escape she had somehow managed to force her body through that slit of an opening onto a narrow ledge. Her face was pressed against the rough stonework of the tower. She had lost her shoes. One stockinged foot scrabbled for purchase on the crumbling sandstone, the other dangled helplessly over the sixty-foot drop to the rocks below.

All her weight was being taken by that one foot on its precarious hold. As we watched, she teetered, the grip of her clutching fingers weakened. For a moment she seemed to recover. Then with a terrible slowness, first one hand, then the other slid away from the wall in the ghastly travesty of a farewell wave. Arching backwards, she toppled down... down...to the waiting rocks below.

Disturbed by the falling body, fulmers darted up through the mist, their eerie call like the wail of a lost soul. From the Japanese came a sharp intake of breath, followed by a long sigh.

As her body fell, I'd squeezed my eyes shut. Now I opened them. With the mist for a shroud, Gina was lying spread-eagled on the rocks. One out-flung arm, plucked by the waves, seemed to be reaching forlornly for a yellow canister drifting slowly back and forth in the surge.

CHAPTER TEN

Mercifully, within a few seconds the eddying haar blotted out the scene below, the sea washing over Gina's body, her skull smashed by the sharp rocks. Legs trembling, I swallowed hard, engulfed by a wave of nausea. Shock, of course. For what seemed a long, long time no one moved or spoke. Then the custodian rubbed his hand wearily over his eyes.

'I'll phone the police and emergency services, Dave. You'd better get your lot back to the coach and tell the driver to take them off to the hotel.' He gave me a quick glance. 'You and the lady here will be needed as witnesses.'

I nodded, and he turned away, his footsteps heavy and slow. No need for haste now. Speaking in low, hushed voices, the tourists trailed back to the coach behind their guide, leaving me alone on the cliff top.

Death was so final. And yet for others life had to go on.

It was not that I was unfamiliar with violent death, but this had been so totally unexpected, so...so...unnecessary. If only that key had still been in position... If only Gina had managed to control her fear enough to wait till we had forced the lock... I couldn't bear to visualise her rising panic. Once she had realised that she was trapped in that tiny room, she wouldn't have been able to control her fear. What rotten luck that a practical joker had slammed the door on her and locked it... It was the sort of silly prank that children indulged in. No children here today, though. It wasn't likely that one of those oh-so-serious Japanese was responsible. And yet... One of them *had* left the others. The Japanese woman in red. I tried to remember whether I had seen a red coat in the group straggling back to the bus. I couldn't be sure – I'd been too upset to take in anything. Who else was here today? A Frenchman, the custodian had said. I hadn't seen anything of him, but that didn't mean...

There was something else... It was hovering on the edge of my memory...so frustrating. Something that didn't quite add up... That was it. Would a practical joker acting on impulse *remove* the key from the lock? And there was something about that keyhole... I reviewed my actions. I'd hammered on the door, looked through the keyhole, listened for movement. Something important that I'd missed was on the verge of surfacing. Perhaps if I went back to the tower...

I stood for a moment staring at the studded door. I looked round to see if anybody was watching, then I mimed hammering and shouting. When I peered through the keyhole, I could clearly see the floor and the wall opposite. Gina wasn't blocking the daylight with her body now. But nothing triggered the elusive something at the edge of my consciousness. Disappointed, I straightened up. But I might as well complete the rerun of my actions...

I pressed my ear to the door. And heard again that faint scuffling, *the scrabble of her feet on the sandstone sill*... The short hairs on the nape of my neck prickled. As if the wood of the door had suddenly become red hot, I leapt back and stood there, heart pounding. At last, I summoned up courage to look through the keyhole again. And saw a scurrying grey shape, and another. *Rats*. Trapped in a small room with rats would be enough to send most people into a panic, even if they didn't suffer from claustrophobia.

With a quick movement, the rat disappeared from my narrow zone of vision. Close to my eye was a bright bead of moisture. Curious, I inserted my finger into the keyhole, rubbed it about inside, and very carefully withdrew it. A thin layer of something translucent and yellowish coated my finger. Cautiously, I sniffed at it. No doubt about it, a releasing agent.

I stared at the incriminating evidence on my finger. The door was locked. Someone had oiled that rusted lock and turned the key. Gina was not the unlucky victim of a mindless prankster but of a cold-blooded killer, her death *premeditated*, the place carefully chosen. By someone who *knew* that Gina suffered from claustrophobia. Whoever had locked the door had calculated that Gina would jump. *Wanted her dead*.

It was hard to envisage one of the Japanese tourists oiling the lock and removing the key. But someone had, so the only other visitors to the castle, the Frenchman and the American, must be prime suspects. And if Hiram J Spinks had indeed been that American...

The old walls with their gun ports now seemed menacing and hostile. In a shaken and thoughtful mood, I made my way back to the entrance and the custodian's hut.

Halfway across the bridge, I stopped for a moment and traced a huge question mark in the grey film of moisture clinging to the smooth metal surface of the handrail. The custodian had said that the American had left after only twenty minutes. Time enough to lock the tower door, but certainly not enough for the releasing agent to penetrate the rust of years. Of course, it was just possible that the red-coated Japanese woman might have been responsible. She *had* been wandering about on her own. But it seemed that the time factor for the releasing agent to work also cleared her, as she had arrived either with the rest of the Japanese, or later than I had. That was something to check with the custodian.

As I rounded the corner, the departing coach revved its engine, its rear lights brightening, then dimming as it drove off into the mist. The door of the hut opened and the custodian emerged carrying a board with the words CASTLE CLOSED TODAY in double size white letters.

'The police'll be here shortly, miss.' He blocked off the castle access with the board. 'They'll be wanting a statement from you, so if you'd care to wait inside...'

He shut the door against the fog and motioned me to one of the two chairs, sitting down heavily on the other while Dave busied himself with kettle and teapot. For a long, long moment he sat slumped in his chair, the silence oppressive. The rattle of teaspoon against thick china mugs sounded unnaturally loud.

He raised his head to look at me. 'I should never have left that key in the lock, but my full strength couldn't move it, so I thought it was quite safe...' His voice trailed off and he gazed wearily into space, seeing not the thin walls of the little hut but worn red sandstone and those fingers clutching desperately at their last chance of life.

Dave raised his eyes interrogatively at me as he deposited a steaming mug of poisonous tarry brew on the ledge beside the custodian's elbow. The sight of the peat-brown liquid instantly extinguished my longing for a good restorative cup of tea. I shook my head.

'Cheer up, George. Don't blame yourself.' Dave patted his colleague's shoulder consolingly. 'It was just a terrible accident. Nobody's fault.'

Dave's well meant sympathy foundered and sank like a stone. In the heavy silence that followed his remark, the faint shriek of a sea bird was a disturbing reminder of Gina's last cry.

I cleared my throat. 'Nobody's fault, you said? I think the police might come to an entirely different conclusion.'

George's hand shook violently, sending a brown tidal wave of tea over a pile of pristine guidebooks and leaflets. Dave set down his mug with a crash and stared at me defensively.

'Now, just a minute. I don't think you can—'

'No, no. I wasn't pointing a finger at either of you. I didn't mean that anyone *here* was to blame.'

They looked unconvinced.

I hurriedly extricated myself from the invidious position of accuser. 'The lock had been recently oiled so that it would operate. That woman's death was not an accident but *murder*.'

A second tidal wave of tea engulfed the guidebooks.

* * *

Some exhausting hours later, I drove back to the White Heather Hotel. Try as I might, I couldn't shut out the awful images that forced themselves to the front of my mind. Those wild staring eyes. The frantically scrabbling fingers. Gina half-submerged in the surf, dead hand stretching out for the yellow canister bobbing just out of reach...

And I was no nearer to identifying the mysterious American. With much wrinkling of brow, George had trawled his memory but been unable to furnish any useful description. 'Just an ordinary American chappie,' was all he had been able to come up with.

After the first shock, he had seized on my startling theory of murder with the fervour of a drowning man clinging to an offered branch, a welcome escape from self-tormenting guilt. The grey-haired policeman who arrived to investigate the reported accident took a lot more convincing. There was much avuncular soothings and casting of knowing looks at his colleague over my head. It was only when I produced my identity card with its security rating that he grudgingly accepted that I was unlikely to be deranged by shock, and that there could just possibly be a grain of substance in my theory. Even then, I had to take him aside and tell him of Gina Lombardini's connection with an international drug ring before he took me seriously enough to summon the Crime Squad and the forensic task force.

The police procedures dragged on for hours. The obligatory statements had to be taken in painstaking detail. The fire brigade arrived with ladders, ropes and other gear, and with practised ease, Gina, more photographed in death than in life, was stretchered off to the mortuary. Then I had to hang around while they dealt with the opening of the tower door. They had to take an axe to it in the end...

I'd hoped to persuade the scene of crime officer to let me have a look at any papers, if Gina's shoulder bag was there. But there was no bag in the room. Only one of Gina's designer sandals lying beneath the window, the strap gnawed by rodent teeth.

I was making good time back to the hotel when a long queue of cars at road works ahead forced me to a halt. I drummed my fingers on the wheel in frustration. The mist had at last thinned to a high ceiling of cloud, though the occasional grey pocket still loitered, reluctant to go. I eyed the dashboard clock impatiently. I was cutting it fine. It would be a black mark to arrive at the hotel after the meal had finished. But when the lights changed, only five cars made it through. I had crawled twenty yards nearer dinner.

The realisation struck me that I hadn't eaten since breakfast. Even a toffee or boiled sweet would be more than welcome. I rummaged in the glove compartment for some form of sustenance. As the red light changed to green, the car first in line leapt eagerly forward – and stalled. The lights changed back. I resigned myself to Mrs Mackenzie's displeasure.

I resumed my foraging in the glove compartment. Tapes, map-reading light, assorted petrol vouchers, tin of sardines, couple of crumbling cat biscuits and a crumpled cellophane bag that had once (but no longer) contained toffees.

Red turned again to green. There was much revving of engines, much inching forward, a lot of tense anticipation and very little progress. A tussle of opinion between an advancing car and one that had jumped the lights from the other direction seemed to be giving rise to some interesting recriminations and heated exchanges. A lengthy delay was definitely on the cards.

I switched off the engine and eyed the tin of sardines, emergency supplies for Gorgonzola. She would be miffed if the emergency supply was needed, but when the cat's away... I made a mental note to buy a replacement, tugged off the lid and tucked into the contents. I was licking my fingers appreciatively when the guilty thought intruded that this was the second of my little moral lapses today.

The first had been when I had sneaked off to Gina's car. That was after the fire brigade had managed to break their way through the tower door. I'd made my way to where her car was standing forlornly in the car park. I knew I'd not have long to find any personal papers before the police turned their attentions to her mode of transport to the castle.

I had the lock picked in three seconds. The door swung open. A leather bag was lying on the passenger seat, where Gina, with her disorganised ways, had abandoned it in full view of any passing thief. A rapid search revealed only the same assortment of junk that for weeks I had been meaning to clear out of my own bag. Nothing in the glove compartment, or in the door pocket. Disappointed, I made to close the door.

Then, mindful that untidy people drop things on the floor, I peered under the front seats, but fished out only a tattered cigarette packet. I turned it over. Eureka! She had torn it open to use as an emergency notepad for a list of places and times. I stuffed it in my pocket and slipped away from the scene of the crime...

Peeeeeeep. The insistent blaring of a horn from the car behind blasted into my thoughts. The vehicles ahead were passing the lights. I made it through, but the car behind didn't. I didn't dare look back. I suppose that counted as my third lapse from grace today.

It was as I had feared. Mrs Mackenzie did not take it well when I appeared in the dining room doorway just as the last guests were finishing off their desserts. After a moment's pregnant silence, her eyes swivelled pointedly to a notice on the dining room wall. *Guests are requested to inform the Management IN ADVANCE if they make other eating arrangements.* For some moments she stared hard at the notice as if to refresh her memory, then marching over to the two tables with their place settings still intact, pounced on the cutlery and carried it off in the direction of the kitchen. Too craven to do more than mumble an abject apology to her retreating back, I fled upstairs to my room.

When I bent down to stroke her, Gorgonzola's eyes narrowed. Her welcoming purr metamorphosed to something remarkably like a snarl as she detected the tasty whiff of sardines on my hand. Then, like Mrs Mackenzie, she stalked petulantly off to stand with swishing tail beside the red *YOURS* holdall. An understandable reaction, I decided charitably, when you're starving and someone has blatantly helped herself to your meal.

I studied the tins in the holdall. What would make the tastiest peace offering? Salmon. That picture on the label looked so enticing. Gorgonzola's mouth was already dripping in anticipation of the gourmet meal to come. An empty rumble from my stomach reminded me that I hadn't eaten for nearly twelve hours, apart from that little snack of sardines, of course. I gazed speculatively at her. Perhaps I could filch her food from under her very nose… No, this was *not* going to be my fourth moral lapse of the day.

After a few minutes of watching Gorgonzola wolfing the salmon, I felt my resolution weakening. I took myself firmly in hand. This would not do. An official of Her Majesty's Revenue and Customs could hardly descend to eating cat food. Anyway, fat chance of being able to wrest what remained of the salmon from an outraged Gorgonzola's tigerish jaws.

Like the mirage of cool blue water materialising before a thirst-crazed traveller lost in the desert, an alluring vision rose up before my hungry eyes. Delicious, crusty, soft-centred rolls and pats of butter. Mrs Mackenzie had meanly snatched the cutlery away, but perhaps she had not yet got round to removing the rolls from the table. I'd make a quick sortie into the dining room and spirit them away. As long as I was careful not to leave any tell-tale crumbs in my room…

I sauntered casually down the stairs, ready to change direction for the lounge if Mrs Mackenzie should appear. I poked my head round the door. The room was deserted. She was obviously still in the throes of tidying up, but could return at any moment. There, only a couple of yards away, lay the tempting basket of rolls and a small dish of foil-wrapped butters.

My mind ranging over some plausible excuses if challenged, I pondered the best method of retrieval – slow noiseless tiptoe, or fast headlong rush. I'd rely on speed. Five or six quick strides took me to the table. I snatched up three of the rolls and a handful of butters. Too late now to regret not bringing a bag to carry them away. I clutched my booty as best I could and beat a hasty retreat, just as the door from the kitchen began to open.

I had reached the turn of the stairs and was congratulating myself on my little victory, when I lost my precarious grip on the rolls. One slipped from my arms and bounced merrily on each step down to the foot of the stairs. It came to rest nestling cosily up against an outsize pair of yellow golfing shoes. My eyes travelled slowly upwards, past the black trousers, past the vivid yellow jersey, and came to rest on the face topped by the yellow and black golfing cap.

'Mighty fine chip shot, ma'am.' Hiram J Spinks raised an amused eyebrow and smiled, but his eyes were cold and calculating. He picked up the roll and held it out to me. 'Guess you missed dinner?' The questioning note in his voice was unmistakable.

I felt a coldness in the pit of my stomach.

'Er, yes,' I said, mind racing. I knew with awful certainty what his next question was going to be.

'You been someplace interesting I should see?' The tone casual, the intent deadly.

It was a Catch-22 situation. If I said that I'd been at Tantallon, and he wasn't aware of this, he would be on red alert. If I said I'd been somewhere else, and he *had* seen me at the castle...

I debated, dithered, took a chance. 'I went shopping in Edinburgh. You know how it is when a woman gets the chance to browse among all those boutiques.' I forced a laugh and took the roll from him. 'I'm counting on you not to tell Mrs Mackenzie about this little foraging expedition of mine.'

He chuckled and winked conspiratorially, but a steel shutter had descended behind those chilly eyes.

Suddenly, I recalled Tantallon, the dipped headlights attempting to stab their way through the thick mist and reflecting on the leaves as I pressed myself against them, the hunched figure at the wheel. He *had* seen me – and recognised me. My presence there must have strengthened any lurking suspicions over the incident at Inchcolm. Looking into those cold eyes, I knew that if I hadn't instinctively pressed myself against the dripping bushes to avoid that approaching car, if I had continued walking in the middle of the road, he would have crushed me under his wheels with no more compunction than he'd brush aside an offending worm-cast on the putting green. Just another terrible accident in the fog. Nobody really to blame...

And my lie about shopping in Edinburgh revealed that I had seen him at Tantallon, *and didn't want him to know*.

I had made a fatal mistake.

CHAPTER ELEVEN

Back in my room, I sank down onto the bed with no appetite for the hard-won rolls and butter. Legs strangely weak, heart thumping uncomfortably fast, I was under no illusion as to the danger that now threatened me. Spinks had killed twice. A third murder – mine – was definitely on the cards.

He couldn't know that I was an undercover Revenue and Customs Officer, but I was obviously taking an excessive interest in his affairs. He'd seen me at the Botanics and Inchcolm, and today at Tantallon, and the clincher for him would be that I had *lied* to him about my presence there. He would now be sure that my turning up at those locations was not a mere coincidence.

Gorgonzola, ever tuned to my moods, uncurled from the comfortable nest she had made in the duvet, stretched lazily, and patted gently at my arm. As I stroked her tufty coat, I grew calmer. That list I'd filched from Gina's car looked promising, and the police enquiry into the identity of the Japanese woman might well provide another lead. With that distinctive gold streak in her hair, it shouldn't be difficult for them to pick up her trail at the group's hotel. As for my own personal safety, forewarned was forearmed. That meeting with Spinks had been unfortunate, but he still would have been suspicious, even if I'd admitted to being at Tantallon. I'd just have to get in there first and pin something on *him*.

That decided, I suddenly felt hungry, broke open one of the rolls, and spread a thick layer of butter over its soft white centre with the aid of a teaspoon from the tea-making equipment. As I prepared to sink my teeth into the soft bread, I found myself drooling in anticipation...

Hunger at least semi-satisfied, I nudged G away from prime position on the bed, and almost immediately fell fast asleep.

...My head was level with his feet. I had a worm's eye view of the studs of his golf shoes. Hiram, unmistakable in an enormous yellow and black golfing cap that floated on the top of his head like some vast hot air balloon, smiled pleasantly at me. Still smiling, he reached into his golf bag and drew out a gigantic butter knife stamped *Made in Japan*. Holding it in a two-handed golfer's grip, he took up a teeing-off stance with my head as the ball. As I stared up at him, he swung the knife high in the air behind his shoulder and brought it down in a slashing power drive...

My eyes snapped open. My forehead was beaded with sweat, my body rigid with fear. For a terrifying moment, I stared uncomprehendingly at the alarm clock on the bedside table. 4.30 a.m. The room was already bright and filled with the chirping trill of birdsong. The white net curtains billowed gently in a light dawn breeze.

Apprehensively, my eyes roved round the room. Nothing. Nobody. Not even Gorgonzola. Relax, it had been only a dream, but I would take it as a warning. No Jacuzzi baths, no wandering alone round treacherous old castles. All Spinks's other killings had been designed to appear accidental. If I kept to crowded, busy places, what could he possibly do? *Plenty*, a small voice inside me whinged. Drowsily, I listened to its craven whine. I would keep out of Spinks's way today by having breakfast in bed...

A few hours later at 7.30 things didn't seem quite so simple. I lifted the phone. 'I wonder if I could have breakfast in bed today, Mrs Mackenzie.'

There was a long silence at the other end of the line. Then, speaking slowly and clearly so that there should be no misunderstanding, she replied, 'I'm afraid it is not hotel policy to offer room service unless there are *truly* exceptional circumstances.' A tinny laugh underlined just how preposterous was my request.

I bit back what I really wanted to say – *I'm afraid too, and desiring to avoid a would-be murderer in the dining room must fall under the category of exceptional circumstances.* Instead, I feigned a humility of which Uriah Heep himself would have been proud.

'I'm *so* sorry, Mrs Mackenzie. I realise I am asking you to go to *enormous* trouble, but I'm feeling so *unwell*. It must be delayed shock after my accident, I suppose.' I played a mean trump card. 'You see, I wouldn't like to alarm the other guests by being taken ill in the dining room. They might find it a bit upsetting if I had to be carried away like poor Ms Lannelle.' A wobble of suppressed laughter made my voice sound convincingly tearful and shaky.

There was a sharp intake of breath at the other end of the line.

I pressed home my advantage. 'I shall, of course, expect to

be charged a bit more to recompense you for all the extra trouble.'

Mrs Mackenzie knew when she was beaten. 'My dear Miss Smith,' she cooed, her voice suddenly dripping honeyed concern, 'of *course* feeling unwell rates as an exceptional circumstance. Why didn't you say so at first? I myself shall bring you up a tray.'

Shutting the window to prevent an untimely entrance by Gorgonzola, I propped myself against the pillows in a suitably feeble invalid's pose and waited. Ten minutes later, there was a tap at the door and the handle slowly turned. I experienced a pang of alarm. Was that yellow and black cap about to appear round the door? Lying in bed, I'd be a defenceless target for an attack.

Then a tray pushed the door open, followed by Mrs Mackenzie's angular features. I let my breath out in a quavering sigh, not entirely feigned.

'I've brought you a light breakfast, not too heavy, feeling as you are.' She placed the tray on the bedside table and with suspicious eyes inspected my recumbent form for signs of health.

I gazed with dismay at the very small boiled egg and two tiny triangles of toast. 'How thoughtful of you,' I quavered, my voice faint with hunger at the mere thought of a large plate piled high with tasty bacon, egg and sausages. The memory of last night's soft buttered rolls rose tantalisingly before me.

'If you're still feeling unwell at lunch time, just let me know, and I'll make you up a special light meal.'

The realisation that she could charge a high price for very little food had brought an avaricious gleam to her eye. It gave a whole new meaning to the phrase Making Much Out Of Little. With an air of quiet satisfaction she surveyed the tray, artistic in its minimal simplicity. A final tweak at the cloth, a precision realignment of teaspoon and knife, and she turned to leave.

Halfway towards the door she abruptly changed direction, crossed to my carefully closed window and flung it wide open. 'A little fresh air will do you the power of good.' Her brisk tone brooked no opposition.

I smiled weakly, hoping fervently that a hungry Gorgonzola would not choose this inopportune moment to make her entrance.

I felt that some comment was required. 'It's very good of you, Mrs Mackenzie,' I whispered, 'to take all this trouble when you have the other guests to consider.'

Inclining her head in gracious acknowledgement, she swept regally from the room.

I left the hotel later that morning, hiding behind a huge pair of dark sunglasses that I hoped lent me an air of wan paleness in keeping with my invalid status. I have to admit, however, they *did* make the negotiation of the dim recesses of staircase and hall a trifle difficult. At the foot of the stairs a sharp pain razored through my shin, and for a long, heart-stopping moment I thought I was under attack from Spinks crouching in the shadows. I wrenched off the glasses to discover I'd been the victim of an ornate Victorian umbrella stand.

A familiar discreet cough revealed the lurking presence of Mrs Mackenzie.

To forestall the inevitable cross-examination, I called out, 'I'm just taking your advice and stepping out for a little fresh air.'

My real intention was to drive towards Edinburgh and treat myself to a huge meal. After that, I planned to call in at Lothian & Borders Police Headquarters and see if they had made any progress towards tracing the Japanese woman. Nestling in my pocket was the cigarette packet I'd found in Gina's Lombardini's car. I would study it over a heaped plate of – well, *anything*.

When I stepped outside, I found that early sun had given way to low grey clouds with more than a hint of rain, a typical Scottish summer's day. Mrs Mackenzie might find it a trifle odd that a supposed invalid was choosing to take the air wearing sunglasses when rain threatened. I whipped off the glasses and thrust them into my pocket. In the car, I sat for a few moments behind the wheel. There was no sign of Spinks's car in the heather-bordered car park, but as I drove along I kept a wary eye on the rear view mirror. Just in case.

After my long fast, I was obsessed with the thought of a gourmet meal, so I didn't stop at the first eatery I spotted, but drove on to find somewhere more likely to provide that special experience.

I picked up the heavy leather-bound menu and took my time studying it, determined to exercise control and discipline. My eyes scanned the main courses... Each dish seemed more mouth-watering than the next.

Branade of Jerusalem artichoke with aubergine caviar
Pickled herring in Madeira brine with side salad
Watercress and mushroom consommé

Grilled fillets of lemon sole with avocado and lemon butter
Delice of Scottish salmon with a fine leek and
mushroom cream
Noisettes of Border lamb with a mint and
cucumber dressing
Panfried supreme of chicken in a bed of sweet peppers and
garlic sauce
Entrecôte of prize Aberdeen Angus garni with mushrooms
and sweet onion

Slowly I reread the list, savouring every item. After much agonised indecision, I at last settled on the artichoke and the salmon. Now I could relax. I fished in my pocket for the torn cigarette packet from Gina's car and studied the list of places.

Inchcolm Cramond May
Tantallon Fast
Longniddry Bents

No other information. No day, no times. Perhaps the Japanese woman would provide a lead, if they managed to trace her.

With the arrival of my meal, speculation was put on hold, so it was an hour later, over coffee served with a jug of cream, that I got out my map and attempted to locate Gina's rendezvous points. I stretched out for a chocolate mint and traced the coastline of the River Forth with my finger. There seemed to be quite a number of islands. Fidra, Bass Rock, Inchkeith, Inchcolm and May. And Cramond Island, facing Inchcolm from the Edinburgh side of the Forth. Interesting. All were within easy reach of Edinburgh and the White Heather Hotel. Thoughtfully, I put down my empty coffee cup.

A waiter hovering with a pot moved forward to offer a refill.

I stabbed a finger down on the map. 'I wonder if you could tell me anything about this Cramond Island?'

'Certainly, madam.' He put down the coffee pot and bent over the map. 'Let's see… You are here. It'll take you about an hour to get there. It's an island only at high tide. At other times you can reach it by causeway.'

I took a pencil and circled the spot. I pencilled another neat circle round Tantallon. Both were on the coast, both within an hour's drive of the White Heather Hotel. If my theory was right… I followed the southern coastline of the River Forth. Longniddry… On the coast. And near a golf course – two golf courses, in fact. That should please Hiram J Spinks. I lassoed Longniddry with another pencil mark. Fast Castle took a little longer to find. It was well to the right of Tantallon, halfway towards Berwick-upon-Tweed. Again on the coast.

I folded the map and pushed back my chair. Two o'clock. It was time I made tracks. Longniddry was the nearest of my targeted places. Perhaps I'd have time to give it the once-over on my way back from Police Headquarters. By now the Japanese woman would have been interviewed along with the rest of the group, ostensibly as another witness to the accident, and the police would be keeping a discreet eye on her movements.

The rain that had been threatening was now coming down in earnest. I shrugged my shoulders inside my thin raincoat and ran for the car.

But at Police Headquarters I met only disappointment and frustration.

'Well, the good news is that we've established the identity of the Japanese woman.' Was there an artificial heartiness in the tone of Detective Chief Inspector Macleod of the Scottish Drug Enforcement Agency? 'Her name is Kumiko Matsuura.' He paused.

'And the bad news?' I said.

'We've lost her. When our man arrived to interview her early this morning, he found she'd left the hotel.' He didn't meet my eye. 'By two o'clock when the group was scheduled to travel north to Pitlochry in the Scottish Highlands, she hadn't returned, so it's "whereabouts unknown" for her.'

Why oh why, had they left it until late this morning to set up the interviews? I hoped that I managed to hide my annoyance. I didn't want to sour relations. That way lay difficulties I could do without. I had to admit it was partly my own fault. I should have stressed the need for urgency. I eyed the clock on the wall, twenty minutes past three.

DCI Macleod intercepted the glance and reached for the telephone. 'Our man will call in if she puts in an appearance.' He spoke apologetically, embarrassed and edgy, sensing my silent recriminations. 'But I'll just see if anything new has turned up.'

I moved away from the desk and walked over to look out of the window. I'd come across a similar view in a guidebook, but not the usual run-of-the-mill sort of publication. It was an interesting mix of information about places to visit and poems about Edinburgh, beautifully illustrated with unusual views of the city, like that rain-drenched Edinburgh roofscape accompanying a poem by Alfred Noyes.

City of mists and rain and blown grey spaces...

Rain and blown grey spaces... Rooftops, grey-slated, precipitously pitched in their perpetual battle against the Edinburgh weather...

Behind me I heard DCI Macleod's noncommittal, 'I see.'

At the sound of the receiver being replaced, I turned. The long black second-hand of the wall clock had hiccupped its way only once round the dial since he had begun his call. Not a good sign. My eyes met his.

'Nothing?'

'She's not come back yet. The rest of the group waited an hour for her, then left for Pitlochry. We've asked the hotel to inform us if she turns up.'

I gazed out at the streaming rooftops. Had Kumiko disappeared of her own free will? If so, why? Was she a frightened witness, who had seen Spinks locking the tower door? Or was she an accomplice to murder? Unlikely. She wouldn't have drawn attention to herself by disappearing from the group. Or was there a more simple explanation – she'd merely gone out for a tour of the city and got lost? The fact remained that the woman seemed to have vanished into thin air.

The heavy driving rain had reduced itself to a mere drizzle

as I drove away from Police Headquarters. By the time I reached the outskirts of the city, the rain had stopped altogether and fugitive patches of blue sky had appeared amid racing grey clouds. If the weather continued to improve, I'd have a look at this Longniddry place. It'd take me only a couple of miles out of my way. Yes, I'd plenty of time before Mackenzie, a flabby version of J Arthur Rank's muscleman, would be beating the gong for dinner. Not, of course, that I was hungry after that magnificent lunch, but I couldn't afford to spend too long there. Turning up late for dinner a second night running would be the last straw in my relationship with Mrs Mackenzie.

The narrow road twisted and turned, trees on both sides, their branches blocking out the view. Where the road ran near the sea, the winds had sculpted the exposed tops of the gorse bushes into rounded shapes as if some topiary artist had been at work.

LONGNIDDRY BENTS. I almost missed the small notice, its lettering blasted by sand and salt. An arrow pointed down a narrow track between high banks. *BENTS?* Had the T originally been a D? I swung the car onto the track. Though narrow, it was tarred, and led after several twists to a surprisingly large car park surrounded by trees and high dunes. I let down the window and switched off the ignition. The cloud-ceiling had lifted and the patches of blue sky were bigger, but the threat of rain was not far away. In good weather, this would be a popular picnic area. Now it was completely deserted.

I got out of the car and took a narrow sandy path leading

to the small bridge over a brackish river. I caught glimpses of the sea as the path climbed gently to the top of the sand dunes through thickets of gorse interspersed with hawthorn bushes and small trees. Faced with a twisting maze of crisscrossing paths, I paused at the top of the first dune. To the left was a line of Scots pines, the silhouette of their dead branches eerily resembling gossiping old women gesticulating with gnarled witchy fingers. To the right, not far off, lay the sea and the distant coast of Fife, its hills patched with fluorescent-yellow rape fields. A cool wind whipped across the dunes rustling the clumps of desiccated grasses.

I gave an involuntary shiver, 'someone walking over my grave', a disturbing thought. Hadn't I promised myself only last night to avoid lonely places? For several minutes I stood perfectly still, every nerve strained to catch the whisper of a footfall, the faintest unnatural sound above the plaintive cries of sea birds, the unceasing rush of the waves, and the soft sighing of the wind through the bushes. Those bushes were so thick *that a corpse could lie hidden among them and never be discovered*. Get a grip, DJ. Why was I scaring myself like this? That faint hum from a passing car meant that I wasn't *very* far from the main road, quite close, really. I chose a path I hoped would take me out onto the beach and quickened my pace.

My shoes made no noise on the sandy ground. *Neither would a mugger's*. There I was – scaring myself again, scaring myself to death. A rather unfortunate turn of phrase. If Spinks poked his head out of the bushes, he wouldn't have to lift a finger, I'd drop down dead with fright. I took a deep breath. This was a popular picnic spot, after all, not the setting for a *murder* movie. There I was, at it again. I gave myself a figurative bawling out, and moved briskly on.

A final twist of the path, and I was standing among low dunes on the edge of an enormous bay. In front of me, half submerged, was an uneven line of jagged stakes, the skeletal ribs of a rotting ship, seawater now its only cargo. I consulted my map. Those white buildings on the far side of the bay must be the golf club. There were no other buildings, making it an ideal spot for landing drugs, isolated, yet near the road for transport...

How peaceful it all was. Blue-green grass spiked the yellow of the dunes. A sudden shaft of sunlight spotlighted a seagull as it flapped its way lazily along the triple line of white breakers at the water's edge. In the distance, a golfer was practising his swings on the hard flat sand, cheaper than paying for a round at the adjacent golf club, I suppose. Golf had started that way, after all, with men thwacking a ball across sand dunes. And now it was a multi-million-pound leisure business.

Yes, a cargo of drugs could easily be put ashore here. How far was Tantallon from Longniddry? Was that island Inchkeith? The wind pulled and tugged at the map, making consultation difficult. Dropping to my knees on the soft sand, I laid it on the ground and weighed the edges down with a couple of stones. Tantallon there... Inchcolm there... Longniddry here... It all made a neat triangle. I spent a few minutes considering the possibilities.

I heard a metallic *clunk* close by. While I had been studying the map, the golfer had worked his way steadily towards me and was practising his bunker shots less than two hundred yards away. All that was visible above the top of the dunes was the glint of sunlight on the head and shaft of his club. Idly I watched as rhythmically it rose and fell.

I turned back to the map. Tantallon... Longniddry... Was it possible to see Tantallon from here? I stood up. That smudge on the coast to my right – was that the castle? I narrowed my eyes and squinted at the distant, blurred outline.

The sand shifted under my feet. I lurched, stumbled over a thin whippy root, and fell forward on my hands and knees. *Swoosh* overhead. Sand fountained up and trickled down the face of the dune as a golf ball driven with lethal force smashed into the sand a yard away from me. For a long moment I stared in disbelief at the embedded ball. It must have been travelling at head height. My mouth opened, but shock constricted my throat. Instead of a shout of outrage, all that emerged was a strangled croak. If I hadn't slipped, the ball would have shattered my skull. That golfer was *dangerously* irresponsible.

A wave of anger flooded through me and broke the paralysis. I scrambled to my feet on trembling legs that barely supported me.

Unladylike language rose to my lips. 'You *bloody fool*. You incompetent *bastard*,' I shrieked. 'You...you...*shitb*—!' The sand avalanched beneath my shaking feet, sending me sliding further down the dune.

I expected a startled apologetic face, red with embarrassment, but there was only silence. And the whisper of another lethal golf ball *thunking* into the sand.

This time I didn't cry out.

The unnerving silence said it all. My assailant was not a carelessly irresponsible golfer. It had to be that coldly efficient killer, Hiram J Spinks. His characteristic modus operandi was murder masquerading as accidental death. First to die, Waldo M Hinburger. Next, Gina Lombardini. Third, DJ Smith. I could visualise the stark headline, *GOLF BALL SLAYS HOLIDAYMAKER*.

My ears, made super-sensitive by adrenalin, picked up the soft slither of moving sand and pebbles from the far side of the dune in front. I hadn't made a sound since my slide down the dune, and the murderer was moving in to view his handiwork, coming to find out if I was lying dead in a hollow. Which was what I *would* be, if I didn't do something about it.

Bending low, I scuttled crab-like away. I had a minute, perhaps less, before the would-be assassin poked his head over the top and discovered that his victim had taken flight. My first instinct was to make straight for my car. I couldn't be far from the car park track and – *there it was*.

I raced along, thankful for the cover of the trees and bushes and the twists in the path. The dead, lichen-covered branches clutched at my arm, plucked at my coat. Heart pounding, I quickened my pace, but had to slow. Wiry roots hidden in the soft sand were too much of a hazard.

Ahead of me, the paths branched, one leading eastwards in the direction of the car park, the other seeming to twist back towards the sea. Which way, which way? Already my breath was coming in great shuddering gasps. Perhaps it was not such a good idea to head for the car. My pursuer might have anticipated exactly that, be lying in wait. Was he ahead or behind? Was that the dry rustle of wind through the gorse bushes...or...?

I darted along the seaward path. Prickly gorse crowded in

on either side. Impossible for anyone to hide there. Unexpectedly, the path turned back on itself, veering suddenly away from the sea in the direction of the road. Sand underfoot gave way to grass and a thick carpet of dead twigs from a huge Scots pine. They'd snap easily. I'd have to be very careful. Cautiously, I tiptoed my way across. I must find somewhere to hide until he gave up the search. I ran on.

The square shape of the building was almost hidden by a clump of hawthorn bushes and trees. I hesitated. Perhaps a double bluff would work. He wouldn't *expect* me to choose so obvious a hiding place. The bushes scratched and tore as I gingerly picked my way through, careful not to leave a tell-tale trail of trampled undergrowth. Overhead, the late afternoon light was blocked by the thick canopy of leaves from the sweeping branches of an enormous horse chestnut tree. In the gloom, the small flowers of a wild white rose glimmered palely. My outstretched hand touched the rough concrete sides of a low shed almost engulfed by the horse chestnut and hawthorn. There was no window or doorway. I edged my way round. On this side, more light came from above. The low concrete 'shed' was nothing more than a couple of huge anti-tank blocks, part of the World War II sea defences. No hiding place here. I ran a tongue over dry lips. I'd wasted too much time. A trickle of sweat ran down my back.

A sudden flurry overhead sent twigs and leaves spiralling to the ground. Startled, I looked up. Two enormous birds, rooks or crows, were squabbling and bickering over a piece of road-kill. In their violent tussle their feet scrabbled for purchase. Wings beating, one snatched the prize, and both fluttered out of sight behind the thickly clustering leaves.

Where I was standing, a great branch hung, half torn off, and the tide of bushes had reluctantly receded, to be replaced by a thick bed of vicious looking nettles. I leapt upwards and hung on. There was an ominous creaking, but it held. By bracing my feet against the concrete, I was able to work my way upwards until I could wriggle onto the top of the block.

I did not stand up. That would expose me too much. From my position I could see high into the tree. My weight had extended the long jagged tear, exposing bright new wood. It all looked dangerously unsafe. Before doubts and fears made me lose my nerve completely, I gripped the branch, and, using it as a primitive ladder, hauled myself little by little into the crown of the tree. As I clawed my way up, the large five-pointed leaves parted, then closed protectively round me.

I stopped when the branches thinned and began to flex and bend in my grasp. It was just as well that my perch was surprisingly comfortable. I might have to stay up here for hours. How long before it would be safe to come down? After dark? That might prove even more dangerous. Anyway, it didn't get really dark till nearly midnight, another seven hours or so. Would Spinks give up his search before that? I couldn't count on it. All he had to do was lie in wait in the car park. Well, two could play a waiting game. I leant back against the trunk of the tree…

My ears became attuned to scores of faint sounds, the wind fluttering the leaves of the horse chestnut, the creak of its branches, the distant cries of sea birds and, closer at hand, the twittering and chirping of sparrows and blackbirds. Occasionally, I heard the muffled hum of a passing vehicle –

the road must be quite close... My thoughts drifted...

Crack...crack... It was the sound of brittle twigs snapping under a careful foot. I sensed a movement below. I pressed myself hard against the trunk and turned my head away. If I looked down into the gloom, whoever was down there might sense he was being observed...

Slowly, ever so slowly, I eased my arm sideways till I could see my watch. Five minutes. Ten. Then *crack...crack...* Spinks coming back? Or had he been standing there all along? Listening. Waiting. Was he even now climbing the tree? As if in answer, the leaves below me rustled and shook, then trembled ever more violently... I bit into my lip to stifle a scream.

I saw no triumphantly grinning face, no homicidal Spinks. With a whirr of wings a small brown bird darted out from its hiding place and flew off. I felt the tension draining out of me. How silly, how dangerous, to let my imagination run riot like that. I had so very nearly revealed my presence. I closed my eyes and forced myself to breathe slowly and deeply. Gradually my heart rate steadied as reason reasserted itself. If I remained in the tree, I was safe. It was going to be a long, long wait...

Salvation came from an unexpected quarter. The hard throbbing bass of a ghetto blaster thumped its way towards me on the breeze. There was an irate shout, then a sudden silence, broken by youthful voices laughing and shrieking. Another shout, and the laughter and shrieks trailed off. In its place came the faint strains of 'Old MacDonald had a Farm', bawled rather than sung. Slowly the volume increased and the words became more distinct. *Crak...crik...crak...crak...* A fusillade of snapping twigs heralded an unmusical cavalry to the rescue.

Carefully, I moved aside some plate-sized leaves and peered down at the path. Into my narrow field of view wound a file of children. No orderly school-crocodile this, but a mad centipede of skipping, dancing legs. Each hand waved a treasured souvenir of the seashore, each throat strove to out-decibel the rest with an enthusiastically hideous imitation of cow, sheep, horse or cockerel. Harassed authority figures at head and rear hustled and chivvied like good-natured sheepdogs. The man at the front carried a cardboard box brimming with squashed tin cans, crumpled crisp packets and empty bottles. Perched precariously on top, in imminent danger of crashing to the ground, was the enormous ghetto blaster, mercifully silenced. The man bringing up the rear lugged along a net sack bulging with footballs, cricket bats and old tennis rackets. Scampering ahead of everyone else, a skinny redheaded youngster took noisy pot-shots with an imaginary rifle at any startled birds that broke cover.

I craned forward for a better view of the bizarre procession. At that same instant, perhaps attracted by the slight movement, the urchin swung his rifle up and round as if tracking a moving clay-pigeon target. His eyes met mine, widened, then narrowed calculatingly. He mimed pulling the trigger. Instinctively, I jerked back.

With a sharp report, as if a rifle had indeed been discharged, the branch under my right hand snapped, sending my body lurching forward. Frantically, I scrabbled, clutched, flailed at branches, twigs, leaves, anything to prevent a headlong plummet to the ground twenty feet below. Debris showered down onto the astonished heads of the temporarily silenced creatures of MacDonald's farmyard. Then my shoulder thudded painfully against something solid, and my arms circled a thick branch in a desperate bear hug.

'Sir, sir!' The young voices were strident with excitement. 'Norrie's just shot a woman out of that tree!'

'What's she doing there, sir?'

'Is she trying to steal birds' eggs, sir? Can we call the cops?'

Eyes closed, I pressed my forehead against the rough bark and waited for my heart rhythm to subside to normal.

'Why's she not moving, sir? Is she dead?' The note of hope was tangible, the word *dead* savoured to the full.

I heard the sigh of disappointment as I levered myself gingerly upright. With as much dignity as I could muster, I brushed assorted twigs from my hair and smiled down at the upturned faces and the goggling eyes. It was going to be difficult to explain my presence twenty feet above the ground in a horse chestnut tree... Then inspiration – all that DVD and video-watching makes kids see people from the US of A as oddballs who do crazy things. If they thought I was American, maybe I wouldn't have to explain a thing.

'Hi there, kids!' I directed a particularly warm smile at the skinny redhead. 'That sure was a *swell* shot, pal. Drilled me right between the eyes. But just let me tell you guys how the Amazon Indians hunt *without* guns, and kill with *poison-tipped* arrows.'

I scrambled my way down, my lurid descriptions of sudden and violent death in the jungle cunningly designed to prevent any more probing questions. When my feet at last touched the ground, my youthful audience was hanging spellbound on every word, desperate to hear yet more gruesome details. The group leaders, less impressed, were eyeing me warily.

The man carrying the rubbish cleared his throat, 'Well, what exactly were you doing up there?' His grip on the box shifted a fraction, the ghetto blaster wobbled dangerously.

'Just a bit of bird watching.' I made a grab for the blaster before it could slide to the ground. 'Hey, I reckon you guys could use some help, so I'll tote this along for you. I'm making for the parking lot myself. Let's go!'

Swinging the ghetto blaster, I turned in the direction of the car park and launched into a spirited rendition of 'Ol' MacDanald.'

Surrounded as I was by my diminutive bodyguards, there was no chance of Spinks getting his hands on me now.

'Ee-i-ee-i-o,' I trilled triumphantly as I marched along.

CHAPTER TWELVE

The wave of euphoria had ebbed by the time I reached the gates of the White Heather Hotel. As I swung into the drive, I slowed the car to a crawl. What if Spinks had gone straight back to his car? What if he had *not* stalked me for hours among the scrub and bushes of Longniddry? My hands clenched the wheel in a vice-like grip. Was he now lying in ambush in the dimly lit hall, or behind the door of my room? I brought the car to a halt and rested my forehead on my folded arms.

The voice of commonsense reasserted itself. It was most unlikely that he would be lurking with murderous intent anywhere in the White Heather Hotel. Another accident there would certainly take some explaining away.

But how was I going to handle our next meeting? Spinks would almost certainly take his cue from my reaction. I stared hard at a brown smear on the windscreen and tried to think myself into his shoes. I had shown too persistent and close an interest in his affairs, so in his eyes, I would not be an innocent bystander, but a police officer…or from a rival drugs syndicate trying to muscle in on his territory. Ye-es, that could be it.

I reviewed the afternoon's happenings in this new light. I

had run away after that second lethal golf ball, indicating that I knew an attempt was being made on my life. How would a rival organisation react to an attack on one of its own? I drummed my fingers on the steering wheel... That smear was irritating me. A quick squirt of screen wash to the windscreen, a brisk movement of the wiper blades, and the accumulation of squashed bugs had almost gone. Yes, attack was the best form of defence. I must make *him* feel threatened...but how?

Frowning, I stared up the tree-lined drive. The squashed body of a fly was still stuck firmly to the windscreen at eye level. After another pump of the windscreen-wash, another sweep of the wipers, it was still there, superglued by impact. To Spinks, I must appear like that; an irritating insect obscuring the way ahead. I got out, and with a flick of my finger dislodged the obstinate husk. That was how he dealt with people who got in his way. That was how he would deal with me if he felt threatened. So...make him think of me as an ally, or at least as someone useful to him and his plans.

By the time I reached the car park, I had worked out a plan of action. There was no sign of him or his car. Good. He'd find a message waiting for him when he collected his keys. I rummaged about until I found the notepad in the glove compartment. The wording would be crucial. After a moment's thought, I wrote in a bold and heavy hand, *How about a meeting to do business*? That would imply I had the backing of a big drug cartel. I hoped.

The rendezvous would have to be somewhere we'd both feel secure. Somewhere quiet. And for my own safety, not too isolated...a place where there'd be plenty of people close by...somewhere in Edinburgh?

I scrabbled once more in the glove compartment and found the Edinburgh guide with its fold-out map. Big green splodges marked parks and open ground in the centre of town. I considered the possibility of a meeting in the Botanic Gardens. I dismissed it – too many opportunities for another little drowning accident. I shut out the memory of Waldo's staring eyes and discoloured face. What about Princes Street Gardens? That would be too public for Spinks...

The most promising looked to be the biggest green area on the map, the Queen's Park and its mini-mountain, Arthur's Seat with its three little lochs. That was certainly big enough to give privacy for our meeting, yet crowded enough on its necklace of roads, and the adjacent Royal Mile and Holyrood Palace, to discourage any ideas Spinks might have. The best place should be a landmark, easy of access, but hopefully not too frequented, and nowhere near anywhere that could become an 'accident' zone. So, not the lochs, nor the Salisbury Crags. *Hunter's Bog*? That name wasn't propitious. *Gutted Haddie*. Weird! And as for *Haggis Knowe*, I sniggered, if I asked him to meet me at either of these places, he wouldn't take me seriously...

My finger hovered over *St Anthony's Chapel (ruin)*, isolated, but only a couple of hundred yards from the safety of one of the main routes through the Park. It was on the edge of a small loch, certainly, but Spinks was unlikely to try to eliminate me in full view of a steady stream of passing cars. I'd meet him there.

I looked again at the message I had written on the notepad. *How about a meeting to do business?* Not assertive enough. I nibbled thoughtfully at the end of the pen, then wrote quickly before any niggling doubts could arise about the wisdom of doing this. *Our organisation could use a guy like you. Meet me in Edinburgh at St Anthony's Chapel in the Queen's Park. 11.30 tomorrow morning. Smith.*

That should hook him.

The hotel hall was empty, though from the dining room there came a murmur of voices and the clink and scrape of cutlery. Should I leave the note in Spinks's pigeon-hole to collect with his keys, or should I slip it under the door of his room? I swithered. Though his car wasn't in the car park, he might have put it round the back. So he might be in his room and catch me in the act. At this moment, I didn't feel up to acting out the role of hard-bitten henchman of a powerful drug baron. But…if his key happened to be hanging up, I'd risk it.

I leant over the reception desk and peered at the rows of pigeon-holes. In the gloom of the hall, it was difficult to see if his key was there. I grabbed the faraway edge of the broad counter and levered myself nearer. One foot maintained a precarious contact with the floor, but the other swung wildly in the air like a novice ballet dancer practising at the barre. I still couldn't quite make out whether… I grunted with the effort of edging that little bit closer… Just as well there was nobody to see this indecorous display.

Someone coughed sharply in the shadows. Embarrassed, I wriggled back to the proper side of the counter and looked round. Mrs Mackenzie, in funereal black, had materialised from nowhere, her angular features tinged with a mixture of unease and alarm.

'Still feeling a little unwell, are you, Miss Smith?' she asked with a look as black as her dress. Sick guests were bad for business, especially those who seemed to be about to vomit on the far side of the reception desk.

'Oh yes, I mean, no,' I stammered. 'I've completely recovered. I just thought I saw er – something, er – scurrying past…'

Her face turned a most pleasing shade of puce.

I babbled on. 'But, of course, there was nothing there. Nothing at all. No. As I said, I've completely recovered, thank you.'

Defrosting now that both her establishment and I had received a clean bill of health, she eyed the paper in my hand. 'How can I help you, Miss Smith?

If I gave her the note to put in the pigeon-hole, she'd almost certainly read it, but I couldn't avoid that now.

I waved the folded piece of paper in her direction. 'I see Mr Spinks hasn't come in yet, but I don't want to be late for dinner.' That neatly skipped over the fact that I was already ten minutes late. 'So could you just slip this little note into his pigeonhole?'

She lifted the flap of the reception desk, lowering it behind her like a miniature drawbridge, and tucked the flimsy piece of paper under Spinks's keys.

'I'll see he gets it as soon as he comes in, Miss Smith.' The words smooth, the eyes sharp, already x-raying the contents.

With a gracious smile in return, I moved off in the direction of the dining room. Ten seconds, I reckoned, before those calculating eyes were scanning the words I had scrawled. I quickened my pace. By handing that note to Mrs Mackenzie I'd certainly burnt my boats. No going back now. I just hoped

I could handle the forces I had unleashed. With an uncanny sense of timing, as I passed the swing-door that led to the kitchen, the air was heavy with the acrid smell of burning.

I did not have long to wait for developments. Just as I was finishing the soup, Murdo Mackenzie, sparse hair slicked down, and otherwise spruced up for evening service in the dining room, delicately edged his way towards me through the cluster of tables. With some difficulty, he manoeuvred his heavy tray past jutting elbows and handbags lying in wait to ensnare the unwary foot. He stopped beside my chair. On the tray stood a very expensive eleven-year-old Chateau-bottled red Bordeaux, its austerely simple label proclaiming its quality.

I was more than a little annoyed. So Mrs Mackenzie thought she was going to pull a fast one by making me pay for wine I didn't want?

'There must be a mistake.' I let the irritation show. 'I didn't order this wine.'

The frown-line between Mackenzie's eyes deepened. He seemed nervous, continuously rubbing one hand over the other like a surgeon cleansing his hands before a difficult operation.

'Er...if you would prefer something else... Morag thought...' He swallowed, 'As you ordered the duck...she thought you might care for something to wash it down. On the House, of course...'

At the word *wash*, his hands unconsciously sped up their soaping motion. Taking my astonished silence for assent, he seized the bottle, uncorked it, poured a little of the contents into my glass, then stood back, anxiously awaiting my approval.

Enlightenment dawned. Mrs Mackenzie must have lost no time in reading my note to Spinks and telling her husband. This was a blatant attempt to ingratiate themselves with somebody more powerful than Spinks.

I picked up the glass and swirled the liquid, colour a warm red, bouquet of ripe redcurrants with a hint of mint. After an appreciative sniff, I graciously nodded my acceptance with the thinnest of thin-lipped smiles, in the manner of Mafia godfathers. Cool, emotionless. That's how they played it, at least according to Hollywood.

My performance had the desired effect on Mackenzie. He stepped eagerly forward to fill my glass, then backed away, nodding and smiling obsequiously. I held up my wineglass to the light and admired its clarity. I took another appreciative sip. As the kitchen door swung behind him, I caught a glimpse of Mrs Mackenzie peering anxiously in my direction. I'd made my mark with the owners of the White Heather Hotel. But I had the nasty feeling that my note would not impress Spinks quite so easily.

Forty minutes later, I pushed back my chair with a sigh of contentment. The food had been excellent. Jitters had certainly not been allowed to spoil what was definitely a gourmet meal.

Back in the (comparative) safety of my room, those jitters surfaced like some time-delayed indigestion pangs. I pulled up a chair to the mirror and studied my reflection. Where was the permanent scowl, the small mean eyes, the cruel mouth of a godfather, or godmother for that matter? Behind my left shoulder, a sleepy Gorgonzola opened one lazy eye. She was curled up on the end of the bed, her stomach swollen and distended after *her* gourmet meal of duck and salmon. How about... I pressed my lips together into a thin line and subjected her reflection to a cold hard stare. Would she sense the naked aggression, arch her back, spit, hiss? Her eye stared thoughtfully back, and ve-ery slowly closed. Verdict delivered.

So much for the hard-bitten look. I'd had a lot more success with the written word, at least as far as the Mackenzies were concerned. I frowned at my reflection in the mirror. Spinks, unfortunately, would take a lot more convincing. He saw people as puppets, to be manipulated by cold-blooded killers like himself. I should be safe enough until tomorrow, though. He would want to find out what I had to offer... After that, I had no illusions about the danger I would be in. He'd had no qualms about ridding himself of his other would-be partners, Hinburger and Lombardini. Up to now, any evidence I had against him was merely conjecture, or purely circumstantial. I was no heroine. Just get something definite on him, I told myself, retreat, then call in reinforcements. So... I stared into the mirror and practised my mean smile.

Gorgonzola's paw patted my cheek and brought me out of a troubled sleep. I lay there, drowsily trying to piece together the disjointed fragments of my dreams. Not for long. She had taken lessons from Attila the Hun, and soon indicated her impatience by parading back and forth, each weighty paw placed with malice aforethought in the middle of my stomach.

Forcing one eye open, I stumbled out of bed and picked my way across the room to the window, where G, tail swishing, had already taken up position. The air coming through the narrow gap at the bottom was cold. Yawning, I pushed up the sash just enough for her to slither through. The early morning sun was already glinting on the surface of the small pool and sending long black shadows across the lawn.

What *was* the time? I peered at the alarm clock on the bedside table. It was still only six a.m. Far too early to get up. Without a twinge of guilt, I climbed back into bed and wrapped the duvet tightly round myself. I'd just lie here a moment and plan...

Trr...trr... I put out a sleepy hand and groped for the switch of the alarm. *Trr...trr...* I fumbled with the switch again. That irritating trill went on and on. I propped myself up on an elbow and managed to get my eyes wider open. The ringing wasn't coming from the alarm, but from the bedside telephone. Who could be ringing me at this early hour? I struggled upright, glancing at the time as I reached over to pick up the receiver. *7.30 a.m.* The alarm should have gone off half an hour ago. I groaned. G must have been at it again. She took a perverse pleasure in patting the alarm-off button with her paw.

'Hello,' I said warily.

'Oh, gooood mo-o-rn-ing, Miss Smith.' It was unmistakably Mrs Mackenzie, but the sweet honeyed tones were totally unfamiliar. 'I was just wondering, Miss Smith, if you would again care to take your breakfast in bed?' There was the genteelest of stresses on the word *again*.

'Uh...' my sleepy brain tried to come to terms with this new Mrs Mackenzie.

My lack of response misinterpreted, she redoubled her efforts to please. 'You could, of course, Miss Smith, state the time you wish Mr Mackenzie to bring your breakfast up to you.'

With some dismay, I visualised yesterday's two tiny triangles of toast. I remained silent.

The same minimalist vision must have also occurred to her, for she hastily added, 'If you feel you could manage the full breakfast this morning, Miss Smith, that will be no trouble, no trouble at all.' The honeyed tones were now definitely forced.

'Well, Mrs Mackenzie, I can't tell you how much I would appreciate that. Your *full* Scottish breakfast and a large pot of tea will be just fine.'

I replaced the receiver and giggled at the picture of Murdo, every step a worry, struggling manfully upstairs, tray laden with porridge, kippers, bacon, egg, black pudding and toast. I wouldn't manage to eat all that myself, of course, but Gorgonzola would definitely appreciate the kippers.

I thought about the note I'd sent to Spinks. *Our organisation could use a guy like you. Meet me in Edinburgh at St Anthony's Chapel in the Queen's Park. 11.30 tomorrow morning.* It was too late to back out now.

The narrow road was signposted *Church of Scotland, Duddingston. Historic Scottish Kirk, 12th Century.* To my right, spacious villas of imposing architecture peeped over high stone walls. I slowed the car and risked a quick sideways glance at the old church with its worn horse-mounting platform. A strange iron collar on the end of a short chain hung from the adjacent wall. I caught a fleeting impression of spiked barred gates, lichened tombstones, crenellated battlements... Then I was past.

The entrance to the Queen's Park lay a hundred yards

ahead. It was 9.45 a.m. That gave me plenty of time to climb the swelling ridge of Arthur's Seat and approach St Anthony's Chapel from the rear. I got out of the car and looked around. In the distance the Pentland Hills smudged the horizon, and on the other side of the road, a reed-fringed loch sparkled in the sunshine. I leant on the waist-high iron railing, gazing down at the geese and ducks sunning themselves at the water's edge. An old man was scattering bread on the ground. Beside him, a small girl, herself not much taller than the geese, was holding out a lump to entice them closer. Reluctantly, I turned my back on the tranquil scene. I was part of a grimmer world.

According to the guidebook, there should be a path from the car park that would take me up over the hill, a much longer route than the more direct approach from Holyrood Palace, but with luck I might catch Spinks unawares, putting me psychologically one step ahead. I scanned the hillside opposite. My way lay to the right of that neat Victorian park-keeper's cottage.

Steps, hundreds of them. I took a deep breath and began to climb. 48, 49, 50. Already my leg muscles were starting to protest. 98, 99, 100. I paused for breath, making an excuse to gaze down over the pretty loch with its border of trees. In the distance, a romantically half-ruined castle rubbed shoulders with some hideous twentieth-century high-rise flats.

I toiled on upwards, a dense thicket of hawthorn to one side, and a high pinkish wall covered with ivy on the other. When I glanced back a hundred or so steps later, the view of the loch was almost totally obscured.

Steps, wall and hawthorn gradually petered out. The path was now a grassy track, still going uphill but much easier on the legs. It was all so incredibly peaceful – tall wild grasses, purple thistles, the hum of insects, the rays of the sun warm on my back. A gentle breeze quivered through the grasses, wafting with it the muted hum of distant traffic. I could have been miles out in the country instead of near the centre of a busy, car-choked capital city.

I scrambled up to an ornate black metal post sprouting incongruously in the middle of the deserted hillside, and, to my surprise, found myself on the edge of a road. I sank onto a thoughtfully placed wooden bench, another unexpected mark of civilisation – like the car park a short distance away. If I'd studied the map properly, I could have driven up here and saved myself a *lot* of effort.

I pulled the map out of my pocket and refolded it with the area of St Anthony's Chapel and Holyrood Palace uppermost. The main route for traffic rounded the bulk of Arthur's Seat and squeezed between Duddingston Loch and the hill, before merging with the street network of south-east Edinburgh at the Duddingston Kirk entrance. I must be about two hundred feet higher up. I swivelled round on the seat. There was the main road far below. This upper road joined the one that ran past the Chapel and Palace, and was quite plainly marked. How could I have missed it?

The sound of an engine starting up broke my concentration. I looked up to see a Range Rover move slowly out of the car park off to my left. I turned my attention back to the map. Should I continue with my original plan and climb up over the hill to my rendezvous point at St Anthony's Chapel? Or should I walk along this road? It wouldn't take any longer, and would definitely be a lot easier…

An engine roared harshly at full rev. A squeal of tyres brought the acrid smell of burning rubber. In that split second I realised the danger I would have been in if Spinks had driven with murderous intent towards me in the Tantallon fog. Instinctively, I flung myself off the bench, curled myself into a ball, and rolled over the edge of the slope.

I came painfully to rest against a sharp and prickly bush. Arthur's Seat is famous for the gorse that clothes its slopes, and here I was getting a close-up view. A hands-on experience, you could call it. I lay there winded for a few moments, in my ears the sharp crack of splintering wood. The engine roar faded...

'Good gracious me, are you all right, my dear?'

I rolled away from the bush's scratchy embrace and looked up. Two horrified elderly faces were peering down at me from the road above. A third face joined them, a whiskery West Highland terrier's. It seemed to be laughing at my predicament.

'Don't be silly, Edith! Of course she's not all right.' This was accompanied by a vigorous shaking of his head. 'She might have been killed. Aye, killed.' The man's white hair fluttered and bounced as shake turned to nod. 'Such driving! And by a woman, even!'

'You do talk a great deal of rubbish sometimes, Harry. It wasn't because she was a woman. It was because she was a foreigner. They're not used to driving on our side of the road, you know.'

'She wasn't just driving on the wrong side of the road, Edith. She was driving on the pavement! Even foreigners can tell the difference between the road and the pavement.'

I tottered unsteadily to my feet and climbed back up the slope. The bench lay on its side, the splintered wood, the jagged pieces of plastic bumper, the sprinkling of orange glass, all mute evidence of Spinks's latest attempt to get rid of me. So he hadn't been taken in by my message...or perhaps he had. And this was his way of getting rid of an unwelcome rival, just as he had got rid of Hinburger and Lombardini. There seemed no point now in going ahead with the meeting at St Anthony's Chapel.

'No, Harry,' Edith was adamant. 'You can't convince me. No *woman* would deliberately try to knock someone down.'

That took a few moments to register.

Edith and Harry, lost in the pleasures of verbal sparring, seemed to have completely forgotten my presence.

I gave a tentative cough. 'Er, excuse me.'

'Oh, Harry! That poor lady – you've been arguing and here she is, all scratched and bruised...' Edith drew breath to fuel another lengthy conversational duel with her husband.

'No, no, I'm quite all right,' I interrupted. 'Did I hear you say that it was a woman driving the car?'

'It was indeed. And a foreign woman at that.' Harry pursed his lips in disapproval.

For once he and Edith seemed to be in agreement. 'Oh yes, definitely foreign,' she nodded.

'Foreign?' How could they possibly know? I had the surreal vision of a Gallic assassin dressed in striped Breton jersey and designer beret.

'We'd passed her earlier, you know... Standing just about here, she was, looking down at the loch.' Edith's eyes gleamed with excitement as she relived the moment. 'I said to Harry, didn't I Harry, "There's another of those foreign tourists." Edinburgh's getting really busy with them now that summer's here and—'

'We said good morning to her. Well, it's only manners, isn't it?' Harry interrupted, unwilling to let Edith monopolise the conversation. 'Not very friendly, she was. Didn't say anything. Just looked at us with those almond eyes and—'

'Almond eyes?' My voice was louder and sharper than intended.

Harry's white eyebrows arched in surprise. 'Why yes, Oriental, you know. Chinese or...'

'Or Japanese?' I said slowly. Had I been right about a connection between Kumiko Matsuura, Lombardini and Spinks?

The sensible thing now would be to let the local police take over, let them handle everything. But Spinks would go to ground as soon as they started nosing round the White Heather Hotel. And he'd not leave anything incriminating behind. Even if they caught up with him, there was nothing they could actually charge him with. Reluctantly, I had to admit that my *only* chance of keeping in touch with him was to continue in my role of Mafia go-between and turn up at our rendezvous. An extremely dangerous course, but it might convince him that I was genuine.

I sensed eyes watching me and looked up. Edith and Harry were gazing at me anxiously. The dog was rootling and snuffling under a nearby bush, paying me no attention at all.

'She looks a bit dazed, Harry. I think we should call an ambulance.' The faintly etched age lines on Edith's face had deepened into worried furrows.

Harry tugged absent-mindedly at the dog's lead. 'We should get the police, Edith. That was a hit-and-run. They might catch that maniac woman before she leaves the Park.'

'There you go again, Harry. There's no chance of that. At that speed, she'll be miles away by now. No, an ambulance is—'

'No, really. That won't be necessary. I'm quite all right,' I said to forestall another lengthy argument. 'I'm meeting somebody at St Anthony's Chapel and I'm a bit late. If you'll just tell me how to get there...' This was a mistake.

'That's the quickest way,' Harry pointed to a broad well-beaten path leading uphill to the right of where we stood. 'Most people take that route, don't they, Edith? It goes right to the top. It'll take you about half an hour.'

At precisely the same moment, Edith pointed to a narrow path winding off to the left through the gorse bushes. 'Now, Harry, I think you'll agree *that*'s definitely the best way.' She turned to me, 'It might take you a little longer, but it's not nearly so steep.'

I winced. I was about to be engulfed in yet another argument. I made an instant diplomatic decision.

'Thank you. Over the top would be the best way, but I don't think I feel quite up to it just now. The other way *does* look a little easier. I'd better go that way. Thanks again for your help.'

Before either could say anything more, I gave them a cheery wave and headed for the path on the left. At a safe distance I risked a glance back. Edith and Harry were examining the remains of the bench. They seemed to be arguing. The dog sat scratching its ear, its hairy head on one side as if trying to decide who was right.

The path slanted gradually upwards. From a sea of waist-high grass the occasional rounded grey boulder surfaced like some smooth-backed creature of the deep. The waspish whine of a motorbike far below competed with the hum of insects. My jangled nerves began to relax.

This pleasant stroll lasted for less than five minutes before the path began to climb steeply and I had to stop for breath. *Not nearly so steep*, Edith had said. Just as well, then, I hadn't taken Harry's route. That brush with death had taken more out of me than I'd realised. I glanced at my watch. No need to hurry, I mustn't arrive too exhausted to cope with anything Spinks might, literally, throw at me.

On the skyline, a paper kite spiralled and swooped, bright against the blue sky. Most of my own clumsy childhood attempts to get a kite airborne had ended in tears. It had seemed like the end of the world then, when it had crashed to the ground or entangled itself inextricably in a nearby tree, but, as I've said, it was a grimmer world now.

If anything, the path ahead looked steeper and narrower, more like a sheep track. Edith and Harry must have the stamina of mountain goats if they thought this was easy. From far below the wail of a siren drifted up. If the hit-and-run had gone to plan, that ambulance could have been coming to whisk away my shattered body. A surge of anger made the incline ahead surprisingly easy going.

Five minutes later, where the hill's brown bones burst through the thin turf, and a tumbled rockery of greyed lava boulders eerily evoked weathered and lichen-covered gravestones, the path levelled out and broadened to a wide grassy track. Was Spinks, that master of planning and opportunity, thinking of me as the late Miss Smith after a successful 'accident'? And what kind of little accident would he have arranged if I had tried to reach St Anthony's Chapel by the direct route, instead of by Duddingston? I'd have to be very careful indeed.

As I came over the shoulder of the hill, the summit lay off to the right, not deserted as I had somehow imagined but really quite busy, with little groups clambering over outcrops, or chattering and laughing as they trudged up the path of volcanic gravel that zigzagged up the reddish summit mound.

Just after 11 a.m. Would I have time to stand for a few minutes on the very top of Arthur's Seat? I hesitated, indecisive, looking longingly at the rocky summit. I made a quick calculation of time and distance. If I made a detour to the top, there should be a splendid bird's eye view of St Anthony's Chapel and its surroundings. I could spy on him, and it would certainly make me feel less twitchy if I could check my route down for any figures lurking behind overhanging rocks. That clinched it, I'd make a quick dash to the top...

Spread out below me lay the grey buildings of Edinburgh, and in the distance glittered the blue ribbon of the River Forth. I could see Inchcolm and the other islands quite clearly, but the chapel was hidden by the shoulder of the hill. Perhaps from over there...

I picked my way carefully across the lumpy summit rock, polished to a black sheen in places by countless tourists' feet. Directly below me lay the small loch shown on the map. Swans floated on its smooth surface. That dark irregular shape must be the chapel itself, perched precariously on an outcrop of rock. I hadn't expected the building to be quite so small or so ruined – only a couple of walls and an outline of tumbled stones. There was no sign of anyone, lurking or otherwise, down at the chapel. No photographers. No tourists. No sinister figure.

My route down was via a wide valley, open and grassy with no ambush places. And quite a few people were toiling up it towards the summit. At least I wasn't alone on the way down.

Just before the chapel, the path dipped sharply into a hollow. I stood for a moment gazing up at the crumbling walls. Byron must have had just such a gloomy place in mind when he penned the line, *Childe Harolde to the dark tower came.*

No bird sang. Utter silence, apart from the whisper of wind in the grasses. I stared back up the way I'd come, up to the summit with its throng of laughing and chattering holidaymakers. It was a world away.

When I looked round again at the chapel, he was there. Standing framed in the ruined arch, outlined against the blue sky, his face in shadow. But I could see that he was smiling. Gorgonzola smiled just such an anticipatory smile when she toyed with a mouse before gobbling it up. I'd thought I was prepared, but my stomach lurched and my throat felt sandpaper dry.

I feigned a confident smile and marched briskly forward. It's difficult to march up a steep incline briskly and with poise. By the time I was face to face with him I was struggling to avoid gasping and gaping like a newly landed fish. Please God, he'd take my flushed face and heavy breathing for signs of anger.

For a long, long moment he was silent. Then he rasped, 'Got your message.'

'And?' I managed, still struggling to regain breath control.

That threw him. I'd obviously hit on the right tactics. He was used to calling the tune and being the one to ask the questions.

Before he could recover, I stepped forward and poked him in the chest so hard that it rocked him back on his heels.

'The thing is,' I said, looking him squarely in the eye, 'I'm not sure if there's room for you in *our* organisation. Know what I mean?'

He frowned, at a psychological disadvantage, the meeting not going the way he'd visualised. I made my move. Whipping out my mobile phone, I punched in my date of birth and my National Insurance number.

'Smith here. He's being stupid. He even tried a little GBH.' I paused, eyes on Spinks.

A voice in my ear said, 'I don't know who you are, but is this some kind of joke?'

Incredibly, my random numbers had found a target. I took my cue from the squawking voice, gazed speculatively at Spinks, and pursed my lips.

'No, I'm not joking.' I paused. 'You want that I should take action?'

An alarmed screech from the voice.

'OK. I'll ask him.'

I severed the connection.

'You want another chance? We'd need to see how neatly you handle your next drop.' I turned my back on Spinks and walked away, heart racing, legs weak. 'Let me know by tonight. I'll be checking out of the White Heather early tomorrow. Your move.' I tossed the words carelessly over my shoulder.

I waited for the impact of the bullet between my shoulder blades, the nanosecond of searing pain, oblivion. But a minute passed...then two...three...

When I reached the road, I risked a quick glance back. I could just make out the thin figure. Still standing in the ruined archway. Still watching me.

CHAPTER THIRTEEN

It was entirely the wrong direction to retrieve my car, but I kept on going. Past the high wall of the Palace gardens. Past the black lacy filigree of the Palace gates. Past the angular modern architecture of the Scottish Parliament. Sure at last that I was out of sight of Spinks, even if he was watching through high-powered binoculars, I headed up the crowded Royal Mile. At a running walk that would have done credit to an Olympic athlete, I weaved my way through the knots of tourists idling along in the June sunshine. I didn't know and I didn't care if those heads were turning in admiration of my athletic fitness, or in annoyance at being hustled out of the way. All I wanted was to put as much distance as possible between Spinks and myself. If you want the truth, my nerve had failed.

The adrenalin-fuelled burst of activity died quickly. Leaden, rubbery legs brought me to a gasping halt. Lungs heaving, I stood there firmly promising myself (yet again) more frequent workouts in the gym, or, more realistically, a few snatched minutes of exercise every morning. Instead of getting back into bed after letting Gorgonzola out, I would get down on the carpet and do a few energetic press-ups.

I closed my eyes, leant against a wall and turned my face up to the soothing warmth of the sun. What on earth had possessed me to challenge Spinks like that? I must have been mad. My heart rate rose again. What on earth was I going to do now? I'd better think of something fast. Should I abandon the investigation, hand over everything to the local police? If I did, *something* would be salvaged. They would be able to arrest the Mackenzies, and that part of the distribution network would be closed down. But the source would be untouched... It would be like leaving a rogue cancer cell in the body... I opened my eyes and searched the sky for a sign. And there it was. A wrought iron one, bearing the words *Clarinda's – the original tearoom*. A good restorative cup of tea or coffee might steady the trembling legs. I pushed open the door.

The place was fairly crowded and I had to edge my way to an unoccupied table at the back of the small room. Snatches of tourist conversation, the muted clink of china and cutlery, the delicious aroma of freshly baked cakes – I let it all wash over me, then pulled the little menu card toward me and studied the list of exotic teas. Earl Grey Blue Flower, Japanese Jasmine, Raspberry Fruit, Mango, Peppermint...I'd taken so many risks already this morning, why not continue to live recklessly? I ordered a pot of Earl Grey Blue Flower and a giant rock bun, to be followed up twenty minutes later by a pot of the Raspberry Fruit and a slice of irresistible orange cake.

An hour after I had come in, I brushed away the last lingering crumb and sat back, jangled nerves restored. Yes, it definitely paid to take risks. And I *would* take another risk by tackling Hiram J Spinks. Buoyed up by that somewhat shaky logic, I drove back to the hotel.

I swung the car into a parking place beside the heather bed

and donned my dark glasses in keeping with the Mafia look. Spinks might be waiting for me. Marvellous stuff those fruit teas. Somehow I felt anticipation more than fear. Now I would be disappointed if he *didn't* react to my ultimatum. Would it be a brief note under the door, a staged meeting at the foot of the stairs – or a bullet in the brain? I crunched my way across the gravel.

It was not Spinks but the formidable proprietress of the White Heather Hotel who lay in ambush in the vestibule. And the bullet hit me straight between the eyes.

'Miss Smith, I must ask you to depart from these premises by noon tomorrow. You have broken one of the *cardinal* rules of this establishment.' Under stress, Mrs Mackenzie had adopted quaint, old-fashioned turns of phrase.

'Ru-les?' Gasped out, strangulated, it wobbled in the middle and tailed off into an ignominious squeak.

She nodded grimly and flung out her arm in a dramatic gesture. My eyes followed her quivering finger. In an awesome demonstration of her direct line to God, a shaft of sunlight illuminated the brass plate.

THE MANAGEMENT REGRETS
NO PETS CAN BE ENTERTAINED

'Pets?' I said, genuinely bewildered. How on earth had she found out about Gorgonzola? What terrible crime had my cat committed? Whatever it was, it must be something so awful it had quite overwhelmed Mrs M's recent fawning deference.

'There's no point in denying it, Miss Smith. I have the proof.'

'Proof?' I croaked. Surprise seemed to have rendered me monosyllabic.

'Naturally.' She drew back her thin shoulders in indignation. 'You do not suppose that I would accuse one of my guests without proper evidence?'

Cravenly, I shook my head. If only I knew what feline crime had been committed... Perhaps I could brazen it out. 'I really think there's been some—'

She silenced me with an imperious sweep of the hand that indicated we should repair upstairs to my room. I trailed behind the ramrod-stiff back, thoughts racing furiously. Had Gorgonzola shredded the curtains, laid out half-eaten rodents in a neat row on the carpet, broken open the Mackenzie birdcage and slaughtered the inhabitant?

Mrs M waited grimly outside my room till I caught up with her, then threw open the door with a flourish. Cautiously, I peeked in. The room seemed just as I had left it. The curtains were unshredded, the carpet was mercifully clear of chewed corpses, and the white sheets of the still unmade bed were unsullied by the stiff little body of a budgie/canary.

I sighed with relief. 'Er, what...?' I said uncertainly.

In her eagerness to confront the culprit with the evidence of the crime, she swept past me, shoudered me aside might not be too strong a term. She stopped by the bed and gazed pointedly at the heaped sheet lying in rather rumpled folds. I followed her over. Surely she wasn't going to accuse me of wrinkling the bed linen?

'*Cat* hairs, Miss Smith. Paw prints. And...' she paused for maximum effect, '...underneath it's even worse!'

With all the assurance of a magician performing a

well-rehearsed trick, she grabbed a corner of the sheet and twitched it back.

Gorgonzola blinked innocently up at us. Half a goldfish dangled from her mouth. Under one enormous muddy paw, another large specimen from the Mackenzie pond lay glassy-eyed, its bright colours already fading.

With a shriek of, 'Oh my God!' Mrs Mackenzie reeled back and sat down heavily on the bedside chair.

'Oh my God!' I echoed.

Two courses of action were open to me: limited admission, something on the lines of 'Oh, I thought it was the hotel cat. Perhaps I *have* rather encouraged it', or complete denial. Unwisely, I chose the latter course.

'I've never seen that cat before. It's certainly not *mine*,' I declared firmly.

I stared menacingly at G, daring her to show any signs of familiarity. She stretched lazily, jumped softly from the bed, and treacherously deposited the half-eaten fish at my feet.

'Cats seem to like me,' I said lamely as she purred loudly and twined herself affectionately round my legs. In desperation, I grabbed her moth-eaten tail and gave it a warning tug. Playfully, she used my leg as a scratching post.

'Shoo! Go away, moggy,' I gritted, trying to keep up the pretence.

I should have remembered that Gorgonzola was a sensitive cat, especially touchy about remarks that reflected on her breeding, or lack of it. Her tail swished angrily, her eyes closed into mean little slits. With a cobra-like hiss she swiped aside the valance sheet and disappeared under the bed.

Nervously, I gazed at the swaying sheet. This was a side to

her character that didn't often surface, but when it did, her sulks tended to last for hours. With a bit of luck, she would stay there out of harm's way. Cheered by that thought, I glanced over at Mrs Mackenzie, who was clearing her throat preparatory to relaunching hostilities.

I got in first. 'Surely you don't think that I could have anything to do with a mangey thing like that?' I snapped. 'I'm really quite insulted!'

Half-convinced by my vehemence, she wavered. A look of uncertainty flitted across her face.

On cue, Gorgonzola shot out from under the bed and pounced on the *YOURS* holdall containing the tins of food. As usual, I had left it invitingly open for any Mackenzie inspection. Deftly, she fished in it with her paw. From its depths she extricated her working collar, a reminder to me of her rank and importance. She deposited it at my feet and sat back with a self-satisfied purr. She had sold me down the river and she knew it.

With the parting shot of 'Laundry charges!' Mrs Mackenzie swept balefully from the room.

And that was how, next morning, I came to leave the White Heather Hotel under somewhat of a cloud.

CHAPTER FOURTEEN

Before that ignominious expulsion I had my little tête-à-tête with Spinks. After the irate whirlwind exit of Mrs M, I slumped onto the chair and stared morosely at the dead fish. The fish stared coldly back. Out of sight, out of mind would be better for *all* concerned. I lifted it by the tail and deposited it in the wastepaper basket. Then I took it out again. I flushed the body down the loo and set about preparing for tomorrow's departure. Gorgonzola left her packing to me, having meanwhile effected a strategic escape through the half-open window.

Before I started the packing I called up headquarters on the encrypted mobile line. 'As of 1200 hours, 25/6, address no longer WHH. Closing in on target. Message ends. Scotch Mist.'

While I awaited acknowledgement and any fresh instructions, I gazed over the trim lawn to the pond, now sadly depleted of some of its inhabitants. Mr M seemed to have been assigned to patrol its margins. And tomorrow, when I checked out, two goldfish, koi-priced, would undoubtedly feature on the bill under 'Additional Items'.

The mobile beeped acknowledgement, but with no fresh orders from their end. I was on my own. Stressed out by the day's events, I straightened the rumpled sheet and lay down on Gorgonzola's paw work. I'd just think things over a little, get things straight in my mind...

Murdo Mackenzie doing his J Arthur Rank act on the dinner gong jerked me awake. I groaned and reluctantly sat up. Apprehension battled with excitement. Ahead lay the confrontation with Spinks. If he didn't accept my challenge, didn't make contact tonight, my chances of keeping an unobtrusive tail on such a violent and slippery customer were almost nil.

The dining room was already quite full, but I spotted him almost immediately, sitting at a table isolated from the rest by a huge potted palm in a stone urn, one of Mrs Mackenzie's attempts to inject a little Victorian ambiance. The table was near the far wall, but he had positioned his chair in direct line with the door to have a clear view of everyone entering. For an instant his cold eyes locked onto mine. I could feel those eyes boring into my back as I made my way, not too fast, not too slow, to a table near the window and chose a chair with its back towards him. He'd have to make the first move.

The message came while I was studying the menu. Mackenzie sidled his way up to my table and gave a tentative cough, the signal that he had something to impart.

'Yes?' I growled. I didn't look up.

He cleared his throat, 'Mr Spinks has asked you to share his table.'

'Tell him I'll come and join him after the dessert,' I grunted, not lifting my eyes from perusal of the card.

He shuffled uneasily. 'You did say after the *dessert*?' he quavered.

I turned over a page of the menu, continued my close perusal, and he scuttled away. I'd quite enjoyed that little exchange. So…Spinks had made his move, and I'd made mine. Pawn to king four, twice, you might say.

'Are you ready to order, Miss Smith?'

I'd failed to notice Mackenzie's silent return. He was standing behind my left shoulder, pad and pencil in hand.

'Why yes,' I said sweetly. 'As you may know, Mr Mackenzie, I am leaving the hotel tomorrow?'

Desperately hedging his bets, he revolved his head in a bizarre half-nod, half-shake.

'Well, since it's my very last chance to sample Mrs Mackenzie's outstanding cuisine, I think I'll choose from the à la carte menu.' Ordering from the most expensive dishes wasn't just gross self-indulgence (though, of course, it was – I really *would* regret no longer being able to sample Mrs Mackenzie's gourmet cooking). It was another move in my dangerous game. You see, I'd calculated it would take quite a lot longer to cook and serve one of the à la carte specialities, and that would keep Spinks on the hook.

I smiled my most dazzling smile, then delivered the body blow. 'That arrangement about meeting him after dessert, did it suit Mr Spinks, by the way?'

He choked. The poised pencil point lunged wildly over the white page. This time his response was a half-shake, half-nod.

I played it cool. 'If I may see the wine list?'

He rushed off to fetch it. Keeping Spinks waiting should give me a much-needed psychological advantage. I hoped it would underline the fact that I was the buyer, he the seller. He wouldn't like it. I'd have to be even more careful. I didn't let this thought put me off my meal.

Most of the guests had finished their meal and left. I laid down my spoon, pushed back my chair and stood up. The moment could be postponed no longer. For one awful instant I thought he had called my bluff and gone, but there he was, glowering over at me. He'd repositioned his chair so that he was partly screened by a drooping palm frond. Face expressionless, I made my way towards him past tables littered with empty wineglasses and crumpled serviettes. It took quite an effort. My heart was thudding furiously, and there was a hollow feeling in the pit of my stomach. This was the moment when I could blow everything with one careless word.

An empty packet of Marlboro lay discarded on his table, the ashtray overflowed with butts. He had been waiting a long time and the wait had not improved his temper.

He consulted his watch with an aggressive flick of the wrist. 'You've sure screwed up my schedule, ma'am. I gotta lot of business to do.'

'Well, Mr Spinks,' I said, beckoning the timorously hovering Mackenzie to bring the coffee pot, 'a good business deal should never be hurried, don't you think?'

That was met with a grunt that could've been either agreement or disagreement.

I plunged on, not wanting to lose the initiative. 'May I ask if you've come to a decision? You'll find partnership with us very lucrative. But we require an indication that you'll meet our standards.'

I took a long sip of coffee, gratified to see that my hand was rock-steady.

Spinks's smile did not reach his eyes. 'I *could* name you a place, time and date. But it's not just a question of dough, ma'am. It's a matter of trust.'

'It is indeed, Mr Spinks,' I said softly and looked him straight in the eye. Perhaps I'd seen too many James Bond films. He picked up the empty packet of Marlboro and slowly crushed it between his fingers. All the time his eyes held mine. Perhaps he'd seen the same movies.

He seemed to come to a decision. 'OK, ma'am, it's a deal.' He gave the mangled packet a final twist and let it fall. 'You gotta map?'

I nodded and reached into my bag. As my fingers closed round the map's oblong shape, my forehead broke out in prickles of sweat. *Those underlinings of mine* were copied from that same leaflet with the red and yellow corner protruding from the inner pocket of his loud jacket.

I fumbled around with bent head as if searching irritably for something I was sure was there, then staged an exclamation of annoyance, 'Sorry, I must have left it upstairs.' In a desperate bluff, I scraped back my chair and half rose.

Spinks raised his hand in a staying gesture. 'Guess we don't really need one.'

I sank back onto my chair.

He made no attempt to produce his own map – didn't, of course, want me to set eyes on those pencilled indications he'd made. 'The drop will be in a few days.'

Yeeesss. Outwardly impassive, inwardly jubilant, I nodded a business-like acknowledgement. I poured myself another cup of coffee, and for the first time in our encounter relaxed. I should have known better.

'There's just one thing, ma'am,' his voice was deceptively casual. 'I'm a careful guy, and I'd feel a whole lot better if you cut me in on one of *your* drops before I fill you in on some more details.'

My throat contracted, sending some drops of Mrs Mackenzie's quality coffee down into my lungs. Through a paroxysm of coughing my mind was racing. Why hadn't I thought of this, had some reply ready? I raised streaming eyes in simulated affront.

'You can't really expect...' I choked. 'The organisation won't like it. Won't like it at all...'

His eyes were on me, calculating, cold. Then he raised his fist and brought it down with a thud on the mangled Marlboro packet. 'No see, no deal. I've gotta be sure too, ma'am.'

I stood up. 'I'll have to check, Mr Spinks. As I told you, I'm leaving the hotel tomorrow. You'll be here *if* we want to contact you?' I hoped the stressed *if* would restore a little of the psychological balance in my favour.

Hiram J Spinks nodded his head and smiled. A smile I didn't like one little bit.

In a last defiant gesture against Mrs Mackenzie and her rules, Gorgonzola spent an untroubled night stretched out on my bed. Which is more than can be said for me. As the brief darkness of the June night gave way to the pale grey of dawn, I lay there open-eyed and sleepless, staring up at a mark on the ceiling. It could be done, yes, it could be done. Though to get Customs to mount a mock drug drop somewhere *would* take a deal of persuasion. Officialdom being what it was, there would be countless obstacles to overcome. But my department carried a certain amount of clout and... Optimism restored, I fell into a deep and dreamless sleep for a whole three hours.

Before I showered, I communicated with headquarters to give them time to mull over my request. Then I packed, subjected the sheets to a close inspection for cat hairs, and disposed of all evidence. There was no other difficulty as far as Gorgonzola was concerned. I could tell she was feeling a trifle guilty about yesterday's little incident, so I was sure I'd find her near the car.

Breakfast was served by Murdo Mackenzie, sleepy-eyed and somewhat rumpled. He'd either been up early loading tins of haggis onto his van, or mounting an all night anti-cat patrol round the goldfish pond.

After breakfast I gathered up the holdalls and went downstairs to face the Gorgon. Mrs Mackenzie had taken up a strategic position behind the heavy reception counter. When she saw me, she compressed her lips into a thin line of disapproval, then mindful of my Mafia connections, stretched them in an ingratiating smile.

'If you'll just present me with my account, Mrs Mackenzie, I'll be on my—'

'I think you'll find it all in order, Miss Smith.' The bill was slapped down in front of me. A bony finger pointed at the items near the bottom of the page under the heading *EXTRAS*.

Breakfast in room
Accommodation of pet
Additional change of bed linen
Restocking of garden pond with fish

All of which inflated the final bill by a totally exorbitant amount. I'd have a lot of explaining to do when I submitted my expense sheet.

I thought it prudent to adopt a chastened and penitent exterior. 'All very reasonable, Mrs Mackenzie,' I mumbled.

With the public side of my business completed, I left the White Heather Hotel.

A superheated gust of air blasted through the half-open window. Outside, roofs and chimneys, rain-sodden on my previous visit, now baked in oven-hot temperatures. I cast yet another glance at the clock opposite DCI Macleod's desk... I took three paces forward, three paces back... I'd been waiting 35 minutes 10 seconds for that call from headquarters... Before my drive to Police Headquarters, I'd spent a couple of hours killing time in Princes Street Gardens, and according to the locals laid out in lunch-hour indolence on the steep bankings, this was the hottest day for ten years, fifty, a lifetime.

Earlier, at Portobello, *Edinburgh-by-the-Sea* in Tourist Information speak, I had found an unobtrusive B&B with a fine sea view where they didn't mind a well-behaved pet. And I'd given assurance that my cat was exactly that. Gorgonzola did her bit by purring loudly and wrapping herself ingratiatingly round the landlord's legs. My cat knew a soft touch when she saw one.

The small fan on Macleod's desk whirred and oscillated, but barely stirred the sultry air in the small office. I sat down on a chair near the desk, too hot to do anything but slump. In another minute I'd be nodding off. Macleod, in shirt-sleeves, looked equally heavy-eyed as he doodled aimlessly on a blank sheet of paper. Both of us willed the telephone to ring. And at last it did.

He listened briefly, then gave me the thumbs up sign. Cradling the receiver behind his ear, he scribbled little notes, interjecting the occasional 'Yes' and 'Right'. With a final 'Right. Understood', he replaced the receiver and sat back, lazily stretching his arms and clasping his hands behind his head. 'Looks like you've got what you wanted,' he said, smiling.

Nearly midnight, and the blue-green northern sky was bleached old ivory above a thick dark layer of cloud on the horizon. Just enough light remained to distinguish features of nearby trees and buildings. Everything else was a blur of dark shapes and outlines.

The red glow of a cigarette showed that Spinks was already waiting, a black form against a deeper patch of darkness.

'Over here,' I called softly.

A silhouette for a brief moment against the light midsummer sky, the faintest whisper of a footfall on tarmac, and he was right beside me. Gone were the yellow cap, the loud jacket. Like me, he was professionally dressed in black.

I led him swiftly past a small cluster of houses with their sleeping occupants, one lighted window showing up starkly in the darkness. A low, padlocked gate barred a narrow road perilously close to the edge of the cliff, and a few paces to the right, broad wooden steps led steeply downwards. As if on cue, a three-quarters moon emerged from behind its bank of clouds, spotlighting the notice *Warning. Dangerous Track.*

Use the Footpath. Sixty feet below, white parallel lines of breakers gnawed hungrily at the semi-submerged remains of eroded cliffs.

I leant over the protective handrail and pointed. 'Most of the coast's like this. Can't get near with a boat.'

I manoeuvred him into the lead on our descent. I didn't want a repeat of that Inchcolm 'accident'. At the foot of the steps we were still high above a tiny harbour nestling in a fold of perpendicular cliffs. The path led round the headland and emerged on the opposite side of the harbour from the tiny jetty. I'd done a quick recce in daylight of Cove, the site selected by HQ for the dummy drop. Even at midday, the mini harbour with its couple of tumbledown fishermen's cottages had been completely deserted, though Edinburgh was only an hour's drive away. Towering cliffs and sparsely populated countryside ensured maximum secrecy. Ideal for smugglers.

In front of one of the cottages, white trumpets of convolvulus shone palely among a pile of lobster creels piled against wind-sculpted red sandstone, and over the wall to the rear, the gentlest of breezes ruffled the moonlit surface of the water, tarnishing its silvered smoothness. The night was warm, yet I felt cold. In the daylight it had seemed a holiday postcard scene, but now it had an indefinable air of menace. *Not* the place to be standing beside a murderer. Would the staged drug drop be convincing enough? I was under no illusions. If he detected something phoney in the staged drop, I would look into the face of Hiram J Spinks, and, like Hinburger before me, see Death.

It was a matter of keeping my nerve. I pressed a button on the side of my watch and peered at the illuminated dial. 23.56.

His eyes were on me, assessing, watchful.

'Four minutes.' I said a silent prayer that everything would run to plan.

I moved over to a lower section of the high sandstone wall that curled a protective arm round the still, dark waters of the harbour. Out to sea, the lights of a distant tanker glittered on the horizon. Waiting. Waiting. The regular shush of the waves counted down the seconds.

Beep. Beeeep. I cut the timer alarm on my watch and signalled with my flashlight. An answering pinpoint of light flickered briefly beyond the entrance to the harbour. With the faintest putter of engine, a dark shape glided towards the jetty. Beside me Spinks stirred. Good sign or bad?

'You guys don't use radio?' his voice held more than a hint of a sneer.

'Old ways. Less likely to be intercepted,' I grunted. 'We know for a fact that the Coastguard scan the frequencies with a tracer.' That at least was true.

Dark figures had materialised on the jetty to receive the crates handed up by other dark figures on the boat. A faint hum came from the darkness at the top of the cliffs, and a huge loading-net on a hook thumped down. With conveyor-belt precision, the crates were passed from hand to hand and piled into it. Another faint hum, and net, men and cargo rose to be swallowed up by the night. Even before the loading was finished, the boat had slipped silently away and melted into the darkness. It was fast, efficient, slick. The whole business had taken no more than four minutes.

'Neat operation,' Spinks grunted.

I was pretty much impressed myself.

'Just one more thing,' he laid a restraining hand on my arm. I turned to face him. 'Yes?'

'Guess I'll have to check on the quality. I deal only in uncut powder.'

I could feel his eyes on me, assessing my reaction, ready to pick up on any hesitation.

'Why, of course, Mr Spinks,' I said smoothly. We had expected that. 'They can't hang around up there on the road, so I gave instructions for a crate to be broken open. A sample will be left under your car.'

In silence we climbed the wooden steps, the only sound the occasional scuff of our rubber soles on the wood and the whisper of the wind through the long grasses. When we reached the top, I let him move ahead. That way, I'd be clear of any suspicions that I'd taken the packet out of my pocket and shoved it under his car.

'Here, you said?'

'On the front axle. Nearside.'

He knelt and felt underneath. I held my breath. This would be the final clincher. I heard a grunt of satisfaction. When he rose and turned towards me, he was holding a small tightly wrapped package.

'Let me,' I stepped forward with a penknife.

Carefully, I made a tiny slit in the plastic. He moistened his finger and touched the powder to his lips.

'Uncut,' I assured him.

For a few nerve-racking seconds he said nothing. I tried to read his expression but in the darkness his face was just a shadow.

'OK, it's a deal. Get yourself to a place called Cramond.

You know it, ma'am? Just beside that famous iron rail bridge. There's a kinda walkway over to the island. Two days from now I'll meet you across there at 2300 hours.'

'Can I ask you to be a bit more precise as to location, Mr Spinks?'

He turned away. 'Don't worry about where to find me, ma'am. I'll find *you*.'

CHAPTER FIFTEEN

Cramond. I leant on the fence and looked at the Roman excavations. Somehow I had expected something more... I struggled to find the right word...more groomed. Weeds flourished – purple weeds, bindweed, white convolvulus, all competing to cover up what man had uncovered. *Please Keep Out.* The notice seemed a plaintively futile request to the encroaching tide of untamed undergrowth.

My appointment with Spinks was a full two hours ahead. If everything went according to plan, the net would close on him tonight. The small radio transmitter nestling in my pocket was disguised as an innocent pen. All I had to do was pull off the top to unobtrusively activate it, and the Customs launches would move in.

A chill gust of wind whipped across the car park. I shrugged on my coat, one of those light reversible jackets that was black on one side, white on the other, and not much protection from the cold of a Scottish summer. I put it on black side out, and set off down a path that led in the general direction of the sea, at present screened from view by a belt of scrubby trees. A sharp turn to the left, and there was a vast expanse of grey water heaving sullenly under a lowering sky. I hunched deeper into my jacket.

Across a wide expanse of promenade, causeway markers stuck up like black jagged teeth above the sand. Cramond Island turned out to be a low-lying grassy mound far bigger than I had expected. According to the guidebook, no one lived there now. The couple of buildings perched on a mini-cliff near the far end of the causeway were relics of World War II. Disused and derelict, like the Roman excavations, they belonged to the past.

On such a blustery evening there was little pleasure to be gained from a stroll along the seashore. I didn't stroll. I jogged down to the stone jetty where a restive sea licked hungrily at the crust of barnacles and long, brown ribbons of seaweed. Apart from the seagulls, I had the place to myself. A blue board with white lettering warned,

DANGER! WATER COVERS THE CAUSEWAY AT HIGH TIDE

A smaller notice advised the safe times for crossing, four hours either side of low tide at Leith. I stood on tiptoe to peer at the tide tables, positioned well above normal head height and printed in the tiniest of tiny print. The tide was on the turn, but the tables showed that there was still plenty of time to cross. In about an hour, however, the causeway would be impassable, and anyone on the island would be unable to leave for several hours. I brushed aside a feeling of unease.

I should have known by now to trust my instinct.

The uneven surface of the causeway made for slow progress. The incoming tide sent angry little rushes of water slapping against the stones, swirling aggressively between markers in the shape of tapered pillars like strange elongated pyramids, encrusted well above head height with grey barnacles and dark brown bladderwrack – another grim reminder that at high tide there would be no escape from the island. If Spinks was intending to arrange one of his little 'accidents' for me, I'd—

My heel caught on a stone, loosened from its setting by the hammer blows of winter storms. I struggled to keep my balance, in real danger of falling off the causeway into three feet of cold water. I'd be better to concentrate on avoiding potholes in the crumbling concrete, rather than speculating on Spinks and his intentions.

From the promenade, the island had looked so near, but the crossing was taking far longer than I'd estimated. I still had a couple of hundred yards of causeway to negotiate before I reached the little beach on the island. I was cutting it fine if I was to familiarise myself with the terrain before the rendezvous time. If he wasn't lying in wait already, that is...

At last, the eroded surface changed to a short stretch of smoother causeway edged by protective sleepers. Now I was making faster progress. In a couple of minutes I stood on the island's shingle beach gazing up at the low brick building perched uncomfortably on sharp-edged grey rock.

He'd said *he'd* find *me*. I stared at the brick walls, searching for any tell-tale movement. He'd make his presence known soon enough. I'd just have to be ready. I mustn't be paranoid. I took a steadying breath and turned away.

No big decisions were called for. I could see only one path, and I took it. It led over a rise too small to call a hill, but high enough to conceal the interior of the island. On either side of the path, patches of waist-high grass swayed and rippled as if a crouching figure was moving stealthily towards me. I couldn't help glancing over my shoulder.

> *Like one that on a lonesome road*
> *Doth walk in fear and dread,*
> *And having once turned round walks on,*
> *And turns no more his head;*
> *Because he* knows *a frightful fiend*
> *Doth close behind him tread.*

I could hear Miss Greeson's prim voice from long ago. 'Commit to memory words like these, my dear, and they will be an inspiration, a comfort to you in Life.' (Always a capital L). Well, I *had* remembered them, and what I felt was not comfort but fear.

On the other side of the rise, bushes trussed by barbed ropes of bramble crowded in on the path. No lurking assailants there, but no way of escape in an emergency, either. I hurried on. The scrubby undergrowth retreated. Boulders pushed their way through earth and grass like bare knees through ragged trousers.

Ahead, the path twisted sharply round an outcrop. It was the acrid smell of wood smoke that alerted me to another human presence. I sniffed the air, then moved forward cautiously. I was standing on the lip of a small tree-fringed depression. In front of me was a gloomy clump of trees, and mossy green stones smothered by ivy and brambles. Grey wisps of smoke curled lazily up from the doorway of a small ruin. There was no other sign of life. The blustery wind in the trees was the only sound.

'Spinks!' I called tentatively.

A reply would have been unnerving. The silence was even more so. After a few long moments, I took a deep breath and moved closer. Set in the crumbling gable-end was a window curtained with ivy. A gust of air sent smoke spiralling upwards from the smouldering ashes like some secret signal.

'Spinks! Spinks! Spinks!' I called again into the oppressive silence. My shouts exploded round the little hollow, shattering the stillness.

Nothing. Not a rustle. Not a whirr of wings from a startled bird. Just my quickened breathing. My fists, thrust deep into my pockets, clenched into tight balls. Why was I letting him spook me like this? He had fallen for my role as middleman in a drug syndicate, hadn't he? So when we met, all we were going to do was clinch a business deal. I rolled this about in my mind for a bit, but was not reassured. The trouble was, I couldn't forget that little way he had of silencing business associates. Waldo's contorted face floated before me. Gina's scream rang in my ears. My fingers closed round the sleek cylinder of the pen-transmitter, my insurance policy. Slowly the wave of panic threatening to engulf me receded. Time to keep that appointment...

The old army buildings huddling on the cliff top seemed a likely place for our meeting, but, closer to, the brick huts were derelict. I scanned the buildings. In the stiff breeze, a shutter hanging drunkenly by one hinge banged noisily. At this very moment, Spinks could be watching me through one of those dark gun slits. Again, my fingers lightly touched the little transmitter.

Now to reassume the role of hoodlum, a hoodlum chafing at being forced to wait. I aimed a vicious kick at one of the battered cans littering the ground, sending it clattering across the cracked and broken tarmac till it came to rest against a clump of nettles.

'Spinks, you bastard, where the hell are you?' I howled into the wind.

Behind me, *creak*. I swung round, the hairs on the back of my neck prickling, a sure sign that I was under scrutiny from watching eyes. A rusty door stood slightly ajar at the bottom of some steps. A tough guy wouldn't just stand there. I charged down the steps and flung my shoulder against the door, sending it crashing back against the brickwork.

The room was empty. Completely empty. There was no furniture, only a rubble-strewn floor and peeling walls splashed and scratched with ugly graffiti. Messages of love, defiance, and death.

Sharon luvs Chaz. True!!!

Independence for Scotland. Revenge Culloden!

Have a good day. Kill yourself!

But from Hiram J Spinks, no message.

Seaview, some wit had scrawled in blue paint above one of the glassless windows. I scrunched my way over and peered out at an expanse of sea. Not much of a view, just cliffs dropping down to slimy green rocks. Useless as a landing site for a drug drop.

Clunk. I whirled round. A white stone bounced across the floor. It came to rest in the shaft of light from the doorway. Round it was wrapped a torn scrap of paper. I stared at the raw splinter it had left in the wooden door. He was playing cat and mouse, trying to manipulate me like a puppeteer controlling his marionette. I'd have to show him I wasn't intimidated, was still in control.

I scooped up the message-wrapped rock and in a couple of strides was standing framed in the doorway.

'You playing silly buggers then, Spinks?' I yelled.

I waited, but he didn't answer. I hadn't really expected he would. To hit the door, the stone could only have come from one direction.

'I don't read messages delivered like this.' I hurled it and its message away off to my right. 'If you want to talk to me, do it face to face, Spinks,' I shouted. 'You've got five minutes before I call the whole deal off.'

I made a big show of looking at my watch, then hunched deep in my jacket, did some serious thinking. All this cat and mouse stuff could only mean that there would be no drug consignment arriving tonight. It never had been on the cards. So why had he brought me here? I knew the answer. *Another little accident.* Should I use the transmitter? Not yet. I'd no proof of *anything.* I'd only blow my cover and achieve nothing. There was still a chance of infiltrating his set-up, and while the tiniest chance remained… There was nothing else I could do here, though. My priority must be to get off the island alive.

I made another show of checking my watch. 21.30. Twilight was not long off. I struggled to remember those tide tables. Had I left it too late? Even if the tide had begun to cover the causeway, perhaps I could still wade across. There was no other option.

'Deal's off, Spinks,' I bawled. 'My organisation won't like

being messed up like this.' The unspoken threat wouldn't do any harm, might even do some good.

While waiting out my ultimatum, I'd been covertly studying my immediate surroundings. Past the block of buildings where he almost certainly lay concealed, a flight of steps in surprisingly good condition led up to raised ground. To my left was a narrow tarmac road edged by brambles and stunted elderberry trees. It would have to be that way. I couldn't risk going closer to him, and I could move a lot quicker on level ground.

Without a backward glance, I set off casually, yet purposefully. Fast, yet not at a tell-tale run. I half-expected a shout or even a bullet, but there was no reaction, no reaction at all. Worrying. I hurried past more ruined buildings, more shapeless lumps of concrete, the flotsam and jetsam from a half-forgotten war.

I was making good progress, but it was definitely twilight now. A sharp turn in the road unveiled a spectacular view of the Forth Bridge, its tracery of iron girders silhouetted against the darkening sky. Soon the light would be gone. I increased my pace. It couldn't be far to the causeway.

Where *was* Spinks? He hadn't enticed me here only to let me walk away. He must have something in mind. And that very moment I found out what it was.

I had subconsciously noted an unusual density about one of the bramble bushes ahead. Now my heart leapt into my throat as a grotesque scarecrow figure loomed from the tangle of undergrowth. Poised for flight, with dry mouth, I stared at it. Then I let out my breath in a long sigh. It was nothing but an old anorak hood stuffed with twigs, and a hand fashioned from a pink rubber glove, pointing to a clump of trees a short distance ahead. A rough cardboard notice crudely lettered in black paint hung round the scarecrow's neck. A large red R had been inserted between the O and the P.

TO THE CO^{R}PSE.

I swallowed hard. He was trying to soften me up with scare tactics. He must have counted on me coming by this more direct road back to the causeway, in fact he probably had something similar arranged whichever route I'd decided to take. The road ran close by the trees indicated by that grisly pink finger. I'd have to pass within a few yards of the little wood. But I didn't have time to turn back.

Trying not to think about what might be in there, I set off. Of course, the effigy might not be Spinks's work. Just part of some childish game. By the time I drew level with the trees I had *almost* convinced myself. One thing's for sure, I'd definitely not be investigating...

Nevertheless, I couldn't help a quick sideways glance as I hurried by. Thick brown trunks, a tangle of undergrowth – and in that darker darkness under the canopy, a splash of scarlet. Resolution forgotten, I slowed, came to a stop. Above the red patch, a paler blob. Someone in a red jacket was crouching at the base of a tree. I saw again Kumiko Matsuura in her red jacket crossing the mist-shrouded courtyard of Tantallon Castle... He'd stationed her here to ambush me.

In a surge of anger, I stooped, picked up a stone, and flung it as hard as I could, aiming to hurt. I heard the soft thump of it hitting its target and tensed myself for a reaction. But there was none. No startled cry, no convulsive leap forward. I hurled another stone. Again it struck home.

Curiosity triumphed over self-preservation. *And that was exactly what he wanted.* I knew it, but couldn't stop myself going over to investigate. Out in the open, there had been just enough light to see. Here under the trees I had to use my torch. Holding it in my left hand, I unzipped my jacket and used the cloth to shield the beam.

The bright spot moved over the rough undergrowth. Fireweed, nettles, a rotten branch – and a soft low-heeled shoe. I let the pool of light rest on it for a long moment before I could steel myself to inch the beam slowly forward and up. A stockinged foot, tight black trousers, red jacket – the ray of light hesitated, then moved on upward.

The oriental face was a waxen theatrical mask, the almond eyes sightless dark wells. The thin gold streak in the black hair shimmered in the wavering light as, involuntarily, my hand shook. I swallowed hard. Lightly, I touched the back of my fingers to the marble cheek. Cold, but not icy. Indisputably dead. But how had death come? Slowly, I let the beam of light travel over the crouching figure. No blood, no horribly distorted features – and no visible means of support against the Law of Gravity. Someone was giggling uncontrollably, and I realised it was myself. Reaction, of course, but not altogether seemly when face to face with a corpse.

Several deep breaths brought my nerves back under control. I put out my hand and gave the limp body a gentle push. As her head tilted slightly to the side, the dead eyes glittered balefully in the torchlight. I jumped back, barely managing to stifle a scream. I'd allowed Spinks to get under my skin again.

Irritation overcoming revulsion, I made a closer examination of Kumiko. Like the invisible strings controlling a marionette, the strands of her wiry black hair stretched tautly between the lolling head and a thorny-stemmed bramble. That, and the savage thorns of the bramble thicket hooked into her clothes, explained the upright head and the half-crouching position of her body. Poor Madam Butterfly, betrayed by her American. A sudden sharp pressure on the carotid artery would have been enough... All he'd have to do was shelter the body under a dark raincoat, and by the time she was found it might very well appear to be a tragic case of a tourist having been taken ill, death hastened by hypothermia in the damp and chilly Scottish summer.

Moral – don't let Hiram J Spinks get too close. And wasn't that *exactly* what I was now doing? He'd killed because it suited him to set all this up, to delay me while he moved in closer for another kill. It was more than time I got out of here. To use my torch would give away my exact position. I snapped it off.

With the torch extinguished, it was pitch black in the little copse. Every sound seemed magnified, every rustle and creak a threat. The hair on the nape of my neck bristled. I spun round. Only the wind. I stumbled through the long grass in the direction of the road.

When at last I felt the smooth tarmac underfoot, I glanced back at the red smudge of jacket, no pale blob above it now. What had been Kumiko Matsuura's last thoughts? The still figure under the trees must have felt secure in the knowledge that *I* was to be the next victim. Instead, she had been the one to die.

Self-preservation must be my priority. Fighting down increasing unease, I hurried on, trying to take some bearings.

The banks of cloud had cleared from the west, revealing a sky bright with afterglow. There was perceptibly less daylight now than before. Far from heading towards the causeway, the road was twisting back on itself. I seemed to be retracing my steps.

There was no doubt about it. The road was taking me back to a point just above those abandoned army huts. Somewhere ahead was Spinks. On the rising ground three hundred yards off to my right, my peripheral vision caught a flicker of movement. There, then gone. I stood stock-still, mouth dry, eyes straining. Nothing. I closed my eyes briefly to rest them. When I looked again, on top of the small hill ahead, black against the greenish-yellow sky, a figure stood silhouetted. Waiting.

My first instinct was to run, the next to drop to the ground. I compromised. Crouching low, and turning my face away, I scuttled sideways into the cover of the long grass that bordered the road. I didn't look back. That waxen face above the red jacket had been visible from some distance. No tell-tale white blob would give away *my* position. Of course, if he had a nightscope… I tried to visualise the layout of the island as I had seen it in daylight. If I cut downhill at this point, it should bring me out at the ruined cottage. From there, it was only a short way back to the causeway.

But an easy cross-country ramble by daylight proved in the semi-darkness to be a nightmare. After crashing to the ground over a boulder and then into a bramble thicket, I had to slow my headlong rush. Grazed knees and scratched arms were painful, but a twisted ankle would spell disaster. I scurried through the long grass, knowing now what it felt like to be a mouse hunted by an owl, a mouse fearful of the cruel eyes watching from the heights, a mouse cringing as a dark shape blotted out the stars before the kill.

That denser patch of blackness ahead could be the trees sheltering the ruin in the hollow. A clump of trees, and that should mean... Without warning, the ground under my feet dipped, and I pitched forward, rolling and sliding, rolling and sliding... Winded, I lay on the damp earth for a moment, staring up at the dark sky slashed by the luminous green and blue of the afterglow. The acrid smell of wood smoke was unmistakable. I'd found the ruin.

For the first time since my discovery of Spinks's latest victim, this moment of inactivity gave me the chance to think clearly. It didn't seem such a good idea, now, to hide in the ruin. These tumbledown walls, even with their thick covering of ivy, would provide little in the way of concealment. At this moment he would see no need to hurry, would enjoy playing with his little mouse. Later, when daylight came, the hollow would become nothing but a trap. He only had to stand on the lip, watch for movement, and...

My only chance lay in making it to the causeway. From here it wasn't far, only about ten minutes – or would have been in daylight. Time was running out. I had to cross before the tide rose above the causeway and made escape impossible. To move quickly I would have to use the torch. And that would tell Spinks *exactly* where I was. But I had no choice.

The broad beam of the torch played over the tangle of undergrowth as brightly, and as visibly, as a searchlight. I was certainly betraying my position and there could be no turning back. What I was looking for was the outcrop of rock that marked the path down to the causeway. There – over to my left.

Sounds carry clearly on the night air. Behind me, I couldn't judge how far, but it seemed frighteningly close, came a shout and the crashing of a heavy body forcing its way through the scrub. Grouse-beaters use the same tactics to flush their quarry. Ignoring the sharp twigs and branches that plucked and tore at clothes and unprotected hands and face, I scrambled up the steep slope. The wavering beam picked up beaten earth. The path at last. I hurried along it, grateful for the easier going.

As I rounded an outcrop of rock, the lights of Edinburgh sparkled, yellow and white pinpricks against the dark land mass. Lights, people, safety. All so near, yet they might as well have been on the moon.

Only eight minutes or so should take me to the causeway. Fighting down an overwhelming compulsion to glance back, I ran on, the bobbing torch pinpointing my position all too accurately. No matter how close he was, there was nothing I could do. The pool of light danced before me along the path, sending black patterns flickering over the knee-high grass and bracken on either side. I tried to keep my mind clear of any thought other than where best to place my feet on the uneven ground... The going had been steeply downhill for quite a few minutes... I risked a glance upwards and ahead. The causeway should be in sight now.

There was no causeway, just water stretching from one shore to the other. Black water under a black sky. I stopped, heart in mouth. Perhaps it was a bit further on... No, there was the squat building, and the small stretch of sand, narrower, much narrower now. My boots sank into the shingle as I raced along the beach. Panting, I scrambled over the rocks and dropped down into ankle-deep water. I heard more shouts from behind. Desperately, I began splashing my way towards the nearest causeway-marker, a good hundred yards further out.

It may have been summer, but the water was icy cold. I had to force my legs forward against the pressure, and by the time I was waist deep my progress had been reduced to a nightmarish slow motion. Small waves sent the water surging chest high. I eyed the ten yards that still separated me from the concrete pillar that marked the causeway. Impossible. I'd have to go back and find a hiding place among the rocks.

A wave splashed up into my face, then another. Salt stung my eyes. My teeth were already chattering, and the cold that was numbing my body began to creep into my brain... Better to take my chance among the rocks than to die of hypothermia here in the water. My mind made up, I began to wade back towards the beach.

A couple of yards in front of me, the water erupted in a fountain of spray. Another fountain, to my left, and closer. A third beside my right shoulder sent water spurting up into my face. Slowly, my dulled brain grasped what was happening. Someone was hurling stones at me from the shore. The creeping effects of hypothermia must have been further advanced than I'd realised, for it took a few seconds longer to work out that the someone must be Spinks. The stones were as efficient as bullets to drive me away from the shore. And there'd be no tell-tale gunshot wound. He was giving me a choice. Drowning after hypothermia, or drowning after concussion, a slow slipping into unconsciousness or a sudden sharp oblivion.

I considered the options and rejected them both. I wasn't going to give him the satisfaction of yet another neatly arranged fatality. A stone splashed alarmingly close. There was another choice, and that was to swim out to sea, using not a fast crawl but a slow breast stroke. With luck, he'd fail to spot my head against the dark water and think that he'd scored a hit.

I struck out in the rough direction of the markers, each moment anticipating the stone that would come smashing into the back of my skull. Any splash would betray my position, but too much caution spelt certain death. I set myself a target of strokes. Eighteen...nineteen...twenty. Then another twenty. My clothes dragged in the water and lead weights seemed to have attached themselves to my arms and legs. Strangely, I no longer felt so cold. Eighteen...nineteen...twenty. Must be close, *must* be. I was.

Immediately in front of me the first marker reared up into the night sky. I lowered my feet and they grounded not on soft sand but on stone. As I moved forward, the water fell to my waist, then my knees. I'd found the causeway. On legs that weren't quite under my command, I waded towards the next marker, and the next, and the next...

...I stopped, chest heaving. I must be a third of the way across. The lights of Cramond seemed a little closer. But the water was deeper, much deeper now. Waist deep. My right foot stepped on nothing and I lurched forward. Cold water filled my mouth, my ears, surged over my head. I rose spluttering to the surface. *Bloody fool.* I'd walked off the causeway. I flailed towards the dim shape of a marker and sobbed with relief as a knee grazed painfully on the causeway's raised edge.

It was no use. My strength was ebbing away. It was time to admit that without help I wasn't going to make it to the mainland. I reached into my pocket and dragged out the transmitter. As I fumbled to pull off the top, the thin cylinder slid from my clumsy, numbed fingers and splashed into the sea. I made a desperate lunge for it…but it had gone.

Tears of weakness and exhaustion coursed down my face. I couldn't continue. I couldn't. Spinks had won. *No, he bloody well hadn't.* In a surge of adrenalin-fuelled rage, I plunged recklessly forward, my target another marker. Then another. Staggering blindly on…

…The cool night air sliced through my soaked clothes. Violent shivers shook my body. *When the shivers stop, that's the time to worry.* Behind me, the northern sky still retained a faint greenish glow. I *must* concentrate, not let my mind wander. Ahead, the pencil line of markers merged with the darkness. I'd have to make sure I was in line with them, or I'd stumble off the causeway again. I passed another one. How many to go? I could vaguely remember counting them on my way across to the island. I hadn't thought it would really matter then. It had just been something to do. *How many?* It suddenly seemed desperately important. 180… 250… 300…? It *couldn't* be 300. I'd never make it. How long between them? I started counting the seconds… One second, two seconds…eight seconds… Level with the next marker. Keep a count. Then I'd know… Know what? I'd reached the next one. Know…my sluggish brain delivered the answer… Know how many I'd passed. Something wrong there. I tried again. Know how many there were… I waded past another two while I thought that out. I'd counted them, hadn't I? On the way to meet that American gangster. What was his name...? Hamburger, Hiramburger...? Two Hiramburgers with tomato sauce, please. I laughed uproariously at my witticism.

It was not so cold now. I was hardly shivering at all. That was good, wasn't it? But I must concentrate on the markers, start counting again. Seconds or Hiramburgers? I giggled. One Hiramburger...two Hiramburgers...ten Hiramburgers. Another marker. Was I going faster or slower? I struggled to work it out. Couldn't. Gave up... How many were behind? More than 150 anyway. 150 out of... I had counted them on the way across. Same as someone's birthday. Mine? July the 28th, seventh month. 728. There couldn't be so many. No feeling in my feet. Legs not functioning much either. Dark water swirling shoulder deep, pulling, tugging...

Half swimming, I pushed forward in a peculiar high-stepping walk like some slow-motion replay. 28th of the 7th. That was it! 287 markers. And I'd already passed... Couldn't quite remember... But it was a lot, definitely a lot. Can't be many more now, *can't be*. Yes, the town lights were really close, no longer just pinpricks. Street lamps, lighted windows. My splashes and the slapping of the tide against the markers were drowned out by a roaring whine overhead, a plane on the flight path to the airport. Its landing light spilt a silvery imitation moonlight across the water. Tourists and businessmen were cocooned and warm in their little capsule, while I...

Too many markers. Might as well give up. Tired, eyes closing... Mouth filled with water. Choking, spluttering. I must have blacked out. I was drifting, no longer resisting the tide, drifting on the current like a modern Ophelia, but without the flowers, of course. Hiramburger's latest victim.

A spurt of rage brought me fully awake, my mind suddenly crystal clear. He'd trapped the claustrophobic Gina, induced panic, left her the one way of escape that was in reality a journey to death. He'd trapped *me*, made me panic. My swim out to sea was to be *my* journey to death. He'd got rid of Waldo, Gina, Madame Butterfly, but not, definitely *not*, DJ Smith. I still had a chance, if I could fight off this overpowering lethargy. Stoke that rage, fuel those flames of anger, and I'd beat that bastard yet.

I blinked the water out of my eyes, straining to make out the dark shape of the next marker. *Where was it?* There it was – off to my left. But with every second I was being carried further *away*. All I could manage now was a clumsy doggy paddle, but after only a few strokes even that seemed too much effort. The tide had me in its grip and I didn't have the strength to fight it. Or the heart. I might as well surrender to that persistent tugging. If I lay back, let the tide carry me, perhaps I'd be washed ashore... No need to struggle anymore. Rest. Just relax... Being Ophelia wasn't so bad after all...

My head knocked painfully against something hard. It bumped again. My fingers touched wood, rough, barnacle-covered wood, then seaweed as soft as silk. I opened my eyes and saw a row of jagged, dark shapes half-blotting out the stars. I'd been snagged, a piece of human flotsam, against a line of posts stretching out from the shore, some ancient jetty, the planking long gone.

My numbed fingers scrabbled for a hold, slipped. Sobbing hot tears of frustration, I tried again. Again my hand flopped back into the water. I summoned up all my failing energies for one final desperate attempt. There'd be no other chance.

I managed to hook an arm round the slimy wood. The next post was now just within reach. Slowly, oh so slowly, I worked my way shoreward till at last my feet sank first into mud, then touched firm sand. Clinging to the posts for support, I lurched out of the water, stumbled up the narrow beach, and collapsed face down in a patch of spiky grass. *Death by natural causes.* No suspicious circumstances. That was what Hiram J Spinks had planned. And that's what he'd very nearly achieved. Still might, if I wasn't found soon...

CHAPTER SIXTEEN

'It's ab-saw-loot-ly essential,' the voice fluted, 'yes, ab-saw-loot-ly essential. Three minutes exactly from the time the first bubble rises. Yesterday's egg was *quite* disgusting. Consistency of the inside of a golf ball.'

I heard a muttered reply, then the *clack clack* of receding heels. Without opening my eyes, I pulled the sheet up over my head. A battle-royal was obviously in progress between Felicity Lannelle and the redoubtable Mrs Mackenzie.

'I don't want to know,' I thought drowsily. All I wanted to do was sleep.

'One wouldn't *believe* the number of ways there are of ruining an egg!' The tones of shock horror were audible through the layer of scratchy cotton sheet.

Mrs Mackenzie's Egyptian cotton bed linen had deteriorated remarkably. After that unfortunate Gorgonzola episode, I had obviously been issued with inferior quality sheets.

'And my researches prove it.' A great rustling and shuffling of papers drove me crazy. 'Firstly, there's the temperature of the raw egg...'

I scrunched the sheet into my ears and slithered further down under the blanket. Why couldn't Ms Lannelle give her lecture in her *own* room? I gave a querulous twitch to the sheet. Mrs Mackenzie reacted badly to complaints, but I'd have to have a word with her about that too...

...I woke with a start and lay there, eyelids closed against the bright light. Felicity's fruity voice was now droning on about toast. The sheet and blanket had fallen away from my head, and her voice had the intensity of a pneumatic drill beating at my eardrums. I bore it for another five seconds, then shouted through clenched teeth, '*Shut up*, Felicity.' At least, that's what I attempted to do, but all that my dry throat managed was a husky groan.

The monologue stopped abruptly. I heard a creaking of springs, closely followed by the long-drawn-out *thud thud thud* of an avalanche of books and papers slithering to the floor. A s*lap slap* of slippered feet, then a hand light as choux pastry stroked my forehead. My eyes flew open. An anxious face hovered above me.

'I'm so glad you've woken up at last, dear. You're looking *so* much better now. Less like a prime piece of chicken.'

'Chicken?' I croaked.

'Your skin had that delightful blue and purple translucence of fresh chilled chicken, ready for the chef's best culinary efforts. Unlike that awful deep-frozen stuff from the supermarket.' Felicity shuddered with distaste. 'Let me tell you, my dear, never...' she settled herself comfortably on the chair beside my bed and launched into an interminable tale of the horrors of factory-farmed chicken.

I gazed dreamily at her. Watching her lips move was incredibly soothing. My eyelids slowly closed. I slept.

* * *

'Are you awake?'

Felicity's voice had become quite mannish. Curious. Maybe it had something to do with gender-benders in factory-farmed chicken.

I was tempted not to reply, to remain cocooned forever in warm torpor, but the voice was insistent.

'Are you awake?'

Reluctantly, I opened my eyes to see the solidly reassuring figure of DCI Macleod standing beside my bed.

'Good.' He dropped onto the chair. 'We won't be disturbed.' With a wave he indicated the curtains that had been pulled round my bed. 'And don't worry about Miss Lannelle listening in. I've arranged for the dietitian to interview her. I'd love to be a fly on the wall for that. She's one formidable lady.' He produced a large brown paper bag and extracted a bunch of grapes. 'Here, munch on one of these.'

I struggled to a slightly more upright position and took one. Macleod popped a couple into his mouth. 'I've pulled some strings. The hospital will tell any enquirers that you're critical. That'll buy us a bit of time.'

'Time?' I croaked, my mind more on the ties of the hospital gown digging uncomfortably into my back.

'Time for you to decide whether you're going to die or not.'

'You sound exactly like Hiram J Spinks,' I said, helping myself to another grape.

'I take it that gentleman had more than a little to do with your being fished out of the waters of the Forth more dead than alive?'

I didn't answer directly, reluctant to relive that cat-and-mouse game on the island. 'Who found me?'

He shot me a glance from under his dark brows, and didn't press for an answer to his question. 'When you didn't signal for the Customs boys to make their move, we knew something had gone wrong. We didn't want to jeopardise anything you were up to, of course, but I asked all shore patrols to keep an eye open for any unusual objects or any unusual activity. Not that you were very active when they found you,' he added dryly.

'Yes, he'd expect me to be dead.' I stopped. The silence lengthened. The distant clatter of metal on china, the faint trill of a telephone came faintly from the corridor outside. I took a deep breath. 'Dead like Kumiko Matsuura. She's on the island... I found her body...' I couldn't go on.

'Take your time,' he said gently. He set a small recorder running as, haltingly, I told my story.

'...I realise now that it was all a set-up,' I finished. 'I did exactly what he wanted.'

'Except drown.' Macleod clicked off the recorder. 'Well, like I said before, *are* you going to die? Could be an advantage.'

'Ye-es,' I crunched on the last of the grapes. 'Let me think about it. Death is so final, isn't it?'

I shouldn't have to wait much longer for Felicity to reappear. It had been more than an hour since Macleod had left, promising to send someone to collect a bag of clothes from my B&B and check that Gorgonzola was being looked after. I was anxious to get going, do something to nail that bastard Spinks, as the late unlamented Waldo M Hinburger might have put it. I'd decided to 'die', and there was something I wanted Felicity to do for me. Again I glanced over at her empty bed. She'd been a long time closeted with the dietitian. Like Macleod, I'd have loved to be a fly on the wall. As if on cue, Felicity surged pinkly through the door on a tidal wave of indignation.

'It's been ab-saw-loot-ly *ghastly*, frightful! When they told me that the *dietitian*,' she managed to invest the word with scornful contempt, 'wanted to see me, I *naturally* assumed she was going to consult me about how to improve the quality of the food served in this place. Well, who better to give advice than I, Felicity Lannelle, gastronome *extraordinaire*? But what happened?'

I shook my head, though I had a pretty good idea.

'The silly woman actually wanted *me* to go on a diet! Subjected me to all sorts of insufferable investigative indignities. Can you *believe* that?' Without waiting for my reply, she flounced down on the bed and lay there quivering like a giant pink and white blancmange.

'It just shows how out of touch they are,' I said diplomatically. 'Whoever heard of a gourmet writer on a diet?' I delivered the final comforting clincher, 'Anyway, you're due to go home tomorrow, aren't you?'

She sat bolt upright. 'You're right, my dear. Forgive, and Eat to Forget.' She rummaged in the depths of her locker. 'I've something in here for just this sort of nasty shock to the system.'

A voice from the doorway interrupted her foraging. 'Excuse me, Miss Lannelle. The dietitian said you forgot to take this with you.' The nurse held up a sheaf of papers. 'It's your personal diet plan.' With a bright smile she deposited the mini-tome on the bed, and effected a strategic and rapid withdrawal.

'*Pshaw*!' Felicity snorted. *Thump*, the offending object hit the bottom of the waste bin.

The rummaging resumed. My stomach rumbled in anticipation. She'd be bound to turn up something edible. With an exclamation of triumph Felicity's hand emerged from the locker holding a small box. In the box were two of the largest chocolate liqueurs I had ever seen, each the size of a quail's egg, each cocooned in a soft green nest of protective tissue. I watched her bite delicately into the top of one of the eggs. The rich bouquet of brandy drifted over.

She looked up, saw me watching every move, and through a mouthful of chocolate and five-star brandy murmured, 'But I'm so rude, dear.' The pudgy hand waved the box with its sole remaining treasure in my direction. 'With all my troubles I forgot about you!' She took another tentative nibble at the rich dark chocolate. 'You know, this afternoon, when someone came and looked at you and then drew the curtains round your bed, I feared the worst.' She tipped up the egg and sipped appreciatively. 'Especially when they packed me off in *such* a hurry to see that woman. If it's not too personal, dear, just how did you—?'

'Well,' I licked my delightfully sticky fingers, 'I was silly enough to go exploring on Cramond Island and got cut off by the tide. Then to make matters worse, I stupidly tried to wade back.'

'We all do foolish things that we regret, dear.' She paused to let the last piece of brandy-encrusted chocolate melt slowly in her mouth. 'But I've never allowed my mistakes to get me down.'

'Not even when you nearly died after eating that haggis?'

Felicity considered carefully, head on one side. 'No-o-o,' she said slowly. Then decisively, 'No, definitely *not*. The haggis episode that brought me here must have been due to an unfortunate allergy. In my line of work, field tests are essential. I pride myself on the accuracy of my reports. Unfortunately, I can't remember what my verdict was. But it will be in my notes, of course. I'm quite looking forward to reading them when I go back to collect my belongings tomorrow.'

This was the moment. I cleared my throat. 'I work for the Government, Ms Lannelle, and I was wondering if you would consider helping us in a little matter?'

A spasm of alarm flickered over her plump face and she shifted uneasily on her bed. 'Not for the Inland Revenue? I can *assure* you that my rather large claims under Expenses, for food, wine and hotel accommodation, are *totally* justified by the need for quality in my line of business. If—'

'No, no,' I broke in. She was beginning to look quite flushed. 'Not for the Inland Revenue. I work in the Public Health Department, and we're running an investigation of the White Heather Hotel. You see, the hospital can't find a medical reason for your collapse, so the possibility is that the food was contaminated in some way.'

I hoped Felicity would be concentrating so much on the food poisoning angle that she wouldn't wonder how I knew all this. It was a calculated risk and I held my breath.

'Contaminated? Food poisoning?' A deep frown creased her forehead. 'But all Mrs Mackenzie's food is ab-saw-loot-ly above reproach.' She shook her head dismissively. 'No, dear. I have to say I gave her a full five-fork rating. Everything is immaculately presented. All cutlery spotless…'

I leant forward. 'That's just it, you see.' My voice was earnest, my eyes impressively frank. 'It's not the food from the *dining room* we're interested in. I checked that out for myself. It's the food in the tins.' I lowered my voice. 'Confidentially, we think the serious contamination might have originated with the canning machines. It's situated in the garage, you may recall. Now, the garage comes under the Factories Act. So we have to give advance warning of an inspection. As you probably know.' I popped in this handy phrase. It invariably gives a ring of truth to the weakest and most mendacious of statements. People don't like to admit their ignorance. Felicity was no exception. She nodded vigorously. 'With advance warning, of course,' I continued, 'any evidence completely disappears. So we desperately need some help. Someone to mount a diversion, and keep Mrs Mackenzie occupied.'

'*Me?*' Felicity breathed, her eyes large and round as dinner plates.

I nodded. 'So that I can make a quick inspection of the canning machines, collect some samples, and that sort of thing. I'd need about half an hour.'

There was a long pause while Felicity thought things out. Then a calculating look crept into her eyes. 'If you *were* to find any evidence, I might be able to sue…'

I'd phoned the B&B to let Jim Ewing know when my taxi would be arriving, so I wasn't surprised when the front door opened as I made my somewhat wobbly way up the short path. What I hadn't expected was for him to rush out and grab me by the arm.

'I don't know how to tell you this, but Gorgonzola—' he stuttered to a halt.

I stared at his flushed face and over-bright eyes. 'Gorgonzola? What's—?'

He hustled me through the doorway into the hall. 'No time to explain. Quick! You'll catch her in the act!'

Not another eviction from a boarding establishment because of my delinquent cat. My heart sank. The thought of having to trail round Edinburgh looking for somewhere to stay was more than I could bear.

He flung open the kitchen door. 'She's in here.'

I closed my eyes, unable to look.

'She started with the fridge. And now it's the walls!'

Reluctantly, I eased open an eye. The fridge was tastelessly splodged with red and black, the walls splotched and splattered waist-high with red, blue, and yellow paint. As I watched, Gorgonzola leapt in the air and brushed a paint-laden front paw along the wallpaper. A smeary red trail now curved across five vertical blue streaks.

Jim's voice behind me said, 'What do you say to that, eh?'

'Oh God, I'm so sorry! I'll pay for redecoration, *of course*.'

'I'll be leaving it exactly the way it is.'

I spun round. He was standing, arms folded, *smiling* as he watched my cat wrecking the décor of his kitchen.

'Don't look so horrified. You're watching a cat artiste at work.' Gorgonzola was now dabbing random white paw prints among the blue streaks. 'I've waited for years to see this. Never thought I would.'

'Cat *artiste*?' Stunned, I pulled out a chair and collapsed on to it.

'Some, of course, dismiss it as mere territorial marking, but that doesn't explain the selective use of colour.'

I was only half-listening. I was staring at the yoghurt pots arranged in a neat row along one wall. 'You mean you *encouraged* her? You filled these with paint, and she dipped her paws in and started daubing the walls...' I trailed off as words failed me.

'I moved her blanket down to the kitchen while you were in hospital, and when I came in the next morning, I found she had hooked the magnetic alphabet off the fridge and put all the letters of one colour together. She was sitting there, eyes half-closed, purring over them. Well, I knew that was significant.' He edged carefully round G, now standing, tail vertical, gazing fixedly at her abstract work of art. 'It's the sign of a cat with artistic leanings.'

I tried to convert a snort of disbelief into a cough, but failed.

'No, *really*. I've a shelf of books on the subject. I'll make you a cup of tea. I can see you've had a bit of a shock.'

While he busied himself with cups and teapot, I stared at her handiwork. Should I repeat my offer to have the kitchen redecorated?

Jim handed me my tea. 'When she's finished, she'll make one more mark, a sort of seal of approval, the artist's signature.'

'But your kitchen,' I wailed, 'it's a—' I hesitated to say *mess*.

'A gallery of cat art,' he said. 'I'm going to frame all the compositions. Each one will have an appropriate title. This one, now,' he pointed at the red crescent smeared over the streaks of blue and dabs of white, 'I think I'll call it *Sun Sinking in the Forests of Siberia.*'

G dipped a paw in the blue paint and smacked it squarely on the lower right hand corner of her latest *oeuvre.*

CHAPTER SEVENTEEN

From my hiding place in the rhododendrons I watched the taxi turn in through the gates of the White Heather Hotel. Time to let the cat out of the bag. While Felicity was paying the driver, I bent down and took hold of the *YOURS* holdall lying at my feet. I unzipped it, just a little. Gorgonzola's moth-eaten head emerged. She crossed her eyes meanly and gave a sharp-toothed yawn, a pointed reminder that being shut up in a bag was one of her pet hates. I ignored this prima donna display, ran my finger round her collar to emphasise that she was on duty, then turned my attention back to Felicity Lannelle.

Relishing her new role as agent of Her Majesty's Government, she was sweeping through the doorway of the hotel, calling in loud fluting tones, 'Mrs Mackenzie! Mrs Mackenzie!'

Under cover of the rhododendrons and the cars drawn up beside the heather beds, I crept to within a few yards of the wide-open front door. I'd warned her not to mention me at all. I could only hope that she wouldn't be so carried away with her role as stand-in for 007 that she'd forget her instructions. I wanted to stay dead.

'Coo-ee, Mrs Mackenzie!' She was clearly enjoying herself.

I heard the sound of a door opening and of footsteps hurrying forward.

'Who—!' The exclamation was cut short as recognition dawned. 'Why, Miss Lannelle... I didn't expect... My, you *are* looking... What can I...?' Mrs Mackenzie gushed, evidently overcome by the embarrassment of greeting a guest resurrected from deadly botulism.

'Well, of course, I came to collect my things. You *have* taken care of them, haven't you?' I detected a genuine note of anxiety.

The unseen Mrs M murmured reassurances.

Then, 'If you'll just let me into my room, I'll—' Felicity suddenly let out a squeal of delight, 'Oh, that heavenly aroma! It's *ab-saw-loot-ly* wonderful. What *have* you got in the oven? My dear Mrs Mackenzie, you *must* tell me.'

The reply was inaudible, but the tone conveyed a maestro's pride.

'Such a combination! And so tricky!' Felicity sounded genuinely impressed. 'One wrong move and you'd have a *complete* disaster. *Could* I prevail upon you to let me visit your kitchen this very instant and observe the next step? Mrs Mackenzie, I, Felicity Lannelle, gastronome *extraordinaire*, implore you!'

My relief evaporated. She had so easily managed to find a way to engage Mrs Mackenzie's attention, but much more of this ham-acting and she'd blow our whole plan sky-high. I hurriedly dodged behind the nearest car, lugging the holdall with me.

I waited. But there was no precipitate exit of Felicity pursued by an irate Morag Mackenzie. Instead, the murmur of voices was abruptly cut off by a closing door. They were on their way to the kitchens. Felicity had done it!

A mature rhododendron shrubbery provides excellent cover for those up to no good. The White Heather Hotel really should have a word with the local Crime Prevention Officer. I lifted a waxy leaf out of my line of sight and assessed my target.

The garage door was closed, as I knew it would be. Ten minutes earlier I had watched Mr Mackenzie's little blue van turn out of the drive and head off, presumably on its routine trip to Edinburgh. With both the Mackenzies accounted for, the coast should be clear. But I have a rule never to leave anything to chance on a job like this. I made a quick, yet thorough, survey of the scene – no sign of an alarm system, rhododendron cover to within a few yards of the garage door.

It should take me five seconds to reach the bell and give it a long strident ring, five seconds to return to the sanctuary of the rhododendrons, minimum exposure. That's what I estimated and that's all it took. I waited. The small access door remained shut. Satisfied, I picked up the holdall. A few tentative probings of my pick-lock and I'd be in...

With a loud *click* the door shut behind me, its position marked by a faint grey outline of light. I've always subscribed to the theory that installing an alarm is as good as pinning up a sign for burglars saying, '*Here lies Treasure!*' I was banking on the fact that the Mackenzies would share the same point of view. They wouldn't want to draw attention to what appeared to be an ordinary garage.

The thin pencil beam of my torch swept over the rough concrete of the ceiling. No security devices there. No windows either, so it was probably safe enough to put on the lights. I'd have to risk it, anyway. Time was the important factor.

As the switch came down, the area flooded with light. I blinked. On the surface, it was just your run-of-the-mill garage storeroom, most of it filled with an impenetrable wall of cardboard cartons, floor to ceiling, wall to wall. By the looks of it, the Mackenzies would have no trouble supplying half of Scotland with a tin of haggis. It could only mean that a consignment was ready to move. I'd come just in time.

But something was niggling at the back of my mind, eating like a worm at my feeling of exhilaration. I stared at the boxes, letting my thoughts drift, hoping that the little seed would germinate, blossom into life… Those tins would take a lot of filling… I had a sudden comical vision of Murdo frantically stuffing a round plump haggis into each tin…of Morag furiously ladling in the deadly gravy before the tin was sealed by the…*the canning machine*. I spoke the words slowly, my voice echoing in the silence. There wasn't one. Not here in the garage. Nor in their kitchen. Yet there had to be one.

I walked over to the nearest pile of boxes and ran my hand over the smooth cardboard. Say twenty tins to a carton. At a rough guess, there must be at least one hundred and fifty cartons in the garage. Three thousand tins…they couldn't do it without a machine. I stood there lost in thought.

A muffled plaintive mew from Gorgonzola reminded me that time was passing. I unzipped the holdall. She stretched one leg stiffly, then another. When all four legs had had the treatment, she leapt lightly out of the holdall and walked over to the boxes, each one fitting snugly against its neighbour like the blocks of stone in an Ancient Greek Cyclopean wall.

Without much hope, I watched her sniff fastidiously along the bottom row. There was little chance of her picking up traces of drugs on the floor or on the cardboard. Anyway, that wasn't what really mattered at the moment. Just where was that machine—?

G had stiffened, head down, ears up, frozen into immobility. I tensed. A paw inched forward. *Thud*. In a gingery blur of movement, she pounced. This was not how she had been trained to behave when she discovered drugs. Natural feline instinct had overcome formal training. Nature had triumphed over Nurture. She had spotted a mouse, been tempted, and fallen. I felt the tension drain out of me. She was now scratching disconsolately at the boxes, hooking her claws on the edge of a small gap in which some defiant rodent was probably thumbing its whiskers. The whole stack juddered, causing the topmost boxes to shift position. A sudden athletic leap upward, a savage swipe at the unseen prey, and she dangled helplessly by the claws of one paw, six feet from the ground.

Her weight and the frantic scrabbling were enough. As if in slow motion, the whole stack tilted, leant forward at a gravity-defying angle, then toppled to the floor with a rumble that echoed like thunder round the confined space of the garage. A cloud of fine dust blotted out the scene.

As it cleared, I could make out the tip of a moth-eaten ginger tail protruding from what was surely her burial mound. For a long moment I couldn't move, frozen to the spot. Transfixed is not too strong a word. Fifty half-kilo tins to a carton. G hadn't stood a chance. Then, with the frantic urgency of a rescuer rushing to dig futilely with bare hands at the scene of an earthquake, I dashed forward, desperate to lift the heavy boxes off the little corpse.

Suddenly the pile lurched and shuddered. The topmost carton rolled onto the floor, and Gorgonzola's eyes, round with fright, peered up at me. *She was still alive.* A tear trickled down my cheek as I bent, took a firm grip of one of the cartons, and heaved with all my strength. It slipped out of my hands and soared through the air to land with a hollow thud at the other side of the garage. Empty. I grabbed another carton. Light as a feather. A hefty kick sent it to join the other one. All the boxes in that column had been *empty*.

I gathered Gorgonzola up in my arms and pressed her furry body to my face. In normal circumstances, she would have spurned such a show of affection. On this occasion, she gave me a shaky purr of gratitude and her rough tongue rasped my hand.

'It was all your own fault,' I scolded into her ear.

The licking redoubled in vigour. G was apologising for her near-fatal lapse. I stroked her head...

'You've just lost one of your nine lives.' I set her down gently. 'If there had been tins in there, you'd be—'

There was now a narrow, dark passageway in the wall of boxes. Tail aloft, a somewhat tottery Gorgonzola strolled towards it, and like Moses and the Children of Israel, we walked between parted walls to the Promised Land.

But at first it didn't seem like the Promised Land, that little, dark space at the rear of the packing cases. I played my torch round the small area. I'm not sure what I expected, but I found only a rusty porter's trolley standing on a threadbare piece of carpet. Just why would anyone want to conceal a trolley behind a stack of boxes? The beam settled on three switches set one above the other on the brick wall. I angled the torch upwards. A dusty, bare lightbulb hung from the ceiling directly above the trolley. One bulb, three switches. Odd. I traced the cable from the ceiling-rose back to the upper switch and pressed it. The dim glow from the overhead bulb revealed a remarkably recovered Gorgonzola sheathing and unsheathing her claws and burying them in the carpet in busy preparation for future victims.

Another switch probably controlled the fluorescent lights in the main part of the garage. I flicked the middle one. The area beyond the stacked boxes was plunged into darkness. So what was the purpose of the third? The cable from it ran *down* the wall and disappeared into the concrete floor. I stared at the disappearing cable. That could only mean... I pushed the trolley to one side. A tug at the square of carpet brusquely disengaged Gorgonzola from her knife-sharpening act and unveiled a camouflaged trapdoor set into the concrete floor.

I heaved at the iron ring recessed into the centre and the trap easily lifted. Whiskers twitching inquisitively, Gorgonzola joined me in peering over the edge of the trap. A substantial wooden stairway complete with handrail plunged steeply downward into darkness. Before I could stop her, she darted down the steps and disappeared. *Scratch. Thump.* Then up from the darkness drifted her special drug-detecting croon.

My hand hovered over the mysterious bottom switch. It was more *likely* to be a light switch than an alarm... I took a chance, pressed it. Light flooded up from below. I went back for the holdall, clicked off my torch and followed G down.

Wheeooo... I let my breath out in a long silent whistle. Two banks of fluorescent lights illuminated a room the size of a large cargo container. Both ceiling and walls appeared to be metal. The floor too. Yes, the secret canning plant for the heroin-haggis concoction was a cargo container, buried deep in the ground. Very clever. Everywhere, stainless steel machinery gleamed in the strong lighting. I reached into my pocket for my camera and methodically recorded everything – the rolls of labels, racks of empty tins, conveyor belts, sealing unit, and two mini-hoppers.

It took longer than seemed prudent, but at last I was finished and shoved the camera back into my pocket. Gorgonzola was picking her way daintily along one of the conveyor belts, a large paw precision-placed each side of the cans lined up ready for filling.

'Time to leave, G.' I gathered up the holdall.

Bzzzz bzzzz. The shrill noise reverberated round the metal chamber, skewering me to the spot. A light above the wooden steps winked a red warning of intruders, and through the open trap came the sound of a key rattling in the lock of the garage door. Discovery lay only seconds away.

On an adrenalin surge, I scooped up G and the tell-tale holdall and flung myself up the wooden steps. A widening band of daylight streamed onto the area beyond the piled-up boxes. Thank God I'd left the main lights off. Gorgonzola wriggled violently, twisting out from under my arm. I made a grab for her, but in a misplaced show of independence she leapt away into the garage.

No time to do anything about it. I flicked off top and bottom switches. In the sudden blackness that pressed against my eyelids, pale patterns danced and swirled. My fingers fumbled for the piece of carpet, found it, jammed an edge in the hinges of the trap to hold it in position, and in one swift movement lowered carpet and trap over my head.

Heart thudding, I sprawled on the topmost step, ear pressed against the wood. I had no illusions and little hope. There was no escape and there'd be no mercy. Cargo container, canning factory, metal tomb. I needed one of Gorgonzola's nine lives right now.

'Holy shit, Mackenzie! Just getta load of this!' The long American vowels were muffled but unmistakable. Hiram J Spinks.

'What's—?' Mackenzie's growl was abruptly cut off.

I heard the thump of boxes being kicked aside, followed by hurrying footsteps. *Click.* A sliver of light showed round the edges of the trapdoor. Would they notice that the trolley had been moved? My throat was dry, no breath in my lungs.

'Looks all right, Mr Spinks...' The voice came from directly above my head.

Hope fluttered.

'Check it out, Mackenzie. There'll be hell to pay if someone's been in.'

Click. The banks of fluorescent tubes flickered and bright light flooded the underground room. Above my head, I heard the scrape of carpet being pulled away from the hatch. I slithered back down the wooden steps in an instinctive effort to hide, then stopped. The slightest sound would betray me. Like a hypnotised rabbit, I stared at the widening gap round the trap as it began to lift...two inches, another two... I saw the scuffed toes of a pair of boots.

'For Chris'sake,' Spinks yelled. 'What's that?'

The hatch slammed down. A series of thumps and bangs was followed by an unearthly banshee wail, the crash of a heavy object and a string of interesting Scottish oaths.

'Bloody cat! It's gone up on top of the boxes somewhere.'

Another banshee wail, suddenly cut off.

'Mr Spinks? Mr Spinks, you OK?'

I heard Spinks's voice, raised but indistinct, and growing fainter. Footsteps came closer, hesitated. With a clatter, the trap's iron ring was lifted, then dropped.

'Don't know what's got into that American bastard,' Mackenzie's voice muttered. 'Nobody's been here. Bloody cat got in, that's all. Bastard expects *me* to search the place for aliens or something when *he's* buggered off. Got more to do than that...'

Footsteps receded. The garage door closed with a crash.

I lay there for what seemed a long time, too shattered even to raise my head, but my thoughts busy. Just why had Spinks rushed off like that? Had I been right about him suffering from cat phobia that time back at the hotel, when he'd thrown down his putter? He'd marched off without a backward glance. Gorgonzola had been sitting primly in the middle of the drive. Was she his Achilles heel?

What *had* happened to G? That abruptly terminated wailing call could have been... Galvanised by the awful thought that she might have been savagely clubbed or kicked to death, and her limp body thrown outside, I pushed up the trap and, on trembling legs, emerged from what had so nearly been my tomb.

In his disgruntled haste, Mackenzie had forgotten to switch

off the overhead bulb. In the dim light, the shadows spilt across the floor in black, fathomless pools. What was that? I prodded hesitantly with my foot. It was only a rumpled piece of coarse sacking. At any moment he might have a change of heart and come back, but I couldn't leave without finding out if G was all right. Fumbling for the sonic whistle, I surveyed the heap of tumbled packing cases. I gave two quick blasts. If she was alive, she'd come...

I lowered the whistle. Ten seconds. Twenty seconds. No response.

Now I had to think of my own danger and get out of here while I still had the chance. It was too risky to put on the main lights. I clicked on my pencil torch and made my way through the darkness towards the grey outline that marked the outer door. With my hand on the Yale latch, I paused. I couldn't leave without one last attempt to find G. I swung the beam round in an arc over the wall of cardboard cartons. Nothing. She *must* be dead.

There was no place for sentimentality in a job like mine, I tried to tell myself. I switched off the torch, and after a pause, eased the door open and applied my eye to the crack. All clear. Or at least, nobody in my field of view. I'd wait twenty seconds before I risked going out.

Fourteen...fifteen... Something had changed. Those purple flowers hadn't been in my line of sight before. Imperceptibly, the door was inching open. *But I wasn't touching it.* So, this had all been a set-up. Spinks and Mackenzie *had* realised that there was an intruder in the canning plant. Now they were coming to deal with him. I stared at the ever-widening gap.

Well, I wouldn't make it easy for them. The element of

surprise might just give me a chance. While disposing of me would be easy in the confines of the garage, they would find it much more difficult to kill me in sight of inquisitive guests peering through the decorous lace-curtained windows of the White Heather Hotel.

I dropped the holdall, flung the door open, and hurled myself through the opening. Just as my mind registered that my headlong rush was meeting no resistance, my feet tangled in something soft. I catapulted forward, sprawling untidily on the Mackenzie driveway.

I lay there winded, unable to rise, expecting at any moment a lethal boot to the side of the head. I felt a sudden pressure on my back, then a sharp pain as Spinks ground his spiked golfing shoes into my shoulders. I wrenched away, at the same time rolling to my left and struggling to my knees.

My mind slowly processed the info that I was staring, not at Hiram J Spinks, gangster, but at Gorgonzola, feline Customs Officer. *She* had pushed open the door, and I'd tripped over her. She stared back, her eyes round and reproachful. I gathered her to me and pressed my face into her soft fur, a lump in my throat. Forgivingly, she submitted to this show of emotion, rubbing her soft body against me. She wasn't one to harbour a grudge, if I was the one grovelling.

The distant slam of a car door reminded me that I was still in danger. I set her down and scrambled to my feet, casting a quick glance towards the hotel. No twitching curtains, no Mackenzie bearing down on me, intent on GBH. Yet. I'd better shut the garage door and get out of here. I scooped her up, grabbed the holdall, pulled shut the garage door, and plunged into the shrubbery.

Not a moment too soon. Boots crunched on gravel. I lay with my chin pressed into a soft carpet of leaf mould. From behind a drooping safety-curtain of shiny green leaves, I watched Mackenzie warily advancing on the garage, an ugly tyre wrench gripped tightly in one hand and a saucer of milk in the other.

He set down the saucer and eased open the access door. 'Here, puss...puss...puss.'

I squirmed cautiously backwards, thankful that I'd managed to zip Gorgonzola safely into her holdall. To my ears drifted strident exhortations from an increasingly impatient Mackenzie. As he finally lost his temper, the door crashed back on its hinges with an ear-splitting report.

'Bloody mog! When I catch you, I'll bash your bloody brains out!'

The stream of invective effectively drowned any tell-tale rustlings that might have betrayed my presence as I slithered through the undergrowth. At what I judged to be a safe distance, I rose to a crouch and, still keeping under cover, made my way back to the road and my car.

I ticked off the gains – the discovery of an active canning plant, a consignment ready to move, and, possibly, the Achilles heel of Hiram J Spinks. I gazed fondly at Gorgonzola, my secret weapon.

Then reaction set in. I stroked Gorgonzola with a hand that shook slightly and gazed thoughtfully through the windscreen. 'Well, G, I think you lost another couple of your nine lives there.'

And I'd so nearly lost my only one... If Mackenzie had lifted that trapdoor a fraction higher...

CHAPTER EIGHTEEN

I found it at the bottom of page four of the morning newspaper. It was quite inconspicuous really. No *Island of Death* headline, only one small paragraph. I sipped my coffee and read about the untimely end of a young woman, identity unknown, cut off by the tide, and drowned in a foolhardy attempt to wade back across the causeway. Kumiko Matsuura fared little better, her obituary rated two column inches. There were no suspicious circumstances, Spinks (and Macleod) had seen to that. Death by misadventure for both of us.

From a long list of eating places in the Tourist Guide, I had selected this little café-cum-gallery solely because it would be on Felicity's route back to Edinburgh. Now, as I spread a thicker layer of butter on my scone, and let the mellow red sandstone walls of the courtyard and cheerful pots of fiery red geraniums draw me back from the shadows of the grave, I congratulated myself on my choice of rendezvous for the debriefing session.

'Coo-ee, dear!'

I looked up to see the gastronome *extraordinaire* billowing into the courtyard and surging towards me.

'I'm s-o-o-o excited. I've had an ab-saw-loot-ly marvellous idea!'

She subsided onto the spindly chair opposite me. Its fashionably thin metal legs bowed ominously, redesigned forcibly from twentieth-century Modern to nineteenth-century Regency.

'But first, my dear, how did you get on with *your* investigations? It all depends on that.' She leant forward expectantly, absent-mindedly helping herself to half of my scone.

'Well...' To play for time, I waved over the waitress and ordered a further supply of scones and coffee. Was Felicity, after all, planning on staying at the White Heather Hotel? If so, she would be a very useful spy in the camp. 'I found no trace of contamination.' I shrugged my shoulders and made a dismissive hand gesture. 'Everything was spotless.'

She beamed, scooped a large bundle of notebooks out of her handbag and deposited them on the table. The pile leant precariously, a multi-coloured replica of Pisa's Tower. 'Then I can include Mrs Mackenzie's establishment in my new project, *Cook Alongside the Master Chefs in your own Kitchen. Learn their Secrets.* It's to be an interactive one-to-one tutorial linked to a computer and CD Rom. What makes this different from the run-of-the-mill is that the student copies a chef's actions *as he cooks.* These notebooks are my research for it.' She seized my cafetière and poured herself a cup. 'Now what do you think of that?'

'Learn from Mrs Mackenzie the secrets of a Scottish Larder, you mean? Learn her Secrets, I like it!' I was positive, however, there was one secret of her larder that Mrs Mackenzie wouldn't be revealing.

'*Everyone* will like it, my dear.' To make way for the new

supply of scones, Felicity deftly resited the Tower of Pisa on top of a nearby table and slid the plate nearer to herself, inhaling appreciatively. 'The heavenly aroma of freshly baked scones really *is* one of the seven wonders of the culinary world.'

With the measured discipline of a Japanese geisha performing the ritual tea ceremony, she raised her knife and sliced the scone. Reverentially, she positioned a square of butter on each warm half, then with a sigh of anticipation sat back, her hands clasped as if in prayer.

I sipped my coffee. Now that I was no longer in the land of the living, I needed someone on the spot at the White Heather Hotel, someone who wouldn't arouse suspicion. Felicity's little project would solve that part of the problem, but to ask her to keep tabs on Spinks and the Mackenzies hardly fitted with my adopted role of Government Health Inspector. Perhaps if I...

'Er...' I said, not quite sure how I was going to broach the subject.

Without taking her eyes from the buttered scones, she leant towards me. 'I know just what you're going to ask, dear. And the answer is, that it really depends on all sorts of factors.'

The mouthful of coffee chose the route to my lungs instead of my stomach. Through a storm of hacking coughs and watering eyes I managed to croak, 'You do?' The woman was a marvel – not just a gastronome *extraordinaire*, but a clairvoyante *extraordinaire*. Even I hadn't known what I was going to ask.

Felicity swooped on one of the pieces of scone. 'Yes, my dear,' she said through a mouthful of crumbs. 'Secret...observation!'

I dabbed at my streaming eyes. 'That's just what I was going to say.' But how on earth had she rumbled my interest in Spinks and the Mackenzies?

'How perceptive, my dear. Yes, the secret is observation. These scones, you must watch them carefully. The time to eat them is *just* as the butter softens.'

'Oh! I quite agree,' I said, swallowing my disappointment, and a mouthful of dark coffee.

She patted her lips with her serviette, picked up the other half of the scone and bit into it delicately. For a few moments there was silence. The gastronome was mulling over her verdict.

'Umm...wonderful texture. It always comes down to timing and observation. But I'm afraid I must plead guilty this morning to a minor lapse in both. Of course, at the time, my mind was fully engaged in planning my new project. Such *possibilities*. Such a *challenge*.'

I refilled my cup from the cafetière, listening with only half an ear. *My* observation problem was with Spinks. I stared at the dark liquid as if it contained the answer.

Indignation raised Felicity's voice an octave, fully capturing my attention. 'I didn't see Mr Spinks's suitcase at all. Well, he *had* left it in a very silly place.'

My cup crashed back onto the saucer, sending a shower of murky brown spots onto the white cloth.

'Suitcase? Mr Spinks's suitcase?' I repeated.

'Well, yes,' Felicity sounded uncharacteristically defensive. 'I gave it just the *teeniest* bit of a knock. I chose that moment, you see, to reverse. Just after the silly man put down his luggage behind my car.'

'He was leaving?' I asked, struggling to sound only mildly interested.

I needn't have worried. She was busy scribbling in a thin notebook plucked from the top of the Tower of Pisa.

'I thought he was booked in till after that golf tournament next week.' Again my tone was casual.

She paused in her scribbling. 'I don't want to think about him *at all*.' Her vast frame shuddered theatrically. 'He made the most *frightful* scene.'

'He did?' I breathed, suitably agog, all pretence of casual interest forgotten.

'I thought I'd just gone over one of those silly edging stones again. So *awkwardly* placed, just where they're bound to catch your wheels!' The hand holding the pen wafted away one of Life's Little Vexations as though it were a bothersome gadfly. 'The next thing I knew, that awful man was banging on the side of my car and shouting the rudest things.' A spot of high colour glowed in each cheek at the recollection.

I clutched at a straw. 'I don't suppose he said where he was off to?'

Felicity closed her notebook with a vicious snap. 'Hell *was* mentioned several times, but I rather presume that he was scheduling it as *my* destination rather than his.'

Long after Felicity had gathered the Tower of Pisa to her ample bosom and left, I sat there trying to work out what to do. Spinks had vanished into thin air, a conditioned reflex to cover his tracks, or a rule of never staying too long in one place? Or perhaps he'd got wind of my resurrection and gone to ground because he felt threatened. Whatever the reason, I'd lost him. I stared thoughtfully at the pots of red geraniums, the same clear red as Gina's coat. The living Gina had led me to Inchcolm and Tantallon. Perhaps the dead Gina could finger Spinks from the grave. I fished out my notebook and thumbed through it to the page where I'd copied her hastily scribbled notes exactly as she had written them.

Inchcolm Cramond May

Tantallon Fast

Longniddry Bents

I ran my finger down the list. Perhaps I'd find a clue to Spinks's present whereabouts. Inchcolm – I was pretty sure he'd been the cause of my 'accident', so I could count that he'd been *there*. Cramond – he'd most definitely been *there*. I was a hundred per cent sure he was that hunched figure behind the wheel in the fog at Tantallon, *and* the murderous golfer at Longniddry Bents. So, for his next scheduled appearance, that left the little island guarding the River Forth, the Isle of May. Or Fast Castle, on the coast, south-east of Edinburgh. I stuffed the notebook back into my pocket and rose to my feet. I'd better consult that map again, and call on Macleod.

'I thought you'd be interested in this.' Macleod pushed a sheet of paper across his desk. 'It came in a couple of days ago. The receiving officer didn't think it merited further action, and filed it with the other reported traffic incidents. It was a bit of luck that the same officer happened to be manning the computer in the Incident Room when the description of the body found on Cramond Island was being circulated.'

'I could do with a bit of luck. The trail's going cold. If Fast Castle or May Island doesn't turn up trumps, we've lost him.'

Without much hope, I scanned the paper, a routine traffic-incident form detailing a case of dangerous driving in Edinburgh's Queen's Park. The witness statement, given by a Mr Henry Crawford, described how a car had mounted the pavement, demolished a park bench and narrowly missed a woman sitting on it. *Description of Car. Colour: red. Make and registration: unknown. Description of Driver: Asiatic female, gold streak in hair.*

Very public-spirited of Harry to report my near demise but where was the new lead in this? Puzzled, I looked up. Macleod was leaning back in his chair eyeing me with what was definitely a smug, self-satisfied smile. 'At the end,' he said.

I glanced down again at the report. At the bottom of the page was a handwritten footnote, dated 29th June. *Ref Road Traffic Incident E8642: Witness H Crawford reports second sighting of Asiatic female driver at Anstruther Harbour, Fife.*

I returned Macleod's smile. 'Time, I think, to have another little word with Harry.'

Edith and Harry were obviously keen gardeners. Window-boxes of pink and purple petunias half-obscured the windows and cascaded in multi-coloured waterfalls down the pebble-dashed walls. Above the door, a giant hanging basket gyrated slowly in the light breeze. Regimented rows of red geraniums and white and blue bedding plants were drawn up around a parade-square of manicured lawn. *Cuidado con el Perro* warned a white and blue ceramic plaque fixed to the wrought-iron gate, a message spelt out pictorially by a line drawing of a fiercely snarling mastiff. A bit of wish fulfilment on the little terrier's part? I suppressed a smile. I dodged the gyrations of the hanging basket and rang the bell.

Edith answered the door, wiping her hands on a blue-striped apron. 'Yes?' she raised her brows in polite enquiry.

Peering cautiously from behind her legs, the terrier gave a half-hearted *wuff*. From the kitchen came the rattle of dishes.

'I don't know if you remember me, but you and your husband were in the Queen's Park a week ago when I was nearly hit by a car…'

'Oh yes, that *was* dreadful!' Edith's eyes widened at the memory. 'You could have been killed. I just said to Harry the other day—'

As if on cue, Harry called from the kitchen, 'Who is it, Edith?'

'Harry, you'll never guess who it is…' She beckoned me in.

For the next hour I heard all about Harry's skill at growing geraniums, petunias and potatoes, Edith's latest adventures at the supermarket, and the dog's visit to the vet. But of their sighting of Kumiko Matsuura, I heard nothing. Whenever I tried to bring up their second encounter with her, the conversation veered off in another serpentine turn as they animatedly reminded each other of some corroborative incident.

At last in desperation, I glanced casually at my watch. 'Good heavens!' I gave an exaggerated shriek of horror. The dog lying on the rug at Edith's feet opened one eye, decided that its guard dog services were not required, and resumed its post-lunch siesta. 'Twenty past *four* already. If the car's not back at the hire company by five, they'll rob me for another day!'

Relying on Edith and Harry's Scottish thrift to imbue them with a sense of urgency, I rummaged in my bag and pulled out a notepad and pen. 'The police say they'll charge the driver of the car that nearly killed me, if I can trace her.' Then, I asked a question that, with luck, would allow no diversions. 'The driver, you saw her again – in Anstruther, wasn't it?'

'That's right,' Edith turned to Harry. 'We'd just parked the car, hadn't we, Harry?'

'No, I don't think so, Edith. We'd been—'

I thrust the notepad under Edith's nose. 'Just write down what she was doing.'

Edith took the pen. 'Well now, dear…I'll need my glasses. Did I have them when I was in the kitchen, Harry?'

He scratched his head and thoughtfully massaged his chin. 'Don't think so, Edith.' His brow wrinkled, his lips pursed, 'Now, you had them when—'

I grabbed back the notepad. 'It's all right. Just tell me what she was actually *doing*.'

'Doing? I don't think she was doing anything much, was she, Harry?' Edith frowned in concentration.

'You're right, Edith. I don't think she was.'

Gritting my teeth, I tried again. 'You mean she was just standing there? In the centre of Anstruther?'

Both shook their heads, Edith from left to right, Harry from right to left.

'No,' she said.

Harry, a fraction of a second later, 'No.'

'No?' My voice rose in a squeak of frustration.

'Not in the *centre*. Down at the harbour on the boat.'

'No, she wasn't standing, she was *sitting* on the boat.'

'Boat?' In striking contrast to the unstoppable flow issuing from both of them, my input to the conversation seemed to have been reduced to single words.

'Yes, the boat. Mind you, it wasn't a good day for going, was it, Harry?'

'Oh no. All those low clouds. I said it would rain, didn't I, Edith?'

'You did, Harry. And you were right.' Edith gazed fondly at her husband. Weather forecasting, it seemed, was another of his accomplishments.

'Boat going where?' I prised the words into the dialogue like a pearl fisher inserting his knife into an oyster.

'May Island, where the bird-watchers go.' Edith looked faintly surprised at my ignorance.

'Isle of May,' said Harry. 'Haven't you been there?'

I shook my head. In my mind was Gina's list and that scribbled word *May*.

'Oh, it's a place to visit for bird-watching, right enough.' Harry nodded wisely. 'Guillemots, gulls, puffins...'

'I do like the puffins, Harry. They're so comical. Do you remember the time we took the binoculars and watched them going in and out of their burrows on the cliffs?'

Harry's weather-beaten face creased into a smile. I slipped in my question before he could embark on another of those lengthy reminiscences.

'So you think that woman was bird-watching, then?'

'Oh no, I don't think so.' Edith was quite emphatic. 'Not with those flimsy shoes. I wouldn't like to walk about the *garden* with those shoes.'

'You're right there, Edith.' They both laughed at the folly of human nature. 'You need shoes with good soles. Now, the fellow with her had the right idea. Golfing shoes with studs.'

'She was with someone?' I said faintly. I'd broken another cardinal rule of witness interrogation. Don't assume *anything*. What else could Edith and Harry be unwittingly hiding? What else could be uncovered with the right question?

'Yes, they had their heads together studying a bit of paper. A map of the island, I think it was, one of those tourist things. You see, the boat was just about to cast off. We do love watching the boats leave the harbour, don't we, Edith? We were standing up there on the quay, and she was down below us and a little bit away. It was when she looked up and I saw that gold streak in her hair that I recognised her. I looked at Edith and she had noticed it too. We didn't know what to do, did we, Edith?'

'No, Harry, we didn't. We could hardly jump on the boat and march up to her and say, "Excuse me, didn't we see you nearly running down a lady in the Queen's Park the other day?" She would have denied it, wouldn't she? Or pretended she didn't understand, didn't speak English. All we'd have got would have been a flood of Chinese or some such foreign lingo.'

'We talked about it all the way back in the car, didn't we, Edith?'

'We did, Harry.' She nodded her agreement.

'Then Edith said to me, "Harry, you'll just have to go to the police. Let them sort it out." So when we got back, off I went straightaway.'

And that was all the information I gleaned from them. No, they couldn't describe Kumiko's companion. No, they hadn't seen her again. On the plus side, the Isle of May was now a definite lead. And that golf-shoe-wearing companion just *had* to be Hiram J Spinks.

I made a show of looking at my watch. 'I really must go.' I rose from the couch and moved purposefully towards the door.

The dog sat up, scratched vigorously, and looked at Edith and Harry enquiringly.

Together they ushered me out. Edith opened the gate for me. 'If we see her again, we'll let the police know.'

Harry neatly dead-headed a red geranium. 'Yes, we will. Right away.'

'That's very good of you,' I said.

But there wouldn't be any chance of them seeing Kumiko again. At Anstruther, or anywhere else.

CHAPTER NINETEEN

Back at my seaside B&B, I sprawled on the floor and spread out the east of Scotland map. Gorgonzola stirred, then stretched out a paw towards her empty food dish, lazily extending and retracting her claws as she calculated how much she could extract from me in compensation for her recent traumatic experiences in the Mackenzie garage. It was a trauma from which she had completely recovered. I knew it. She knew I did.

'It's no use. I'm not going to give in, G,' I said.

I smoothed a crease out of the map. Anstruther was...here. I marked the spot with my finger. So the Isle of May must be... Yes, there it was, a lonely speck guarding the wide mouth of the Forth estuary, not easily accessible from anywhere. The dog's head peninsula of the Fife coast was the nearest land. Which explained why Kumiko had been sighted there.

G manufactured a piteous mew.

'Nice try,' I said cheerfully, my eyes on the map.

Inchcolm, Cramond, Tantallon, Fast Castle, Isle of May, I lassoed each of them with a red marker pen. Five red circles on the map, just like a magnified version of a child's Join-Up-The-Dots game. I took my pencil and linked them up.

They formed a triangle, with the Isle of May at its apex. Significant?

I got up and stared out of the window for inspiration. At this hour, the promenade beneath my window was almost empty. A cool sea breeze had sent all but the hardiest holidaymakers scurrying home. Waves broke gently on the yellow sand in little crispy lines of foam, like lace-edging to a ruffled garment. Off to my left, and just visible if I craned sideways, the grey shape of Inchcolm smudged the blue waters of the Forth. I pushed up the window and leant out. To my right, purpled by distance, lay the peak of Berwick Law, my marker for Tantallon.

I left the window open and went back to pore over the map again. The western point of the triangle was Cramond, where the tidal estuary narrowed to meet its feeder river, the Forth. The apex of the triangle, the Isle of May, lay at the mouth of the estuary, almost in the North Sea. An ocean-going ship could easily drop a cargo there and go on its way without exciting undue attention. And then... I drew a series of somewhat wobbly red lines radiating from the Isle of May to each of the ringed places. I sat back on my heels and admired my work of art. The rays of the rising sun, the Japanese flag. Rather appropriate, really.

The map rustled and crinkled, the Isle of May was obliterated by a large ginger paw. When she saw that she had my undivided attention, Gorgonzola collapsed slowly onto her side and closed her eyes in quite a passable imitation of a dead cat, a cat who'd starved to death.

I capitulated. 'You win, G.' But I wasn't going to give in completely. I rummaged through her tins till I found *my* favourite, salmon and trout mixed chunks. Hmm, supplies were getting a bit low. I'd have to do something about it soon. 'Salmon and trout,' I said loudly.

She lay motionless but a tell-tale drool of saliva glinted at the corner of her mouth.

I dug in the side pocket of the bag. My searching fingers found the spoon but no tin-opener. I scrabbled among the tins, tossing them out onto the floor, upended the empty bag and shook it. Not a sign of the opener.

A furtive glance revealed that Gorgonzola had raised herself from her recumbent position to a predatory crouch. Two slitty copper eyes, a twitching tail. I recognised the signs of an aggrieved cat.

'I know you deserve it, G, but what can I do?' I spread my hands placatingly. 'Now just let me fold up that map.'

I tugged at the corner. She made no attempt to rise, bracing her sturdy front legs and digging her claws into the smooth paper. A pink toothy yawn made it clear that a battle of wills was in progress.

A soft tap at the door broke the impasse.

'Come in.' I gave the map a surreptitious tug in the futile hope that her attention had been diverted, then another tug, more forceful this time.

To the sound of ripping paper Jim Ewing poked his head round the door. 'I was wondering if the cat would like some fish?'

Gorgonzola responded by bounding across and twining herself ingratiatingly round his legs, her allegiance pointedly transferred.

'You've got your answer, Jim.' She had won that round. I

gave in gracefully. 'I've mislaid the tin-opener. Can you lend me one? I'm getting a bit of aggro from the cat for not opening the tin.'

'No problem. I've got a spare one downstairs.' He glanced at the ragged map still clutched in my fingers. 'Bring that down and I'll rustle up some sticky tape.'

Gorgonzola stepped daintily down the stairs in front of us. 'Perhaps she's ready to do another painting.' An excited look came into his eye. 'I've left her easel up and the paints ready.' He pointed to a large piece of paper taped to the kitchen wall.

But Gorgonzola Van Gogh had other ideas. She marched over to the fridge, stood on her back legs, and pawed at the handle.

While she noisily wolfed down the fish, I fixed the tape to the back of the map.

'Heard of a place called Fast Castle?' I asked.

'Been there on a walk.' Jim raked in the drawer for the spare tin-opener. 'Funny to think that it was so important five hundred years ago. There's nothing much there now, though.'

'Not worth going to then?' I folded the map and stuck it in my pocket.

He leant on the worktop watching G's tongue chasing a last flake of fish round the bowl. 'Only if you're an artist or one of those historian types.'

'So not many people go there?' I dropped in the question casually.

'It's pretty well deserted nowadays. When I was there last, I didn't see a soul – apart from a couple of fishermen, that is. Why anybody would want to fish from the top of a cliff, beats me.'

'From the *top* of the cliff?' I said. 'That's unusual.'

'Must be the challenge, I suppose. They've got special rods.'

Thoughtfully, I slipped the tin-opener into my pocket. *Curiouser and curiouser*, as Lewis Carroll's Alice said.

Back in my room with the bedside radio tuned softly into the Classical channel, I chewed on a soft mint and thumbed through the East Lothian tourist guide till I reached the section on castles.

Fast Castle. Ruined 14th century castle dramatically positioned on the cliff edge one hundred feet above the sea. The Wolf's Crag of Sir Walter Scott's novel, The Bride of Lammermuir. *Cross to it from the main cliff by a small wooden bridge. Danger of vertigo.*

Gorgonzola, energetically engaged in cleaning the last of the fish dinner from her whiskers, was eyeing me speculatively. I tossed my mint wrapper at her, just to remind her not to chance her paw.

The radio music faded on a long violin note to be replaced by a male voice murmuring indistinctly, '...tonight's concert...weather forecast...'

I leant over to turn up the volume, and helped myself to another mint.

'A high pressure system is stationary over the British Isles. Tomorrow, everywhere can expect high temperatures and sunshine, except for a narrow band along the east coast stretching from Fife to the Lothians, where an onshore breeze will keep the temperature down, and there is a strong likelihood of sea mist...'

Spinks and castles, DJ Smith and east coast haar. I moved over to the window and, chin in hand, propped my elbows on the sill and studied the distinctive triangular shape of Berwick Law. Beyond it lay Fast Castle, and the next round in the no-holds-barred combat with Spinks. I mulled over Jim Ewing's remark about the fishermen and their special rods. Now, *that* sounded promising.

Linda's scissors flashed, and dark chunks of my hair fell to the floor.

'Yes, a blonde, spiky cut.' I smiled. The hairdresser looked at me, then schooled her expression into one of polite attention. 'I'm in a show at the Festival, and I've got to get into the part,' I explained.

With a mixture of satisfaction and consternation, I watched the transformation of my neat hairstyle into something that resembled a bleached lavatory brush. My only trump card in this deadly game with Spinks was the fact that he'd written me off as dead. And dead I was going to stay. He wouldn't recognise me now, even if I had the bad luck to meet him on my daylong stake-out of Fast Castle.

She dabbed away industriously at my roots. 'Fringe, is it?'

'Fringe?' My thoughts had been miles away. Momentarily at a loss, I stared at her reflection.

'You know, the unofficial side of the Festival. Amateurs, and students and such like.'

'That's right,' I trilled, and launched into a totally fictitious account of my dramatic career.

'How'd you come to pick up a male part, then?' She stood back and surveyed her handiwork with a critical eye, then with a mutter of satisfaction drew off her rubber gloves and dropped them neatly into the sink.

'Oh, um,' I wasn't prepared for this one. 'Bob dropped out at the last minute,' I flannelled.

She chatted brightly on, but I listened only abstractedly. I must have been a bit off-beam in one of my replies, for she'd paused and was looking enquiringly at me in the mirror.

'Sorry,' I waved an apologetic hand. 'What was that? My mind was wandering there for a moment. I was just thinking about something you'd said.'

And I was. Male part. What a great idea! Why hadn't I thought of that? A change of sex as well as hairdo. That should definitely fool anyone, even the wary Spinks.

I left a lavish tip for Linda and made a beeline for the nearest theatrical costumier.

The bearded young man with the spiky hairdo stared unblinkingly at me in the bathroom mirror. He put up a hand and tugged thoughtfully at his wispy blond beard. It didn't come away in his hand. I smiled. He smiled.

When I flung open the bathroom door, Gorgonzola arched her back and hissed, then crept forward and cautiously sniffed at my trouser leg.

'Same old me, G,' I reassured her.

I sat down on the bed and pulled on a pair of hiking boots. In front of the wardrobe mirror I shrugged on the large rucksack with artist's board and sketchpad prominently displayed. I was now the hiking artist, suitably clad in baggy red-checked shirt, faded jeans fraying in the right places. That was to be my protective shield.

I bundled Gorgonzola out of the window to fend for herself

till my return, and clumped somewhat noisily down the stairs in my new boots. Jim Ewing emerged from the breakfast room carrying a tray loaded with dirty dishes. Bowls and glasses clinked and rattled as he stopped short in surprise.

'Good morning, sir. How can I help you?' The tone translated to, 'What the hell are you doing here in my establishment?' He manoeuvred his bulk between the front door and me, making it plain that this stranger owed an explanation for his intrusion.

'Er, hello, Jim. It's just me, DJ Smith.' I'd asked for a breakfast tray that morning and had hoped to exit unseen and unquestioned.

He took a step forward and peered closely at my face. 'Good God! What *have* you done to yourself?' His mouth hung open in utter astonishment.

'There's a friend I've not seen for ages. I've made a bet with him that he'll not recognise me when he sees me again.' I gave an embarrassed laugh. 'A substantial bet.'

'Well, my money's on you!' he moved slowly aside.

With a cheery wave, I strode down the path into the early morning sun. When I looked back, he was still standing there, a stunned look on his face.

As usual, the forecasters had got it all wrong. No mist, no haar, just the pale sky of early morning. A few fluffy clouds drifted lazily across the expanse of blue. I heaved the rucksack into the car and stood for a moment on the promenade gazing at the flat expanse of damp sand left behind by the retreating tide. Lanky sea birds paddled and poked at the water's edge and Berwick Law was a smoke-grey cone on the horizon. It was definitely an artist's scene. Any artwork I did at Fast

Castle would definitely have to be in the naïve style. My attempts at drawing even simple things, like houses or cats, never turned out right. I had to admit that, as far as ability in painting went, Gorgonzola had a head start.

Fast Castle. The notice pointed along the cliff top to my right. I eased the rucksack to a more comfortable position on my shoulders. Perhaps I shouldn't have been so authentic with the artist's gear. Already it seemed to be weighing a couple of kilos more than when I'd started off. At least the walking boots were a good buy for the rutted and uneven path. 'Not much frequented,' Ewing had said. Except by Spinks's henchmen – if I had an accident, I certainly wouldn't want first aid from *them*.

I had descended quite a distance from the main road to reach the cliff top path. It now meandered across grey lichen-covered rocks, only to disappear again over the shoulder of the hill. I paused at the top of the rise and looked down. From my vantage point I could see for miles along the coastline. Fingers of red sandstone poked their way inquisitively into the ocean, and gulls drifted lazily midway between soaring cliffs and wrinkled sea.

I'd scanned the tumbled outcrops of rock on the steeply sloping hillside for some time before I spotted the remains of the castle, grassy undulations barely distinguishable from the grey boulders. Only one ragged fragment of wall had survived six hundred years of weather and war.

It was certainly a lonely spot. Six hundred years ago the air must have echoed with shouts and cries, the whinny of horses, the clang of metal on metal. Now, the piping call of a sea bird, the faint whisper of the sea against the rocks far below, the noise of my own laboured breathing, served only to emphasise the silence.

The path plunged steeply down the grassy slope that lay between me and the still distant ruins. At times when it narrowed to the width of a sheep track or to nothing more than a ledge over a dizzying drop, it took all my concentration to place my feet safely, but at one point, steps had been cut into the hillside and I was able to unglue my gaze from the path immediately in front of my feet and look up.

Less than three hundred yards in front of me, the surviving fragment of wall reared skywards, its weathered red sandstone merging with the surrounding cliffs. I caught my breath. Even in its ruined state, the castle still had a brooding presence, with the power to shock and send a shiver down the spine. The long-dead builders had chosen their site well. The castle was perched, not on the cliff edge, as I had supposed, but on a piece of ground split off from it by some ancient cataclysmic event. To bridge the gulf, wooden planks and heavy chain handrails guarded against a headlong tumble to the rocks and crystal-clear water far below.

I crossed quickly, feeling safer when my boots trod again on firm ground, skirted past the remains of the castle and moved out onto the exposed cliff top. Just as well the weathermen had got the forecast wrong. In mist or haar the place would be a veritable death trap.

My nostrils twitched as they were assaulted by a pungent rancid odour. *Death*. The unmistakable stench of death. Over to my left was a deep fissure. At the bottom, half-hidden in a cushioning bed of nettles, I could make out a loose scattering of white wool and bleached bones, the putrefying carcass of a dead sheep. What had I expected as I steeled myself to look into that cleft? Something a good deal more sinister.

With a sharp intake of breath – definitely not a good idea in the circumstances – I turned away. Better finish exploring and find a place to set up my artist's sketch-board before I had company. And I was sure there would be company. Gina's list had proved accurate for Tantallon and Longniddry, and Fast Castle had also been on her list. Perhaps I was already under scrutiny through high magnification lenses.

The thought galvanised me into tourist mode. Ostentatiously, I rubbed my fingers over the ancient mortar binding the worn stones. Delightedly, I peered at the bright yellow lichen and the colourful carpet of pink thrift at the cliff edge. Hand shielding my eyes, I followed the swooping flight of birds circling and drifting in the thermals against a cliff white with droppings and tufted with old nests.

It would not do to spend too long staring at one spot, but I was increasingly convinced that Fast Castle, for a drug consignment, was indeed the perfect drop site with its grey shingle beach, inaccessible except by boat. The 180 degree arc-of-view eastward was seascape, unbroken to the horizon, empty except for a solitary fishing boat bobbing gently in the swell. To the north, dimmed by distance, lay the hills of Fife – and the Isle of May. I took it all in.

I shrugged off the rucksack and untied the sketch-board. Holding it up, I slowly turned full circle, as if seeking the best viewpoint. Near the top of the hill a quarter of a mile away, a brief flash of sunlight on glass hinted at a possible watcher. It could, of course, be the sun reflecting off harmless window glass. I didn't think so.

I found a good position on the hillside and set up my gear a couple of hundred yards above the castle, and slightly to the right. That way I would be out of the line of anybody coming along the path. One problem solved, but with the board balanced comfortably on my knee another one loomed. As I have said, my artistic skills are – to put it succinctly – nil, but if someone came along, I would need to have some sort of picture ready. People seem compelled to peer over the shoulders of artists, so I must be prepared for my efforts to be eyeballed by passers-by, innocent or not.

When I'd first had the inspiration to disguise myself as an artist, I'd rushed enthusiastically to the nearest art shop, grabbed a brush or two, a drawing pad and board, a case of watercolour paints, and a small booklet entitled *Watercolour Made Easy*. I'd intended to read it up beforehand, but, as they say, the road to Hell… I skimmed the first page. *Watercolour is perhaps the most difficult technique in painting.* My heart sank. So much for becoming another Turner. But weren't some of Turner's later paintings a blend of wishy-washy (but admittedly glorious) colours? Indeed, oh heresy, nothing but smudge. I brightened. *My* painting would be in the style of the later Turner. There was no need to paint a photographic representation of the scene in front of me. With a few rough outlines, and some washes of paint, I could have a passable picture – *Fast Castle in the Sunset,* or *Fast Castle in the Haar,* if someone was curious enough to ask. Anyone who insensitively enquired where *was* the sunset, or where *was* the haar, would get a pitying look. I would inform him (or indeed her) with the unshakeable confidence of the born artist, that we do not restrict ourselves to what is actually *there*, if the scene before us is *mundane*. We improve it with a sunset, or a haar – much more romantic.

Humming happily to myself, I sketched a few wobbly outlines of the ruins. A quick zigger-zagger of the pencil represented the cliff edge, and I was ready to begin painting. Impasse. *Water*colours need water to mix them. I'd forgotten that elementary fact. The nearest water – salt at that – was a hundred feet or so down the cliff. Gloomily, I chewed the end of my newly purchased brush. Nothing for it but to sacrifice some of the can of lager I'd brought with my packed lunch…

I was just getting into the swing of things, applying an artistic purple smudge over rather uninspiring grey and black smudges, when a shadow fell on the paper. Startled, I looked up. Surely I hadn't been so engrossed that I'd missed someone coming along the path?

'Got it wrong there. We thought you were painting the castle.' The voice came from behind me. The tone was sarcastic, the transatlantic accent unmistakable. 'Yeah, guess we got it wrong.'

Slowly, I swivelled round. Not one face but two peered down at the paper. Though they were carrying fishing rods and a tackle box, I sensed the men weren't fishermen. Bright tartan shirts seemed de rigueur for those pretending to be something they were not. I should know. I was wearing one myself.

'Of course it's the castle!' Just in time I remembered to deepen my voice. 'It's Fast Castle and haar.'

The more thuggish of the two frowned aggressively. 'What's with this her? Where's the dame? You having me on, mister?'

Gratified at the 'mister', I daubed on another splodge of

purple. 'Not her, haar. H-a-a-r. It's a Scottish word meaning 'sea mist'. I know there's none at the moment, but mist adds that romantic touch to a picture, doesn't it?' My voice was deadpan with no trace of the amusement welling up inside. If I could get them to dismiss me as some sort of harmless crank, I'd become just part of the scenery, and they'd get on with whatever they'd come to do.

'But where's the goddamn castle?' The aggressive one seemed to be spokesman for them both. The other remained silent and watchful. The more dangerous of the two.

'How can you expect to see anything in a haar?' The wisecrack was forming on my lips, when the instinct for self-preservation prevailed. 'Well,' I stroked my wispy beard earnestly, 'I haven't *quite* decided where I'm going to put the castle. Or how much of it's going to be visible. These things take time, can't be rushed, you know.'

Head on one side, I made a tentative daub on the paper. Out of the corner of my eye, I saw a sneer of contempt replace the look of ready suspicion. With a shrug, he and the silent one turned away.

Reaction set in. I watched their retreating backs, and knew with a cold certainty that if the slightest of doubts had crossed their minds, my body would have been tossed into the fissure beside the remains of the dead sheep. For a moment, I saw my own body crumpled there, eyes staring sightlessly up at the changing sky. Death by misadventure, no suspicious circumstances.

In keeping with my mood, I splashed a sombre grey wash all over the paper. An inherent characteristic of watercolour (later confirmed in my artist's book, Chapter 4, Wet on Wet) is that wet colours run untidily into one another. I made this fascinating discovery for myself when I added a few impressionistic black squiggles to represent the outline of the castle. I picked up the paper and, holding it at arm's length, studied the effect. Not at all what I had intended, but definitely intriguing.

Spinks's minions had disappeared behind the spectacularly ruined remnants of the castle, but I could track their position by the bobbing tips of their rods. They now seemed to be somewhere near the cliff edge, right above the little beach. Even to one who knew little about the sport of angling, those rods had seemed unusually long and strongly constructed. I resisted any temptation to find out what they were doing. A move like that could be fatal for the mission – and myself. So, no creeping forward on hands and knees to spy upon them from behind a rock. No slinking up to the castle wall and straining to hear their conversation. At all costs I must appear totally absorbed in my painting. My life depended on it. With luck, I might get a clue from something they said or did on their next visit to check on me. For they would come back to check me out. For them, it would be routine security. It's what I would have done myself.

When they came, I was ready. I'd changed my position, and was now facing westward, sitting half-turned away from the castle, as if no longer interested in it. *Fast Castle in the Sunset* was three-quarters completed, ready for their inspection. Using my newly acquired wet-on-wet technique, glorious yellows, oranges and reds had replaced the muted purples and greys of my first masterpiece.

Out of the corner of my eye I saw them approach. The line of conversation 'Good catch today, guys?' was definitely a no-go area.

I heard a soft footfall, laboured breathing, and once again the shadow fell across the page. I barely acknowledged their presence.

The aggressive one peered over my shoulder. 'What's it this time, fella? *Exploding Cheeseburger over Fast Castle?*' The words were accompanied by an unpleasant snigger. 'Yeah, you got it made. You play your cards right and maybe McDonald's will use it for promoting their quarter pounders.'

The Silent One's tight lips relaxed a fraction. His eyes remained watchful.

Exploding Cheeseburger. Wounding words to the genuine artist, but to me a source of satisfaction, carefully concealed. It seemed I'd passed the scrutiny test.

I donned an injured expression. 'Actually, it's *Fast Castle in the Sunset,*' I whined.

The aggressive one picked up the tackle box that he'd deposited on the ground while he insulted my masterpiece. It was only then that I noticed it was dripping wet. As if it had been immersed in water. Sea water. In a flash, I knew exactly why. They'd been doing a trial run, using that box as a substitute floating package.

I averted my eyes hurriedly from the evidence and pointed upwards. 'You see that sky?'

Both heads tilted up. A bank of grey-edged clouds now stretched as far as the eye could see. Only random patches of blue remained.

'There's not enough impact in that for a picture. Stronger

colours are needed – like you get at sunset.' I waved my brush knowledgeably. A splatter of almazarin crimson fell from it onto the aggressive one's buff trousers. Fortunately, he didn't notice.

The two exchanged meaningful looks. 'You mean you're going to hang around till sunset, fella?' On the surface it was a casual, innocent question, in reality heavy with danger. It was, after all, only mid-afternoon.

'Oh no, I'm never out painting *that* late. The light's just not good enough. The imagination is *so* much better.' I stuck the crimson-tipped brush into the water substitute and swirled it briskly round. 'I'll be packing up soon. Looks like rain. That's fatal for watercolour.'

Another unspoken message passed between them. 'Loada crap,' drifted back towards me on the wind as they turned their backs and trudged off.

I finished off *Fast Castle in the Sunset* and signed it with a flourish. Two masterpieces in one day. Gorgonzola Van Gogh would have to look to her laurels.

Even without the beard, my spiky yellow hair was a bit of a shock to Macleod, but he was suitably impressed with what I'd found out.

'So you think they use these long rods to fish packets out of the sea?' He twirled a pen thoughtfully between his fingers.

'Yes. And that was the trial run, using their tackle boxes for practice. I'm pretty sure the real thing's going to be tonight. They were quite uptight at the thought that I might still be there after sunset. That reminds me. What do you think of these?' Proudly, I placed my two masterpieces on his desk.

I regret to say that his reaction was rather similar to that of Spinks's two thugs, only more tactful.

There was a long pause while he studied them. He picked up *Fast Castle in the Haar* and turned it upside down. 'Er...'

Mutely, I pointed at the signature and he flipped it the right way up.

'I know I'm a detective but...is this meant to be Fast Castle?'

'That's *Fast Castle in the Haar*,' I said a little defensively.

'Ah, I see,' Macleod struggled to be diplomatic. 'A companion piece to *Fast Castle*...er...'

'...*in the Sunset*,' I finished modestly.

Fast Castle in the real sunset was no match for my painting. To be honest, there wasn't much of a sunset. Only the faintest of pink tinged the tiny area of sky visible behind the lowering clouds. Macleod and I had agreed on a one-person reconnaissance – me – to watch Spinks's men, and follow them discreetly from a distance. Two watchers would be twice as difficult to conceal, half a dozen, impossible. What I *hadn't* mentioned was that I intended my role to be a little more active. I would try to intercept any packages that floated my way. Macleod would have tried to talk me out of it. That's why I didn't tell him. From a study of the tide tables, I'd calculated the narrow window of opportunity when a vessel could drop its illicit cargo close to the cliff and count on it washing up onto that little beach. The pick-up party would have done their homework too, but to avoid arousing comment would leave their arrival till after dark. I was counting on that. My life in fact depended on it.

To get hold of a package and be able to analyse the contents was worth the risk. But it wouldn't be *too* much of one, I told myself. Spinks's mob couldn't be certain that all his contraband cargo would arrive safely at the beach beneath the castle, so one package missing would go unremarked.

After that apology for a sunset, all colour had drained from sky, sea, and land. I had perhaps an hour before it would be difficult to distinguish one object from another. And soon after that would come the dark. I shook myself free from the clump of spiny gorse. For the last couple of hours I'd shifted and turned as the needle spikes impaled different parts of my anatomy. In all that time, nobody had come along the path. As far as I could tell, I was the only human being on this lonely stretch of coast.

I myself had now become a creature of the night, clad in black jacket, trousers, and gloves. A black silk balaclava concealed my spiky yellow hair and any tell-tale pallor from my face. In my hand I carried an extendable and strong carbon fibre rod, purchased from a fish-tackle shop near my Portobello B&B. My intention was to slip down to the ruins, fish up a package, and return to my prickly hidey-hole long before the arrival of Spinks's gang. I had it all worked out.

At first, everything went according to plan. Without incident I negotiated the wooden plank bridge that crossed the chasm, skirted round the forlorn remnant of wall pointing jaggedly skyward, and stretched myself out full length on the short springy turf of the cliff top. When I peered over the edge, a hundred feet straight down, there they were. Ten dripping, black-wrapped bundles lay half off, half on the shingle beach, lifting and falling in the swell, their shapes already camouflaged by the dusk and the dark sea.

But *the best laid schemes of mice and men gang aft agley*. Robert Burns was right. My big miscalculation was the skill required to hook up a package. I'd forgotten the formula: Difficulty of task multiplied by Degree of Inexperience in handling fishing rods adds up to Time Spent. A long time. Too much time.

For a vital five minutes, I made clumsy attempts to assemble the extending rod and the purpose-made grappling hook, a special one with opening jaws, designed to retrieve small items from unlikely places. It was a larger version of those infuriating amusement arcade grabs where you struggle to pick up a soft toy and drop it into a hole before the time runs out.

At last, my giant fishing rod was ready, and I lowered the hook steadily downwards. With a spurt of white it splashed into the water, just to the right of one of the packages. I reeled in and tried again. And again. The third time, the hook landed squarely on top of a package that had been nudged up the beach by the rest. I raised the tip of the rod a fraction. One of the claws slipped over. I held my breath. The techniques honed in those misspent youthful years at the arcades flooded back. No movement must be hurried. I eased and joggled the jaws. A fraction here, an infinitesimal amount there. How long had I been desperately fishing? No idea. Just concentrate.

I closed the jaws and slowly, slowly, started to reel in. As the line took the strain, the package lurched and one corner rose in the air. *Careful now, careful*. I mustn't lose my nerve. Pressure, pressure of time. If time ran out, the price of failure was not money, but a life. Mine. The package shifted, rose slightly, snagged. I tugged. The jaws slid off the shiny waterproof covering and the package crunched back onto the shingle. I should have quit at this point. But you know how it is, there's always the temptation to make just one more attempt. I reeled in a little, and opening the jaws wide, swung the tip of the rod sideways. The grab landed with a faint thump and this time the jaws took a secure grip. I closed my eyes and breathed deeply for a couple of seconds to steady myself. This was my last chance. I was already pushing my luck. By just how much, I was about to find out.

I tentatively tightened the line. The jaws held. Apply steady pressure...no jerks. The package trembled, then rose cleanly into the air. I nursed it upwards as quickly as I dared. Steadily, but agonisingly slowly, the rectangular shape rose to meet me. At last, it came level with the cliff top. I drew the rod towards me and reached out for my prize. My gloved fingers touched it.

It was at that precise moment of triumph that I heard the metallic rattle of the chain handrail. Faint but unmistakable. Someone was crossing the bridge. Spinks's men, it could only be them. I had about thirty seconds before they came round the ruins and spotted me. If they hadn't already.

There was no time for me to rise to my feet. In one fluid movement, I clutched the package, jettisoned the rod over the side of the cliff, and rolled towards the sole piece of cover on that exposed cliff top. The cleft with its rotting carcass. To find it, all I had to do was follow my nose.

A split second before the first dark figures rounded the castle wall, I curled into a ball and dropped over the edge.

CHAPTER TWENTY

My mouth tasted foul, full of something unspeakably awful. What a hell of a headache! Some hangover, I thought muzzily. And the *smell*. Surely I hadn't passed out on some ghastly rubbish tip. I forced an eye open. *Ouch.* Green and white flashes shot across my vision. I hastily closed the eye and rested for a minute. Till that foul smell again jolted me into wakefulness.

I was aware of hushed voices, soft footsteps padding to and fro, a thump from somewhere above my head.

'Be careful with that!' the low voice was impatient.

'It's slippery. I can't get a grip...' I'd know that apologetic whine anywhere. It was Mackenzie.

Memory flooded back. And with it fear. Fear of discovery. Fear of death. Fear more powerful than the stench that surrounded me. It was that alone that prevented me from vomiting. Even in my fuzzled state I knew that the sound of retching would draw unwelcome attention.

Disjointed words floated my way. '...only nine...must have...can't spend...search...'

More grumbles from Mackenzie. Suddenly, closer and loud, his whine, 'What's that stink?' A dark shape blotted out part of the night sky above my head.

I shut my eyes. Cats' eyes reflect light, so would mine. If he shone a torch down here, I'd be done for.

A distant '…only a goddam dead sheep…get your butt over here…' An American voice, but not Spinks's.

I opened my eyes. Mackenzie had gone. I could breathe again, but that's about all I *could* do. My left arm was trapped under me as I lay wedged in the bottom of the cleft. Something sharp was digging into my arm, hurting like hell. If I shifted position, I might dislodge something that would betray me to the killers above. A rock on my head, that was all it would take to finish me off. But I'd *have to* move. The pain was now excruciating. No, I *mustn't*. OK, I'd count up to a hundred, then move.

I made it as far as forty before the pain became unbearable. If I could just ease the weight off my arm a fraction… I tried to twist onto my right hip, but I was wedged too tightly into the bottom of the cleft. A little leverage…my free hand felt for something on which to get a purchase. A stone dislodged by my scrabbling fingers rustled through the nettles and long grass. Another bounded down and hit me square between the eyes. The groan that escaped from between my tightly compressed lips sounded frighteningly loud.

'What the hell was that?' Mackenzie's voice, thin and edgy. 'It came from over there.'

'For Chris'sake, Mac! Never heard of methane gas? That sheep's belly'll be full of it.'

'I tell you, somebody's there!' His voice was much closer.

I lay, heart pounding like a sledgehammer. Pounding so loudly that I was sure they'd hear it. Even the pain and the indescribable stench had faded into the background.

Adrenalin, I suppose. I sensed him standing there directly above me.

'Methane gas, I tell ya. Quit bitching and give a hand here.' The voice was full of menace. 'We've gotta be back at the van before the moon rises. Now move your ass!'

Mackenzie muttered an imprecation. A cigarette stub arched through the air in a shower of sparks and soft footsteps reluctantly retreated.

After fear comes overwhelming relief, then a draining exhaustion that shuts out everything else. I managed to lie still for what I calculated to be another ten minutes. Till, that is, my eyes adapted to the dark and I saw the maggots. Fat, glistening, *loathsome*. My stomach churned, muscles tightened, and I threw up. Copiously and noisily, an involuntary reaction that I could not control. No question of secrecy now. Weakly, I waited for retribution. None came. No cries of alarm, just the silence of the night, the gentle wash of waves against the shore. They'd gone.

There was no need now to worry about noise and discovery. I wriggled free from that awful clinch with the dead sheep, propped myself upright, and thought hazily about how best to drag myself out of the fissure. What else was in the cleft apart from the mouldering sheep – and now myself? Nettles, I could recall nettles. And quite steep, rocky walls. Falling in had been easy, climbing out was going to be a bit more of a problem. I was weak and dizzy and probably suffering from a touch of concussion. I sat there among the nettles and the stench, summoning up enough reserves to claw my way upward.

It took a long time, but at last my hand was reaching for the edge. I was gathering myself for the effort of pulling my aching body over the top when I remembered the package. Getting hold of the damn thing had nearly cost me my life. How *could* I have forgotten all about it? That touch of concussion must be worse than I'd thought. I grabbed a handful of tough wiry grass to steady myself, and looked down. From above, the bottom of the cleft was an inky pool of darkness. I could see nothing. The very factor that had saved me from Mackenzie's searching eyes was now working against me. I gritted my teeth and slid all the way back down.

I found it in the end. Though by the time I was sitting with my back against the castle's worn sandstone blocks, well away from the noxious perfume of my friend the sheep, I was too exhausted to feel any elation. A full moon was now peeping over the black land mass behind me. I peered at my watch, but my eyes refused to focus properly. At a guess, it was now well after one a.m. I eased myself to my feet, and clutching my prize, began the long trek back to the road.

The moon was well risen by the time I reached my car. I threw the precious package onto the back seat along with the balaclava and gloves, and wearily slid behind the wheel. Before switching on the ignition, I tilted the rear-view mirror. A deathly white face stared back at me. Below the lavatory-brush haircut was a bruise, already turning an interesting shade of purple, and a bump the size of the proverbial duck's egg. A jagged cut crusted with dried blood zigzagged across my cheek. Altogether, I was a truly ghastly sight. I wished I hadn't looked. It had made me feel worse than I did already. I slipped the car into gear and set off.

Five miles outside Edinburgh, my blissful contemplation of

a long hot shower and a soft, soft bed was rudely disrupted by a waving torch. As I slowed, my headlights picked out a yellow-jacketed figure with its arm raised. Drawn up on the other side of the road was a police car. There must have been an accident of some kind. I lowered the window, selfishly hoping that I wouldn't be held up too long.

The figure with the torch stepped towards me and bent to peer in the window. 'Just a routine check of…'

With an awful sinking feeling I realised his torch was illuminating my suspiciously battered features.

'Good evening, officer,' I said brightly. 'Has there been an accident?'

There was no answering smile. His narrowed eyes were taking in the dried blood, the bruise, the bump. 'Are you reporting one, sir…er, madam?'

The package. Suddenly, I remembered the package on the back seat.

'No, no,' I babbled nervously. 'Oh, I see what you mean. No, no. All this is just make-up that I didn't have time to wash… I've been at a first aid accident course…as a victim.' I gave a rather too high-pitched laugh. Confronted by his look of scepticism, my voice faltered and trailed off.

He straightened. 'I'll just check your rear lights.' He moved away.

In my mirror I could see the discreet signal to his colleague seated in the car opposite. Mesmerised, I watched the driver's door open and the bulky figure ease itself out from behind the wheel. I knew what was coming next. The polite invitation to leave my vehicle. The hallo-hallo-hallo-what's-this-then routine when he spotted the incriminating balaclava and gloves. The discovery of the drugs. Alluring visions of shower and soft bed imploded to a pinpoint faster than you can say Lothian and Borders Police. It was going to be a long, long night.

Just how long, I underestimated. Not that it took much time for them to whisk me into headquarters. The questioning lasted all that night and most of the next day, in fact. Only one person knew my true identity, and that was Macleod, not contactable by phone, landline or mobile, or even carrier pigeon. He had nipped off with his fishing gear to some misty, rain-soaked Highland loch. He was incommunicado. And so was I. An undercover agent, undercover, and under arrest.

The thick finger stabbed down again on the record button. Tape hissed quietly as the spools revolved.

'I'm asking you once more. Where did you pick up that packet of drugs?' The grey eyes were as hard as the voice.

I stared at the bare walls of the interview room. Was that drab paint part of psychological warfare to cow the spirit? Or due to sheer lack of funds and imagination? I found it hard to believe that this same wishy-washy hue was this year's fashionable colour for kitchens and bathrooms.

I cleared my throat. 'OK, I'll talk—' I paused. Those trendy young designers who make over other people's houses on television, what would they do to those boring walls? Slap on black and white stripes to represent the prison gates about to close? 'Yes, I'll talk.' They leant forward expectantly. 'But only to DCI Macleod. Alone.'

I'll say this for them. They were persistent. Eventually, though, I wore them down. After the tape machine had recorded an hour of silence, they gave up. They marched me off to the cells. The key turned in the lock and I resigned myself to a longish spell in durance vile.

But the summons came late that evening. Fishing, it seemed, had been good on the remote highland loch – so good that Macleod had headed back a day early to stash his catch in the freezer, and workaholic as he was, had popped into the office on his way home. That unscheduled return got me off the hook.

Neither the name I'd given nor the drugs charge had prepared him to meet the DJ Smith he knew. When I was escorted in, it took him quite a few seconds to register that the Debbie Jones on the charge sheet was myself. His mouth gaped as wide as one of his dead fish, and he darted frequent sideways glances at me as the minion recounted my misdeeds.

'God, you look awful!' he burst out when we were left alone.

'Are you referring to the hair style or the bruises?' I collapsed gratefully into the chair in front of his desk. I fingered the tender lump on my forehead. 'It was worth it. We've got a new lead.' I pointed at his fishing gear propped against a filing cabinet. 'And that's it. No, I'm not suffering from concussion. I've been fishing too. And my catch is worth a lot more than yours. "Found in possession of a packet of a Class A drugs", wasn't I? Well, here's how I acquired it.' I filled him in with all the details.

It was round about midnight when I quietly let myself into the B&B and tiptoed upstairs. As soon as I opened the door to my room, I knew I was in trouble. Even before my hand hit the light switch, a loud *hissssss* followed by a soft thud heralded a confrontation with a very irate Gorgonzola. Though I'd left the window open for her and a dish of water handy, I had expected to return before dawn, so I'd not left any food. As the light came on, we sized each other up. Straight legged, tail swishing, eyes narrowed to menacing slits, she fluffed up her fur into spiky tufts.

'Come off it, G,' I murmured. 'You know it's me, and I know you've been fed by Jim Ewing. You've been down at the back door piteously asking for food at least three times today. Come on, admit it.'

She had the grace to look just a tiny bit ashamed. I scooped her up in my arms and pressed my face into her soft moth-eaten coat.

'I missed you, G. Really I did.' I mumbled into her fur. Truce was declared. Gorgonzola's rough tongue rasped at my cheek, and a throaty purr indicating forgiveness vibrated deep in her chest, as relief at my return overcame an indignation fuelled by anxiety. To celebrate our reunion, we both tucked into a midnight feast, G of duck, me of a couple of chocolate hazelnut bars kept for emergencies.

I'd slept most of the day in the cell waiting for Macleod's return. Mental and physical exhaustion had made the narrow bed with its coarse grey blanket seem almost comfortable. So now, after my feast of choc bars, instead of slipping beneath the duvet, I subjected my lavatory brush hairdo to a close inspection in the mirror above the basin. The spikes of bleached hair glinted brassily in the strip light. I pursed my lips. If we chanced to meet again, it wouldn't do to jog the memory of those two thugs I'd encountered during my artistic endeavours on the cliff top. There wasn't anything I could do about the length, but I could definitely do something about the colour.

No time like the present. It shouldn't take more than half an hour. On the way back I'd bought some dark brown hair dye at a 24-hour store. Opening the packet, I pulled out the plastic gloves and rapidly skimmed through the instructions. *Towel round neck…apply to damp hair…use liberally…* Easy! I seized the bottle and splashed it on. I soaked each strand thoroughly, as per instructions, until brown drips trickled down my forehead and splattered into the basin. Even so, my hair was so short that I used less than half the bottle. When I looked in the mirror, my hair still shone golden and undulled.

Through the drips I squinted at the instructions. *Do not worry about the colour. It is no indication of the final result…* Of course. The colour had been bleached out of my hair. It would need a lot of dye to return it to its former self. Repeatedly, I massaged the lotion into each strand until I had used up every last drop. Now what? *Wrap hair in towel and wait 30 minutes.* I did as instructed and sank onto a chair. Well, that had taken a bit longer than I'd anticipated, but a quick burst of the hair dryer, and in three quarters of an hour all that yellow would be gone.

I might as well read up on the Isle of May while waiting. Edith and Harry's sighting of Spinks and the late unlamented Kumiko had got to be an important lead. And it was the *only* lead I had. The boat they'd been on had been heading for the Isle of May and that meant they had business there as Spinks wasn't one for sightseeing.

What info did I have about the island? I padded over to the shelf by the window and rummaged through my multi-coloured collection of leaflets. *Golf Courses of East Lothian, Castles of the Lothians, Historic Edinburgh, Excursions from Edinburgh. Shopping in Scotland's Capital...* Reluctantly, I put that last one down. Perhaps when I'd finally nailed Spinks and his gang...

Another leaflet fluttered to the floor. *Edinburgh Botanic Gardens and The Glasshouse Experience.* 'I don't think lurking in their tropical pool was meant to be part of the experience, do you, G?'

Gorgonzola paused in mid-postprandial wash, stared consideringly at me, yawned, then resumed her clean-up more vigorously than before.

Islands of the Firth of Forth. Bound to be something in here. But there was only a brief paragraph about the Isle of May and a distant picture of the cliffs. And that was it.

I subsided into the chair, nearly dislodging my towelling turban. Absent-mindedly, I tucked in a loose end. I poked my tongue round a tooth, trying without success to dislodge a crumb. That was the trouble with chocolate hazelnut bars...

I closed my eyes in concentration. Hadn't Macleod given me something about the Isle of May? He'd shoved some sort of nature magazine into my hand after I'd told him what Edith and Harry had said. I'd given it a quick glance and stuffed it into my bag. I got up and pulled the bag out of the wardrobe. Yes, the magazine was still there. The picture on the front was of a cheeky-looking black and white bird with a fat beak. A toucan? No, puffin, that's what it was. I scanned the contents page. *Isle of May National Nature Reserve in the Firth of Forth. This month's cover: Puffin colony at Pilgrims' Haven, Isle of May.* Quite a big article – and a map.

Gorgonzola had seized the opportunity of my temporary absence from the chair to curl up on the warm cushions. Easing her aside with a murmured, 'Move over, Fatty!' I settled down to mug up on Spinks's destination.

My head fell forward with a jerk. I must have nodded off there. I yawned. Full of best duck, Gorgonzola had also succumbed, her head turned to the side, pink tip of tongue protruding, one paw dangling limply over the edge of the chair. I yawned again. Hair-dyeing time must be up. A quick wash through, and I'd be ready for bed. I rubbed my eyes and reached for the alarm clock. I'd left the stuff on my hair half an hour over the recommended time. Well, that shouldn't make much difference. It would just be a bit darker than normal.

I trotted blearily over to the basin and unwound the towel. I wouldn't mind a shade of brown so dark it was almost black. It would be—

Aaargh. I couldn't hold back the involuntary shriek. I stared at the mirror. A punk, Frankenstein-featured with scar, bump and vibrant acid-green hair, stared back open-mouthed. I closed my eyes and clutched the edge of the basin for support. Slowly, I counted to ten, eased one eye open to the thinnest slit, and darted a sly sideways glance at the mirror. The green-haired punk swivelled her eyes sideways. A streak of brown ran like war-paint down the side of her face.

I shut my eyes. I opened my eyes again. It was no trick of the light. Without doubt, my hair was a vibrant and shimmering green. And despite a whole bottle of shampoo, vigorously and desperately applied, so it remained.

* * *

Before nine next morning, hair discreetly under wraps, I paced up and down outside Linda's salon waiting for her to appear. At last her car swung into the parking bay. Head down, fumbling in her bag for her keys, she didn't notice me until I placed myself squarely in front of her.

She looked up, startled. 'What *fantastic* make-up! I didn't recognise you for a minute. What play did you say you were in?'

'Not make-up. I fell off the stage,' I gabbled. 'I need an appointment. I *must* have one.'

She shook her head doubtfully. 'I'll look at the book but I don't think...'

I followed her into the salon. 'It's an emergency.' Dramatically, I whipped off the balaclava, converted for my present purpose into a pudding bowl hat.

To her credit, Linda kept a straight face, though the twitching corners of her mouth and the firmly pressed-together lips betrayed inner whoops of mirth.

'Oh dear.' A guffaw was barely converted into a cough. She ushered me into a seat and whipped a multi-coloured salon cloth round my shoulders. 'The first customer's not here yet. I'll see what I can do.'

She busily sorted through various bottles of lotions and liquids. Little snorts and burbles of suppressed mirth rose above the sound of running water.

'What went wrong?' I whinged. 'I was only dyeing my hair back to its original colour.' I stared gloomily at the awful apparition in the mirror.

'Don't worry about it.' Linda patted my green spikes. 'Red dye. That's the answer.'

'Red!' I yelped. Had I delivered myself into the hands of a madwoman? I threw off the covering and tried to rise from the chair.

Linda pressed me back down. 'Trust me. I'm a hairdresser! You know, you really shouldn't have attempted to dye bleached hair yourself. But you're not the first. I've seen it all before.' She gave a peal of unseemly laughter as she recalled previous DIY hair disasters.

'Well,' I sulked, 'there wasn't a warning on the packet.'

'People usually don't read instructions, anyway. That's where I get a lot of business,' said Linda, cheerfully dabbing at my hair.

'*Voila*!' she cried, whipping off the towel with a flourish like a magician unveiling his favourite trick.

A slow smile spread across my face. No more eye-stopping green. My hair was just an ordinary nondescript dark brown. Now I was ready for that dangerous trip to the Isle of May. With the aid of a little make-up – well, a lot of it – plastered over bump and scar, I wouldn't stand out amongst the scores of other day-trippers to that bird sanctuary in the River Forth.

From the sea, the tall cliffs were scored with clefts and fissures deep enough to swallow a boat and hide it from prying eyes. It was easy to understand just why Spinks might be interested in this windswept island. The launch nosed into the little natural harbour and was tied up at the concrete jetty. I shrugged on the photographer's gadget bag and, as my fellow passengers surged ashore, allowed myself to be swept along in their midst. A Court of Law needs hard evidence, and I aimed to get it. My surveillance equipment – binoculars and camera with its powerful zoom lens – was nothing more than the essential gear of the enthusiastic wildlife photographer. It should arouse no comment.

On each side of the jetty brown wracks of seaweed draped the rocks in a slippery blanket. Tiny fish darted in the shallow pools left by the receding tide, and sea birds swooped and circled overhead, their strident cries cutting through the excited chatter of the crowd milling around me. None of them looked like puffins. The birds, I mean, not my fellow trippers.

I made a show of consulting the simple map provided with the ticket. Others, too, might not be as innocent as they seemed. It was important, therefore, to establish a harmless amateur profile, blend into the mass. Just in case.

I waved the pamphlet at a florid-faced man standing nearby. 'Where's the best place to take pictures of the birds?'

'No idea.' He pointed up the path towards a distant wooden building. 'You might get some information there. Maybe get a drink, too,' he added hopefully. He trudged off in search of something probably a bit stronger than a cup of tea.

The crowd were beginning to disperse. I'd better make a move myself. Yesterday, a study of the Ordnance Survey map had familiarised me with the topography of the island and its place names – the South and North Horns, Maiden Rocks, Pilgrims' Haven, and Kirkhaven, the little bay where we had just landed. All had been just meaningless names on a map with no indication of how suited any of them would be to Spinks's schemes. I'd have to do some reconnaissance on foot.

At a leisurely pace, camera dangling ready for instant use,

as if I'd nothing more on my mind than to snatch a few bird photographs, I set off up the rough grassy path towards the South Horn. I hadn't realised till now that the Horn really was a horn, a foghorn, that is. Standing on its concrete plinth, it looked remarkably like a giant re-creation of an old His Master's Voice gramophone.

A stab of pain shot through my ankle. Caught up in this fantasy, I'd caught my foot on one of the tussocks of grass in the centre of the path. Paths like this would not be good for any reconnaissance in the dark. I hobbled on a few steps and rested for a moment at a gateway flanked by small stone pillars. In the small field beyond, a rabbit scuttered across the grass through wild flowers, campion, I think, growing as thick as daisies on a neglected lawn. Quite pretty things, wild flowers. I hummed a few bars of 'An English Country Garden'. As I gave an experimental twirl of the affected ankle, a purple-topped thistle, asserting its Scottish identity, clawed viciously at my leg, piercing through my thin trousers with its barbs. Not all wild flowers are dainty fragile things, are they? Just like women.

Behind me I heard the quick patter of running feet and high-pitched childish shrieks, then a crescendo of howls. Ignoring the jab of pain, I sidestepped smartly through a gap between another two stone pillars on my left. Shutting my ears to the mayhem going on behind me, I took a deep breath of tangy salt-laden air overlaid by the more pungent guano of nesting sea birds. Weak rays of sun filtered through banks of cloud. Where once a road had run, grass and weeds ruled.

A deep slash in the cliff ran almost to my feet. I approached the edge with caution. The sheer black sides were splashed with brilliant white layers of bird droppings. Far below gleamed water, water so clear it was hard to tell where the rocks cut the glassy surface. A shallow cave, a darker shadow among the other shadows, broke the waterline. A slow swell nudged at a pile of flotsam, crunching it against the unforgiving rock. This would be ideal as one of Spinks's collection points, if they used those long fishing rods as at Fast Castle, or sent in a small boat. But a bit risky if even the slightest swell was running. I aimed my camera at a shaggy black bird perched on a jagged outcrop of rock. The cave was nicely in the bottom of the frame. I pressed the shutter.

Where exactly was I on the map? It was hard to say. The basic outline of the simple guide leaflet wasn't much help, but in the bay below, that stack shaped like the Old Man of Hoy should be a good landmark. I delved in my rucksack and pulled out the Ordnance Survey. That outcrop must be Maiden Rocks. I marked the map. Alongside I wrote, *Possible sighting* of cormorant, underlining the first two words. The map might fall into enemy hands. One couldn't be too careful.

I seemed to have the cliff top to myself now. It was amazing how such a small island could swallow up a boatload of people. There was no sign of peevish, crying children, or anyone else. So why did I have that prickling feeling in the back of my neck? That unmistakable feeling of being watched.

Slowly, I folded up the map and slid it into the rucksack. As I heaved the strap onto my shoulder, I swung casually round, my back to the sea. Nothing. Nobody. Only a dead sea bird under a scrubby bush, its head tucked under its wing in a grim parody of sleep. Perhaps I was being observed from the sea through a periscope... I tried to smile at my feeble joke. I was just being twitchy. I trudged on along the cliff top.

Pilgrims' Haven turned out to be a grey, stony beach disfigured by the usual rubbish thrown up by the tides: a rusty jerry can, a broken lobster creel, a couple of old tyres, a bit of green plastic sheeting. At the water's edge, a yellow plastic canister grated noisily against the rounded pebbles as it rolled to and fro. That lump of rock on the horizon must be... I consulted the Ordnance Survey again...the Bass Rock. And Tantallon was more or less straight across. The Spinks Triangle.

A seal broke the surface of the sea. I watched its dark sleek head appearing and disappearing in the lapping waves. I gazed out to sea, teasing at the thread of memory...and I remembered...Gina. Gina floating face down below the red crags of Tantallon, and, bobbing beside her dark head, a yellow canister. The seal submerged. One minute it was there, the next, only a ripple marked the spot. Divers – they would be another way for Spinks to retrieve or deposit his packages, perhaps in a lobster creel. A lobster creel marked by a brightly coloured float...

Pilgrims' Haven's secluded beach, enclosed as it was in the arms of a little bay, would be an ideal collection point from Spinks's point of view. On the map I wrote, *Probable sighting of seal*. I crouched down and took my second photograph, this one featuring in the foreground the broken creel.

'A load of trash. Why'd ya wanna take a picture of a loada trash?' The voice was nasal, oddly threatening.

When I looked up, he was standing there, a cigarette cupped in his hand, the Silent One from Fast Castle. To generate so many words, maybe that lobster pot *was* something special.

Crouching down again, I took a close-up. 'Photo comp.' I smiled up at him engagingly, searching in those dark suspicious eyes for that disastrous start of recognition. They remained mercifully blank. I straightened up and clipped the lens cover back on. '*Fruit of the Sea*, that's the theme... You've got to interpret things to catch the judge's eye, you know.'

'Yeah?' After this effort he lapsed into silence again. Those eyes were giving a thorough once-over to my powerful binoculars and the camera with its 400mm lens.

I forestalled the questions. 'Bird photography, that's what I'm really into. Do you know, it's dead birds that earn me more money than a great pic of...say...' under the unwinking scrutiny of those eyes, my mind searched desperately for a likely species, '...one of those cuddly puffins. Would you believe *that*?'

His stony expression indicated that he'd have a hard time believing anything.

I plunged on. 'The Environmental Lobby can't get enough publicity pics of oiled sea birds and that sort of thing. It's a nice little earner.'

'No sweat?' The Silent One tossed the glowing butt of his cigarette into an advancing wave. He no longer seemed interested in me. I tucked the map into my belt, and with a cheery ''Bye' crunched off up the beach to rejoin the path. Beads of sweat formed on my hairline as I relived those last tense moments. I had just reached the top of the cliff with its banks of white campion, when I heard quick steps behind me.

'Hey there,' he called. 'Don't I know you from some place?'

Every instinct shouted *Run*. I turned and waited for him to catch me up. I made a show of studying his face, then slowly shook my head.

'We-ll, we were both on the boat, weren't we?'

He hadn't been. I would have spotted him. I treated him to a disarming smile and prayed that he wouldn't recognise in me that weedy artist on Fast Castle cliffs. His turn to shake his head. It was bothering him. Any moment now the connection might be made.

In a crisis I become wildly inventive. It's a knack much admired by my colleagues. Self-preservation, I suppose.

'I know!' I cried with what I hoped was the right degree of pride. 'You've seen my picture in the *Guardian*, yesterday's paper. Page 7, or 8, or was it 17? I was the winner of their Wildlife Photo Competition.' He definitely wasn't a *Guardian* reader. 'It was in the first edition. Do you know,' I worked myself into a state of indignation, 'I actually bought five copies of the second edition to send to my friends and it wasn't there! What do you think of *that*?'

While I was gabbling on, my mind was racing. What if he made the connection – this wildlife photographer and the artist with the spiky yellow hair? Would he buy it that I had an artist brother? I didn't think so. He lit another cigarette, cupping his hands over the flame, his eyes watchful. He wasn't listening. His brain was searching its hard disk.

I smiled a 'sorry can't help' smile and turned away. What could he do about it, anyway? He could hardly strike me down in broad daylight, in full view of anyone coming along. But no one was coming along. We were quite alone. 'Amazing how such a small island can swallow up a whole boatload of people', I'd thought only a short while ago. I'd been quite pleased to be away from the madding crowd. Now I was desperate for witnesses. The cliffs here above the bay were low, only about thirty feet high, but quite high enough for a fatal accident. A quick push and...

I forced my legs into a casual stroll. Not too fast, just keep it natural. I mustn't look round. I strained my ears for the soft sound of running feet, braced myself for the sharp blow on the back. Or the rabbit punch to the nape of the neck. He would know how to kill silently. That wild soaring of the imagination I was boasting about just now has its downside.

I shouldn't have been worrying about a rabbit punch. It was a rabbit hole that caused my downfall. Literally. I pitched headlong, nose-diving into the coarse turf. When I picked myself up and looked round, he was nowhere in sight.

I could see quite a distance along the cliff top. Had he gone down to the beach again? If so, why? Worth investigating, but risky. I trotted back along the path. At a spot I calculated would be just out of sight of somebody on the beach, I did another nose-dive, this time controlled and deliberate. I wriggled forward on my elbows, camera with telephoto lens at the ready. And there he was, doing a beachcomber act, getting those fancy shoes of his wet as he made a grab for the lobster creel. Before he turned my way, I raised the camera, snatched a quick shot and wriggled my way backward.

I made a low crouching run back along the path, slowing to an upright, less Neanderthal position when I felt it safe to do so. I consulted my watch. I had only an hour till the boat left, but there was time for a quick recce of the rest of the island. There must be other landing places and I needed to suss them out. I found another couple of possibilities. One was the oddly named Mill Door, a narrow finger of greeny black sea below a small dam (I cautiously marked it on my map as 'sight of

<u>rare</u> white-billed puffin'). The other was the North Horn and low-lying island of Rona, joined to the main island of May by a metalled bailey bridge ('<u>second sight of rare</u> puffin').

The sharp blare of the ship's siren boomed across the island. That meant fifteen minutes to get back to Kirkhaven, or I'd be left behind. It wasn't far back to the harbour, and the going was easy, an old metalled road, then a broad grassy track. I made it to the path leading down to the jetty with five minutes to spare. Already the boat was half full, the best seats commandeered, the jostle for places encouraged by the thin drizzle that had set in.

Another sharp toot from the siren encouraged stragglers to quicken their pace. Because of the tides, the ship couldn't delay its departure. We'd been warned about that on the way over. Should I just slip behind that wall and allow myself to be left behind? I can't deny I was tempted. What removed the temptation entirely was the sight of the Silent One standing, silently of course, at the top of the path. I noted the salty tidemark on his expensive shoes, and the damp patches getting damper on his expensively clad shoulders. He'd been there for some time in the drizzle, studying the faces of those embarking. I joined the queue shuffling slowly forward. I didn't meet his eyes. That might betray the fact that I was taking a special interest in him.

There beside me was the florid-faced man, heaven sent.

'Get your drink, then?' I asked, conversationally turning my head.

The gloomy look gave me my answer before he replied. 'Aye, I'd the choice of orange or cola.'

Suitable commiserations took me safely past that dangerous

scrutiny. As we passed the Silent One, I sensed a sudden quickening of interest, then a relaxation of tension. That inquisitive photographer was leaving the island. The Silent One was satisfied.

But I'd be back. By night, when he was no longer watching.

CHAPTER TWENTY-ONE

'Something *ghastly's* happened at the hotel!' The voice on the phone was distraught. I recognised at once the rich fruity tones of Felicity Lannelle.

'What—?' I began. 'Tell me—'

Several times I tried, Canute-like, to stem the flood of long drawn out wails and breathless gasps, but with as little success as that hapless monarch. Before one sentence ended, another began. From the incoherent babble the only really intelligible words were 'my cooking project', 'Mrs Mackenzie' and 'ab-saw-loot disaster'. Had Mrs M, arms akimbo, refused to divulge the secrets of her larder, aborting the Cooking Experience before take-off? Yes, that must be it. Felicity had revealed to Mrs Mackenzie that she would be just one of many chefs to be featured. Mrs M would brook no rivals. Perhaps she had dictated that *her* kitchen, and no other, must be the star in Felicity's great work. Perhaps in a fit of jealous pique, she had ordered Mr Mackenzie to make a bonfire of Felicity's precious notebooks. All her research had gone up in flames.

But even a frantic Felicity Lannelle had to draw breath sometime, and when she did, I swiftly cut in, 'Where are you? At the White Heather? Right. Be with you in about half an hour.'

I slammed down the phone before I could be engulfed by another tidal wave of lamentation. I'd help her out. It would be a chance to nose around the hotel. No matter how disapproving Mrs Mackenzie might be, she wasn't likely to further upset a lucrative guest like Felicity by sending me packing.

I drew up in the White Heather's car park. An ambulance, its doors flung wide, was drawn up to one side of the front door. Had Felicity's woes precipitated a hysterical collapse? In the silence after I'd switched off the ignition, I heard the hum of a car engine coming up the drive behind me, and in the narrow rectangle of my rear-view mirror saw a police car. Its wheels crunched noisily on the gravel as it drew to a halt. Surely Felicity hadn't… My stomach lurched.

The nearside door opened and Macleod clambered rather stiffly out. A pebble of ice formed in the pit of my stomach. I shouldn't have been so abrupt with her. I should have foreseen that under extreme pressure her volatile personality might succumb to suicidal tendencies. If she couldn't cope with the present moment, to wait half an hour for help would have seemed impossible. I could see that now.

I pressed a button and the car window slid smoothly down. I didn't get out. I sat there allowing Macleod to come over the gravel towards me. It was silly, but it meant I wouldn't hear the news I dreaded for another twenty…fifteen…ten seconds. He rested his hand on the roof and stooped till his head was level with mine.

'I think that man of yours has been busy again.' His face was grim. 'Not that there'll be any proof, of course. At least not at first, till we get Forensic to have a good poke around.'

The icy pebble in my stomach became a boulder. Spinks must have stumbled across my link with Felicity, and been waiting for her to put the phone down before he struck.

'Dead?' My voice was a croak.

'Definitely. Oh yes, definitely dead.'

Plump, unscrupulous Felicity, with her fruity tones, teetering pile of multi-coloured notebooks and excited plans for the future. Somehow, I felt it was all my fault. I looked away, not trusting myself to speak.

'You seem a bit upset. Didn't know he meant anything to you.' Surprise sharpened Macleod's voice.

It took a second or two for the pronoun to register. Then, '*He?*' I said blankly, raising my eyes to his face.

'Mackenzie. Who did you think it was?' He stood up and held open the car door for me to get out.

'I—' Over his shoulder I caught sight of a large figure surging down the steps towards us.

'It's *frightful*! A calamity!' Felicity's face crumpled. She dabbed at her swollen eyes with a napkin-sized handkerchief.

Usually impassive, Macleod failed to hide his incredulity at this unexpected and public show of grief for the unfortunate, and not much lamented, Murdo Mackenzie. His face was a study – as, of course, was mine.

'*Felicity*…!' was all I could splutter before I was enfolded in her arms and crushed to her woebegone bosom.

Macleod's authoritative, 'Excuse me, ladies!' accompanied by a loud clearing of the throat, rescued me from suffocation in the nick of time. I disengaged myself from her watery embrace.

'If you'll just go along and wait in the lounge with the others, I'll send someone to take your statements as soon as we've finished at the garage.' He fished a notebook out of his pocket. 'If I might have your names, ladies…?' Discreet as ever, he was being careful not to blow my cover.

'Ms Smith. Ms DJ Smith.'

'*Ms* Lannelle – *gastronome*,' Felicity growled, disgruntled at not being instantly recognised as the celebrity she was.

As I steered the tear-stained gastronome in the direction indicated, I mulled over the information he'd slipped me. Whatever it was that had prematurely ended Mackenzie's life, it had happened in the garage. But how? And why? And not an accident. Macleod had been sure about that.

'Where *were* you when you heard the awful news?' I asked, careful to phrase my question so as not to open the floodgates once more.

Felicity teetered to a halt in the vestibule. She put her hand on the elegantly spindly table to steady herself. It wobbled alarmingly under the onslaught, sending the potted fern on its top sliding towards the edge.

'I just can't bring myself to talk about it. It's…it's so ab-saw-loot-ly awful.' Her mouth trembled. Her fingers caressed the soft green fronds of the fern. Absent-mindedly, as she spoke, she plucked at it. In a thin green stream the pieces fell and gathered on the pristine Victorian tiles. Not that Mrs Mackenzie would be bothering about that today. She had far weightier considerations on her mind.

'You've had a terrible shock,' I soothed. 'We'll go to the lounge and I'll get somebody to rustle us up a cup of coffee – or perhaps something a little stronger.'

Her fingers paused momentarily in their plucking.

'I don't want to say *anything* in front of the others,' she hissed dramatically. 'Commercial secrets, you know! People are *so* unethical when it comes to stealing a winning idea!'

At these last words, her mouth trembled again. My initial guess about the source of her anguish must have been correct. Mackenzie's untimely death would certainly have directed a cold blast at the towering soufflé of her cooking plans.

'That's just it, Felicity!' I cried, seizing my chance. 'A winning idea can't be crushed even by a setback like this. Now we'll go to your room, have something restorative there, and you can tell me everything in confidence.'

'So there I was, sitting in the conservatory waiting for Mr Mackenzie to serve morning coffee. Such a fine establishment. They serve a full range of speciality coffees.' Fortified by perhaps too many tumblers of her cooking sherry, Felicity waved a plump hand expansively. 'Jamaican Blue Mountain, *of course*, and Monsoon Malabar Mysore', she rolled the exotic syllables round her tongue, savouring the roasts in a sort of virtual-reality coffee tasting. 'Do *you* have a favourite, my dear?'

I was about to administer another dreadful shock to her fragile system by admitting to a partiality for a well-known brand of Instant, but she swept on.

'*My* favourite is Sumatra Mandheling. Its *hint* of chocolate is ab-saw-loot-ly divine.' A dreamy faraway look softened the gastronome's plump features.

'Well, there you were, just gasping for your first sip of Mandheling...and it never came?' I paused encouragingly.

'No, it never came.' The soft faraway look was supplanted by a flush of annoyance at the memory of the deprivation. 'And I must admit I was wondering if standards were beginning to slip. Then…then…' she faltered and took another swig from her glass, 'there was the most frightful high-pitched scream from out the back somewhere.' Her vast frame shook at the memory. 'Do you know, it reminded me of the cry a lobster makes when you throw it in boiling water.' Thoughtfully, she contemplated past culinary incidents. 'Well, of course, we all looked at each other, wondering. No one liked to say anything. Then we all rushed over to the windows. There was nothing to see. And then Mrs Mackenzie came staggering out of the garage. She just stood there in the sunlight with her hand up over her mouth. Swaying. She started this frightful moaning noise. Just like…' Felicity paused, searching for a familiar culinary comparison, and failing to find one opted for, '…one of those ghastly grey pigeons that go *woooh, woooh, woooh*.' She emitted a creditably pigeon-like croon. 'My dear, it quite made my hair stand on end. A well-bred woman like her, always so refined, so austere, so *private*, reduced to this.' She shook her head sorrowfully and fell silent, gazing for a long time into the amber depths of her tumbler, as if seeking an answer to one of Life's Great Mysteries.

I was silent too. Was Mrs Mackenzie reacting to the sudden death of a beloved spouse, or to the realisation that she and her husband had paid the price for double-crossing Spinks with some little scheme they'd hatched together?

Felicity finished off her drink with one gulp. 'One of the staff came out and led her indoors. We all stood there looking at each other, not saying a word. The silence was eerie. Then someone came in and told us there had been a dreadful accident and Mr Mackenzie was dead. I just went to pieces.' She shuffled her feet in embarrassment. 'You see, I'd had it all set up for just after lunch. Mrs Mackenzie was going to let me into the secret of one of her most successful recipes. But *now...*' Once more Felicity stared gloomily into her glass.

'In a few months when she begins to get over all this, she'll *want* a new interest,' I suggested tentatively. 'Perhaps you could make an approach then.' I didn't think it at all helpful to mention that the only approach she might be making would be through the gates of one of HM's prisons.

Men in white coveralls and hoods were busy in the garage. A full forensic investigation was in progress, then. Supplementary lighting had been brought in, and an area cordoned off with coloured tape near to where Macleod and a balding man were standing. They were watching the police photographer taking pictures of a heap of cardboard boxes.

When Macleod saw me, he beckoned me over. 'He's only been dead about two hours. We've a real chance of nailing our man this time.'

I suppose most people subconsciously expect a murdered body to be slumped with a knife sticking out of its shoulder blades, or its skull shattered by some blunt instrument. But all Spinks's murders appeared, on the surface, to be mere accidents. No suspicious circumstances, that's how he worked. What had he set up this time? I was both curious and apprehensive.

The boxes I'd last seen neatly stacked to ceiling height against the side of the garage now lay in a jumbled and untidy pile. Some had burst open, spilling tins in all directions. I didn't notice the hand at first. When I did, I couldn't drag my eyes away. The fingers seemed raised in a mute appeal for help. The rest of the mortal remains of Murdo Mackenzie were mercifully hidden by the tumbled heap. Had death been swift, or... I swallowed hard.

The balding man answered my unspoken question. 'Instantaneous, I'd say.'

I picked up a tin. 'There must be some weight in even one case of these,' I said speculatively.

He pursed his lips. 'Severe head injuries – not from those boxes, though. A good attempt has been made at disguising the weapon, but we can usually tell.'

'You mean he *wasn't* crushed by the boxes?'

'I think we'll find he was already dead.' The strong lights glinted on his scalp as he peered over the top of one of the boxes at what must be Mackenzie's head. 'Imprint abrasion, you see.'

'Imprint—?'

'Human skin picks up the imprint of what hits it. For example, a rope, a shoe, a car bumper, or, as in this case, a thin metal tube.'

'Like the shaft of a golf club,' I said slowly.

The pathologist stooped to make a closer inspection of what lay behind the box. 'Spot on. Not just the shaft. The head of the club too. Tramline marks, curved edge. The heel of a putter. Yes, I'd say it was a putter.'

Spinks had been counting on Mackenzie's death being dismissed as just an unfortunate accident. This time he had slipped up.

* * *

From behind the anonymity of the one-way glass I tried to guess at Mrs Mackenzie's thoughts. Drawn and grey, she sat in front of the interview table, her back still ramrod straight. She'd been the strong one of the partnership, dominance, not love, the relationship. She would recover. Was she clinging to the hope that the police had not discovered the underground lab? It was well hidden, and if they were concentrating their attentions at the front of the garage…

Macleod was saying, 'I know it's painful for you, Mrs Mackenzie, but we *had* to ask how you discovered the body of your husband. It's quite understandable that you can't remember much about it.'

A swift nod of acknowledgement from the upright figure. 'The accident…such a terrible shock…' Her lip trembled.

'That's just it. You see, we don't think your husband's death *was* an accident.'

The ramrod figure suddenly sagged as if Macleod had struck her a physical blow.

'*Not an accident…*' she whispered. Her eyes were wild and frightened.

'He was already dead when the boxes fell on him.'

'No!' The word was the faintest whisper.

'Now can you think of anyone who would…?'

But she wasn't listening. Her eyes stared straight ahead. A muscle in her cheek twitched.

'Don't you want to know how he died?' Macleod waited. She brought her eyes back to meet his.

He repeated, 'Don't you want to know?'

'How?' her lips barely moved.

'Severe head injuries – the weapon, a golf club.' He made

it sound like an incontrovertible fact.

The effect on her was startling. The sagging figure snapped back to its former stiffness. A small red spot burnt in the pallor of each cheek, her slack mouth reset in a thin grim line. I realised with some astonishment that Mrs Mackenzie's overriding emotion was rage.

Macleod fed the flames. 'Crushed his skull like an eggshell.' He pushed a brown envelope across the table towards her. 'Would you like to see the photographs?' His tone was casual, as if he was offering to show a collection of holiday snaps.

I winced at the calculated brutality. But it had the desired effect. The gold band on her wedding finger glinted in the harsh lighting as her bony hands gripped the edge of the table.

'I told Murdo that he was dangerous! I told Murdo not to—' She stopped.

'If you're worried about incriminating yourself, Mrs Mackenzie, I have to tell you that we know *all* about the lab under your garage and what it was used for.'

Her back slumped against the hard wooden chair. I could see all resistance drain from her. She pushed wearily at a strand of iron-grey hair. 'What else do you want to know?' she said dully.

Now that he'd won, Macleod exchanged the bludgeoning stick for the tempting juicy carrot. Kindly, concerned, avuncular, he leant forward. Hyde replaced Jekyll. 'We've got to catch your husband's murderer. Can you help us to do that, Morag?' he asked softly.

CHAPTER TWENTY-TWO

In the brief dark interlude between the end of the long summer twilight and moonrise, the coastguard cutter, engines throttled back to a whisper, nosed into a tiny inlet on the most northerly part of the Isle of May. I was one of the dark shapes that scrambled ashore and took up position in the lee of the concrete platform of the North Horn. It would be an hour until the full moon rose above the horizon, the full moon, the smuggler's friend. But not this time.

Moonlight. The dictionary definition, 'Light from the sun reflected from the moon's surface', is neutral, scientific, correct. But poets write verse after verse dedicated to its beauty...

The dark figure beside me shifted his weight to ease cramped muscles. To distract myself from the mind-numbing boredom of waiting, I listened with closed eyes to the night sounds, Nature's Moonlight Sonata...the sharp slap of waves on rock, the sad sigh of the night breeze through sea grasses...the distant, ghostly scream of a sea bird... In my mind I heard the tense opening bars of that classic film *Dangerous Moonlight*...

The big drop had been scheduled for tonight, the night of the full moon. That was all Mrs Mackenzie knew. She'd left that side of things to her dear departed while she cooked the gravy. That had been their little scam – cooking the books, so to speak. 'Surplus' gravy had been siphoned off and sold. All very profitable – until Spinks did some probing.

By one a.m. the moon was fully above the horizon. As forecast by the Met Office, a stiff easterly breeze sent clouds scudding intermittently across its face. Nothing else moved. With the wind from this quarter, any landing would have to be at Altarstanes bay, three hundred yards to the south-east. Our laser nightscopes would have no difficulty in picking out detail at that distance. Starlight was sufficient, even if the range had been half a mile.

But there was no need of artificial aid to eyesight at the moment. In the cold light of the moon even the bird droppings were visible on the timber floor of the old iron Bailey bridge below. The path from the bridge forked down to Altarstanes bay a hundred yards further on. Though the beach of the bay itself was hidden from our observation point, nothing could approach unseen by land or sea.

My earpiece squawked into life. 'Target Zero.'

Target Zero, our name for the ship dropping the drugs, was on its approach run. My earpiece wouldn't speak again until our quarry was in the bay. The signal had come from a member of the Rapid Reaction Force in heavy oiled jersey and yellow oilskins working the winch of one of the little fishing boats a mile distant. Target Zero, a silent moving shadow, would have suspiciously swept the fishing vessels' decks with its own nightscope before turning towards the drop zone.

The glittering interplay of moonlight and shadow on the sea

made it impossible, even fleetingly, to detect with the naked eye a small moving shape. But through my nightscope...yes, there it was, a powerful motor launch slipping up from the direction of Pilgrims' Haven, the only other possible landing place on this side of the island. Altarstanes or Pilgrims' Haven – the drop could have been at either. To ensure the drop was here at Altarstanes, *The Maid of the Forth* had been anchored off Haven's small beach. On board, masquerading as a wedding reception party, a lucky squad of the RRF had been noisily drinking and dancing for hours at the taxpayers' expense.

The smudge on my nightscope vanished as the cliffs folded round the outline of the launch. Cautiously, I shifted my position. Was it going to leave a yellow canister in the bay to mark the drop, or were Spinks's men already in position on the beach? Our spy on the high ground above the bay would—

'Meeting,' said the voice, tinny in my ear. Monosyllabic, the breaking of radio silence, minimum. But it told us all we needed to know.

'Go. Go. Go.' No excitement in the voice, just a level calm. Beside me dark shapes rose from the long grass and ran swiftly forward. I followed. Over the bridge, up a slight rise, onto the cliff top. They raced along the path down to the bay. I stopped. Orders. I was solely an observer. *They* were the experts in violent action.

From my vantage point behind the cover of a large boulder, I could see the narrow strip of beach and the outline of the launch, black against the moonlit waters. A muffled shout, a splash, the high-pitched scream of an engine as the launch tried to make its escape. A creaming wake as it turned in a tight circle and roared towards the entrance of the bay. White lights erupted in a sparkling necklace across that neck of water, as the RRF flotilla, no longer blacked-out, left their cover in the fishing fleet. The lights merged. Now the RRF were moving in for the kill.

Its engine howling in a mad bid for freedom, the launch raced forward. Momentarily silhouetted, then illuminated by powerful searchlights, it hurtled seawards. Over to the far left, there was a gap between the lights. The driver spun the wheel and took his chance.

The next moment, the reason for the gap in the lights became clear. With a screech of tortured metal and a crunch audible even to me on the cliff top, the nose of the launch reared skywards, as if escape lay that way. It hung there, then in a graceful slow motion back-flip, smashed beneath the surface. I shuddered. More deaths.

With the howl of the engine abruptly cut off, shouts and cries from the beach were sharp in the night air. By now, the searchlights from the line of approaching boats had illuminated the beach like a stage. A body, from the clothing not an RRF man, lay at the water's edge rolling lazily from side to side in the surge of the waves. The element of surprise seemed to have been complete. Below me a cluster of dark balaclava-clad figures were pinioning three men face down on the shingle. Two reports rang out over the bay. *Shots*. One of the RRF men catapulted backwards and lay motionless. The searchlights swung away to probe the cliffs, leaving my side of the beach in shadow. A heat-seeking device locked the light onto a jumble of boulders.

'*Customs. Immediate surrender required in ten seconds. Repeat. Immediate surrender required in ten seconds.*'

In the jumble of rocks, no movement.

'*Five seconds, four, three...*'

At *two seconds,* shouts from the rocks. I craned round the smooth sides of my boulder. Orange flame spurted from the shadows. *Pfftt.* One of the lights exploded. An answering shot sent up a puff of dust. Splinters of rock pattered like raindrops into the sea. Silence.

It was then I heard the scrape of a shoe, the faint rattle of a pebble, the rapid breathing of someone running up the path from the beach. One of the RRF? I'd play safe, anyway. I shrank back behind the boulder. Not having a weapon had its disadvantages.

The sounds were louder, more definite, very close now. I slid slowly down until I was flat on the ground. A face at that level should escape the notice of someone running desperately to evade capture. Or so I hoped. I snatched a look. The figure was little more than a silhouette against the glow from the beach below. But I'd seen enough. It was Spinks's unmistakable profile and crewcut.

Option – try to arrest a serial killer, though I was unarmed.

Option – follow him, and call in the cavalry as soon as possible.

Option – lie low, and inform control.

I didn't really *have* a choice. I would need to stick close to him to have any real chance of bringing him to book. But I could strengthen the odds in my favour. I activated the throat mike all of our party were wearing.

'DJS. Target Two heading south. Following.'

By now Spinks was more than a hundred yards ahead. In the bright moonlight it wasn't going to be easy to keep in contact without being seen. I started to run, ready to drop flat if he looked back.

He didn't look back. Speed seemed to be his overriding priority, and the noise he was making covered any I made. He was taking the upper track over high ground. When I was sure of his direction, I spoke into the mike. 'DJS. Heading to Main Light.'

The Main Light is quite distinctive, a square Victorian tower complete with gothic arched windows and battlements. You couldn't mistake it even in the dark. Adjoining it, a rectangular building housed the modern version of the old light, in the shape of a radio mast poking a needle finger into the night sky. My eyes struggled to adjust as racing clouds obscured the moon. I stopped, wary of tumbling headlong on the rough ground or falling into the small pond grandiosely designated on the map as *The Loch*.

Spinks's shadowy figure had merged with the dark mass of the buildings. My eyes weren't giving me any information, but my ears might. I closed my eyes to aid concentration. I tried to blank out the rustle of wind in the grass, the thump of my heart after that burst of running. Was that the sound of a door softly shutting? I opened my eyes and peered at the impenetrable blackness at the foot of the tower. Nothing. Had he gone to earth there till the Customs' operation was over and he could slip away unseen? Time to summon reinforcements.

Wheeep... From off to my right came the sharp startled cry of a sea bird. Had it been disturbed by Spinks as he made his escape down to the sea? Abruptly, like a light being switched on, moonlight flooded down once again. Out of the corner of my eye, I caught a flicker of movement against the whitewashed walls of an old tower perched on the cliff edge. I tried to visualise what I'd seen on my previous visit as camera-toting tourist. Beside the tower was a mini ravine leading down to a small dam and power station, below that, a narrow finger of sea with a funny name...Mill Door. I'd marked it on my map as 'Sighting of rare white-billed puffin'.

'DJS. Mill Door,' I said tersely into my mike. They'd know Target Two was attempting an escape by sea, and send a boat to cut him off. All I had to do was make sure that he didn't backtrack before they got here.

I headed down into the ravine. The walls rose up, cutting off the moonlight, but there was just enough reflected light from the sky to enable me to break into a swift trot. Noisier, yes, but I had to take another calculated risk. Spinks too would be concentrating on speed.

Now that I was clear of the shadow of the ravine I had no cover. But it was unlikely that eyes were watching. He wouldn't have gone to ground here. He'd be making for a boat tied up in the little inlet. Looming up in front of me was the concrete block of the power station. I hurried past and stopped abruptly.

Below me a long concrete ramp sloped down to the sea. My quarry was clambering into a powered inflatable moored to an iron ring. And the distance between us was as bare and as brightly lit as a mortuary slab. The outboard motor spluttered and died. He heaved at the cord again. I tensed myself to run forward with some desperate idea of waving wildly and shouting to distract him and gain time, I suppose. For the RRF to respond to that last signal, all I needed was five minutes. I didn't get them.

There was a whisper of sound behind me. An arm clamped itself round my neck, forcing my head roughly backwards. A voice, cold and deadly, said, 'Freeze!'

My muscles did exactly that. You don't argue when the sharp point of a knife is pressed against the side of your neck. Spinks hadn't looked back. Neither had I. It had been a fatal mistake. Fatal as in Death. Death in the next few seconds...for me. The arm tightened.

The instinct for self-preservation told me to struggle and scream. I did neither. Close proximity to death sharpens the mind wonderfully. I made myself go limp, closed my eyes, and sagged at the knees, letting my assailant's arm take the whole weight of my body. He gave a grunt of surprise, and the arm lock round my neck loosened slightly. But before I had time to work out my next move, the supporting arm was whipped away and a violent punch between the shoulders sent me sprawling winded on the rocky ground. I was dazedly aware of being roughly turned onto my back. A foot stood on my stomach, the knife-point again nicked my throat, and the balaclava was torn from my head.

The recognition was mutual. The Silent One, true to type, said nothing. Gasping for breath, and with a heavy boot pressing into my diaphragm, neither did I.

Suddenly he waxed loquacious. 'Seen you before.' Another press of the boot.

He stood up, keeping his foot in place, and half-turned his

head, looking past me off to my left. He seemed to be waiting for something.

I heard the scrape of a shoe, then Spinks's nasal twang. 'What is it, Al?'

The Silent One jerked his head in my direction. 'Spied on us coupla days ago.'

I had a worm's eye view of Spinks staring down at me. His eyes glinted as the moonlight caught his face. Despite the Silent One's attention to my solar plexus, my breathing was now capable of coherent speech. *Make it good! It may be the last thing you say.* I took as deep a breath as possible under the circumstances. I mustn't allow a tremble.

'Revenue and Customs, Mr Spinkssss.' The last word ended in a spluttered hiss as the Silent One transferred more weight to the foot on my diaphragm.

I clutched at his leg, digging in my nails in a desperate attempt to pull him off balance. Futile. My lungs laboured frantically to drag in air, but oxygen starvation drained me of strength in seconds, and I sank back limp and semi-conscious. Just as blackness rushed towards me, the weight lifted, allowing me to breathe normally again – if drawing in air in great gulps could be called normal. As I tried to lever myself up on an elbow, the Silent One applied his foot to my upper arm, pinning me to the ground. Spinks stood on my other arm. They looked down on me, considering for some moments.

'Kill her.' Spinks's voice was sharp, decisive, and unemotional. He could have been ordering a caddy to throw away a dud golf ball.

The Silent One nodded, his face blank, showing no

emotion. I stared up at him. How would he carry out Spinks's orders? Funny thing, looking into the eyes of my murderer, I wasn't paralysed with fear. My mental defence mechanism under stress had gone into overdrive. One part of my brain was coolly listing possible ways he could go about it. Knife. Foot on throat. Bullet. Skull bashed in... Another part of my brain was whining in querulous outrage, *What gives them the right to kill me, wipe me out with no more compunction than swatting an irritating fly?*

In a surge of anger the words came. 'I think you're making a *big* mistake, Mr Spinks.' My God, I sounded like a character in a bad B movie. All it needed was for him to say, 'I think not'.

Spinks smiled coldly. 'I think not.'

That did it. I couldn't help myself. Tension, I suppose. I giggled.

'You know what they say, guys. She who laughs last, laughs longest.' I smiled brightly up at them.

They looked at each other. Spinks removed his foot from my arm and at the same time snapped his fingers with a flicking gesture. The Silent One stepped off my other arm and hauled me roughly to my feet. As I staggered trying to regain my balance, he viciously twisted my right arm up behind my back and held me in a tight neck-lock. He turned me so that I faced Spinks.

'You've got thirty seconds to explain yourself before Al breaks your neck.' He sounded as if he couldn't wait for Al to begin.

Start with what they perceive to be the truth and the suckers will believe anything. It's the art of the con artist the world over. I looked him in the eye as best I could with my chin pointing skyward.

'I've got a throat mike. When I saw you leaving Altarstanes, I radioed in. It's been picking up everything I've been saying.' The pressure of Al's arm on my neck muffled my voice and made it difficult to breathe. 'Kept track *gasp* of your movements *gasp*. They know *gasp* you're here at *gasp* Mill Door *gasp* with an inflatable.'

Back at base they knew *now* about the inflatable.

Al's arm tightened cutting off my air. A roaring in my ears, a red haze before my eyes, I fell into blackness. Then I could breathe again as his arm lowered and held me across the top of my chest. As I sagged, desperately sucking in air, I felt fingers pulling open my jacket. I heard a grunt of satisfaction or perhaps surprise. A sharp pain sawed at the back of my neck before the mike cord snapped as the mike was torn off. Bait taken. Now for the hook.

'We've a cordon of Customs' boats all round the island,' I lied. 'You'll need me if you want to break through.' If you're going to tell a lie, it might as well be a quality one. 'I'm Deputy Controller, Revenue and Customs, Scotland.' It sounded impressive, anyway, and might buy me a little time. But I was under no illusions as to what Spinks had in mind for me. Even if he fell for this, once he'd made his escape, he'd get rid of me. He'd not even bother to stage one of his little 'accidents' to cover it up.

He stared at me. In the silence we all heard the faint hum of a powerful engine approaching from the direction of Altarstanes. Al's arm shifted back to a neck-lock as he awaited Spinks's order. Was it to be life? Or death? The hum had increased to a muffled roar, perceptibly nearer.

Spinks turned his head to listen. 'Get her down to the boat.' Without looking back, he hurried down the slope of the dam, confident in Al's ability to carry out his orders.

Al hustled me forward, taking silent pleasure in giving my arm an agonising jerk whenever I slowed or stumbled. Though I'd gained those precious minutes of life, I had to admit that the outlook didn't look too promising. Deborah J Smith was definitely not a good risk on the books of a life insurance salesman.

As we reached the inflatable, the engine spluttered once, twice, and caught. Al gave my arm a vicious upward twist. A searing pain arced through me so fiercely that I was barely aware that he had released his grip. My shoulder and upper arm were on fire, but from the elbow down I felt only a curious throbbing numbness. I became aware of the knife pricking again, this time between the vertebrae of my lower back.

'Get in and lie down on the floor.' The tone was expressionless, casual, the underlying message clear. *Do what you are told, or this knife will sever your spinal cord.* I did what I was told.

The boat rocked as Al clambered in. A foot pressed on my kidneys, forcing my face hard against the damp, cold duckboard slats. This position as a floor mat severely limited my outlook. Even when I twisted my head round at an almost neck-dislocating angle, I could see very little, only a wedge of night sky above the bulging sides of the boat. Face down, and pinioned to the floor as I was by Al's size 12s, it was hardly going to be a case of 'in one bound I was free'.

'*Do something before it's too late*!' screamed a panicky little voice inside me. If I could suddenly heave myself up to my knees...butt Spinks with my head, catch him off balance, knock him overboard...fling myself into the sea before Al could recover from his surprise...

Slowly, slowly, I bent my elbows. Calculating. They would be looking ahead, watchful for the first sign of the forces of Law and Order. So if I avoided any rapid movement...levered myself up... I tensed my arm muscles. *Now.*

'Quit that.' Al delivered a sharp blow to my right elbow bone of such searing intensity that a wave of nausea welled up, leaving me gasping for breath. A warning kick to my ribs followed.

I closed my eyes and concentrated on quelling the pain-induced retching. Fantasising over plans of escape definitely took lower priority than the prospect of lying with my face in vomit. It's a funny thing about the human brain. It can deal properly with only one set of incoming signals at a time. So while all my attention was focused on my heaving stomach, the pain in my elbow was little more than a background throb.

Spthash! Half the ocean flung itself into my face. I hardly had time to blink my eyes clear, before more water splatted over the side of the boat. My brain forgot about the nausea and started analysing this new data. Bigger waves. That meant we had left the shelter of the land. Which way were we heading? *Think.* Whether he had believed me or not about the cordon of boats, Spinks wouldn't have headed north towards Altarstanes and the approaching launch. And he hadn't headed straight out to sea, because up till now we had been in sheltered waters. So he must have gone south. I had no idea how much time had passed since we had set off from Mill Door, but the rougher sea meant we were nearing the tip of the island – and Pilgrims' Haven.

For the first time since Al had hooked me round the neck, I felt a flicker of hope. If we were still close inshore, the inflatable would pass across the mouth of the Haven. And anchored in that small bay was *The Maid of the Forth* with its exuberantly partying RRF. I might be able to hear the blare of their music blasting out to ensure their presence was well and truly advertised.

I strained to hear above the roar of the outboard. Nothing. I squinted upwards at the silhouette of Spinks. There was no tension, no indication of a sudden awareness of possible danger. A niggle of doubt threatened to snuff out that flicker of hope. Maybe we weren't heading south. I stared up at him again with my one available eye. But the moon had set or gone behind a cloud. He was only an indistinct dark mass against the stars.

We *must* be approaching Pilgrims' Haven. Or even have passed it. The flicker of hope died. No music. There was definitely no music. I'd been clutching at straws. Once the RRF on *The Maid of the Forth* had heard the go-ahead for the raid at Altarstanes, they'd have packed up and headed back to port. They'd performed their function. Once Spinks was clear of the island and any sign of pursuit, he'd dump me overboard as casually as a litter lout throwing a cigarette pack out of a car window or a beer can into the harbour. So this was it, then.

Th, th, th, th – th – th – It took several seconds to register the sudden silence as the outboard engine stuttered and cut out.

'*Holyssshit*.' Spinks flicked the starter switch impatiently. The engine roared for a couple of seconds – and died.

Did I dare to let that little glimmer of hope rekindle? If our fuel tank was empty, there was a good chance that the RRF launch I'd heard approaching from Altarstanes would catch us up. And then...

Click. A lighter's flame flickered shadows over Spinks's arm. Al's voice said, 'Half a tank of gas.'

Off to the right, a burst of Scottish dance music erupted. A few seconds later, it was abruptly cut off as if by a closing door. I heard a woman's high-pitched laugh, two voices raised in a raucous duet. *The Maid of the Forth*. It must be, but I couldn't tell how close.

'Goddamn electrics must be wet!' The boat rocked as Spinks leant over and fumbled with something out of my field of vision. 'For Chris'sake grab the oar while I dry them out. We're drifting towards that goddamned ship.'

If only I could *see* something other than boots and the side of the boat. Even the patch of sky had been blotted out as Spinks and Al shifted position. What were my chances of attracting *The Maid of the Forth*'s attention?

Nil. Al anticipated me. As I filled my lungs in preparation for a good loud scream, my head was jerked back and a foul-tasting oily rag was stuffed into my mouth.

'Move to take it out and I'll break your arm.' He performed a trial demonstration on my left arm, twisting it back and up.

To scream you have to be able to take in a gulp of air. My scream of pain came out as a muffled whine that wouldn't have been heard a couple of yards away. Pain, rage, fear and a grudging admiration for Al's efficiency battled for ascendancy.

'OK, that's it.' I heard the rattle of metal as the engine cover was replaced.

Don't let it start. Don't let it start. The pursuing Customs cutter had a good chance of catching up if our engine wouldn't fire.

It fired.

'Guess that's fixed it.'

The steady beat swelled to a roar as Spinks revved experimentally. The boat surged forward.

Without warning, the engine cut out again and we jerked violently to a halt. *Whoomph.* The breath was knocked out of my lungs, as Al landed on top of me.

'In a spot of trouble, there? Want a hand?' The words, slightly slurred, carried clearly on the night air from *The Maid of the Forth*. Tantalisingly close.

I eased my neck round and squinted upwards. Clouds had obscured the moon and stars. Spinks loomed above me, a silent bulk. In the distance, we could all hear the steady hum of the approaching cutter.

A woman's voice giggled, 'They've come to join the party, Jim. Letsh invite them aboard. Need some new talent.' A shriek of laughter.

Spinks stooped down, leant over the side for a long moment. 'Some kind of plastic trash seems to have tangled with the shaft.'

A coarse hiccup bounced across the water. 'No need to be like that, Jim. Of coursh they want to come. Go on, ashk them,' slurred the woman's voice again, pouting, sulky.

Al levered himself upright by jabbing his elbow into my kidneys. 'Drunken assholes. I'll—'

'Can it, Al! Cut the prop free from all this garbage.' Spinks's voice was low, urgent.

'*Oh, ye'll tak the high road and I'll tak the low road,*' came warbling slightly off-key from *The Maid of the Forth*.

A new voice broke in, 'Hey there, guys! Great ceilidh here, don't miss out on it. Lots of booze and women!' Another few bars fortissimo of 'The Bonnie Banks of Loch Lomond' assaulted the eardrums. 'Hold on! We'll come and get you. Won't be a jiff!'

The cavalry were coming to the rescue. Elation. Euphoria. But were they overdoing it, laying it on a bit too thick?

'For Chris'sake, hurry it up, Al. We're in trouble if these drunken bastards get across here.'

Al grunted a reply. They were leaning out over the back of the boat, neither of them paying attention to me. I'd never get a better opportunity. My left arm was still paralysed from Al's attentions. My right arm was pinned against the side of the boat. I tried a cautious tilt sideways to free it. Yes, could do. Once I'd made my move, I'd only have seconds. It was the last chance I'd ever have.

I made a lunge for the rubber bung – pull, or twist? *Pull*...

Solid as a rock, it didn't budge an inch. I twisted desperately at the bung. Another twist, my sweaty fingers slipping...

'What the f—?' Al put a foot on my back, grabbed a handful of my hair and wrenched my head backwards. The knife in his hand slashed down at my fingers.

I felt a searing pain and a spurt of wet against my throat. But a cold, not warm, wetness. Before I could analyse the implication, the boat rocked violently, and my face fell forward into *water*. I was drowning, my nose full of water, mouth stuffed with a foul oily rag, air supply abruptly cut off. Fuelled by panic, I tensed my right arm, drew my knees under me and with superhuman strength, heaved my head and shoulders upward.

I was dimly aware of a splash and Spinks shouting. I half spat, half clawed the evil-tasting rag from my mouth and flung myself sideways, throwing up an arm to ward off Al's follow-up attack.

It didn't come. No slashing knife. Indeed, no Al. Only Spinks, backlit by a powerful searchlight, clutching the engine cowling and staring at me open-mouthed.

A shout of 'Revenue and Customs'. Under cover of all those Scottish reels the cutter had approached unheard.

The dance music shut off abruptly. In the sudden silence, Al splashed and threshed frenziedly on the other side of the rubber gunwale. Suddenly, he rose from the deep, arm flailing, knife still clutched in his hand. The blade flashed in the beam of light. Descended. Razor edge sliced down.

Whuuush. A section of the inflatable collapsed like a soufflé that had caught a chill. Al's contorted face appeared, only to sink out of sight. The knife glinted and fell again. *Whuuush*. Like some frightful monster of the deep, or a rerun of a Hitchcock film, Al reared in the gap. Drowning. His eyes locked onto mine. In them I read death, his death – and mine. He wasn't going to go quietly into the dark. He intended to take me with him.

Pwhit. The knife slashed into the floor a couple of inches from my outstretched hand. As the knife rose for the fourth time, I scrabbled onto hands and knees and flung myself backwards over the side. I caught a glimpse of Spinks's arm outstretched, frozen into immobility, then the cold waters closed over my head.

CHAPTER TWENTY-THREE

Al's dark eyes stared at me, his lips pulled back in a silent snarl. Even in death he had the power to chill. I let the sheet fall back over his face. I wondered if Macleod had noticed the tremor in my hand.

'That's him.' With a nonchalance that didn't fool Macleod for one moment, I turned away.

He nodded to the mortuary attendant. The man pushed back the sheet. Looped round Al's wrist was a white plastic tag.

Macleod flicked a finger at the label. 'Alberto Pettrini, a nasty piece of work. We took his prints and got an ID on him from the lads in New York. There's a Mafia connection. He's one of their heavy mob.'

I've never found it easy to stand in a mortuary and look at a dead body. But by concentrating on the clinically impersonal stainless steel and harsh shadowless lighting, I can control the nausea welling up in me. No, it's not the body itself, or the mark of violence on it that brings the rush of bile to my throat. It's the little reminders that the lifeless flesh on the metal table had once been an individual like myself, with vanities, hopes and fears like my own – the dark undyed roots of blonde hair, the painted toenails, the plaster on the finger.

In Al's case it was the black crescent-shaped mark on a fingernail. A toe on my right foot bore a similar mark where it had intercepted a tin from Gorgonzola's larder.

'Lucky for you he never learnt to swim.' Macleod's voice reached me from a distance.

His comment steadied me. Al had been a killer, cold and ruthless. He would have dispatched his victims with just about as much emotion as... I searched for an apt comparison...a mortuary attendant tagging a corpse.

I turned away from the sheeted body. 'Even luckier that the inflatable broke down where it did.'

Macleod shot me a quick glance. 'It wasn't a question of luck. When they heard you were heading their way, the RRF boys laid out a plastic line at propeller level between *The Maid* and a buoy.'

My recollection of the episode was disjointed, hazy, chaotic – the heart-stopping shock of sudden immersion in cold water, lungs bursting, then the sweet inhalation of night air. I remember screwing my eyes shut against blinding lights playing over an inky sea, swimming desperately for the nearest boat, water closing over my head again, fighting for breath...choking...then smooth grey metal blotting out the stars, rough hands pulling at my arms, the bone-jarring impact on the metal deck...retching, gasping...hands rolling me over onto my side.

Al hadn't been so lucky. One last Excalibur-like appearance of his knife glinting in the beam of the searchlight, and with this virtuoso re-enactment of *Morte d'Arthur*, it was all over. By the time they'd picked me up there was no sign of him.

There was no sign of Spinks either. Out of the range of the

cutter's searchlight, the few hundred yards to the shore would have been a relatively easy swim. I had a gut feeling that in the darkness and confusion he had made good his escape.

Macleod seemed to be able to read my thoughts. 'We're still searching for the body of the Spinks fellow. He *might* just have managed to get away, of course.' From his tone he didn't seem to think it likely.

'Mmm,' I said non-committally.

'Not convinced?' Macleod raised an eyebrow. 'Though we fished this one out after six hours, it can take some time for a body to surface – depends on what they've had for their last meal. I believe curry's a good resurrectionist.'

'Er...?' I said.

'For raising the dead. Gases, you know. Maybe he hadn't eaten for some time.'

As the doors of the mortuary closed behind us, I caught my last glimpse of the Silent One. Silent for all time, his sheeted form was being filed away in a refrigerated drawer.

After tidying up a few loose ends for those obsessive form-fillers in Records, and filing my report on the case for Head Office, that was that. Operation Scotch Mist wound up. They expected me back at my desk on Monday. I thought about claiming injury time, pleading incapacity for wounds received in the course of duty, but aching arms, multiple bruising and a couple of taped-up fingers from Al's knife would be greeted with derisive grins. I had to admit that after a quick rasp of the tongue and curious sniff, even Gorgonzola had appeared to show little concern, her way of underlining her displeasure that I'd once again abandoned her overnight.

One person gratifyingly took note of my delicate condition – Jim Ewing. He gave me a hand down the stairs with the *Yours* and *Mine* holdalls and stowed them in the boot. Once again, he was the soul of discretion and refrained from commenting on my battered appearance.

I turned my attention to Gorgonzola, who had already taken up position on the back seat. 'An artist has to take care of her paws, G,' I said as I clipped her into the special harness. If I had to brake sharply, there would be no repetition of that nose-dive when we had first arrived at the White Heather Hotel.

'Come back any time. B&B free of charge on production of a Cat Art masterpiece.' He slammed down the boot lid and stood on the doorstep waving. Through the open door behind him, hanging in pride of place on the wall, was G's red, blue and white oeuvre, *Sun Sinking in the Forests of Siberia*.

So, here I was with some free time on my hands. We'll give you a whole weekend, they had said generously, but that would be barely enough time to drive the four hundred miles back to London without blowing the head-gasket of my old banger. I might as well go by the tourist route, see the sights, wind down. I'd leave Edinburgh by the A1, drive past the White Heather Hotel for old times' sake, and make for Newcastle. Then I planned a detour to squint at the Roman Wall before heading for Durham and its cathedral. I'd spend the night in York and…well, after that it would depend on the weather…

A few fluffy clouds dotted the brilliant blue sky. A warm breeze blew in the open sun-roof and ruffled my hair as we bowled along the southern shore of the Firth of Forth. There was no sign today of that clammy haar I'd come to associate with this part of the east coast. I drove, and Gorgonzola lounged in the sun, eyes tightly shut and tail twitching gently.

I jabbed at the radio button in search of some soothing mood music.

'...a light onshore breeze with a high of 20 degrees.' The local radio station's short jingle followed, then, 'Looks like it's going to be *per*fect for the first day of the Scottish Golf Championship at Muirfield.' The background music swelled into a discordant heavy beat. Hastily, I jabbed at another button. That was more like it – smooth, classical, tuneful. I screwed up my eyes against the glare from the road. Even with the visor down, the sun was really bright. The traffic was heavier than I expected, most of it going in the same direction as me. It was the weekend, of course, and a sunny day. They'd be making for the long stretches of beach between North Berwick and Longniddry. The sand dunes at Longniddry... *I* hadn't enjoyed my visit there, but on a day like today and with no one stalking me and intent on murder...

The car in front slowed to a halt behind a long line of queuing traffic. There was no point in getting stressed, drumming the fingers on the wheel, that sort of thing. This was much more pleasant than being stuck in a London traffic jam. I hummed along to the music on the radio and thought about Spinks... If he had escaped, where would he go to ground? I'd no clue at all. He probably *had* drowned, after all. Why let it niggle at me? Better to draw a line under it and move on.

I peered ahead at an AA notice, the black lettering stark against the yellow background. *SCOTTISH GOLF*

CHAMPIONSHIP MUIRFIELD. Below that, an angled arrow pointed off left, *1 MILE.* What if Spinks *was* still alive? He'd feel safe, wouldn't he, with everybody thinking he was dead? And a golf fanatic would be drawn to this championship like a moth to a candle flame. I felt the excitement building up in me. Then, like a drench of cold water, came the depressing thought that to take a detour to Muirfield would just be a wild goose chase, three or four hours wasted. And if I wanted to visit York, I'd have to miss out on the Roman Wall, and probably Durham Cathedral too. The marker for the junction crept slowly nearer. The car in front turned off left. I'd have to decide. Should I? Shouldn't I? I signalled left.

Within five minutes I was regretting my decision. Trapped in a nose-to-tail line of cars, progress was now a series of long stops and short starts, making my previous snail's pace rocket-propelled in comparison. The sun beat down on the roof. I lowered the window and drew in a lungful of carbon monoxide. Hastily, I pressed the window-up button. My fingers drummed a tattoo on the steering wheel. Bad sign.

I became aware of a petulant scratching on the back of my seat. Another bad sign. Fur coats and high temperatures don't make for happy owners. Gorgonzola had lost her cool in more ways than one, and was indicating that she wanted out of this oven *now*.

'Not long, G,' I said soothingly.

We crept round the next sharp bend. Smooth stretches of grass with strategically placed sandy bunkers swept down to the road on either side. Red and yellow flags fluttered in the stiff sea breeze on billiard-like greens. All this naturally led me to believe the end to the slow crawl was...well, just round the corner.

Wrong. The line of cars stretched interminably ahead. What on earth had possessed me to act on that crack-brained impulse to check for Spinks? I could have been walking on the Roman Wall by now, taking my ease, drink in hand, at some country pub...

Fifteen frustrating minutes later, I made it slowly into Gullane, a small town of grey stone houses. I found myself opposite another yellow AA notice indicating a route to an official car park. The vehicles in front veered sharply left and I swung after them. Houses of elaborate Thirties design sporting white-painted wooden verandas peeped over high walls and hedges, exclusive and excluding. In the distance the sea sparkled and glinted, in the foreground, a vast expanse of short-cropped grass served as a giant car park. Deliverance was in sight.

Well, it was and it wasn't. Ten cars ahead, a sweating red-faced marshal was orchestrating the parking. With exaggerated sweeping motions, like a portly businessman misplaced in an aerobics class, he directed cars to their designated positions. Suddenly, he slapped a hand down on the bonnet of the car four places ahead of me. His arm shot out dramatically, pointing off to the right. The word 'overflow' drifted towards me on the breeze. The thwarted red 4x4 roared off down a bumpy sandy track between head-high prickly bushes. The rest of us crawled meekly after him, nursing our suspension over the bumps and potholes.

Exactly one hour after my mad decision to go in search of a dead man, the car came to rest at Muirfield, the home of the

Honourable Company of Edinburgh Golfers. I released
Gorgonzola from her harness, and, with doors and windows
open, sat there letting the breeze waft over me. G trickled over
the sill like marmalade spilling out of a jar and flopped, a hot
and sticky orange blob, under the nearest bush. All around,
car doors slammed, voices called. I levered myself stiffly out
and stood flexing my leg muscles. Now that I was here, I
might as well get on with it. I reached back into the car and
rummaged in my bag for a mug shot of Spinks that Macleod
had managed to winkle out of the NYPD. Leaving
Gorgonzola to look after herself in the shrubbery, I locked up
the car and followed the crowd.

I don't know what I was expecting. Perhaps an imposing
wrought-iron gateway with golf clubs rampant or passant,
picked out in gold leaf. The entrance to the Honourable
Company's grounds looked nothing like that. Beneath the
banner advertising the Championship was a rather
insignificant gate adorned with a brief notice, plain and
plainspoken, *This is a private golf club. No admittance.* A bit
of a disappointment, really. I had more than enough time to
study its non-existent finer points as I queued with a couple of
thousand others to hand over a fortune in return for my
ticket. I wouldn't be able to claim this on expenses, unless a
miracle happened and a resurrected Hiram J Spinks rose from
his watery grave.

Never having been to a Championship Match before, I had
no idea what to do next. Maybe I'd get some help from the fat
booklet that came with the ticket. *History of Muirfield...
1744...oldest golf club in the world... Rules of the Club...
Ladies are permitted to play provided they are accompanied*

in play by a gentleman... How was that for political correctness! I thumbed on through the glossy pages... *Open Championships held at Muirfield have been the Ryder Cup, Walker Cup, Curtis Cup*...all very impressive.

The map of the course looked a bit like a microscope slide of some deadly virus – the greens were pale green squiggles on a darker green background, the bunkers picked out in sandy beige. I skimmed through the accompanying description. *Hole 1. The most difficult opening hole in Scotland... Hole 2. Innocent looking but treacherous... Hole 4. Short hole but uphill...menacing bunkers... Hole 5. Elevated position. Magnificent views to Edinburgh and Fife... 16 bunkers...* If I found the golf boring, I suppose I could view the scenery. Maybe from that hole I'd even spot the yellow-checked cap of Hiram J Spinks!

From where I was standing in front of the rambling stone clubhouse – Victorian pavilion-style, all white wood and red-tiled roof – I could see the whole course laid out before me, as in the booklet's double spread map, and round each green, a small horseshoe of people. The loud speaker behind me boomed, 'Players 7 and 8 will be teeing off in five minutes.' That's where I'd start. Hole 1.

I paid no attention to the man beside me at first. I was too busy scanning the crowd.

'Security are you, then?' the words were muttered in my ear.

Startled, I glanced sideways. He stood there at my elbow, ginger-headed, angular, a huge blue and green golfing umbrella hooked over one arm. Just one of two hundred others clustered round the hole.

'I couldn't help noticing the way you're looking at the crowd. You didn't even see that bit of action there, did you?' His Adam's apple moved up and down his throat like a yo-yo on its string.

I watched fascinated. It was huge, as if, when his mouth was open, a golf ball had flown through the air and lodged in his throat.

'There's a lot of famous names here today. And a lot of weirdos about. I suppose you've memorised all their faces from their mug shots? Well, am I right?' He didn't wait for a reply. 'Have you a—' he paused and lowered his voice furtively, '—a *name*?'

'Smith,' I said out of the corner of my mouth.

A shadow of disappointment crossed his face.

I couldn't resist it. 'Well,' I whispered, looking theatrically around to make sure nobody was listening, 'I'm also known as S.'

He tapped the side of his nose knowingly and winked. ''Nuff said! Mum's the word!'

I stared at him, fascinated. He not only looked like a character from a television comedy, he talked like one too.

The two players, their caddies and most of the crowd, had melted away. My turn to ask a question. 'Where's everyone gone?'

The blue and green umbrella was raised to the horizontal position till its tip pointed along the fairway. 'The ball landed in the left-hand bunker. They're all off to see the fun. We might be in time to catch some of it.' He loped off towards the distant knot of people.

I hesitated. I'd pictured myself going from hole to hole

scanning the faces – maybe an hour's work. I hadn't realised the crowd would change so much, some remaining at a particular hole, some following their favourites round the course. I would have to enlist my odd companion's help. Two legs good, four legs definitely better.

I caught up with him at the bunker. Somehow he'd managed to infiltrate to the front row of onlookers, but when I tried to join him, backs, shoulders, elbows and craning heads formed an impenetrable barrier. When brute force fails, guile has to take its place.

'First Aid! Need to get through!' I invested as much urgency into my voice as if a disaster of spectacular magnitude had occurred. Reluctantly, but instinctively, the crowd parted, and I slipped to the front.

Ginger Head or Adam, as I had privately named him after his most distinctive feature, acknowledged my arrival with a sideways glance and a conspiratorial wink. It seemed that I had arrived at a critical moment. With all the deference of an attentive butler, a caddy was handing a club to a harassed-looking player.

'Sandwiches are no good.' Adam's voice was gloomy.

Sandwiches? I glanced at him, startled. Was this a password? Some sort of coded message to which I was expected to give the response, 'Cake is better'?

Just before I opened my mouth to make a complete fool of myself, the Adam's apple gave a convulsive jerk. 'No, he shouldn't be using a sand wedge. Much better with a long iron.' The ginger head nodded sagely.

I choked back the phrase I'd been about to utter. Instead, I said, my tone heavy with meaning, 'I'd like to talk to you.'

His attention remained riveted on the play. 'Whatever it is, S, it'll have to wait till he's sorted this one out.'

A puff of sand spurted up. A sigh rose from the spectators as the ball did a jiggly little dance on the lip of the bunker, then trickled back, leaving a long flattened trail on the neatly raked sand. The player and his caddy went into a huddle. Another club was pulled out of the bag.

'Told you!' Adam said triumphantly.

A short smooth swing, an audible *snick* as the club made contact, and the ball soared from the sand and rejoined the fairway.

At the green, while we watched the putting, I tried again.

'When I said I'd like to talk to you, I meant professionally.'

'Shh!' he hissed, bony finger on lips. I thought he was about to launch into cloak and dagger mode again, but he jerked his head towards the players. 'Mustn't speak while they're concentrating on their putting. Bad form.'

The red-shirted golfer hunched over the ball. He made several trial putts. Then *click*. The ball rolled wide of the hole and finished up a yard or so behind it.

Adam sucked air noisily through his teeth. 'Too much force and didn't allow for the slope.'

Red-shirt launched into a repeat of the putting pantomime. A sympathetic sigh rose from the crowd as his next putt stopped well short of the hole.

'Overcompensating.' Adam sniffed disparagingly.

It wasn't till red-shirt had lost the hole and we were regrouping round the players at hole 2 that I finally managed to corner my companion's attention.

'Your country needs *you*,' I whispered, investing the stirring words with all the overblown drama of the spymaster in a cheap B movie.

His head snapped round.

'Yes, the operation here has international implications, A.' I paused and looked at him searchingly. '*Can* I call upon you, A?'

His eyes bulged. 'How did you know my name was—?'

I placed a finger to my lips. 'No names. We're the *Secret* Service.'

The golf ball in his throat danced up and down.

'Well, A?'

I held my breath, my stock of clichés almost exhausted.

'I'm your man, S.' His eyes gleamed with suppressed excitement. 'Is it a Snatch?'

'I'm not at liberty to say. But have a look at this.' I whipped out the mug shot of Spinks. 'Here's the man we're looking for. Tall, skinny. Favours loud checked caps. We've had a tip-off that he's going to turn up here. He's a *very* dangerous customer. On no account is he to be approached.' I consulted the map. 'I'll nip across to hole 17 and from there I can cover holes 16 and 15. You work forward from hole 3. If you spot him,' I glanced up at the sky, still deep blue with only the barest trace of cloud and no chance of rain, 'signal with your umbrella. Raise your brolly and open and shut it two or three times.'

Adam took the photo of Spinks, devouring it with avid eyes. 'Right, S. I've a good memory for faces. If he comes my way, he'll not slip by.'

A man with a mission, his angular figure merged with the crowd now trooping off in the direction of the green at hole

2. I felt a prick of conscience. What if he *should* stumble across Spinks? What if he indulged in some flamboyant spy-catching behaviour that attracted unwelcome attention and perhaps a bullet? Had my little game of clichés from the world of 007 put him in mortal danger?

It was too late to call him back now. In any case, there was only a snowball's chance in hell of Spinks being around. No, I'd never see that blue and green umbrella raised as a signal.

But I did. On the edge of my vision, a way off at the 5th tee. Held aloft and opening and closing three times.

If I was still talking in clichés, I'd say that my heart missed a beat. Could he be mistaken? 'I've a good memory for faces. If he comes my way, he'll not slip by,' he'd said. My throat felt suddenly dry. It looked like mission accomplished. I'd have to make sure, of course, before I called out Macleod and his boys.

It was easy enough to get to tee 5 from the hole at 14, easy enough, but it took time. I had to wait till the players at hole 3 were on the green so that I could pass behind the encircling crowd. Then it was a case of darting round the unoccupied tee 4, before trotting the hundred yards to where the umbrella had signalled discreetly above the shoulders of the crowd. I arrived just as the players were preparing to drive off.

What I hadn't taken into account, if I tracked down Spinks, was the scaffolding erected for the television coverage of the event. Bulky black cameras perched vulture-like on tall platforms, ready to swoop on their prey. And everywhere, men with shoulder-mounted cameras accompanied bands of commentators roaming the ground like cartoon Martians, each sporting a cap sprouting a mini-aerial, and earnestly, urgently, murmuring into their microphones. The commotion accompanying an arrest, a mob of armed police rushing onto the course interrupting play, would all be on live television. The thought brought me out in a cold sweat. I took a deep breath. First things first. Establish beyond doubt the identity of the man fingered by the brolly.

Adam's head was swivelling like a meerkat on lookout as he kept tabs on his quarry and at the same time searched for me. When he saw me, he raised his eyebrows and rolled his eyes, inclining his head and the brolly to the left, holding that position as a gun dog points at a downed pheasant. It was sheer bad luck that at that moment play was held up for some golfing technicality or other. Eyes, that a minute before had been riveted on the competitors, now roved around for some other point of interest. And what was more interesting than a man with a crick in his neck looking as if he was auditioning for a living statue competition? I was the only one approaching the tee across the rough, in direct line with Adam. Anybody looking at him couldn't fail to see me.

There was nothing I could do about it. I scanned the faces. *And there Spinks was*, shock in his eyes. A jolt like an electric current ran through me as our gaze met. Away to the right in the direction of hole 12, a burst of applause broke out for someone bringing off a difficult shot or winning the hole. Around me, another world away, voices murmured, faint, indistinct.

'Mission accomplished, S.' Adam swung his brolly off his shoulder and planted the tip firmly in the ground in a symbolic gesture of victory.

At precisely the same moment, I leapt forward. I don't

know what I had in mind. Place a heavy hand on Spinks's shoulder shouting, 'You're under arrest'? Wrestle him to the ground then sit on his head? I never found out. My spring turned into an inelegant nose-dive as my foot executed a fancy tango with Adam's umbrella. With a cry he crashed to the turf, landing on top of me with bone-jarring impact. Groggily, I tottered to my feet. Spinks hadn't stood around politely waiting for us to disentangle ourselves. He had disappeared.

The *thwack* of club meeting ball caused the crowd to lose interest in us. They pressed forward round the tee, heads craning for a better view. I tried to elbow my way through. Not a hope. The detour round their backs cost valuable seconds. I glanced to right and left. A couple of yards of grass separated the fairway from a stony path running parallel with the course. Of Hiram J Spinks there was no sign at all.

Heavy breathing behind me heralded the arrival of a chastened Adam. Before he could launch into a long-winded apology, I scribbled Macleod's number on the back of my Championship booklet and thrust it into his hands.

'Get to a phone and call reinforcements, A.' I slipped into B movie mode, knowing that this would be guaranteed to galvanise him into action. 'Give them the code words *Operation Scotch Mist*. Tell them to bring dogs and set up roadblocks.'

'Got it, S.' He scurried off. When it came to a choice between golf and espionage, there was no contest.

To the right, the path provided no cover for a couple of hundred yards. If Spinks had gone that way, he would still be in sight. But to the left, a smaller grassy track branched off through a dense clump of sea buckthorn and conifers. A weather-beaten notice indicated *Path to Gullane village*. He'd have to get back to his car. And that would be parked near the village. I broke into a run.

With an impenetrable barrier of head-high buckthorn on either side, I raced along. He couldn't be far ahead. After a couple of minutes, I was faced with a decision – take the narrow twisting path through the buckthorn, or the broader track through a dense growth of conifers? I hesitated. There was no point in plunging on in the wrong direction. The thump of my feet on the hard ground had drowned out any other sound. Now, off to my right, above my laboured breathing, I could make out the distant soft swish of waves on the shore. I listened for the sound of running footsteps ahead. Nothing. Through the buckthorn, or through the conifers? *Which?* Speed was the priority, for both of us... I turned down the broader track.

My feet sank into a soft carpet of old pine needles, fallen cones crunching underfoot, in my nostrils the earthy smell of damp soil overlaid by the scent of pine resin. In the struggle for light, the trees had shed all greenery except for their topmost branches. Black cones hung from their dead limbs in funereal decoration, and the occasional splotch of pale filtering sunlight only accentuated the gloom. Even at midday, under that thick canopy, it was perpetual twilight. Spooky, definitely spooky. The path twisted, turned, so that I could see only a few yards ahead. Reluctantly, I slowed my pace. A twisted ankle would put paid to any pursuit.

At last the trees thinned out. Here and there, where the light was stronger, patches of moss, startlingly green on the bare ground, had gained a precarious foothold. Now there was a perceptible incline to the path. The trees ended abruptly, and I found myself staring at the top of a low hill, its flanks clothed in impenetrable scrub.

The narrowing path zigzagged its way upward, the scrub giving way to thick-leaved grasses studded with thistles. Sand under my feet indicated that I'd reached the dune barrier behind the beach. The sound of the unseen sea was very close. At the top of the dune I stopped for a moment to catch my breath. I'd have the best chance of spotting him from this vantage point, but there was still no sign of a fleeing figure. *Shit*. Had I chosen the wrong path?

Another row of grassy sand-hills stretched ahead. A way off to the left, some kind of hunting bird hovered near the ground. Below me was a valley of blue-green buckthorn laced by a network of paths, any of which could have been his escape route. It was impossible to tell where any of those paths led. They might just circle and peter out. I tried to put myself in his shoes. *I'd* make for the shore and a sure line of escape.

I plunged downward into the valley, then on faltering legs panted to the top of the next thirty-foot dune. Out at sea, a bright red oil tanker snailed its way up the Forth past the blue-grey hills of Fife. Then, behind me, *chkk chkk chkk chkk*. With a chattering cry, a bird fluttered up from a clump of stunted pines just visible over the shoulder of a neighbouring dune.

If Spinks *had* gone to ground there, it would be fatal to make a direct approach. I'd have to use the buckthorn as cover and infiltrate from the rear. I slithered down a narrow sandy gully, digging my heels deep into the soft sand. Wincing as fierce thorns tore at my clothes and hands, I fought my way through the bushes. On the edge of the thicket, I lay flat and squinted through the tangle of twiggy branches.

In my battle through the buckthorn I'd overshot my target. The pines were still on my right, but behind me. I'd come out high above a large bay of greenish blue water. White waves curled crisply onto golden sand, a dream scene from a holiday brochure.

I sucked at a long scratch oozing blood on the back of my hand. I couldn't face the torture of the buckthorn again. A few yards away, a sandy path twisted and turned through some scrubby bushes. I'd follow that track down and cut along the narrow beach where it would be easy going. Any figure hurrying along the beach would be visible for miles in either direction.

Halfway down the track, I slowed to manoeuvre past an overhanging bramble. A defiant tendril whipped out and latched onto my sock. I bent down to unhook it, and froze, hand outstretched. In the smooth powdery sand were deep impressions. Impressions of footprints, sand *still trickling into the hollows*.

Something hard thudded onto the nape of my neck. The blue sky turned black, my knees buckled and I felt myself falling...sinking into the soft sand. A sensation of sliding, sliding...

Perhaps if I opened my eyes I could... I could what? Can't remember...it doesn't matter. *Yes it does*. Why? Don't know...sliding...floating on my back down a sandy river just like Ophelia. She sang as she drowned, didn't she? What should I sing? Can't think of any...

A jab of pain as my back and shoulders bumped on riverbed... My clothes were wet now. Wet clothes are – heavy, aren't they?

...garments, heavy with their drink
Pulled the poor wretch from her melodious lay
To muddy death...

Muddy water...no, salty water...floating, floating...sun warm on my face...

I was aware of a flickering shadow against my closed eyelids. A voice thick with menace grated, 'Those who try to get one over on Hiram J Spinks don't live to regret it. You've messed with me once too often, sucker.'

Hands were beneath me, lifting, rolling me over onto my face. I was swallowing water...choking...choking...

Too much of water hast thou, poor Ophelia
Alas, then she is drown'd
Drown'd, drown'd...

EPILOGUE

The Lazarus syndrome, I think they call it, better known as the Near Death or Out of Body Experience. Black void. A long dark tunnel. A bright light at the end. Warmth, peace, quiet. The sensation of looking down from a great height...I had it all.

Quite interesting, really.

A body is floating face down and wearing my clothes. I *think* I remember watching Adam splashing through the waves towards it. He seemed to be shouting, but no sound...

Nausea was welling up. I couldn't raise my head from the pillow without the room whirling and spinning in a stomach-churning gyration. I'd been here a week in the Royal Infirmary Edinburgh, though I don't remember much about the first couple of days. I had a room to myself, must be kept quiet, they say, the blinds drawn against the light. Actually, I didn't feel too bad, apart from a dull headache – as long as I lay back against the pillows. There was nothing to do but look at the walls and study the sheets embroidered RIE in spidery red thread. I wondered what they did in the Royal Infirmary Perth... I dozed off.

'Feel like a visitor?' asked Macleod's voice.

Cautiously, I opened my eyes, careful not to move my head. I groaned feebly. 'No, I feel like a seasick sailor with a hangover.'

'Serves you right,' Macleod was unsympathetic. 'What the hell did you think you were doing chasing after Spinks without backup? If that chap you'd recruited hadn't commandeered somebody's mobile, then followed you, we'd have had another 'accident' to bury. While he was dragging you out of the surf, he saw a man leaving the scene. From the description it could have been Spinks.'

Adam splashing through the surf...

I must have looked uncharacteristically contrite and repentant, because he sat down by the bed and patted my hand, in a definitely avuncular manner.

'He *might* not have got away with it, of course,' he said consolingly. 'We're always suspicious when a healthy adult drowns in shallow water. And then there's the bruise on the back of your neck.'

I thought it time to steer the conversation round to a less embarrassing subject. 'Thanks for your message that Gorgonzola's being looked after by Jim Ewing.'

He nodded. 'I knew when we found the car that she would be somewhere near. I remembered that you'd said the B&B man had taken a special interest in her.' He plonked a cardboard tube on the bed. 'I nearly forgot to give you this. It seems that your cat has taken to vandalising the walls. Strangely enough, Ewing is delighted. He says she's an artist.' A twitch at the corner of his mouth was at odds with his deadpan expression.

I made an attempt to lean forward, then thought better of

it as the room swirled alarmingly. 'I can't raise my head off the pillow,' I said apologetically.

He up-ended the tube and drew out a rolled-up sheet of A3 cartridge paper.

'What was I saying?' He looked thoughtfully at the paper, and turned it 180 degrees. 'Spinks has slipped through our road blocks. I think we've lost him. He's a tricky customer. If you'd drowned, it would have been difficult to charge him with murder. All we had to go on was your recruit's somewhat sketchy description of the man leaving the scene.' He turned the painting a further 90 degrees. 'Your chap seemed to think he had been enlisted by MI6 for some reason.'

'I expect he called you M.' I reached towards Gorgonzola's work of art.

'Dead right, S.' He ignored my outstretched hand. 'You know, this artist, Picatso, *has* a certain flair. I've seen worse in exhibitions at the Academy.'

'Perhaps if I could see it…' I made a grab, only to sink back with a groan.

It was Macleod's turn to look contrite. 'Sorry, I forgot about your head. Here's the feline masterpiece.' He held it up.

I was quite impressed with the broad bands of green, spatters of yellow, and intriguingly random trails of red and black. In the bottom right hand corner was the signature, a blue paw print.

'Put an armed guard on that, M. It's worth a fortune.'

'Yes, yes,' he said soothingly.

'You don't believe me? According to Ewing, paintings by cats can fetch $15,000 in the States. I think a suitable title might be *Impressions of Muirfield*.'

Macleod held the paper at arm's length and studied it with exaggerated reverence for a long moment. '$15,000, eh. Get that blue paw print on *Fast Castle in the Sunset* and *Fast Castle in the Haar* and you can take early retirement.'

I adopted a wounded expression. 'Too much flippancy, Chief Inspector. That's—'

What I was about to say was interrupted by raised, heated voices outside.

He frowned. 'We've put a police guard in the corridor. There shouldn't be any—'

The door edged open a fraction, then slammed shut with the sharp report of a pistol shot.

He threw the painting onto the chair by the bed and in a couple of strides was across the room. The noise of argument raging in the corridor increased by several decibels as he flung open the door. Mindful of the dire consequences of sudden movement, I lay still, eyes closed.

'—ab-saw-loot-ly preposterous…' The unmistakable fruity tones sank to an indistinct murmur as the door clicked shut again.

I was left in suspense for several minutes until I heard Macleod's, 'Do you feel strong enough for a visit from the gastropod *extraordinaire*? She insists she has something *absolutely* important to tell you.'

I opened my eyes and swivelled them in his direction. 'Gastro*nome*,' I said sternly. 'A gastropod has a flattened muscular foot and eyes on stalks…'

His mouth twitched. 'Exactly. Fair description, don't you think?'

I choked back a gurgle of laughter.

'She insists it's a matter of life and death. Do you want to see her, or will I send her on her way?'

The decision didn't have to be made. The door opened a few inches. Through the narrow gap I could see a young police officer engaged in an unseemly tussle with what appeared to be a billowing purple chiffon sheet.

'It's all right!' I cried. 'Let her in.'

Felicity surged into the room, red-faced and perspiring.

'My dear, how ab-saw-loot-ly ghastly you look! Pale as a ghost. Not a smidgeon of colour in your cheeks. But never mind, I've brought you a couple of little things to build up your strength.' With some difficulty she disentangled a white insulated box from the voluminous folds of her caftan. 'Here we are! You'll find this will slip down just a treat.'

Before my eyes floated a vision of ice cream, silky, creamy, refreshing. One of my partialities. 'Wonderful!' I drooled. 'What flavour is it?'

'Flavour?' The folds of Felicity's ballooning caftan deflated gently around her as she sank heavily onto the bedside chair and the $15,000 *Impressions of Muirfield* Picatso. Would I have to retitle it *Impressions on Muirfield*? 'Flavour?' she repeated. 'Well, very subtle, of course, but definitely,' she pursed her lips in thought, 'definitely fishy.'

'*Fishy*! Would this be a new gourmet recipe of yours, Felicity?' I asked, somewhat stunned.

'Oh no, dear. I can't take the credit for that. It's quite traditional.' She opened the lid and peered at the contents. 'I think this one...' Between finger and thumb she held up for inspection the warty shell of a medium-sized oyster.

Macleod's eyes met mine. Apparently his aversion to oysters

equalled my own. 'Time for you girls to have your little tête-à-tête.'

I heard the door open and close as he made his escape.

'Your project, Felicity? Something's happened?' I said, desperately hoping the question would distract her from force-feeding me with a slimy mollusc.

Her eyes moistened. Unnoticed, the bi-valve slipped back to rejoin its companions in the box.

'There *is* no project! I *have* no project!' A tear roller-coasted over the plump contours of her face and added itself to the briny oyster pool. 'There's been a *ghastly* development. Mrs Mackenzie has been,' she dropped her voice to a dramatic whisper, 'has been *arrested.*'

I could hardly say, *I know. And I'm responsible*! Well, I hadn't *personally* snapped on the handcuffs, but you know what I mean...

I opened my eyes wide in feigned astonishment. 'Arrested! Not for the *murder* of Mr Mackenzie?'

'No, no, no,' she sobbed. 'It's in all the papers. On *drug* charges. I've built *everything* round her marvellous recipes. But who will want to read the recipes of a *criminal*?'

'I'm sure there's *some* way of retrieving the situation, Felicity.'

I cupped my hand to my face in prostrate emulation of Rodin's The Thinker. I didn't hold out much hope. The watery gastronome *extraordinaire* was in no fit state to participate in a brainstorming session. Wallowing in gloom as she was, her mind was as cloudy as uncooked cornflower sauce. Thanks to Spinks's administrations, my thought processes were pretty ropey too.

As barely suppressed sobs shook the purple tent, it suddenly came to me. I patted her hand reassuringly. 'Your project *will* be a winner,' I smiled. 'All you have to do is entitle it, *Gourmet Recipes from a Prison Cell.*'

Her woebegone face uncrumpled. 'Ab-saw-loot-ly super!' she breathed.

Beaming, she delved into the depths of the insulated box. With a flourish, she whipped out two glasses and a small bottle.

'Oysters and champagne. Time for a leetle celebration, don't you think, my dear!'